A BRIDE IN STORE

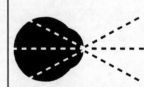

This Large Print Book carries the
Seal of Approval of N.A.V.H.

A Bride in Store

Melissa Jagears

THORNDIKE PRESS
A part of Gale, Cengage Learning

GALE
CENGAGE Learning·

Farmington Hills, Mich • San Francisco • New York • Waterville, Maine
Meriden, Conn • Mason, Ohio • Chicago

GALE
CENGAGE Learning·

LIBRARY OF CONGRESS CATALOGING-IN-PUBLICATION DATA

Jagears, Melissa.
  A bride in store / by Melissa Jagears. — Large print edition.
    pages ; cm. — (Thorndike Press large print Christian romance)
    ISBN 978-1-4104-7458-2 (hardcover) — ISBN 1-4104-7458-5 (hardcover)
    1. Mail order brides—Fiction. 2. Triangles (Interpersonal relations)—
Fiction. 3. Choice (Psychology)—Fiction. 4. Frontier and pioneer life—Fiction.
5. Kansas—Fiction. 6. Large type books. I. Title.
PS3610.A368B77 2014b
813'.6—dc23   2014035991

Published in 2015 by arrangement with Bethany House Publishers, a division of Baker Publishing Group

Printed in Mexico
1 2 3 4 5 6 7 19 18 17 16 15

To Easton and other EB Butterflies:
I pray God grants you and your families
extraordinary perseverance and wisdom.

Chapter 1

Kansas, 1881

The *thwack* of the train door jolted Eliza Cantrell upright. Acrid coal smoke whooshed through the muggy passenger car.

"Now, don't nobody get any ideas," a menacing voice growled.

The one time she traveled by train, it had to be robbed? Her breath froze like jagged ice in her lungs as she dared to glance over her shoulder.

"We ain't gonna harm ya none, iffen you cooperate." A lanky man with a blue bandanna covering his face waved two pistols above the crowded seats. "The train's near-empty safe didn't make us happy, so if you'd hand over your money and valuables, we'd be much obliged."

Two more masked men with their hats pulled low slipped in behind the leader. One was hardly taller than a boy; the other's wild white eyebrows and whiskers obscured the visible portion of his face.

Eliza gripped the edge of her seat and shot a glance across the aisle toward the Hampdens. Carl hadn't seemed the heroic type during the hours Eliza had conversed with his wife, but surely concern for his family might bolster him into action?

Carl sat slumped beside Kathleen, who clung to their two children.

Eliza scanned the rest of the crammed seats. No men stood to face the robbers, and at the front, a porter lifted his hands in surrender.

"Let's do this nice and easy and we'll leave happy. And you want us happy, unless you fancy ending up like your expressman." The lines around the lanky leader's eyes bunched as if he were smiling under his filthy mask. "We tossed him out the window."

The woman behind Eliza moaned.

Eliza peered down at her handbag and swallowed. Could she hide her money without getting caught?

"I'll take that wedding band and whatever else you got." The short robber thrust a bag under the nose of a man sitting across the aisle two rows behind Eliza.

She had to do something quickly. She wore no jewelry, but her every last dollar was in her bag. Her brother certainly

8

wouldn't cough up more money if she lost what he'd unwillingly given her in the first place, and of course, she wouldn't bother to ask her mother for any help — not that she even knew where her mother was.

Easing open the clasp of her leather traveling bag, Eliza rocked with the sway of metal wheels whirring over iron rails.

The lips of the elderly woman beside her moved in harried prayer.

Prayer.

God, I know I haven't been talking to you much, but if you care . . . I need some time.

She looked over her shoulder.

"I'll take that necklace." The lead robber pointed at a woman two seats back who whimpered while fiddling with her chain's clasp.

The short robber was still standing in front of the passengers in the back seats, and the older robber with the shotgun was leaning against the wall keeping an eye on the crowd.

Eliza turned and fished out her money clip with jittery hands. Should she put a few dollars back in the bag for them to find?

The tall robber knocked the back of her seat.

Eliza pushed the entire wad under her leg.

The thief stopped beside her, a gun in one

hand, his empty palm out. "Your turn, pretty lady." His voice was strange and gravelly.

Had he called *her* pretty? She shoved a soggy wisp of hair off her cheek and anchored it behind her ear, her hands shaking. Turning over her handbag, she dumped out the letters from the soon-to-be husband she'd never met, crackers wrapped in a handkerchief, unfinished needlework, and her embroidered purse. She opened its clasp. Three pennies, a nickel, and a half dollar fell into her lap.

He kicked her foot. "Where's the rest of it?"

"That's all I have."

The robber's eyelids narrowed over his light blue eyes. Blond stubble meandered up the sides of his face above the bandanna. "Fifty-eight cents?" His eyes raked down her body, and she hunched as if she could hide from his licentious leer. "That's not homespun you're wearing, though it ain't pretty." He leaned closer, his body odor overwhelming. "You got more than that."

She dug her fingers into the seat cushion. "I've got nothing for you." She pressed her teeth into her lower lip. Surely God would understand her evasiveness.

He squatted, shoved aside her skirt, and

10

glanced under the seat. "No carpetbag?"

"I only have two trunks in the freight car." She moved her legs farther to the left lest he touch her again — or ask her to move her legs the other way. Despite being covered with layers of skirt, flesh, and bone, the wad of bills felt conspicuous.

The robber stood, swiped the coins off her lap, and deposited her measly change into his breast pocket. He thrust his empty palm toward the old woman beside her. "Stop with the mumbling, lady. Give me your ring."

Eliza pressed against her seat, creating space between his hot sweaty body and her offended nose.

Mrs. Farthington stopped praying, her damp eyes pleading. "This was my late husband's. Please, sir, if you'd only allow me —"

"Don't 'sir' me. Just hand it over. Didn't you hear the part about keeping us happy?" The cheek muscle beneath the robber's eye jumped.

Eliza tensed. Surely he wouldn't throw the widow out the window.

"*Now,* old woman." He jiggled his open hand.

Eliza stared at the scar beside his pinkie and ran her tongue over her teeth. How

11

she'd like to sink her teeth into the faint half circle.

The widow pulled the thick gold band off her thumb. The robber snatched the pretty piece and slid the ring onto his finger atop two others. "Hand over your cash."

The old lady fumbled with her reticule's drawstrings.

He leaned over, reaching for the widow's purse, but a sudden lurch made him grab for the shelves above them instead.

"What's this?" His hand grazed Eliza's leg, and the wad of cash slipped from under her thigh as he pulled out a bill. He waved the dollar in front of her. "No money, eh? Just a poor girl down on her luck?" He grabbed her by the waist and hefted her out of the seat.

She shrieked as he tossed her over his shoulder as if she weighed no more than a bag of oats.

Holding her with one arm, he dipped down. "Look, fellas. I found the goose that lays the golden eggs."

"Let me go!" She flailed her fist at his head, but he dumped her back onto the seat before she could make contact.

His eyebrows rose as he ran his thumb across her thick wad of cash. "Mighty obliged."

If things didn't work out in Salt Flatts, what recourse would she have without a penny to her name? She snatched at her money, and the robber gave her a murderous look.

He leaned down until his eyes were so close they seemed to merge into one. "You realize I oughta make an example out of you so others don't get any funny ideas."

His hot slop-pot breath made Eliza want to turn away. Instead she narrowed her eyes at the man inches from her face.

He drew back and cocked his head, then gestured with his arm to the other passengers. "I don't care if you're a woman, a child, a saint, or a sinner," his strange, gravelly voice boomed. "You will not hold out on us."

He raised his hand and cracked his pistol against her cheek, setting fire to her face. Her body hit the plump side of the woman beside her, and the sunlight dimmed. Eliza pressed her palm against the pain, moaning deep and low to keep from crying out.

Across the aisle, the Hampdens' son, Junior, whimpered.

Eliza forced herself upright.

The robber shouted at the passengers up front. "Now, let that be a lesson to ya. If anybody else don't cooperate, losing your valuables won't be the worst thing about today."

Blood oozed between Eliza's fingers. Gritting her teeth, she crossed her ankles to keep from kicking the vile man in the shin. The brand-new patch on his trousers would make an excellent target.

The Hampdens' one-year-old daughter, Gretchen, broke into a full bawl as the man pivoted toward them. Kathleen's desperate shushing only made the baby's sobs more frantic.

Eliza ignored the impulse to slam her bootheel down on the robber's instep before he walked away.

The white-haired bandit stomped forward, the fringe of his leather jacket swaying. "We're coming up on Solomon's Bend."

Through the window, Eliza spied a line of trees on the horizon, indicating a river's bank. A cluster of saddled, riderless horses grazed in the waist-high prairie grasses.

The small thief rushed to gather the loot from the remaining passengers on the car's left side while the blond thief made quick work of the right. When they reached the front, the leader drew his hat down farther and tapped his foot impatiently.

Gretchen's shuddering breaths and the muffled sob of a lady in the back were the only sounds besides the rhythmic chug of the train and the drone of its wheels.

After handing her crying daughter over to her husband, Kathleen reached across the aisle, a handkerchief dangling from her hand. "Here, Eliza."

Eliza frowned despite the ache in her cheek and took the offered linen square. Blood would ruin its pristine white lace, but she couldn't find her own handkerchief. "Thank you."

"You gave it a good try," Kathleen whispered.

"No, it was stupid," muttered Carl. "She could have gotten herself killed. Could have gotten us all killed."

At the front, the littlest robber pocketed his last trinket, and the older robber backed up until he bumped against the other two. "Have a nice trip to Salt Flatts, folks."

When the train slowed to take a sharp bend, the gang spilled out the front and barred the door. One by one, they jumped and rolled into the sea of green grasses.

Several women burst into sobs, and Mrs. Farthington's prayers turned grateful.

Eliza put more pressure on her pulsing wound and slumped in the seat. Once again God had seen fit to take away everything she had. Why had she even bothered to pray?

■ ■ ■ ■

The bell above the door to the Men's Emporium jangled madly, stealing William Stanton's attention from replacing a Winchester's loading gate.

The train depot manager's son, Oliver, stood out of breath at the front of the store.

Will sighed. Not a customer. Wiping his grimy hands on a towel, he sidled around the ammunition bench at the back of the store. "What can I —"

"Pa needs you at the depot, right quick." The boy — not much more than a collection of animated elbows and knees — beckoned him, looking ready to dart back outside within a breath. "The train was robbed, and a lady needs you to give her stitches, and then this one old man —"

"Hold it." Will pointed toward the white stenciled letters on his front window. "Under *Men's Emporium, Purveyor of All Things Gentlemanly,* I've listed gunsmithing — nothing else."

"Oh, c'mon, Mr. Stanton. We all know you're gonna be a doctor someday, even if you don't put it up there."

"I'm not practicing. Get Dr. Forsythe."

"But the lady needs stitches." He stuck

his hands on his hips. "On her *face*."

Will gritted his teeth but untied his oil-smudged apron. The county doctor adamantly declared that the best surgeons — whether the surgery was major or minor — were fast surgeons. Coupled with the man's sorry bedside manners, his speed would ensure the woman's face would be stitched up in seconds to spare her pain, but the work would be shoddily done and certain to look terrible.

How could he allow a horrible scar to disfigure a woman if he could possibly suture her wound so people wouldn't stare at her for the rest of her life? He'd learned at his mother's knee to sew and sew well. "Does she truly need stitches?"

"Yes, sir." The boy backed out the door. "Mrs. Hampden insisted I get you while Dr. Forsythe cares for the man with chest pains."

"Anyone else hurt?" Leaving Oliver standing in the doorway, Will strode to the back to grab his medical kit — a small wooden box his father had fashioned with a carving of Jesus' nail-pierced hands on top.

"No." The boy placed his hands at his sides, as if he were gripping holstered six-shooters. "I heard Mr. Hampden say the gang tossed the expressman out the window,

17

though. Posse went out to see if he's still alive before they chase after the gang. Pa says they likely won't pick up a trail, since they jumped off at the Solomon River. Probably rode through the water a ways."

Will flipped his sign to Closed and hustled after Oliver, who wove through the onslaught of pedestrians from the train.

"William!" Mrs. Hampden flagged him down from across the street.

Will turned and waited for a wagon to pass. He dodged a donkey cart and almost stepped in the unmentionable pile an animal had left behind on the dusty road. "I was just heading to the depot."

As soon as both his feet hit the sidewalk, Kathleen pivoted toward her store. "I had Carl bring her to the mercantile. She doesn't need half the town watching you stitch her up."

He strode after her, barely nodding at the people passing by. For a short, pregnant woman, Kathleen could sure eat up the ground.

When they entered the mercantile's back room, instead of climbing the stairs to the family's apartment, Kathleen led him into the office, where a lady wearing a wrinkled black dress sat on a crate pressing a wad of blood-soaked fabric against her face. The poor thing looked exhausted.

Carl stood by the door jiggling his fussy little girl, his eyes wide with frustration. "I sent Junior upstairs for a nap, but Gretchen won't lay down without you."

Kathleen took the one-year-old from his arms and rested a reassuring hand on the injured woman's shoulder. "Eliza, this is William Stanton. He delivered Gretchen. No finer doctor in the county — even if he is rather young."

Will frowned, not sure whether he scowled more because she called him a doctor or because she made him sound like a child, though Kathleen was indeed closer to his parents' age. He sat on a crate next to his patient. The deep red color plumping her cheek made his fists curl. How he'd like to make the perpetrator's face match hers.

Will forced himself to smile though, knowing his demeanor would affect his patient. "I wasn't really given a choice in attending Mrs. Hampden. She has a knack for giving birth so quickly that whoever happens to pass by gets the honor of attending the delivery."

"You're highly competent, no matter what you say." Kathleen shook her finger at him, then took a pouting Gretchen out the door.

Carl turned to follow.

"I'll need your help, Mr. Hampden." Since he'd run out of cocaine powder, Will grabbed the laudanum from his medical box.

"Um . . ." Carl shifted his weight, taking a long look at the door. "I don't do well at the sight of blood. . . ."

"You can close your eyes."

"Or screaming." He looked a bit pale already.

Will blinked innocently. "I don't intend to scream."

Eliza, who looked much calmer than he'd expected, glanced at Carl, a smile tugging at her lips. "Me neither."

"Great, two jokers." Carl took a reluctant step closer.

Will winked at Eliza before unscrewing the bottle's cap and measuring a small dosage. "Unfortunately, all I can do is help you get very relaxed and not notice the pain so much. You'll still feel every stitch."

Carl groaned, and Eliza's face scrunched. Was the needle he'd pulled from his kit making her anxious or was it Carl's unmanly apprehension?

She sucked air through her teeth, then quickly relaxed her face. The blotch on her handkerchief grew bright red around the edges.

20

Will handed her the medication, and she gingerly placed the cap against her lips.

"You're not going to want to sip that — drink it right down."

She threw back the whole measure, and forced it down with a hard blink.

He left to wash up in the Hampdens' upstairs apartment, giving the medicine time to work.

Carl was pacing the tiny office when he returned, yet the lady seemed relaxed.

Will sat beside her and reached for her makeshift bandage, his hand cupping hers. "Let me take a look."

She removed her hand and stared straight into his eyes. Her irises were a rich brown, like the cloves she'd used to sweeten her breath.

He forced himself to break from her gaze and focus on her gash. She'd most likely need eight stitches. He pressed the cloth back against her skin to staunch the blood. The heat of her cheek through the handkerchief was uncommonly distracting.

Mr. Hampden swayed and put a hand on the wall to keep himself upright.

"Carl, get behind her so you can't see, and I need you to clamp your arm across her forehead and against your side to hold her still."

She shook her head slightly, the loose tendrils of hair tickling his knuckles.

He should anchor her hair behind her ear, but that would be too intimate a gesture for a doctor. Not that he was one. Maybe that's why he almost desperately wanted to do that very thing for some reason.

"I won't move." Her eyes were steady and as dark as the hair trailing across his hand.

He blinked and refocused. She didn't realize how many stitches he was going to have to put in. "Dr. Forsythe might close this up quick enough you could stay still without help, but you wouldn't be happy with your scar. Stitches hurt no matter how much Mrs. Hampden talked up my abilities."

"I've had stitches before," the lady mumbled. "I'll be fine."

Maybe she would. At least she appeared more resilient than Carl. The man was turning whiter with each passing second, and he wasn't even looking at Eliza.

Maybe he should wait for Kathleen to return, but was she strong enough to hold this woman still?

"When do you plan on starting?" The lady's eyebrows arched as she tried to peer down at his hand cupping her cheek. She actually looked amused. A woman who could laugh in this situation was a strong woman indeed.

"I'm giving the medicine time to work." He glanced down at her hand but saw no wedding ring, then rolled his eyes. The robbers would have stolen it. "What's your last name, Eliza?"

"Cantrell." Her eyelids sagged, then flew open. If she was feeling sleepy, the medicine had done its job.

"It's time."

His friend anchored her head under his arm, his muscles flexing tight, his Adam's apple running up and down his throat.

"Just look at the ceiling and think of lots and lots of sales, Mr. Hampden. Happy thoughts." Will smiled at Miss Cantrell and scooted closer. "You should close your eyes."

She tried to shake her head, but Carl thwarted her. Good.

"If I can't watch, I'll flinch."

"All right." Grabbing a little piece of leather with his free hand, he offered it to her. "Bite down on this. It'll help steady you."

When she nodded, he lowered the handkerchief and began his first stitch. Impressively, she only tensed and forcefully exhaled.

Will prayed for a steady hand with each poke of his needle. If she stayed motionless and silent, Carl would remain upright and her scar would be minimal.

After seven stitches, he knotted the silk. "I'm finished." He smiled into her droopy eyes.

Carl let go of her head and sighed. "That wasn't so bad, but I need to go, um, outside for a moment." He moved toward the door on wobbly knees.

Will couldn't suppress a chuckle at the man's melodrama, not that Carl was paying attention to him. "You impressed me, Miss Cantrell." Will wiped his hands and pulled out some bandaging. "I should have taken your word for how you'd fare."

She gave him a weak smile before her head drooped and her shoulders sagged.

He frowned. He hadn't given her enough medicine to cause her to sleep sitting up. "Are you all right?"

Maybe she'd counted his stitches and realized the extent of the damage. She wasn't the prettiest woman in the world. She had a fairly long face and big eyes, but every woman wanted to be beautiful, and stitches and the resulting scar wouldn't help. Though, if she was tough enough to endure sutures without a peep, she'd rise above a fading scar. "In a few years, I don't think you'll see any evidence of what happened today. Unless you look really close."

He held out the bandage, trying to figure out the best way to wrap her head. "You'll need to cover your wound until it no longer oozes. Then you should let it air dry."

"I'll be fine." She handed him her unadorned bonnet and reached for the gauzy roll. "At least my face anyway."

"Are you hurt elsewhere?"

She sighed as she lifted the strip to her face. "My pocketbook."

Will put her hat on the edge of the desk. "Where're you headed? Folks in my church could donate money to get you home."

The bandage's end kept slipping from where she tried to anchor it against her neck with her chin. Will reached out to hold the piece against her skin, velvety like butter. His fingers itched to run along her jawline.

Watch it, Stanton. You don't manhandle patients just because they feel soft.

After she got the first round of gauze started, he let his hand slide down, his double-crossing fingers lingering seconds longer than necessary.

She stopped unrolling the bandage and looked at him out of the corner of her eye. Was she trying to figure out why his hand

25

loitered so long where it shouldn't have? He met her gaze and tried to breathe normally.

She watched him for a second before continuing with her head wrapping. Without the aid of a mirror, she smoothed the cloth as she unrolled the bandage.

He should help her, but he was afraid his fingers might decide to take a trip down her long neck.

"No need to send me anywhere. I'm Salt Flatts' newest resident."

"Oh." Will scurried to think of any Cantrells in the area, but none came to mind. His tongue suddenly felt dry. "Are you alone?" She had to be, since no one was with her, but why had she come? There weren't many available jobs in Salt Flatts for single ladies. "Do you need a place to stay? Maybe a member of my church could house you until you can send for money to stay at one of the boardinghouses."

She tied a neat little bow under her chin and indicated she wanted her hat. "If you're wondering when I will pay you, don't worry —"

"Oh no, ma'am." Will handed her the bonnet. "I don't charge people."

She cocked her head and scrunched her brows, as if witnessing nuts falling out of his ears. "You aren't charging me because of the robbery?"

"No. I don't charge for my services because I'm not ready to hang out my shingle as a doctor."

She puckered her mouth as if he'd said something that didn't make sense. "People seem convinced you're better than the county physician, so why wouldn't you ask for payment?"

Why did he feel as if she'd pulled out an augur, readying to drill a hole in his skull to check for brains? "I just don't."

She shrugged. "You're selling yourself short. If Mrs. Hampden insisted I see you because you do such great work, then you're worthy of being paid." She flung up empty palms. "Not that I have any money at the moment."

"As I said, don't worry about it."

"But I'll pay soon." She took a sidelong glance toward the door and leaned forward to whisper. "You're looking at a woman who's going to be running the most prosperous mercantile in town. Just wait and see."

His eyebrows froze near his hairline. "A mercantile?" Salt Flatts had one too many stores already, if his financial woes were an indication.

"Have you heard of F. W. Woolworth of Pennsylvania?" Her serious face had transfigured in the same way his little sisters' did when they talked about kittens. "I'm going to —"

The door creaked open, and Kathleen came in, arms void of children. "Are you done already, Will?" She smiled upon seeing Miss Cantrell's bandaged face. "I didn't hear anything while I was putting Gretchen down — not even my husband's unconscious body hitting the floor."

Kathleen giggled and squeezed Will's shoulder before taking a seat next to Miss Cantrell. "Do you need Carl to get your things? I should've asked who was waiting for —"

"No need." Miss Cantrell clamped both her hands around Kathleen's. "I've got plans."

Will turned to pack up his box, pushing his emaciated savings purse farther back into the corner.

Great. Another mercantile owner. If Miss Cantrell was about to compete with the Hampdens, the Lowerys, and him and Axel for Salt Flatts' sales revenue, he'd never make enough to afford medical school.

CHAPTER 2

"William!"

Will stopped and turned in the middle of the road, barely avoiding being hit by a mule cart.

Carl waved at him from the front of his store. The man's color was looking better.

Will sighed and jogged back. "Did I forget something?" He mentally checked his medical supplies. He'd repacked them while trying to ignore Eliza chattering to Kathleen. The less he knew about their newest business competitor the less depressed he'd get.

Competing with the Hampdens' hadn't hurt their friendship . . . but he had no time for sparking, and for some reason, he wanted to sit and stare at the woman who'd proven herself tougher than his mother — and few ladies in this world could hold a candle to Rachel Stanton.

"Do you want lunch?" Carl rubbed a hand across his flat stomach. "We've got nothing prepared, and I'm starving."

Will glanced over his shoulder, though he couldn't see his store past the bustle on the street. "I don't know." If Miss Cantrell was about to open another store, could he afford to be closed for lunch? "Do you know anything about the name Woolworth?"

"Might've heard the name." Carl rubbed his chin. "But it's not coming to me. Why?"

"Doesn't matter." No need to alarm him. Nothing was likely to come of a single woman trying to start a store with no money anyway.

"Let me get the women so we can head to the hotel."

Both women? "I'm not so sure —"

The door slammed behind Carl, and Will huffed. Too rude to just walk away. He liked Carl — he really did — but the man wasn't the greatest conversationalist. And from the way Miss Cantrell ceased divulging her business plans the moment Kathleen returned, she surely wouldn't speak of them in front of the Hampdens. So the next hour would be him listening to what? Talk of knitting and fashion?

Miss Cantrell walked out of the store, her hat repositioned to hide the bandage knot crowning her head. Handfuls of eastern women had arrived over the years, and none

30

of their outfits had been so . . . so . . . dull.

So they most likely wouldn't be talking fashion during lunch, since his mother's mourning dress had more ornamentation than the flat black cloth Miss Cantrell sported. Not that her plain dress didn't accentuate her curvy —

Miss Cantrell's hands latched above her hips, and she cleared her throat.

He looked up and blinked, trying to find an excuse for his wandering gaze as she walked closer and asked, "Is something wrong?"

She had no way of knowing what he'd been thinking, but that didn't stop the heat from rising to his face.

"I got lost in thought." He hoped his skin hadn't turned as red as it felt. Doctors shouldn't blush. He'd studied enough medical diagrams to know what a woman looked like under —

He rubbed his hand across his eyes as if he could wipe away the image he'd pulled up. What was wrong with him? Miss Cantrell wasn't pretty enough to tempt a man into immoral mind wanderings.

"William!" Mrs. Graves called out a few yards away.

Oh, how he wished his cheeks weren't burning at the moment. He took a step away from Miss Cantrell and turned to face the woman hustling toward him.

"Glad I caught you." She took a deep breath and smiled. "I've run out of whatever concoction you gave me last month. It has worked wonders on my —" she glanced between him and Miss Cantrell — "complaints. Better than the elixir Dr. Forsythe gives me. Might I bother you for more?"

"I'll have to make some, but yes."

She put a stout hand to her ample bosom. "Thank you." After sighing, she took a good long look at him and then peered down her nose at Miss Cantrell. "I don't believe I've seen you before." She turned back to him, eyebrows furrowed. "Are you two together?"

He took another step back and tipped his head toward the woman in question. "Miss Cantrell just arrived on the train, and since the first Kansans she met robbed her of her purse, Carl and Kathleen are taking her to lunch."

He really shouldn't join them. If he did, the glint in Mrs. Graves' eye did not bode well for him and Miss Cantrell in the rumor mills.

Mrs. Graves' eyebrows rose. "Oh, I heard about the robbery." She snatched Eliza's hand and petted her knuckles as if she were a frightened puppy backed into a corner.

32

"I'm sure that was just dreadful. Did they accost you? Is that what happened to your face?"

The growl of his stomach protested the inevitable minutes about to be lost trying to escape the town's worst gossip. Why did he have to mention the train robbery?

Miss Cantrell took a step away from the older woman. "I'm afraid we've yet to meet, Mrs. . . ."

His face warmed again. How rude of him not to introduce them formally, but Mrs. Graves wasn't exactly well-mannered. Being a fancy easterner, Miss Cantrell probably found them both boorish.

"I'm Mrs. Graves, and there was a time I was this close" — she held out two stubby fingers pinched together — "to being this man's mother-in-law."

Of course the busybody would bring up his failed engagement to her daughter, Nancy, with a complete stranger. He rubbed the back of his suddenly hot neck. Things were going from bad to worse.

Carl backed out of the mercantile's door with a child attached to each hand. "Kathleen will be just another minute."

"I don't have much time before the ladies meet." Mrs. Graves patted him on the arm as if he were naught but a youth. "So I'll come by your place tomorrow for my medicine."

"Looking forward to it." Will retained his fake smile as she scurried to cross the road toward the millinery, where several ladies were quilting behind the huge glass windows — no doubt changing topics of gossip as fast as pedestrians passed in and out of view.

The scuttlebutt would surely revolve around him and Miss Cantrell for the next fifteen minutes or so.

Hopefully he could leave the tincture for Nancy's mother with Axel and lie low when she came to retrieve the medicine.

"So you're treating Mrs. Graves? That's mighty considerate of you." Carl eyed him, both of his children pressed against his legs.

"I just can't keep from —" He cut off his own excuse with a shake of his head. Of course, he could tell the woman no, but not when Dr. Forsythe's harsh purgatives, blistering, and other heroic treatments had done nothing for her. If Forsythe would bother to listen to him, the man could've learned of the herbal concoction one of the women in town recommended for Mrs. Graves' female complaints.

But should he be prescribing contrary to a medical-degreed doctor? He hadn't read even a quarter of the medical volume he'd purchased from a battlefield surgeon. Still, Nancy's mother's health had improved with his tincture.

Will glanced toward Miss Cantrell, who seemed exceptionally interested in their conversation. He looked back to Carl. "Well, it's just awfully hard to refuse Mrs. Graves anything."

Carl snorted. "You can't refuse *anybody* anything."

Since Will had delivered Gretchen, Kathleen had refused anyone's counsel but his, and how could he withhold something to ease Junior's cough or clear up Carl's hay fever? "Would you like me to start refusing your wife's requests for medical advice?" Will gave little Gretchen a big smile, which she returned.

"Don't you dare. Kathleen won't even look at Dr. Forsythe after his treatment of Junior's whooping cough."

"So you don't charge the Hampdens either?" Eliza's gaze bored into him.

"If you were to refuse someone services, it should be Mrs. Graves." Carl let go of Junior's hand and scooped Gretchen up into his arms. "The woman encouraged Nancy to leave you, so she shouldn't be able to wring free services out of you."

And there it was — the topic he was hoping to avoid. Will gritted his teeth. "Must we speak of this now?"

"Why not?"

"My past is not exactly a topic I want to discuss in front of Miss Cantrell."

"She'll find out sooner or later." Carl shrugged. "Nancy Graves jilted Will because he can't make up his mind whether or not to become a doctor."

Will wrapped his hands around the top of the hitching post, strangling the wood. "And Carl stole my neighbor's mail-order bride."

Carl's cheeks pinked. "All right, I won't share anymore."

The air rushed out of his lungs. "I'm sorry, Carl. I shouldn't have said that." Definitely not in front of the children. Thankfully, Junior looked as if he were daydreaming, and Gretchen was certainly young enough not to understand.

"Though it's not like Miss Cantrell won't hear about that either." Carl glared at him before turning to Eliza. "I didn't know Kathleen was promised when I fell in love with her, and Everett Cline got himself a pretty wife not too long afterwards. Everybody's happy."

Miss Cantrell smoothed her hands along her plain bodice. "I feel like I need to air something uncomfortable about myself to set things to rights."

"Oh no. We're —"

"My former fiancé pretended to be interested in me long enough to steal my father's business contacts." She smiled, though she winced with the effort. "Now we're all equally embarrassed."

Will ran a hand through his hair. At least his soon-to-be competition seemed honest and forthright. "You could have kept that a secret. We didn't need to know."

She shrugged. "Might as well tell you before the town speculates."

The door to the mercantile opened, and Kathleen stepped outside. "Are we ready?"

Will cleared his throat. "I think I'm going to bow out. This is the day my family comes into town." He sneaked a glance toward Miss Cantrell, but she didn't seem disappointed. Not that she had a reason to be. "I'll eat with you another day."

Will had no sooner picked up the pistol he'd been trying to repair all morning than the store's bell kicked into a tinny chime up front.

He'd returned from stitching up Miss Cantrell to find two men waiting impatiently at his door and had just finished helping them load their wagons and then downed some crackers and dried fruit. When would he be able to finish this pistol? Watching the store by himself proved impossible for getting gun work done. Gunsmithing was more profitable than the store, but repair work alone wouldn't keep them afloat.

"William?"

"Back here, Nettie Bug!" Reaching under the desk, he snagged some lollipops and stuffed them into his pants pocket. He walked out from behind the counter to wait for his littlest sister, an awkward flurry of ruffles, lace, and brown ringlets. Her tiptoe gait nearly sent her into a shelf before he swept her up.

His taller-than-average pa, Dex Stanton, and another little sister, Becca, strolled up the middle aisle while Nettie patted his chest pocket.

He grinned. "Not even a hello for big brother, eh? Candy's more important?"

"Pwease." She batted her long eyelashes.

Sighing, he pulled out the lollipops. "I give in."

The bell clanged again. Hopefully his brothers were coming in with his mother and Emma. They'd be handy for a quick unloading job.

Instead Miss Cantrell stepped through the doorway and walked straight to the display of wilting wild flowers. Though he never would have considered fresh flowers to sell well in a store meant to carry anything and everything manly, they sold enough to be worth the trouble.

Pa squatted beside Becca to help unwrap her candy. "Guess we ought to wait until after you help your customer."

Will lowered his voice. "She's not here to buy anything." Snooping on her competition most likely. Why else would she have come in?

"Oh?" Pa smiled as he scanned Miss Cantrell. "Should I know this girl?"

"No, nothing like that. It's just . . . I met her today. You heard the train was robbed?"

His father nodded.

"Unfortunately, she no longer has any money." Will craned his neck. Miss Cantrell was absorbed in picking through the flowers, apparently safely out of earshot.

"So she's here to see you?"

Will shook his head vehemently. "No, she —" Had the Hampdens told her he co-owned the place?

Miss Cantrell moved to a pile of unopened boxes and frowned.

"I'll introduce you, but don't volunteer any information about me." If she didn't know he was the proprietor, maybe she'd

39

discuss her business plans now that the Hampdens weren't around. Then he could determine whether or not she was a real threat to their business.

"This sounds promising."

Did Pa actually rub his hands together?

As if Mrs. Graves seeing him blushing over Eliza weren't bad enough, Pa was likely to tease him to death.

"It's not what you're thinking." Will jiggled Nettie. "Come and meet a friend."

Pa glared at Nettie settled in his arms, but Will ignored the look. He insisted his parents make her walk on her own, but he could break his own rule. It was, after all, his fault she had Little's disease and walked so poorly, often tripping and falling over nothing.

Becca grabbed his free hand and checked on the ring she'd made him a year ago. Thankfully, he'd spun the grinning bead back up after successfully stitching Miss Cantrell's cheek, otherwise Becca would have scolded him for not wearing the ring right.

"Miss Cantrell?" He turned the corner. "I'm surprised to see you in the Men's Emporium."

She startled and bit her lip, then immediately winced.

He sucked air through his teeth in sympathy. That couldn't have felt good.

"Yes . . . well . . ." He'd expected a blush to creep into her cheeks at being caught spying on her competition, but not so. She shoved her hands behind her back and glanced over his shoulder toward the back. "Good afternoon, Mr. Stanton." She took a quick look at his sisters. "Are you out shopping?"

Ah, so she still didn't know he owned the store. Good. "My family is." Will gave his father a look, pleading for silence. But the giddy gleam in Pa's eye wasn't promising.

"May I introduce them, since they're rarely in town?" At her nod, he jiggled the bundle in his arms, who kept her hand tightly gripped to the sucker stick in her mouth. "This little one is Nettie, and the butterball staring up at you is Becca, and this is my father, Dex Stanton. Everyone, this is Miss Cantrell, Salt Flatts' newest resident."

Pa tipped his hat. "Pleased to meet you. I've got a wife and three more children down at the mercantile. No, wait — here they are." He rushed to open the front door.

Will took a step back. No use giving Ma any reason to assume he was interested in Eliza. "That's my mother with Emma."

41

Ma and his oldest sister bustled through the door, his gangly brothers behind them.

"And my two brothers, Ambrose and John. Be careful with your lunch; they eat anything that doesn't move."

Both boys pulled off their hats. "Ma'am."

Pa walked Ma up to Eliza, his eyes twinkling. "Miss Cantrell, let me introduce my wife, Rachel Stanton. She's ever so happy to meet you."

Will cleared his throat as loud as he could without hurting his vocal cords.

"What happened to your face?" Becca blurted.

Pa set a huge hand on Becca's head. "Now, that's not a polite question to ask a stranger."

"That's all right." Eliza attempted a small smile. The laudanum's effect had to be wearing off, so she'd likely endured a painful pull with the gesture. "Your brother sewed up a gash on my cheek this morning."

Again Eliza glanced toward the back. What was she looking for?

Ma took a step toward Eliza, but Pa put a hand to her arm. "Well, I see we're intruding. We'll be back later."

"We will?" Ma's face was as confused as Eliza's. She normally did all the talking, and she'd yet to say a thing.

With a smirk, Pa took Nettie from Will but then let her slip to the floor, keeping a firm grip on her. "I forgot we've got business with, uh, Mr. Raymond, and the girls should eat their lollipops outside. Nice to meet you, Miss Cantrell. Hope to see you *very* often."

Did Pa just wink at her? He shot his father a warning glare, though it would likely do no good.

"Yes, good to meet you." Ma gave Pa a sizzling look, but those big brown eyes would sparkle with a matchmaking gleam the second Pa filled her in on his assumptions.

Will sighed.

But he had to admit the thought of his parents playing matchmaker didn't sound so bad if they set their sights on Miss Cantrell.

But he'd only met Miss Cantrell a few hours ago. What was wrong with him?

The doorbell dinged several times as his family cleared the door.

"I didn't mean to scare them away." She fingered a dying daisy. "Though I don't know why my presence would keep them from shopping."

Will shrugged. "Can't shop with sticky lollipop hands." He pointed to the wild flowers. "Are these what brought you in?" When would she admit she wasn't there to shop but snoop?

She stared at the lackluster display. Why hadn't he replaced the sad bunches this morning?

"I think it's rather clever for the store owner to provide men with an easy way to show affection for their ladies, don't you?"

"Would you want someone to buy you one of these?" He pulled out the bouquet in which he'd stuffed some whitish-pink flowers he'd found. Frowning, he tugged out a wilted one.

"I'd find them pleasant enough." She waved at the sorry mess he held. "While they aren't spectacular, most women, I assume, would appreciate something over nothing. Though it'd be better if the man picked these weeds himself if he wanted her to experience any romantic notions. Imagine the money . . ." Her voice lowered. "Imagine how much the proprietor could make if these weren't flowers you could find in a ditch."

Will frowned at the lifeless bundle tickling his hand. It wasn't his fault only spindly yellow and white flowers seemed to be blooming. "I suppose a woman like you would want a hothouse bouquet."

"Oh no. I don't expect a man to offer me flowers."

Why was that? "Miss Cantrell, you sell yourself short. A man would feel foolish offering you weeds if he had roses."

"What?" Her visible cheek pinked.

Some part of him — an inane, irrational, senseless part, to be sure — desperately wanted to tell her he'd picked these himself . . . but of course, not for her. He shoved the flowers back into their hole. "Well, if a man could get you a better bouquet, he'd do so."

"Is there a hothouse around here?"

"No." As a city girl, she was about to get a rude awakening. "This is the middle of Kansas, not . . . Where are you from again?"

"Pennsylvania."

He snapped his fingers. "Starting a hothouse might be a good idea." Maybe he could get her interested in a business not directly in competition with them. "I don't know how big of a town you'd need to support such a thing, but that's something to check into."

She shook her head, the smile patronizing. "I've never grown a thing, and that's a limited venture."

Limited, eh? "Well, it's not that these sell

a lot anyway, so you might have a point."

She pulled a nosegay out of the bucket and peered in. "There's no water in the bottom. It would help if . . . Wait." She looked at him. "How do you know whether these sell or not?"

Blast it, he'd ratted on himself. "I'm the one who sells them."

She looked toward the windowed storefront, her lips soundlessly forming the words *Men's Emporium.* "Um . . ."

"But you know what? I need a woman's advice on things like these. Maybe we could work together and —" He clamped his lips. What was he thinking? They couldn't afford a clerk.

She certainly seemed to think she could run a store, but the only way they could take on a woman business partner was if one of them married her. With her being penniless and their needing help so badly . . . He coughed against the knot in his throat. "I mean, let me think about a way we could help one another."

"I don't need help."

The woman was as stubborn as his mother. Of course she needed help. "Sure you do. First thing we need to do is find your family." Why hadn't Carl or Kathleen escorted her to them earlier?

"Um . . ." She glanced back at the window again. "I expected to find him here."

A man?

"Your father? An uncle?"

She swallowed twice before wincing as she spoke. "Fiancé, actually."

"Oh." Whatever had clumped in his throat earlier sank into his gut. "You thought he'd be shopping?" Of course, the first woman since Nancy who made him inexplicably jittery was spoken for. "Why didn't he meet you at the station?"

"Because I came earlier than expected. You don't happen to know an Axel Langston?"

Will's face cooled instantly.

"I thought he ran . . . the Men's Emporium . . ." Eliza's face paled as well.

"You're . . . his . . ."

"Mail-order bride." She put a hand to her chest. "So that makes you . . ."

"His business partner."

The finger she'd pointed at him slowly descended. "Yes, I should've guessed."

They stood staring at each other.

"Where's Axel?"

"Not here." He had no notion of his friend's whereabouts — like too often lately. "I last saw him two days ago."

"I was afraid of that." She sighed. "He

mentioned he did some trapping to offset the store's losses. When do you expect him back?"

Why would Axel tell her that? The scraggly pelt Ned Parker had brought in months ago hadn't sold — and Axel wasn't much of a hunter. "I don't know when he's returning."

Why, oh why, had he ever persuaded Axel to pursue mail-order brides?

CHAPTER 3

"So . . . this is the store." Eliza frowned at the mostly unorganized merchandise behind Mr. Stanton.

Axel couldn't be gone for long. He knew she was coming. She'd arrived early, so she'd figured on being a surprise, but not penniless with no one to turn to.

How would working with William go while her fiancé was absent? She'd basically told him she planned to run this store after he'd stitched her up. What did he think of her boast now?

"Yes, the store." William fiddled with the ring he'd played with after stitching her up. A simple braided multi-thread band with a bead featuring a smiling face in the center. "I thought you might've come in to observe our methods . . . not because you intended to run *this* store. But, well . . ." He swung his hand halfheartedly at the three aisles of rough shelving. "What do you want to see?

It's not much."

He turned away, but his muttered *obviously* didn't elude her detection.

The man's confidence had flattened within seconds. Was he afraid she'd belittle him for their struggling store? "I can see you've worked hard with the setup."

Probably best not to mention the things she wanted to change based on Axel's correspondence. Not today anyway. "The flowers —"

"Yes, Axel suggested that a month ago. I told him flowers in a men's store was silly, but they haven't done too poorly. I think the window display helps sell them."

Yes, the dapperly dressed mannequin holding a bouquet of fake flowers, giving any passing woman the idea her husband might turn into a dashing, flower-wielding man if she'd encourage him to shop there. But Axel hadn't concocted the flowers and the display, she had. "This was Axel's idea?"

"He's had several good ones lately. I was skeptical of this one, but it didn't hurt anything."

Ah . . . if William hesitated to accept Axel's ideas despite the rationale, he'd no doubt question the efficacy of a woman's ideas.

At least Axel believed in her enough to

implement them.

She fingered the rows of various shaving soaps, colognes, and brushes sitting on a nearby shelf, wreaking havoc with the floral scent by adding hints of sandalwood and bay rum. "I see you've arranged these attractively." She'd move them away the first chance she got, so no customer would get a headache.

"Yes, another of Axel's suggestions. If customers can easily access often-needed items, we won't need to waste time gathering things for them."

"Exactly." She smiled. "Care to show me around?"

"We could wait until —"

"No, I'd like your opinion on how things are displayed, what you think needs improvement . . ." Might as well start working. "See if I can suggest anything to help."

William's features transformed from uncomfortable to wary. "How do you know about retail, exactly?"

"I've worked behind the counter of a successful mercantile since I was nine." Since her mother had abandoned them. She'd omit the part where her father died and left everything to her brother, who'd hardly done anything in the store beyond push a broom and who somehow thought her un-

51

necessary once he inherited the store.

Zachary was lazy and she'd told him so, told him how quickly he'd lose the store if he didn't let her manage it. Soon he'd discover the truth of it, but she'd not go back to save him. Especially after he told her not to return and beg him for money when her inheritance ran out. And it had definitely run out — out a passenger-car door and into the tall prairie grass in the pocket of some lout.

"So why'd you come to Kansas, then?" William scratched at the back of his head.

She bit her lip. No sense in making herself seem less capable than she was. "A long story."

He glanced at his timepiece. "It's close to quitting time. Has someone gotten your things from the depot and taken them to . . . Uh, where are you staying?"

"Good question. I've no money. And without Axel . . ." Where could she stay?

William looked up at the ceiling and gritted his teeth. "I'm not sure it'd be right for you to stay upstairs in Axel's quarters while I'm downstairs in the back room."

"No, that won't work." She'd known Axel lived above the store, but William stayed in the building too? "Well, today's fiasco is my reward for spontaneity. I'll never do that again." She'd thought her early arrival would be a fun surprise for her husband-to-be, but with him out of town, what was she to do?

She had wanted to work in the store this afternoon and learn as much as she could from Axel, but now she'd have to find a place to stay. "With Axel unexpectedly gone and me without money, do you have any idea of where I could go?"

William's cheek twitched as he stared out the window at the fairly busy street. Not that it was as busy as the main thoroughfare her father's shop had been on. "My parents don't have room and neither do Axel's, I'm afraid."

He ran a hand through his hair and stilled. "Mrs. Lightfoot." He marched to the front door. "You could stay with her." He opened the door and hollered the name again.

Eliza walked to the large front windows. Will crossed the street and offered his arm to a woman with a rounded back who wore a face-obscuring scarf. Was he going to suggest she stay with her? Surely it was wrong of her insides to cringe because the woman hid her face. Unless Axel returned before nightfall and made other arrangements, she really didn't have many options.

Mrs. Lightfoot listed to one side as she moved toward a chair. Will slipped his arm under hers to ease her leg strain.

She sat down with a huff. "I haven't been able to get into town until today. I've been out of medicine since last week."

Hadn't he checked on her last Sunday? "I didn't realize you'd need more already."

"Because I shouldn't. I use more than I ought trying to alleviate the pain. It's been terrible lately." She settled against the back of her seat with a sigh that fluttered her head scarf, then glanced toward Eliza. "What's your name, dear?"

Will held an open hand out toward Eliza. "Mrs. Lightfoot, this is Miss Cantrell. She came in with the train that was robbed this morning."

"Oh my, is that what happened to your face?" Her voice wheezed as she threw a compassionate look toward Eliza.

She touched her bandage. "Unfortunately, yes."

"Miss Cantrell is Axel Langston's intended." The last word tasted like camphor in Will's mouth, bitter and cold. Why had Axel not mentioned he had arranged for a mail-order bride? "But he's not in town at the moment, and she needs lodging. I was hoping you could take her for the night. I'll compensate you once —"

"No," both women said in chorus.

"I mean," Eliza said, stepping forward, a hand to her mouth, "it's not that I don't need a place to stay, but I didn't realize Mr. Stanton meant to pay. Surely Axel will settle my bill when he returns. He doesn't know I'm already here."

Irena waved a dismissive hand. "I'm not worried about it, child. William refuses to let me pay for treatments, so this being the first thing he's asked for, I won't take his money."

Will frowned. He let Irena feed him dinner as payment every time — which he shouldn't continue allowing since he obviously wasn't helping much.

"And no need to have Mr. Langston pay either. You're welcome to stay with me." Mrs. Lightfoot straightened a leg and moaned. "If I can get back home, that is."

How had she managed to walk the eight blocks from her boardinghouse just outside of town? Half a dozen wagons had probably passed her, yet no one offered a ride? He hardened his jaw. Of course not. "My parents can take you home — Miss Cantrell as well."

Mrs. Lightfoot narrowed her eyes. "But the question is, will Miss Cantrell want to come? Does she know what I am?"

"I haven't had the chance to tell her anything." And what would he have said? "Probably best you do that yourself."

She straightened in her seat and turned her piercing blue eyes toward Eliza. "Have you ever gone to a freak show, Miss Cantrell?"

Well, that wouldn't have been how he'd have gone about it.

Eliza blinked. "A freak show?"

"Yes, a circus sideshow where you pay money to see people with —" she moved her hand toward her scarf but dropped it back into her lap — "peculiarities."

"No. I did read about General Tom Thumb's wedding years ago though."

"Well, I used to work for a traveling circus as a bearded lady."

Reaching up to his jaw, Will tried to imagine his stubble defining his character — or rather his whole life.

Eliza's eyebrows tilted in confusion. "I thought such things were a disguise or a costume or —"

"Oh no. Many things were disguises, but some of us are truly the real thing." Mrs.

Lightfoot leaned forward on her cane. "My one and only pregnancy changed my life in more ways than one. My son turned out to be very small in stature, similar to General Tom Thumb, and he still travels around billed as the Smallest Man on Earth. But for some reason, in the months following his birth, I grew a beard."

Eliza nodded slowly, doubt flickering in her eyes.

"When society shunned us, the circus provided us the best opportunity for employment, but I can't travel anymore. So I settled here and established a boarding-house." She readjusted herself in the chair. "People often aren't comfortable around me, so I don't have many guests, but you're welcome to stay with me. Right now, you'd be my only occupant."

"What do you say, Miss Cantrell?" Will held his breath. Would she turn down the offer? Had he invited Mrs. Lightfoot inside only to face more rejection? "She's got room."

Eliza scratched her head. "I don't want to take advantage of you just because you have no boarders."

Irena's bushy gray eyebrows arched above her bright blue eyes. "You're not opposed to lodging with a bearded lady?"

Eliza put her hands on her hips. "If you're kind enough to take in a penniless lodger, why would I be?"

Mrs. Lightfoot settled back against her seat. "I like you, Miss Cantrell." She stretched out her right leg again. "Now, if only I found my knees and ankles as agreeable."

"Let me get your medicine." Will beckoned to Eliza with his head to follow him. "Thank you for not snubbing her," he whispered as they walked down the center aisle.

"Why should I be thanked for looking past a woman's beard? I stick out like a sore thumb myself at the moment."

"Your stitches will heal and the scar will fade." He walked around the back counter and flipped open his medical case.

She stopped on the other side. "Though it certainly won't make me any prettier."

Did she think that scar would keep men from noticing her when there were so few eligible ladies in town? It certainly hadn't hindered his wandering eyes.

The bell rang. Probably best she return to the front before his eyes wandered again. "Would you mind telling whomever that is I'll be up as soon as I mix this for Mrs. Lightfoot?"

"Of course." Eliza turned and walked the aisle with purpose.

Evidently his heart was completely over Nancy. Unfortunately it was tripping up over Eliza.

Probably because she was new in town.

Yes, that was it. He grabbed an empty bottle and unstopped a few others. He was merely attracted to her because she was novel. If he wanted to keep thoughts of Eliza from his head, he should crowd them out by mingling with other single ladies.

But where could he meet new women? He capped his bottles and shook up Mrs. Lightfoot's tincture. Perhaps once Axel returned, he could go on the rounds he'd once attended with Dr. Forsythe. Surely the little towns around Salt Flatts needed medical help, and if he went to church elsewhere, he —

What was he thinking? Doctoring to meet girls? What a self-serving way to use his little bit of medical know-how.

He shook his head and repacked his supplies. He'd get over this sudden fascination with Eliza as soon as he could mentally picture her together with Axel.

Which at the moment his imagination stubbornly refused to do.

CHAPTER 4

Instead of using the reflection of the emporium's window to make sure her shirtwaist and skirt lay nicely, Eliza smudged her finger through its thick layer of street grime peppered with tiny handprints and bug trails. She pulled out her notebook and added *Clean the building's front* to the list she'd started last night.

A single wagon traveled down the road. So few people this morning. Was Salt Flatts only as large as her neighborhood back home? Axel had told her Salt Flatts was a large, booming town. Evidently, he'd never seen a truly booming town. Or was this as big as western towns got?

Without money, she really had no choice but to find success in this town, no matter its size. Her business acumen was all she now had to persuade Axel to keep his word and marry her, so she'd conduct herself as if she came for a job interview rather than a wedding ring. If Axel could look past her face, attire, and empty pockets, and was reminded of the contents of their correspondence, he'd surely choose her as a business partner.

She entered the Men's Emporium to the door hinges' protest. Another item to put on her fix-it list. Everything about shopping should be easy. Like opening the door . . .

Or seeing a shopkeeper upon entry.

She crossed her arms. The bell tinkled a second time as the door shut behind her. Would Axel greet customers faster than William? Might he have returned overnight? Suddenly she was short on breath. How would her fiancé react upon first seeing her?

No one came, so she started counting.

At nine, William shouted. "Be with you in a second."

Right — a second. Yesterday she'd perused the shelves for more than a minute before he came. Might Axel be with William? Her heart pulsated down into her fingertips as she forced herself to walk to the back.

William was sitting behind his gun counter fiddling with a rusted rifle — alone.

She glanced around. "Do you think working on guns while attending the shop is wise?"

61

"Why not? I can work while no one's here."

"Perhaps no one's here because they waited too long for service one day and have decided to shop elsewhere."

He narrowed his eyes at her. "When there's two of us, we don't have a problem. I can't twiddle my thumbs waiting for customers."

"So Axel hasn't returned?"

He shook his head as he popped out a part.

Tension leaked out of her muscles, and her heart stopped ramming her ribs. Being relieved that her fiancé was still gone had to be a bad thing. They had to meet sooner or later. Was she going to have to wait the whole week, until the day she was scheduled to arrive? All this heart-fluttering anticipation followed by instantaneous stress release couldn't be good for her.

Leaning against the long counter that sectioned off the back area, she took in the store's layout. Two huge display windows up front flanked the door, but she couldn't see much of the door from back here — and not at all if she were to sit at the desk piled with papers and catalogs behind the counter on the right or at Will's gunsmithing table on the left. The two untidy shelving units dividing the store into three sections obscured any ability to see incoming customers. "Why don't we place the counter up front in that empty space to the left? People would see you immediately, and you could greet —"

"Nobody puts their counter up front."

"Doesn't mean we can't." She smiled, trying to dislodge the wary look in his eyes.

He picked up a pair of tweezers. "Perhaps we should wait for Axel before we change things."

A mountain seemed more willing to consider budging than this man.

The door's bell sounded, but William didn't move. With his tweezers, he tried to finagle a tiny something back inside the rifle. "Be with you in a second!"

Yelling at customers from the back seemed to be his normal way of greeting. She grabbed an apron off a hook. "I'll watch the store."

He dropped a spring, slapping his hand on it before it rolled away. "Now, wait a minute. There's no need."

She huffed and cinched the apron. Was he as much against businesswomen as her brother? Axel had not named him, but he'd described his business partner as a pleasant, helpful chap who'd welcome help, but those weren't the traits she'd observed in William. More like jumpy, uncomfortable, and leery. "I came to help Axel. I might as well start now."

Walking to the front, she plastered on a smile for the elderly gentleman who'd straggled inside. "Can I help you?"

The man's bushy white eyebrows rose. "With what?"

"Finding something." Maybe he was right to question her. What if she didn't know if they carried the first thing he asked for?

"What I need is William. Is he not here?" He cocked his head. "Who are you?"

"I'm . . ." She'd already mentioned being Axel's intended to a few people, so shouldn't she admit to her relationship? But if Axel didn't find her agreeable, that'd be embarrassing to explain later. "I work here."

He scratched behind his ear. "I still need William."

"He's in the back." Would the people of Salt Flatts be prejudiced against women clerks?

The man grabbed a handful of cigars from a box, took them to the counter, and placed his hands in his pocket and fished around. He slapped down a coin and then went back to his pocket.

"Hello, Mr. Harbuckle." William wiped

64

his hands on a grimy towel. "Anything else I can get you?"

"No thank you." The man pulled out a five dollar bill. "I just came in to give you this for helping my wife last year."

"I didn't help much." William shoved the money the man dropped onto the counter back toward him. "Besides, you gave me eggs."

"Take it, son. I'm leaving town to move in with my boy. Don't want anyone saying I left without paying my bills."

William stared at the money as if he didn't know how to pick it up. Evidently the price was fair, since he didn't protest the amount. Why wouldn't he want to be paid? "All right then, but the cigars are on sale, five for the price of four, so I'll get you a nickel."

Eliza looked at the shelf with the cigar box. No sign stated such.

After the older man left the store and William returned to his work, she said, "I bet collecting on a debt was nice."

"I wouldn't call it nice." William's tongue worked as he fiddled with something in the gun. "I couldn't help her. She died."

"I'm sorry." Working with life and death had to be hard. "But that doesn't mean you aren't owed for the work you did."

"She was Dr. Forsythe's patient back

when I followed him on rounds." William put down his tool. "But he refused to help, told Mr. Harbuckle his wife's case was hopeless."

Eliza cringed. "He said that to his face?"

"Unfortunately, yes. Dr. Forsythe and I have a long-standing disagreement on how to deal with patients." He leaned back in his chair and crossed his arms. "I think the anxiety that comes with heroic medical procedures won't help a person get well, and Dr. Forsythe says real doctors don't bother with weak homeopathic cures."

What could she say to that? She didn't even really know what he was talking about. She'd only seen a doctor maybe twice in her life.

But a store? She'd been in one her entire life and definitely knew more about running one than he did. "Do you have anything pressing you want me to do? If not, I'd like to clean the front windows. And do you have a blackboard for advertising sales? Are there others besides five cigars for the price of four?"

"No. I just created that one for Mr. Harbuckle. I couldn't refuse his payment, so I gave him a discount on the cigars."

So her future business partner placed items on sale without a plan? She pinched the bridge of her nose. Axel had written that the store was floundering, and now she knew why. How did he deal with William's sporadic attention to the business and his impulsive decisions?

"Are you all right, Miss Cantrell? I have some headache powders."

"No, that's not necessary." She dropped her hand from her face.

She'd have to step lightly — Axel might soon be her husband, but he was surely more attached to his childhood friend than to her. She'd have to figure out a way to work with William — she had no choice.

Will couldn't keep from glancing around his customer to where Eliza stood with Lynville Tate. The farmer evidently couldn't decide which cologne smelled best on his own. Not that he'd ever had a difficult time choosing before — he bought whatever was cheapest. But today, he was sniffing each uncorked bottle Eliza held to his nose — more than once.

"I only need one of these. You gave me two." Mr. Grant pushed a package of Veterinary Fever Remedy across the counter toward Will. "I need a cough powder."

"My apologies." How long would it take before he didn't feel compelled to watch

Eliza work? She certainly wasn't incompetent. In two days, she'd practically taken over helping customers. Another two days and she might take over the whole store.

He returned to the medicine shelf and pulled off a similarly shaped package, double-checking the label this time. "I'm sorry your horse feels poorly. Have you applied hot poultices to his hooves or stomach?"

"No, but I'll try it. Throw in some licorice. And do you have any saw-handle screws? I only need one."

Crossing over to the licorice bin, Will could hear Eliza's lilting voice respond to Lynville's sickeningly charming rumble. He shouldn't eavesdrop, but someone ought to make sure Lynville wasn't trying anything untoward. Will took a piece of paper off the top of the bin and rolled it into a paper cone.

"I still think plain old bay rum's the best." Lynville's chest puffed out a little. "It's what a real man wears."

"A good choice. I'm going to assume you could use more soap?"

"Of course."

Why did Lynville just step closer to her? To prove he stank? Will flipped the licorice lid open, smacking it against the wall.

"How is your brush holding up, Mr. Tate? Badger bristles are the best."

What on earth was she talking about? Had Irena taught Eliza how to shave her face last night?

Will dug the scoop in, hitting the bottom with a clang. Lynville looked over his shoulder and gave him a lazy smile. Hadn't Lynville started sparking with Sarah? She was prettier and dressed nicer — and was silly enough to consider the clown.

"My brush is perfectly fine, miss, but I'd like your opinion on a hat. I've wanted a new one for weeks but can't decide which one makes me look more dashing."

Will scrunched the paper cone in his hand. Lynville hadn't so much as looked at a hat since he'd started frequenting their store.

He had to commend Eliza, though, for appearing oblivious to the man's flirtations and acting as if every customer wore a grin too big for his face.

Will grabbed a saw screw and forced himself to walk out of earshot. He'd never sold as many things to Lynville as Eliza had stacked on the counter. Surely men wouldn't continue to buy more than they needed because of some lady clerk. They'd run out of money eventually.

And once a wedding ring appeared on her finger, the excitement would die down.

"You seem preoccupied with that girl." Mr. Grant leaned against the counter and glanced at his watch.

"Just checking on her. I haven't trained her yet." He put the licorice bag and screw in the man's box.

"Doesn't look like she needs training."

Will forced himself to attend to his sums instead of looking at her again. "I think I have to agree."

"So where'd she come from, and why's she working for you?"

Will rubbed his lower eyelid and hemmed. "She was robbed on the train and needed work." He didn't know why he skirted telling the truth, except for some reason he hoped Axel wouldn't like her.

Even so, Axel and Eliza should share the news, not him.

"You always were a sucker for pity cases." Mr. Grant counted his coins and slid them over. "Much obliged."

Will drummed his fingers on the counter, watching Lynville's hands as he reached above Eliza to get a hat off a shelf, leaning more than necessary. He caught Lynville's eye and glowered.

The man just smirked.

Before he could march over to assist with the hat and send Eliza to the back room for a good half hour, she pointed to the hat he ought to purchase, brought it back to his pile, and tallied his bill.

And what a pile of things she'd sold to the rascal.

Once his old classmate left the store, Will leaned against the counter. "I hope Lynville Tate didn't pester you too much."

She wiped her hands with a bandanna. "I bet he bought more today than ever before." She fluttered her eyelashes, and Will almost laughed at the comical exaggeration. Lynville deserved the pocket cleaning she'd given him for his outright boldness.

"He'll be disappointed when he finds out Axel sent off for you."

"You make me sound like something you order from a catalog."

"Or a newspaper ad." Will clamped his mouth shut — her bald-faced honesty was rubbing off on him.

She blinked a couple of times. "I suppose that's right. But since I no longer come with the money advertised, he might just send me back."

Would Axel be that shallow? A possibility. Maybe he ought to mention her penniless state as soon as Axel returned. Then his

71

friend would form no attachment, and Eliza would be free to entertain other suitors —

No. His thinking was going haywire, almost immoral — definitely unethical. Will ran his hands through his hair. "I've got to leave for a bit. Do you want to run the store, or shall I close?"

"Me?" She paused on the lowest rung of the ladder she'd just stepped onto. "You trust me already?"

More than he trusted Axel to work hard when no one watched. "Sure." He forced himself to turn around and grab his hat rather than soak in the beaming smile brightening her face. "I'll leave keys in case I don't return quickly. Close whenever you wish."

Her hand grabbed his arm. He tensed, yet she kept a firm hold.

"You've got another gun to fix, and you told that one man you'd have his purchases ready by five."

"I have plenty of time to finish the gun." He extricated himself and found the customer's shopping list. "Nothing unusual you can't find."

She stared at the paper with a stern tilt to her lips. "This isn't exactly a good way to do business."

"That's right — it's not." And being

fascinated by an unattainable, frumpy co-worker was definitely not good for business either. "Your fiancé should be here helping. I'm going to go find him."

He'd find Axel and drag him back before nightfall.

CHAPTER 5

If Silas Jonesey hadn't been sitting on the porch of his tiny cabin watching him approach, Will would have turned around in defeat. This was the last place he could think of to check for Axel, but his gelding wasn't tied here either.

Will surveyed his friend's impressive spread. At only twenty-six years old, Silas had cultivated his fields and improved his buildings more than some who'd owned property twice as long.

"What're you doing up my way?" Silas called from his rocker, where he was busily sharpening a knife on a whetstone.

"Looking for Axel Langston." Will slid off his saddle and led his horse to the thick green grass under the hackberry tree. "Has he been by lately?"

"Naw, told him I didn't want his company if he only came to drink." Silas crossed his arms over his broad chest. "Those fancy

74

pills of yours didn't help, by the way."

Will shook his head and tried not to sigh too loudly. "I told you they wouldn't, but you insisted on trying something."

"Well, if Dr. Forsythe's medicine turned me back into a drunk, then some other medicine ought to fix it."

A pill for everything? That'd be nice. Then he wouldn't have to go to school; he'd just consult a list and cure the world. "I'm sure Dr. Forsythe didn't intend for you to drink like a fish."

Silas drew his dark eyebrows together. "It was supposed to cure melancholia but didn't do a lick of good."

"Potions and magic won't cure you." Will tromped up the stairs and slid onto the porch rail. "You have to face the fact that your wife is gone and work through those feelings with God's help — not medicine. When Nancy left me for —"

"Don't go comparing your girl calling things off to my wife leaving. You have family and can get married anytime you want."

Will scanned the horizon, too pink for him to stay much longer. "I don't know about that — the pickings are slim."

"Just don't choose a mail-order bride," he spat.

Will kept the smile off his face. "Not all

mail-order brides are bad — I'm sure Everett and Carl would vouch for them."

"Not Axel's father, not the man who married the German woman, and not me."

Will rubbed his jaw, his stubble as scratchy as Silas's personality lately. "There're plenty of unhappy couples without the brides being ordered by mail."

"At least they're unhappy *together.*" Silas thunked his legs onto the railing.

Will pulled a mint from his pocket. "Try taking one of these a day."

Silas caught the candy and frowned.

"It'll sweeten your disposition."

Silas chucked the mint back at Will.

He pocketed it and wiped off his grin. "I still wait outside church in case you show up."

"Isn't it enough I got off that tonic?" Silas stared at his hands as he rubbed them together.

"God wants you back, Silas. You. As you are."

He clenched his jaw and shook his head. "He doesn't want me angry."

"You're only angry because you want to be." The man knew exactly what he ought to do yet refused. "Anger has gotten you nothing but years of gut ache. Give it up."

"So what if it's turned me sour? It's fueled me into getting my back forty under control and then some. I've got more wheat growing than any other homesteader in the area. An orchard even. Lucinda wouldn't complain now that I'm better off than almost anyone around these parts."

Will took in the man's pristine acreage. "Treasures that rot."

"I don't recall asking for a sermon," Silas muttered. "Actually, I don't recall asking you over at all."

"What's stuck in your craw today?"

"Today I've been alone again for six years." Silas played with a cracked fingernail. "Seven months of having someone to call my own wasn't enough."

Will laid a hand on Silas's stiff back. No use in any more talk. The man had probably used his vocal cords more in the last five minutes than the last five weeks — though his isolation was more Silas's own fault than anyone else's. Silas had been dealt a bad hand, though. Will couldn't imagine the life of an orphan, let alone how an orphan would feel upon being abandoned a second time by the person who mattered most in his life.

Maybe one day Silas would return to God and lay down his anger. In the meantime, Will couldn't do much besides pray. "Well,

I'll get out of your hair, then. Got any idea where I might find Axel? No one's seen him at any of the saloons."

"Have you asked his pa?"

"His parents' is the only place I haven't checked." He'd hoped to avoid them — he just couldn't imagine Axel willingly staying home for more than two days. And learning of his absence would only aggravate his father's normal irritability.

Forcing her sleepy eyes to stay open during a jaw-dropping yawn, Eliza followed her nose to the dining room table. The baked sugar smell that had woken her turned out to be a stack of muffins. Enough for ten people, not just two women.

Irena Lightfoot pushed through the kitchen door with a plate of scrambled eggs in one hand and a pitcher in the other. "I hope I didn't wake you." Though a fancy white-and-blue scarf obscured her face, her low-hanging brows suggested a frown.

"I couldn't sleep any longer." She took the pitcher from Irena's knobby hands and filled their glasses. "I'm famished."

"You should've come home last night for dinner." Irena didn't look at her. She likely disapproved of her being out so late but kept her opinions to herself. A good trait for someone running a boardinghouse.

But Eliza had nothing to be ashamed of. She sat and grabbed a muffin. "I didn't want to leave the store until the displays were just right, and then I had to clean up."

"Was William helping you?" A faint hint of censure colored her voice.

"He left to look for Axel around three. That's another reason I stayed late. I wanted to be there when Axel returned." She picked the nuts off the top of her muffin. "But William didn't find him."

Irena only hummed, as if she'd expected that answer.

Was no one else concerned about her missing fiancé? Why was William the only one trying to locate him? What if Axel was dead?

Her hostess finished setting the table and said a brief word of prayer, but didn't mention Axel's disappearance to the Lord.

Eliza took a bite, but even the sugary muffin wasn't sweet enough to make her feel better. Did Mrs. Lightfoot know anything about her future husband?

Irena leaned over the table, letting her scarf swing forward so she could get a forkful of eggs to her mouth.

"This may be rude of me, but why don't you remove your scarf to eat?"

Irena held up a finger, probably indicating she hadn't finished chewing. "I've found it easier for my guests."

"But not easier for you."

"Well, no." She chuckled. "However, my job is to make you comfortable."

"Does it bother you if people stare?"

"Oh no, honey. I used to accept money so people could stare at me. I'm quite over that."

"Then, if you don't mind my saying so, I'm uncomfortable staying with you for nothing yet physically inconveniencing you. If you'd like to take off your scarf, I'd probably stare for a bit. I've never seen a bearded lady, but I'm sure the oddity will wear off and then I'll think nothing of it."

"Well, that was honest." Irena laughed. "I'll tell you what, as long as you stay honest, I'll take the scarf off. If you find you can't get past the distraction, let me know. I'd much rather have company than eat with ease."

"All right." Eliza touched the bandage swathing her whole head for a two-inch gash. She hadn't taken it off because the stitches looked even worse. "I do believe I've been given a taste of what you must feel. I get lots of second glances as I walk down the road. Makes you sensitive to the rest of your appearance — though I've never been one to care about fashion and the like."

Irena fiddled with her scarf's knot tucked behind a pile of salt-and-pepper curls. "You do dress rather . . . dowdy."

"I don't think anyone's come right out and said that to me before."

"I figure if *you're* going to be forthright, I'd make this a completely honest relationship." She finished untying her scarf but didn't drop it. "Ready to commence staring?"

Eliza cupped her hands under her chin like a child eager to see something spectacular. "Ready." She winked.

Irena wound her scarf around her hand but cut eye contact. Her beard was grayer than her hair, close-cropped and neat, yet sparse.

"My former fiancé cut his beard much like that, but my brother lets his grow scraggly. Half the time his mustache hangs in his mouth." Eliza shuddered. "Yours looks so much better."

Irena looked up and swallowed hard. "Thanks, I guess."

Eliza shrugged and picked up her fork to spear some eggs. "So if we can be honest with each other, and I ask a question, can I expect a truthful answer?"

Irena laced her fingers atop the table. "I believe I'm about to regret this honesty thing already, but at my age, I'm afflicted with tell-the-truth disease anyway. You young'uns need lots of help, though you hardly listen."

"I do want advice though." She set her silverware down. "Why do I get the impression something is wrong with Axel?"

Irena scratched at a sideburn. "In what way?"

"No one's worried or surprised that he's disappeared."

"I'm afraid I don't know Axel personally." She rubbed her nose. "I've heard a bit about him, but I avoid believing or spreading prattle. The gossips will tell you I turn into a wolf at night or that I became this way by consorting with the devil." She gave a weak smile. "You've written to him and talked with William, so you know more than I do from better sources, and nothing I've heard has been too alarming."

Eliza frowned but let the topic drop. She'd not push Irena to gossip just for honesty's sake.

Yet if Irena had heard positive hearsay, she wouldn't have evaded the question.

Eliza walked into the Hampden Mercantile

even though she was rather late for work. The muffins she'd consumed — and she'd eaten quite a few after Irena refused to divulge anything about Axel's reputation — rolled around like lead shot in her gut.

She was crazy, just like Ruth had said, except her friend back home had only worried Axel would be gap-toothed and pockmarked. Not some irresponsible wastrel who flitted in and out of town without breathing a word to anyone.

A gap-toothed man, if responsible, would be the better option.

Surely a convenient marriage couldn't be worse than choosing from the Pennsylvanian men who'd come courting after her fiancé jilted her. But none of those had any interest in her business ideas, and Axel had. He'd promised her a store, offered her exactly what she'd wanted her whole life.

Yet what if the man was something worse than ugly?

She stopped midstride. What if he didn't return because he'd died? She would be stranded in Salt Flatts with no store and no husband.

Kathleen walked out of the back room with a stack of bolted fabrics.

"Here, let me help you." Eliza rushed over to take several bolts off the top.

"Thanks." Kathleen smiled but then frowned when Eliza pulled off the rest. "Just because I'm in a family way doesn't mean I can't handle the inventory."

Eliza gave her friend's overly large abdomen a pointed glare. "No need to tax yourself."

"You're as bad as Carl."

"Then at least Mr. Hampden's got his head on straight."

Kathleen pshawed. "Acting like an invalid won't get things done around here." Her waddling steps made the boards creak beneath her. "Say, what are you doing here anyway? It's past nine."

Eliza dropped the bolts onto the fabric table and began to place them with like colors, keeping her gaze on her sorting task. "I had a talk with Mrs. Lightfoot about . . . Axel, and well, I didn't get any real answers and thought maybe you might have some, but then . . ." She looked up and scanned the store's few customers. "Maybe I should come back later."

Kathleen leaned heavily upon the table. "Well, if you're wanting to ease my burden, what better way to make Carl do everything than keep me busy talking?" She smiled mischievously, but Eliza couldn't smile back.

"Do you think I could find a job in Salt Flatts if I don't . . . end up marrying?"

Kathleen's face sobered. "I don't know. You already think you're incompatible? How long has Axel been back in town?"

"He's still not here." She picked at some loose threads on a bolt of gingham.

"Then how can you be certain —"

"Surely if anyone in this town could understand how hard it is to marry someone you've never met, it's you." She leaned closer and whispered. "William mentioned you were a mail-order bride like me."

Kathleen grinned. "No need to whisper. There's more than one woman in this town who's come that way. And not many ended up with who they were intended for."

"They didn't?"

"No. Let's see. . . . Me, of course, and well, the man I jilted, Everett Cline, was jilted by more than me. I think maybe three? Perhaps more. Kind of a town joke."

"Three? Poor man." How sad to be rejected so many times by desperate strangers.

"Ah, but he got one that stuck." She smiled. "And I think Axel's mother was a mail-order bride too, or tried to be — wanted to marry William's pa."

"So I'd not be the only one to jilt a man

who brought me here through a mail-order bride service?" The heaviness clotting her breath broke up, allowing her lungs to draw in more air than she'd managed all morning.

"No, but why would you? I thought you wanted a store. No other single men around here own one. Well, except for William, but it's more Axel's store than his."

Then there was William. She'd known he'd held an interest in the store, but how much sway did he truly have? He didn't want to move the counter, didn't greet the customers, created sales off the cuff . . .

If she married Axel, would William treat her as if she held half of Axel's percent? Or would he fight her every suggestion, just as he did now? Was Axel the kind of man to back up his new wife over his childhood friend if they disagreed? It wasn't as if she had won Axel's affection — their marriage was a business deal.

Eliza looked out the mercantile's front windows, watching the town's busy street. "William mentioned the day I arrived he'd been jilted too." With everyone jilting everyone else, maybe she should be less worried about deciding whether or not to jilt Axel, but whether or not she could keep him from jilting her.

"William?" Kathleen frowned for a second, then shook her head. "Oh yes, Nancy Graves. For a second I thought you meant a mail-order bride had jilted him."

A desperate woman like herself was surely beneath the notice of a man as handsome as William. He'd never have to consider marrying a stranger. At medical school, he'd likely find plenty of attractive city girls interested in courting. Though why *had* he been jilted?

"Why did this Miss Graves leave him? I mean . . . unless he has some terrible dark side I don't see, what reason would his fiancée have had to call it off?"

"No dark side." Kathleen repositioned herself with a groan. "Couldn't make up his mind about going to school quick enough for her taste. She really wanted children, if I recall correctly, and married a widower with a slew of them."

"She must not have loved William very much then."

"I think that's what hurt him the most. They were together since they were young'uns."

"So why doesn't he go to school? Is it just because he hasn't enough money?"

"I'm sure that's part of it, but three years ago, when his mother gave birth to his twin sisters, they came too early and William was the only one there." She pressed the heel of her hand against her stomach for a moment and made a little hissing sound. "Something went wrong. He saved his mother, but lost one baby, and the other has . . . problems."

"That's awful." She bit her lip. Talking about babies being born early and having problems was likely not the best conversation to have with Kathleen at the moment. "Though I'd think that would make him more eager to learn what to do in an emergency." Would he be able to help Kathleen if she and the baby were in crisis?

"He blames himself for not riding off for the doctor — which he refuses to acknowledge would have been the worse choice. He couldn't have known how bad it was going to be. But then Dr. Forsythe had the audacity to tell him if he'd taken a few minutes to make sure the babies were breathing well before helping his mother, the girls could have been fine."

How terrible to feel responsible for a sibling's death. "Why would the man say such an unkind thing?"

"That's Dr. Forsythe for you — facts and statistics, no compassion. Told William what page in his book to read about what was wrong with his little sister and that nothing could be done. William blames himself for not having known."

"Yet he still doctors against his will."

Kathleen gave her a half smile. "Because, unlike Dr. Forsythe, he cares."

"And his fiancée left him while he grieved his mistakes?" At Kathleen's nod, Eliza tried not to scowl. "This woman doesn't live in town anymore, does she?"

"No, she moved away after she got married."

Good, because she didn't want to serve such a woman. Not that it was likely this Nancy person would visit the Men's Emporium . . . where Eliza ought to be already. "So you don't know anything about Axel's character that would make you advise me not to marry him?"

Kathleen pulled at a loose thread at the end of a bolt. "I'm not going to say the young man has no flaws. Who doesn't?"

She narrowed her eyes. Would Kathleen refuse to talk about Axel too? "What are his faults exactly?"

"Well, he was a rather smart-mouthed youth. My husband used to natter on about how the boy was more of a hindrance at barn raisings than a help. . . . But truth be told" — she leaned closer to Eliza — "I'm not sure my husband is good enough with a hammer to know."

She straightened back up and shrugged. "When Axel got that inheritance after his grandfather died, he tried to put it to good use, buying some property and setting himself up with a store.

"He should've asked for advice, so I guess he's a bit headstrong, but at least he didn't throw the money away at a tavern or bet it all on some silly scheme. He tried, then realized he needed help, and begged William to join him. Then he realized that wasn't enough, so he sought you out."

"I guess no one can go through life without learning some lessons." She certainly shouldn't have mouthed off so badly to her brother about how he'd fail to run the store as well as she could. Oh, why had Father gone with convention and left all his property to his lazy son instead of her? She bit her lip. Because she'd been a silly girl, moonstruck by attention from a handsome man. A handsome, swindling man.

So what if Axel wasn't the prince of perfect choices? Which would be better? Doing the work she dreamed of with a less-than-stellar husband, or looking for some man to keep her who didn't believe in her ambitions, who might even stomp on them?

And wouldn't Axel be better than trying

to make it out here alone with nothing?

"Kathleen!" Carl's call was accompanied by a child's whimpering, which quickly escalated into a full cry.

"I'm sorry." Kathleen grimaced. "Gretchen woke up this morning with stomach problems, and Carl doesn't handle illness well."

Eliza forced herself not to guffaw at the understatement. "I know. He was there when William stitched my face."

"I better go." She pushed herself away from the table. "If you want to talk more, come by for dinner."

Eliza scratched her temple. "Thanks for the offer, but Mrs. Lightfoot's expecting me."

Kathleen waddled off and looked back over her shoulder. "Feel free to come another time, then."

Did she need to do any more talking? It's not as if she'd ever expected a fairy-tale wedding. A mail-order bride was not a princess, and a struggling mercantile owner was not a prince. If only she could find the man and drag him home so she could decide whether he was worth the trouble of marrying before her stomach tied itself into any more knots.

Stepping out into the wind, she anchored

her loose hair behind her ears to keep the locks out of her eyes and walked toward the Men's Emporium, nodding at the few men who nodded to her. Clearly, a scarcity of women garnered her more male attention than she'd ever received back home.

Could she find someone here willing to court her if she jilted Axel? Considering the three smiles she was given after walking only a block, it seemed it wouldn't be too hard. Lynville Tate definitely appeared interested. But if she married him, she'd be mucking stalls and milking cows, not running a store.

She blinked her eyes against the heat behind her eyelids before entering the Men's Emporium, careful not to let the door slam shut with the wind. Customers filled the store's aisles, and taking a steadying breath, she looked around, hoping to find someone who didn't appear to be a customer — her Axel.

They all seemed to be shopping, though, and William only raised his hand in greeting before returning his focus to a man who appeared to be arguing with him. Nobody seemed to need her help, so after the contentious man left, she trudged back to attend the sparse cashbox.

"Could you gather this for Mr. Carmichael?" William handed her a piece of paper. "He's coming back in an hour."

"I can. Has Axel . . . ?" She couldn't say more for fear she'd give away the worry, frustration, and downright apprehension she had at meeting the man.

The door chimed, announcing another customer whose heavy tread thumped on the floorboards.

"Good afternoon, Mr. Langston," William called.

Her heart stopped. Axel? She summoned up a smile and twirled toward the front.

His dark head had a lot of gray at the temples. Could he have lied about his age? Though his face was quite handsome, and he was certainly tall.

"Hello," her voice squeaked.

Axel gave her a sideways glance and frowned.

She hadn't beauty enough to make a man do cartwheels, but was she that disappointing? She reached up to touch her bandage but quickly dropped her hand, wiped her sweaty palm on her apron, and moved forward. "I'm Eliza."

He gave her a scrutinizing look, as if trying to recall her from memory.

This did not bode well.

"Let me introduce Miss Cantrell." William came up behind her and laid a firm hand on her shoulder. Surely he felt her nerves tightening every last muscle. "She's working here."

"Where's Axel?" The older man looked past her, then to each side of the store.

Her knees turned to mush. Of course. William wouldn't have greeted Axel so formally. A relative?

"We don't know. I intended to stop by your house tonight to see if he was laid up there." William turned to her. "Eliza, this is Axel's father."

She nodded. If his son inherited half this man's good looks, she had nothing to worry about on that account. She tried to smile but couldn't quite do so with his scowl directed at her. "I look forward to getting to know you."

"Why's that necessary?" He looked at her as if she were nothing more than a squashed bug, then turned his frighteningly direct gaze onto William. "How long's Axel been gone?"

"Five days, sir."

Mr. Langston cut his eyes at her. "And how long you been working here?"

Why was he interrogating them? "Three days. Did you come in for something I could help you find?"

The man stared at his ink-stained hands,

then turned his glare back on William. "You hired her without Axel having his say?"

Did he not hear her name? "I'm Eliza Cantrell, sir."

He turned a blank look at her.

William cleared his throat. "This is Axel's mail-order bride. She came earlier than expected."

Mr. Langston blinked. Twice. Then started to shake his head slowly. "Axel wouldn't order no mail-order bride."

She swallowed. Hadn't Axel informed his parents about her? "I'm so sorry. I thought he would have mentioned my coming."

"No." His jaw worked hard. "My boy'd never do such a thing."

She clasped her hands in front of her, trying not to shrivel like a piece of bacon in the hot, roiling stare he aimed at her forehead. What did he have against mail-order brides? Hadn't Kathleen said he'd married one? And why hadn't Axel informed his parents she was coming?

She did come six days earlier than planned, but surely Axel wasn't planning to spring her on his family the day of their wedding. Especially since Mr. Langston didn't seem to be taking the news well.

William squeezed her shoulder. "Maybe we should wait until Axel returns to discuss this further. Did you come in for something?"

Mr. Langston took his lethal stare off her and handed William a broken steel pen point. "I need another handful of these."

William left to gather the pen points, leaving the two of them alone.

Her hands trembled as she smoothed her apron skirt. "I'm sorry I'm such a surprise."

"Not a surprise — a blow straight to the gut is what it is." He looked to the ceiling. "That boy ain't got no brains."

All right, maybe talking to him wouldn't be beneficial. Though if she jilted Axel, she definitely had a supporter. "I have a love for business, sir. I grew up under my father's tutelage, and Axel wanted help running the store. I'm not . . . I'm not worthless."

"Right." His jaw set like concrete, he looked over her shoulder. "Will's got my tips." He sidestepped her as if she were nothing but a pothole in his path.

She shivered in the wisp of air he left behind and fingered a flannel shirt dangling off a shelf's ledge. For once, she had no desire to fold an item up nice and crisp and lay it perfectly atop the others in the stack.

She dropped the sleeve. It could hang there for now.

Or not. Snatching it off the shelf, she

flicked the shirt out and started folding.

"What's wrong with her face?" Mr. Langston's voice was lowered, but not enough that she couldn't hear.

"She came the day the train was robbed —"

"Well, that's not a good sign."

"Evidently, she held out on one of the thieves and he made her into an example." William put the nibs and a bottle of ink in a small sack. "Could've been worse."

"Worse?" He grunted. "Seems to me stubborn women usually get what they deserve."

Stubborn? Would he rather she'd thanked the man for stealing her savings? She creased the shirt's collar with more pressure than necessary.

William rolled the top of the sack and tallied the price.

Why didn't he defend her? He'd seemed sympathetic. Or maybe he'd simply been pretending, knowing he'd have to work with her.

Mr. Langston swished around in his pocket for coins. "Put it on my account." He scowled back at her for a second. "Heard the sheriff nabbed the train robbers this morning. Got some loot back."

"Thanks for the information, Mr. Langston." William handed Axel's father his purchases. "Have a nice day."

"We'll see." He clomped past her, but she kept right on folding.

Maybe there was a divine reason her fiancé had not been around when she arrived. Though she'd not really asked God what to do, was He warning her not to marry Axel through his father's misgivings?

And if that was so, would He provide her with a way out of Salt Flatts? The sheriff having hauled the robbers in this morning might not be a coincidence. Maybe it was her train ticket home.

CHAPTER 6

The next day, Eliza quit an hour early so she'd be certain to catch the sheriff. She tried not to run, but yesterday the lawman's doors had been locked after she'd left work.

If she chose not to marry Axel, she'd need money to fend for herself until she found work or figured out where to go.

Something wasn't quite right. William seemed uncomfortable talking about Axel, Irena refused to tell her anything she knew, none of the townsfolk who'd learned of her impending marriage had congratulated her, and Axel's father hadn't even known about her.

The jailhouse door stood ajar, and she stopped to catch her breath before entering.

She stepped into the jailhouse and wrinkled her nose at the smell of unwashed bodies. A short man with a leer stared at her from the cell in the back, his hands hanging through the bars.

She quickly broke eye contact and headed for the lawman behind the desk. "Sheriff Quade?"

"Yes." The older man with a long, well-groomed mustache looked up from his work and squinted. "Have I talked to you recently?"

She put a hand to her stitches, no longer covered with a bandage but still painful, and quite itchy. "Yes, sir, the day one of those men backhanded me with a gun."

"Ah, yes. I suppose you want your stuff back." He sighed.

Didn't everybody want to claim their things? "I'm sorry to inconvenience you, but I really need —"

"No need to apologize." He rubbed the top of his brow. "No one's been happy with me today, and I've had to deal with *them.*" He jerked his thumb back at the cell.

Behind the short thief, a man with a long yellow-white beard slumped in a chair and leaned over to spit. The other criminal lay prone on a bunk with his hat over his head twiddling his thumbs. Thankfully, he seemed content not to look at her. He'd probably smile proudly at the damage he'd done to her face.

It looked like the sheriff had captured them all. "I'm Eliza Cantrell. Is there some process I have to go through to get my money?"

"No, ma'am, but you won't get much unless we find their stash — and they haven't been helpful in that regard."

The short robber smashed his face between the bars. "I might be able to find you a few dollars iffen you want to come in and entertain us for a while." His sloppy kissing noises ran cold chills up her torso, which bloomed into heat.

"Shut up, boy." The sheriff glared toward the cell, but didn't so much as move. His lips pursed sympathetically. "Sorry, can't exactly hang 'em for running off at the mouth, nor expect manners from a bunch of reprobates."

"Oh, I'll be real sweet to her, Sheriff."

Sheriff Quade stood and beckoned her outside, the front door shutting off the string of profanities hurled at her.

She put her cold hands against her cheeks.

"I should've known better than to let a lady come inside." He pointed to a bench, and she sat. If only she were still wearing her bandage, her heated face would be at least partially hidden from sight.

Who'd have thought she'd want that horrid piece of cloth back on?

Sheriff Quade thumped his boot onto a

crate and leaned over his knee. "The thing is, they didn't have much money when we captured them. My deputies went back to look for a hideout that may or may not exist, but I don't want you holding out hope."

Her stomach sank low. "So I may be out of my money forever?"

"Highly likely, ma'am."

"I've got nothing?" She couldn't leave town if she had no money. As a last resort, she could write her brother, but he'd given her all she was due.

She definitely shouldn't have told Zachary she'd be just fine without him. He was spiteful enough to make her eat her words.

"We recovered a little — what was on their persons when we caught them — so I can get you a percentage according to the claims made." Without waiting for a nod from her, he slipped inside. His muffled command for silence only caused loud laughter.

She took a deep breath through her nose and let it out slowly through her pursed lips. If she found a job right away, maybe Mrs. Lightfoot would let her stay a little while longer for nothing . . . but if she jilted Axel, would she be able to find a job in the town he'd grown up in? Would she even want to stay?

The door swung open again, and the

sheriff handed her ten dollars. "That's all I can give you."

"That's it?"

"As I said, we didn't recover much, but tell me where you're staying, and if we find anything, I'll personally deliver any more that comes in."

She slid the single bill from his grasp, turned her head away from his sympathetic brown eyes, and blinked back moisture. Ten dollars. She had no choice but to stay. "I'm residing at Mrs. Lightfoot's."

"Ah, yes. At least you can pay your board now."

But not for next week and the week after that.

"If you can't find me there, I'll soon be . . ." She bit her lip. If she did marry Axel, the sheriff would figure out her new living arrangements. "Well, you can inquire after me at the Men's Emporium. I'm working there." Working. Maybe she could convince William to pay her for helping at the Men's Emporium. Though a week's wages wouldn't be enough to do much either.

"Interesting choice, but I'm glad you found work." He tipped his hat. "I best get back."

Eliza watched the sheriff disappear, then

stared at the cash in her hand. All night she'd tossed and turned, anticipating getting her money, having the freedom to say no to Axel. But ten dollars instead of five hundred wouldn't get her anywhere. She folded the bill until it was a tiny little square.

She hoped her fears over Axel were unfounded. Though she'd hated her mother for ruining their family twelve years ago by disregarding her vows and abandoning her father to pursue acting, Eliza had spent all day yesterday fabricating reasons to go back on her commitment to Axel.

Was an inclination for turning one's back on a promise an inheritable trait?

Had she just about let emotions and a fear of the unknown turn her into her mother?

Will sped up to overtake Eliza as she turned off Main Street. He didn't want to hold on to this letter and prolong the inevitable. He felt his chest pocket, making certain the missive was still there. Thankfully, Axel's father hadn't seen the note for Eliza tucked into Will's when he'd delivered it. Mr. Langston would have been sore that his son had written to her and not to him.

How would Eliza react? Would she sigh in relief or act disappointed? Would either reaction keep his wandering thoughts contained?

He couldn't think around Eliza, and his productivity had decreased. The gun he'd been working on for two days should have been finished in one, but he couldn't keep his eyes off her. She wasn't flirting with the customers, but the more time she spent with one, the more he wanted to count how long she made eye contact or smiled as if he were the only man in the world.

Why didn't she smile at him that way?

He groaned at the overwhelming desire to know the answer.

Eliza stopped and looked over her shoulder. "William." She turned, waiting for him to walk the last few feet to catch her, hiding her stitches with a palm pressed against her cheek. Which was silly, since he'd examined them before she left work.

"Are you coming to check on Irena?"

"Yes." He ought to anyway. "Can I walk with you?"

She shrugged and returned to walking. "You might as well hear about my trip to the sheriff's." Her lips twitched, and she glanced toward him. "I only got ten dollars back. Enough to pay for my board and maybe —"

"Now, wait a minute." Will shook his

head. "My doctoring's supposed to pay for that." If she paid her room and board, she'd have nothing left.

She sighed and trudged along.

Had she really believed she'd recover all her money? She was lucky to get ten.

He played with the bead on his ring. He might as well broach the topic now. "Axel sent me a letter."

Eliza stopped midstep. "So where is he?"

He halted beside her, his mouth suddenly fuzzy. "Don't know."

Her eyebrows gathered together. "Still?"

"He didn't tell me where he was."

She narrowed her eyes. "That seems to be a habit of his."

A habit Will had never been more annoyed with than now. "He's evidently laid up at some ranch outside of Atchison. His horse bucked him. He hit his head and messed up his leg."

With her hand over her mouth, Eliza looked misty-eyed. "And here I'd thought . . ."

"He said he'd be fine." He certainly would be, once he learned he had a woman like Eliza in tears over him. Would he have risked the ride home if he knew his fiancée was waiting?

Eliza's face seemed to go through a series

of emotions, some downright heartrending, others contemplative. What was she thinking so hard about?

"Did he say how long he'd be gone?"

"Some doctor told him to stay put until he could ride his horse safely." Why Axel was that far away to begin with, Will couldn't guess.

"Since Axel will be gone awhile, why don't we work to get the store's counter up front while we wait?"

Will snapped up straight. That's what she'd been thinking about? Even though he'd said they should wait for Axel to return? "We don't have the money for that."

Her adorable pout made him want to smile.

He dropped his eyes. Finding another man's intended adorable was a bigger problem than if Eliza destroyed all his shelving and ordered him to build new ones from uncut trees. "Though I suppose I could do most of the work without purchasing much."

Her eyes brightened.

"But how could I attend customers if I'm playing carpenter? And I'm no good at woodworking. You'd be unhappy with the wait — and the result."

She scrunched her lips. Surely thinking

up an argument for the project.

"And how many customers would be annoyed by the construction mess and leave?"

"A few days of lost business would be worth it if the result was more customers in the future."

"Again, we ought to wait for Axel to return." He tugged the note from his pocket. "He sent this for you with my letter. He didn't know you were here, of course. He asked me to meet you at the station." He tried to smile. If he'd known about her and Axel before she arrived, could he have steeled his heart enough to deflect that jolt he'd felt while stitching up her cheek?

"Too bad I didn't come when scheduled." She pursed her lips and took Axel's letter. "I'd still have money."

He couldn't figure out what to do with his hands, so he anchored them to his belt. "If your letter gives you a better idea of his location, I could fetch him while you run the store."

Her big eyes widened, a small glimmer dancing within her dark pupils. "You'd trust me to watch the store?"

He shrugged. "If it would get Axel back sooner . . ." Because he really, really needed Axel home.

"Of course." Her voice descended as if

he'd given the wrong answer.

Did she not want Axel to return? He gripped the back of his neck and shut his eyes tight against the desire to hope she didn't.

Starting slowly back down the road, she opened the letter. No seal, no envelope. Did she know how tempted he'd been to read it himself?

She scanned the paper as they walked. At the bottom porch step of Mrs. Lightfoot's boardinghouse, she sighed. "No more information than you had. He did tell me which bank I should put my money in." She snorted. "And that I should hold off introducing myself to his parents."

She folded the letter. "Guess it's you and me for a while. Hopefully not too long."

"Right." How many days could he be alone with her before he said something he'd regret?

She stopped at the front door, her hand on the knob, and turned to face him. "Would you visit Axel's family with me tomorrow after work?"

He rubbed his temples. Spend more time with her away from the store? "Axel told you to wait."

"Yes, but he didn't know I'd already revealed myself to his father."

"I don't think it would be wise to —"

"Fine. I'll go by myself."

He crossed his arms. "And that definitely wouldn't be wise."

"Then, you'll come?"

The woman was bound and determined to trip him up. If she only knew what a mess the Langstons were.

"I can't let Axel's father's anger fester any longer than it has if I'm going to stay, so I need to visit them as soon as possible and make amends. They'll be more comfortable with me if you come."

He cupped the back of his neck and pinched the tense muscles running across his shoulders. He hadn't visited the Langstons much since childhood. He had no idea why Axel's parents didn't get along, but it didn't take an adult to understand the marriage wasn't good — at all. After Jedidiah's reaction to Eliza the other day, Will expected their marriage hadn't improved over the years.

"Why don't you stop thinking and tell me yes?"

He shook his head at her bossiness but couldn't smile. "I guess a bad relationship with the in-laws isn't a good way to start a marriage."

"Exactly."

"Then I suppose I shouldn't say no." But how he wished he could.

CHAPTER 7

Axel's parents' home sat on a quiet lot at the edge of town, apart from the other houses. Weeds were growing over the rock pathway meandering up to the front door, and a scraggly bush obscured most of the ivy climbing the walls. The intrusive vines had pried off the siding in places, and sun-bleached curtains hung behind grubby windows.

Eliza gripped the wagon's seat as Will pulled his horse to a stop. Perhaps she should have brought a gift, or waited another day and baked something. Something that might mitigate Axel's father's displeasure, something that would've made a good impression. She looked down at her best dress — not fancy by any standard. Her looks certainly weren't in her favor.

She wiped her palms on her skirt before William helped her down. "You still think this is a bad idea?"

"Would it change your mind if I did?"

"Maybe."

If he had misgivings about her and Axel, why didn't he say something? "Don't keep things from me. I'm going to have to marry the man, for goodness' sake. And you . . ." She poked him in the chest. "You know him best and have nothing at stake, so why not spit it out? If there's something I should know about Axel, as the woman planning on tying myself to him for the rest of my life, you need to tell me. Now. Before it's too late."

William's jaw worked back and forth, and she backed away from his intense glare.

Maybe she shouldn't have been so direct. "Please?"

He rubbed a hand down his face. "That's just it. I really can't say anything bad about him, except . . . except . . ."

"What?"

"He drinks occasionally, and sometimes he's not the best worker." William huffed. "But sometimes a man only needs a wife — and a child or two — to get himself straightened out." His hand massaged the back of his neck.

She glanced at the front door. "So why doesn't anyone seem . . . happy for me?"

"He wasn't exactly a well-behaved kid.

He's been working on being a better person, though. But people in small towns have long memories."

"Are *you* happy for me?"

He licked his lips. "Should I not be?"

"I suppose you don't know me well enough to know what would make me happy, but what about Axel? Are you happy for him?"

He cleared his throat. "I couldn't wish for him anything better."

His intense gaze was unnerving. He hadn't wanted to visit the Langstons' with her, and here she was interrogating him. "Well, since I dragged you here, I might as well get on with it."

"Hold on a second." He grabbed her hand. "When making a big decision, you shouldn't be careless. You should be picky."

"That's why I'm here. To help me decide."

William dropped her hand and put his back in his pockets. "I wish I could help you know what to do."

She beckoned for him to precede her. "Well then, say a prayer this visit goes well."

"Is that what you want?"

After she nodded, he scurried up the uneven stone sidewalk and knocked.

Eliza tried to peer into the window speckled with prairie dust, but sunshine obscured everything. Silence stretched between them until William knocked again, louder.

The door creaked open, and a woman with a messy blond bun peeped through the crack. "Can I help you?"

"Mrs. Langston?"

She tilted her head back and pushed her wire-rim spectacles closer to her face. "William Stanton?"

He nodded, swallowing hard. "I've brought a visitor. This is Miss Cantrell."

"Eliza?" Mrs. Langston swung the door open, but instead of the scowl her husband had worn, her frown lines disappeared with a smile. "From Pennsylvania?"

"Yes." She took a step closer. "I suppose your husband told you I'd come?" Apparently, his anger hadn't affected his wife.

"Oh no. Axel's told me about you several times."

He had? But why keep their engagement from his father?

"Come in!" Mrs. Langston swung the door open wider.

William smiled at Axel's mother, and Eliza's breath caught. She closed her eyes, hoping he'd not noticed the mouthful of air she'd swallowed. Had he ever smiled at her like that?

Yes, her first day in Salt Flatts. However

she'd only gotten half smiles since then. Why was that thought troubling?

"Let me get some refreshments." Mrs. Langston bustled away.

Eliza walked in behind William and blinked against the dimness. The front room wasn't exactly well kept. Fabric was strewn everywhere, a half-made dress hung from a rafter, and several trouser legs lay across the back of the sofa.

Mrs. Langston walked around the corner carrying a plate of rolls. "I baked these this morning. I have company so rarely. Please ignore my mess and find a seat. Can I offer you coffee or tea?"

William grabbed a roll for each hand and slumped in his chair. "Tea, please."

Once Mrs. Langston disappeared again, Eliza leaned over to whisper, "Do you think Mr. Langston's here?"

"Nah," William mumbled around a mouthful. "Mrs. Langston's too happy."

"I suppose her being excited to meet me is a good thing."

"Very good." His chewing slowed, and he got a faraway look in his eye.

When Mrs. Langston reappeared, Eliza mirrored the lady's smile. Axel's mother appeared careworn, with harsh lines framing her mouth and a dull color beneath her eyes, but she'd been pretty in her day. Perhaps Axel *was* as handsome as William. If so, he might easily be too handsome to want her. She rearranged herself in the lumpy chair, removing the beginning of a man's coat sleeve from underneath her.

Mrs. Langston set a glass of tea in front of William, then handed her one. She sat, adjusted her skirts, and smiled expectantly.

Eliza's tongue felt glued to the roof of her mouth, so she grabbed her drink and sipped the overly sweet liquid.

Then Mrs. Langston's face fell, and she glanced between them. "Where's Axel?"

William straightened and cleared his throat. "We don't rightly know, ma'am. Didn't your husband mention the letter I received?"

Mrs. Langston massaged her palm nervously. "No."

William frowned. "Axel wrote that he fell off his horse and is recuperating at a farm near Atchison. Didn't ask for someone to get him. Probably shouldn't be moved."

Mrs. Langston sucked air between her teeth. "This is my fault."

"Do you know why he's in Atchison?" He leaned forward in his chair.

Eliza couldn't help but lean forward too.

"He's out looking for stores willing to

stock my ready-made clothes. The seam-stress in town is unhappy with the quality of my work." She stared at her lap. "She's stopped hiring me."

Eliza frowned at William. "Why aren't you selling them at your store?"

He scowled. She leaned back.

"I didn't know anything about Mrs. Lang-ston's clothing."

"You wouldn't, honey. Until recently, I've only been doing dresses. I've been working on some men's shirts and trousers Axel thought you could sell." She rubbed a hand repeatedly over her other arm. "The more places we find for my work, though, the bet-ter I can support myself."

William stopped munching and set his bread on the table. "Why would you have to support yourself?"

"Oh dear." Mrs. Langston picked up a ladies' magazine and fanned her face. A vis-ible reddening crept up from her collar. "This is why I should be content with no visitors." She reached over to pat Eliza's knee. "But I'm quite thrilled you've come."

Eliza clasped her hand. Though the wom-an's cheeks were flushed, her hands felt like icicles. "Are you insinuating your husband's planning to div—"

"Oh no." Mrs. Langston's harsh smile was

anything but happy. "He don't abide scandal. I've just been 'put away.' We attend church together, but other than the money he gives Axel to pay for my groceries and kerosene, I'm to fend for myself."

"How horrible."

She shrugged. "Caleb's moved so far away he doesn't know what's goin' on, but I still have Axel, and he's a wonderful son. Better than I could have hoped for after he learned —" She abruptly stood. "I forgot my tea. Excuse me."

Eliza nodded as if Mrs. Langston needed her consent. After her future mother-in-law walked out of the room, she wilted against her chair, closed her eyes, and smiled.

Axel treated his momma right. That's why he'd been secretive about where he'd been. His parents forced it upon him. "So he's a good man."

"I've misjudged him." William stared at his feet. "I should've helped him more."

"Well, as she said, you wouldn't have known." Eliza took a sip of her tea and relaxed. No reason to fret over Jedidiah Langston not liking her — Axel's mother did. If Jedidiah could treat his wife so poorly, he wasn't worth impressing.

Mrs. Langston returned and plopped down in her chair. "I'm sorry I rushed off.

I'm out of practice hosting." The tea sloshed as she set her glass on the end table. "We should talk more about you, not me."

"Before you do," William said, scooting to the edge of his chair, "is something wrong with your hands?"

Mrs. Langston clasped her hands tightly in her lap, stuffing them in the folds of her dress. "It's nothing."

"They seem to trouble you. Numbness? A sensation you're trying to rub away?"

Eliza blinked at William. He'd figured that out in the few minutes they'd been there?

"Too much sewing, I suppose. That's why the seamstress is unhappy with my work. She only wants expensive dresses, perfectly stitched." She briskly rubbed her hands together. "Nothing seems to help, but I'm all right. I deserve worse for my sins."

Worse than being abandoned by her husband and made to work when her hands wouldn't cooperate? Eliza scooted forward in her chair. "Now, Mrs. Langston —"

"Call me Fannie."

Eliza smiled. "Fannie. Maybe William can help."

Fannie tucked her hands behind her back. "No more fussing over me. Tell me about you."

William seemed content to drop the

subject and fiddle with his ring.

She cleared her throat, but he said nothing more. "Well, I haven't much to tell that I didn't relate to Axel in my letters. My father died and left the store to my brother instead of me, and Zachary doesn't want my bossy self telling him how to run things, though he never paid attention to the store before." She rubbed her forehead, trying to contain the headache that always came from stewing over the unfairness and ignorance of her brother.

"Surely some man back home would've wanted your help." Fannie reached over and put a hand on her arm. "Not that I'm sorry you came."

She wrung her hands in her lap. "A man courted me while my father was sick, but he only wanted access to my father's information — contacts, suppliers and . . . bank account. To my shame, his sweet talk enchanted me for a while." She thumped the armrest. "No one should use a person like that."

Did Fannie actually shrink into her chair and blanch?

"Sorry, just the thought of the man infuriates me."

"Rightly so," William muttered.

She startled. She'd nearly forgotten he was

121

there. "Anyway, I figured someone out west might be open to my help, my experience, so I advertised, and your son answered." She smiled at the memory of his first letter. Perhaps the robbery and the turmoil of his absence had jumbled her emotions too much to remember how pleasant he'd been in his letters and very interested he was in her help. "I figured we'd fit."

A man who sacrificed for his mother and believed in a woman he'd never met? Axel couldn't be too upset she'd be a penniless bride. She'd almost run away for nothing.

Will sighed at the sight of his parents' homestead and slowed the borrowed horse and buggy. Eliza had whistled for nearly the entire two-hour ride.

She'd been humming, whistling, or singing to herself practically nonstop since they'd visited Mrs. Langston, making it pert near impossible to concentrate on whatever firearm he was supposed to be fixing. Her melancholy of the previous few days had disappeared. Now she was determined to unpack every box and arrange every last bit of inventory, pestering him to rearrange things so they were more "accessible" and "convenient."

And ever since she'd asked him to describe

Axel in detail, she'd been eagerly inspecting each customer the second they walked through the door.

He'd been looking forward to visiting his family after church so he might have a break from his seemingly constant need to keep tabs on Eliza, but his mother's invitation for her to join them for Sunday dinner had wrecked his plans.

As they approached his parents' house, Will's brothers rushed up from nowhere and jumped into the wagon bed. Ambrose's skinny body scrambled up behind him and he pointed. "Ma says to park on the other side of the barn. She's putting the table outside."

"Hey there, lady." Thirteen-year-old John leaned over Eliza and reached for the basket at her side. "Whatcha got in there?"

Eliza snatched the basket away. "Does liver and onions sound good to you?"

John wrinkled his nose, but Ambrose's curly head turned, tickling Will's ears. "That don't smell like no liver and onions to me. I smell sugar."

Will laughed. "You can't fool them. They're sugar hounds."

Eliza gave John the eye. "Maybe I season my liver with sugar."

John reached for the green-checked cloth

covering the basket, but Will pulled his horse up short beside the barn, and his brother chose to save himself from flipping over the seat instead.

John was a bit too friendly at times. Will beckoned for him to take the reins. "Why don't you take care of the horse."

"You oughta take care of him, don't you think? I can escort the lady in."

Will glared at his brother's mischievous grin. "Because you want to steal the good-ies."

John flashed Eliza a smile. "I'll be back."

Will leaned over to whisper in her ear. "Run."

She chuckled, her eyes dancing. Intoxicating. What wouldn't a man do to keep this woman laughing? She transformed into a beauty with the slightest hint of merriment — scar notwithstanding.

"Admit it, William. You want Irena's tarts for yourself."

"Exactly." He gave her a warm smile.

Maybe too warm, since she quickly schooled her playful look.

"Are you going to help me down, or do I have to employ this strapping young man to assist?" She squeezed Ambrose's bicep. "What's your name again?"

"Ambrose, ma'am." He flexed his muscle.

"Don't even think about it." Will dropped the reins and hopped down. He caught John in a headlock, roughed up his hair, and playfully pushed him aside. He walked to Eliza's side of the wagon. "Hand me the basket."

"Not on your life." She scrambled down without putting a hand out for assistance, as if she truly feared for the tarts.

He put his hands at her waist to help her down anyway.

A mistake. He wanted to wrap his arms farther around to feel the rest of her.

The second she hit the dirt, he let go and shoved his hands into his pockets. They felt as near to on fire as hands could without being engulfed in flame. If there'd been a water trough nearby, he'd have thrust them in. "Don't worry. I won't touch your basket until it's fair game."

And he'd try not to touch her ever again, because she'd never be fair game.

She looked at him with a cocked eyebrow. "I don't trust you."

For good reason. Will stepped back. "John, why don't you take Miss Cantrell to the house? You're small enough for her to pummel if you get too friendly with the tarts."

"Mmmmm." John licked his lips. "What kind?"

Eliza glanced over her shoulder as John

escorted her toward the house.

If Axel knew the thoughts that had popped into Will's mind while helping down his fiancée, he'd not be obeying his doctor's order to rest — Axel would be racing home to take his friend out behind the barn for a good pounding.

CHAPTER 8

Near the tables the Stantons had set outside, Eliza spotted a woman she'd never seen before setting out plates. Eliza's hand unconsciously covered her fresh pink scar. Even without facial flaws, she had never looked a fraction as beautiful as that dark-headed woman.

John jabbed her in the side. "She's pretty, ain't she?"

Eliza blinked. How long had she been staring? She nudged John. "Are you going to introduce us, young man?"

"Right." He walked her closer and threw out his chest as if announcing royalty. "This is our neighbor, Mrs. Cline."

The woman held out a hand. "Call me Julia."

Eliza smiled. "Julia it is, then."

Was this the mail-order bride who'd married the man Kathleen jilted? A woman this beautiful should have had her pick of men back east. She didn't look as old as William's parents or the Hampdens, only mid-twenties maybe.

Eliza tried not to let the woman's dazzling smile intimidate her. "I'm Eliza Cantrell."

John rocked up on his toes. "She came from the East — just like you did — to marry Axel."

Heat crept into Eliza's face at his jumbled wording. "Somehow I don't believe, if *you* came here intending to marry Axel, he'd choose me over you."

Julia's laugh lilted like a bird's song at the beginning of spring. "No, not Axel." She gestured to the table. "Why don't you put down your basket."

John gave the tarts a longing look, but when his father called him, he left immediately.

"Eliza!" William's mother barreled out of the house.

The unexpected motherly arms around her felt good . . . and sad. Twelve years next month since her mother had abandoned her family to pursue theater. Had she been hugged once in those twelve years? Eliza squeezed her hot eyelids shut lest she embarrass herself over a simple gesture. Her father had loved her, but he'd never been a man to show affection, and her brother had been more concerned with proving himself superior.

When Rachel didn't let go, Eliza let out the breath she'd been holding and returned the squeeze.

That seemed to satisfy her. Rachel pushed her to arms' length and looked her over. "Glad you came."

"Thank you for the invitation." Did the dear woman notice the sheen in her eyes?

Julia laid a gentle hand on Eliza's arm and tipped her head toward a blond-headed man carrying a dark-haired boy with grass-stained knees. "This is who I came to town for. My husband, Everett Cline, and our son, Matthew. He's two. Everett, this is Miss Cantrell."

Everett was older and definitely more handsome than Carl, in an earthy, rugged way. He leaned down to give Julia a quick peck on the cheek before handing Matthew to her. "Pleased to meet you."

Dex called for everyone to come to the table, and Julia took Everett's hand and flashed Eliza a parting smile.

William walked over. "Ready to eat?" He held out his hand.

And for a split second, she imagined intertwining her fingers with his as Julia had done with Everett's.

William dropped his hand and frowned before turning away from her. "Why don't you follow me?" he called over his shoulder.

Was he angry she'd hesitated to take his arm? He should be. So very rude of her. If he could have read her thoughts though . . . if Axel could have read her thoughts . . .

William pointed to an empty chair. "They thought you'd want to sit between me and Julia." He rushed over to help Nettie get up on the bench with her sisters.

Everett pulled out Eliza's seat, then sat on his wife's other side. "I hear you're marrying Axel."

"Yes, whenever he gets here." She pulled her gaze off William and lowered her voice. "Though the wait's quite nerve-racking. How did you handle meeting each other for the first time without fainting?"

Both Julia and Everett's faces contorted in silent amusement . . . or maybe embarrassment?

Dex stood and clinked his glass with a spoon. "Let's pray."

Everyone at the table bowed their heads. Even Matthew, though he didn't stop talking, but rather whispered quite loudly, "Leg hurt. Bad."

Julia gave his knee a quick peck.

"Lord, thank you for good friends, your

provision, and the beautiful weather you provided so Rachel didn't natter my ears off all day stressing over dark clouds and wind. Keep the kiddos glued to their chairs. Bless our conversation. Don't let me embarrass the newcomer so badly I receive a lecture tonight."

Rachel snorted.

"Amen." Eliza chimed in with the rest of them.

Everyone began passing around food, the adults fixing plates for the children. Julia handed her a bowl of potatoes.

"So, concerning your question about not fainting at your first meeting, have you written to Axel?"

"Oh yes, many times."

"Everett and I hadn't even written. In fact, he didn't know I was coming." She sent a furtive glance toward William's mother. "Rachel played matchmaker."

"So this mail-order-bride thing isn't a completely stupid thing to do?" She took a glance at William's mother. "My friend Ruth insisted I'd lost my mind when I told her why I was coming out here." And maybe she had, considering she'd resolved to marry a man in order to run a store.

Julia cringed. "I'm not saying marrying a stranger is the *wisest* thing to do."

Everett's face showed up behind his wife's back. "What she means is, I was very stupid."

"When you're stuck together, however, you're forced to make things work." Julia's smile lit her soft brown eyes.

Everett shrugged as he dished some green beans onto two plates. "Or you don't. Marriages don't always turn out — even for people in love. A young friend of mine's wife left after a few months, with no warning, and another mail-order bride near here was abused."

Great. If only Ruth were here to add the horror stories she'd heard. But Axel wouldn't be a horror story — no man who cared for his mother could be evil. Eliza took a platter of sausage and onions and spooned herself a small helping. "I was hoping for a little more reassurance."

Julia squeezed her shoulder. "If two people are committed and have the Lord on their side, you aren't doomed. Have you talked to Axel about your commitment to God? What you want from life? Why you're marrying? If I'd advise anything, it'd be to talk about everything before you say 'I do.' If you have a secret, eventually the person you marry *will* find out." Julia cast a glance at her husband, who gave her a sad smile.

What deep dark secret had this beautiful woman attempted to keep?

Julia kissed the top of her son's head. "So the sooner the better."

She had no secrets. Nor anything enticing to a man other than her experience running a store. Hopefully that would be enough. "I've got nothing to hide."

"Then you'll be fine."

Unless, of course, Axel was hiding something. No, she needed to stop letting her mind go back to thinking the worst of him just because no one talked him up. He was laid up from an accident because he was helping his mother — he was a good man.

The conversation picked up around her, and she tried to concentrate on eating. Axel's mother and his letter had explained his whereabouts, but her heart still wasn't at ease. Maybe because William seemed so edgy. But why? She'd asked him if he thought her marrying Axel was a bad idea, and he'd said nothing terribly contrary. Though the drinking bit had her concerned.

The surrounding prairie grasses and the lowing of cows made the dirt yard possibly the prettiest dining area she'd ever eaten in. Smiles, laughter, and good-natured teasing swirled about her. Would she be able to manufacture this for her own children, since she'd not known such warmth? Could Axel? It seemed he hadn't experienced a very loving family either.

On the other side of the table, William finished making a plate for his littlest sister. He pressed her nose with his index finger, and she scrunched her face but clearly enjoyed the attention.

Eliza's stomach twinged. Would she be in Kansas hoping a man who didn't love her would fulfill her vocational dreams and stay faithful if her mother hadn't run and her father had been as affectionate as the Stantons?

A chill wrapped around her despite the unobstructed sunshine.

"Are you cold?" William stood beside her, gripping the back of his chair. "I could get you one of Mother's shawls."

"No, I'm all right." She shook her head and sat up straighter. "Didn't Mrs. Langston say her hands felt cold all the time? Do you have any idea what is wrong with her?"

He sat and took the bowl of corn Ambrose passed him. "Unfortunately, I don't. All I can do is search my medical books and hope to run across a remedy. She's better off visiting Dr. Forsythe."

Rachel's head perked up on the other side

of Ambrose. "What's wrong with Mrs. Langston?"

"I don't know." William tore off a hunk of bread and stuffed it into his mouth. "She didn't ask me for help, so I'm not going to push myself on her."

"Why do you always give up so easily?" Eliza eyed him. "If something needs doing, or a goal is worthy, you should pursue it with your whole heart."

"Sometimes no matter how hard you work for something, the dream hops in a wagon and leaves you behind."

She bit her lip. He probably meant Nancy Graves. "Maybe a dream's particulars need to be abandoned, but not the dream itself. Change the plan. Readjust your expectations. Take your doctoring for instance . . ."

The table grew quiet, and even little Matthew quit his monologue, though the tapping of silverware grew louder. Perhaps a close-knit family was not as free with criticism as hers had been.

"What about my doctoring?"

She glanced around the table. Besides the girls chattering away, everyone's face was blank. Perhaps she needed to extricate herself.

But at the same time . . . "I don't understand why you don't practice medicine freely now. People want your help, and evidently, you've done a lot of good. Why not do the best you can — throw everything you have into your calling — despite not having a degree? Why not return to Dr. Forsythe and resume your apprenticeship rather than think yourself incapable?"

Ambrose coughed on something he must have swallowed wrong. John slapped him hard on the back while William kept his gaze on his plate.

"Maybe doctoring isn't what I'm supposed to do right now." He stood and took the empty pitcher from the table. "I'm getting more lemonade."

He stomped off, and the sound of silverware clinking against dishware began again.

Eliza felt Julia's eyes on her, and she turned to the Stantons' neighbor. "I hope I didn't ruin dinner." She sighed. Maybe this was why her family hadn't treated her affectionately — she was too free with her critical thoughts.

"Oh no, you said nothing we haven't wanted to say. But he's such a wonderful young man, we hate to jab at something so sore." She gave her a slight smile. "I guess I shouldn't have bothered advising you to be open with your feelings. Seems you're not the kind to keep things inside."

Eliza ignored the food on her plate and reached for her basket of lemon tarts. Perhaps one — or four — would make her feel better about the disturbance she'd caused.

Would William despise her now that she'd embarrassed him in front of his family?

For some reason, her stomach was more upset over the possibility of his having a poor opinion of her than the uncertainty of her future with Axel.

Will handed his empty dinner plate to Ma, then crouched, waiting for Nettie to toddle toward him. He frowned at the lurching progress she made across the grass-patched yard.

"You need to work on keeping your heels down, sugar bug." He swooped her up in his arms and kissed her soft forehead.

Ma gave Becca a narrow-eyed glare from across the table. His little sister let go of one of the barn cat's tails, blinking big innocent eyes.

"I've had enough trouble getting Becca and Nettie to mind this week. If I wasted my breath insisting Nettie walk right, she'd never get out of the corner."

"So you've been a sugar *pill*."

Nettie shoved her thumb into her mouth.

"I'm more worried about her character right now. Besides, if her walking can't improve, like Dr. Forsythe says, I —"

"He didn't think carbolic acid would save Julia's leg either."

Ma narrowed her eyes at him. If he'd not been too old, she'd have ordered him to go cut himself a switch.

"Sorry, Ma, didn't mean to interrupt, but I think it's crucial while she's young. She can put her heels down — she's done it before — so I don't believe Dr. Forsythe when he says she can't."

He squeezed Nettie tighter. "I'm the reason she's like this." He swallowed hard against the lump that invaded his throat every time he thought of that awful day. "I have to try."

Ma's gaze seared into him until he had to look up. "No one blames you."

He shrugged.

Nettie twisted his ring. Even she knew the little happy face taunted him. He slid his ring around his finger to hide the silly smile.

Becca reached up and slipped it back around. "That's not how you wear it."

He let her put the bead back on top, but he wouldn't promise to leave it there once he left. "You're right." He couldn't help but melt at her pleading eyes. Ever since he'd stitched up her knee, she'd thought he was the best doctor in the world and annoyed their mother into helping her braid the band and bake the bead for him.

Everett and little Matthew walked past the barn and into the pasture.

"Excuse me, Ma. I want to talk to Everett." He handed over his little sister and strode toward the pair.

When he came within talking distance, Everett looked up and smiled. "Trying to get out of cleanup, eh?"

"Seems you've found yourself a good excuse." Will shrugged and smiled at Matthew, who was readying to poke a cow chip with a stick. "Do you mind if I ask you something?"

"I don't see why not." Everett leaned over to guide his son away from the unpleasant lump. "Let's go this way, son."

Will ambled behind them. "How do you stop thinking about a woman?"

"You mean forgetting one?"

When Will nodded, Everett shook his head. "Once Julia stepped off the train, I couldn't keep her out of my mind no matter how hard I tried . . . and I was miserable. So why bother?" He took away his son's stick before he speared another cow chip. "But Nancy's been gone —"

"Oh no, not Nancy. Unfortunately, this woman's engaged to someone else." Will crouched to pick up a stone. He had to admit it: the spark of . . . something . . . was stronger with her than it had been with Nancy. Perhaps because he was older. Perhaps because Eliza had more backbone than Nancy, more backbone than he. "And I don't have the luxury of time to help me forget."

Everett frowned and looked over his shoulder. "You mean Miss Cantrell."

"Yes." He stood and threw the rock at a nearby tree.

Everett didn't say anything.

Will crossed to the hackberry tree and leaned against the trunk as Matthew plopped down to dig in the soft dirt between its roots. "I'm finding excuses to watch her. I can't stop thinking about her, and I've only known her for a week." He'd heard of love at first sight, and this had to be what people meant, but if so, it was as dangerous as lightning, striking with no thought as to what it hit.

Everett sat on the ground by his son. "You shamed me years ago by saying life isn't always about what we want when it comes to a woman. You should remember what your sixteen-year-old self said."

"This time it's harder for some reason, but it shouldn't be. She's engaged."

Everett propped his arms up on his knees. "Well, then I'd say you've got thought problems. Second Corinthians tells us to bring every thought into captivity and make it obedient to Christ. If you memorize that verse — every time you realize your mind is not where it's supposed to be — you can recite it, turning your thoughts in a God-honoring direction."

"What if another pops into my head soon after?"

"The Bible says *every thought*. God knows we're going to have to capture more thoughts than one. The passage uses a lot of war terminology . . . because it is war." Everett leaned back, a pained expression dulling his face. "And war never lets up. It's day after day, hour after hour, and the enemy keeps coming, the musket balls keep whizzing."

Everett's voice grew scratchy, his eyes unfocused. "Though your friend dies in your arms, you have only one boot, and you weep at night for your mother — you still have to clean your gun and take your turn standing watch. Fighting isn't easy, but it's what you do."

Will rarely heard Everett or his father talk

about the war. He held his breath lest he interrupt the man's recollections.

Matthew crawled into his papa's lap and laid his head against his shoulder.

Everett exhaled. "But then, wars end. If you survive, you can move on to better things." He kissed the back of his son's head. "Though the battle with your sin nature doesn't end this side of heaven."

"Then there's no hope?"

"For you to conquer sin with willpower? No." The corner of Everett's mouth lifted into a crooked smile. "But the good news of the gospel is still the same. Jesus died for your sins, all of them — the ones you committed yesterday and today, and the ones you'll commit tomorrow. I think God often uses our defeat to force us to depend on Him."

Will nodded, looking far out into the fields. He knew God was faithful to forgive, but how he conducted himself affected his relationships here on earth. He had to stop thinking about Eliza. Otherwise he'd not survive working at the store after she and Axel married.

He needed to fight to get himself under control — immediately.

God, please help me. I need to conquer this.

CHAPTER 9

One hundred thirteen or just thirteen? Will blinked, the numbers blurring worse than usual.

Just thirteen, like it should be.

He'd stayed up all night trying to finish checking the store's ledgers — for naught. It seemed he'd done every one of his sums correctly. So why didn't they match what the bank said he had in the store's account? Finding a huge problem on the last page was unlikely, but he wanted to finish. Business was slow, and Eliza handled the morning customers easily without him.

Which was good. Ensconcing himself at the back desk had kept his mind from wandering to her very often. He'd managed not to look at her for an entire hour and a half today.

Eliza's warm voice selling Lynville more soap tugged at him, but he refused to look their way. Was Lynville bathing his pigs with store-bought soap? No man needed as much as he'd bought this last week — unless he was washing livestock by hand.

"Do you need anything else, Mr. Tate?"

"I'm going to get one more thing."

Behind Will, the thud of Lynville's purchases hitting the counter and the scratching of Eliza's pencil against paper endangered his focus.

When Lynville's boot steps stopped, he caved and looked toward them. Lynville's cheeky grin was surely the most annoying thing on the planet. Not that it was working on Eliza at the moment — she evidently had no problem focusing on sums.

"Add this, would ya?" Lynville laid a bouquet on top of his pile. "You pick these? They're right pretty."

"Yes." She fingered a leafy purple stalk. "I've never seen these before. Probably a weed, but they make the yellow stand out."

Will turned back to the ledger, the numbers jumping around more than usual. Once Lynville left and Eliza busied herself elsewhere, then he could focus. Hopefully.

He was thankful medical schools were lecture based. He could absorb information better by hearing than reading, and the hands-on portion would help.

He scanned over to the negative number

at the end of the last column.

Or maybe he'd been dreaming about school for nothing — he'd never get there.

"That'll be $8.65."

Will pursed his lips in appreciation. This week alone, Lynville had spent more than he had in the past year. How would his spending habits change when Axel showed up and claimed —

No. He wouldn't imagine Axel and Eliza together — that would steer him toward trouble again. He pulled out his notepad of verses and started reading to keep his mind from envisioning Eliza's smile, Axel's arms around her . . . or how she'd feel in his own.

He jabbed his pen into his paper. *Focus on reading verses, Stanton.*

"Put it on my account, if you would, Miss Cantrell. And these are for you."

"What?" Eliza's confused voice stole Will's attention again.

Lynville tipped his head forward in a mock bow, bouquet extended over the counter.

"Oh, Mr. Tate, I . . . I can't."

Eliza held the nosegay of yellow wild flowers loosely between two fingers, as if the bouquet had molded.

"Of course you can." Lynville's smile was more saccharine than the taffies he'd purchased. Were those for Eliza too?

Would she tell him about Axel?

She visibly swallowed. "That's kind of you. I'll get a vase and set them on the counter for everyone to enjoy." She disappeared into the back.

He shook his head. She was too concerned about profit. What mental gymnastics had she done to justify keeping her engagement secret?

Not that he minded that she didn't appear eager to announce her engagement. Perhaps that meant — *No, stop hoping, Stanton.*

War. He was at war with his stupid thoughts.

The door chime jangled again. Another victim for Eliza's eyelashes to overpower? Though she'd not yet come out of the storage room.

A woman's voice echoed through the store as she called to her husband, and Lynville's fancy bootheel clicks followed their footsteps outside a minute later.

Will grabbed a ruler, positioning it under an annoying line of wriggling numbers. One more page to go. At least doctoring didn't require much math, only dosages — though he could kill someone if the dosage was wrong. Oh, why had God seen fit to give him his father's reading problems?

146

Eliza's slippered feet shuffled back from the storeroom. The sound of a glass vase thunked behind him.

Forty-five cents plus —

"Are you almost done?" Her sleeve tickled his shoulder.

He flicked the ledger shut. Too bad there weren't any customers to keep her busy — to keep her away from him. "Did you need something?"

"Do you want me to double-check the figures?" She frowned at the closed ledger.

"No, thank you." He'd not let her see the records right now, not until he figured out why his books weren't matching up. Maybe he needed to dig out every one of the invoices they had piled up in the back . . . somewhere.

Relief filled him as she left and busied herself with a stack of denims.

He picked up his ruler and finished checking the last page.

The final negative number did not change. Should he deposit a sum from his savings into the store's account to make it balance? Would that be the right thing to do or just another wrong piled on top of many others?

How could he have miscalculated so much? Where was his mistake?

■ ■ ■ ■

Eliza walked into the Men's Emporium seconds before tiny raindrops turned into big splats. It hadn't looked like threatening weather when she'd left the boardinghouse a few minutes ago. What a way to return to work after staying home for a couple days to avoid William.

She swiped at the tiny water pearls on her sleeves and forced herself not to grit her teeth as she stood at the front — not being greeted.

Was William still mad about the stupid comment she'd made at the picnic? She couldn't believe she'd faked an illness to get away from his coldness, but since he'd stopped talking to her . . . Well, for some reason she couldn't bear another day with him like that.

But cold-shouldered co-worker or not, she couldn't make herself hide out at the boardinghouse another day. And for some reason she needed to see William, even if he wasn't talking to her.

She could hear him fiddling at his gun counter at the rear of the store. She sighed and walked back.

When a board creaked under her foot,

William looked up and lifted his hand in acknowledgment but continued working.

"I hope you haven't been overly busy the last two days."

He gave her a side glance and grabbed a slender screwdriver from a bucket. "I had a few busy moments. Glad you're feeling better."

If he truly was relieved to see her off her sickbed, shouldn't he at least smile?

Not that she'd been sick . . . or in bed.

She turned and scanned the store's three aisles, then blew out a breath, straightened her shoulders, and pivoted back to face him. "I'm sorry for what I said at your parents'."

He flicked his hand, without deigning to look up. "Forgotten."

Forgotten? He'd given her a week of cold shoulder for her big mouth. "So . . . this is how you treat someone you're on good terms with?"

He fiddled with something in the gun. "I don't hold it against you. Everyone thinks I'm wrong for not returning to Forsythe's tutelage, but I can only do what I feel is best." He picked up another tool.

Evidently, he was as intent on not talking to her as he'd been since the picnic, so she'd broach the other topic she'd been stewing over. "Do you think I could be paid for the work I've done here? Mrs. Lightfoot hinted at me starting to pay her room and board this morning — she said she was kidding, but still, I think it's fair. I've stayed there much longer than anticipated."

"Sure." He snagged the cashbox and pulled some bills out from the back corner.

She held out her hand to stop him from dragging out more. "That's more than necessary."

He put two more dollars on top and handed her the stack. "You've worked hard." He reached for the ledger.

She licked her lips and looked down the center aisle to the front door. She couldn't see the street for all the rain. No customer would wander out in that. "Can we talk?"

He said nothing. Confounded man. Well, if he wasn't going to utter any objections, then he'd have to endure her prattling.

"Do you no longer . . . like me?"

That at least got him to look up for a second. "I don't know what you mean."

She meant whatever he wanted that to mean. She had to understand what had caused his change in behavior if she was going to keep working with him. "Why are you acting like this? What happened to the William I first met?"

"I still don't know what you mean." A part

flew from the table, and he leaned over to snatch the piece off the floor.

"I thought maybe . . ." Her heart started to gallop. What could she say without ruining their business relationship?

He looked over at her, his mouth pursed.

She tucked her hands in the crook of her arms. "Forget it."

She'd made a commitment to Axel — uncomplicated by questions, uncertain futures, or . . . the sudden strange fluttering in her stomach when Will looked at her now . . . or refused to.

A roll of thunder rumbled close by, and rain slammed against the roof for a few minutes before lagging. She stood beside him, listening to the rain while he went back to disassembling his customer's gun.

She needed to occupy herself with something.

Stomping to the household section, she stacked the boring sheets and empty ticks more compactly on the shoulder-high shelf and stood on tiptoe to grab the goose-down pillows. To entice customers with their plumpness, they needed to come down a level or two. But her fingers could barely brush them.

With the windows up front fogging, no one would see her, so she jumped and caught one by the corner. The pillow slipped from her hand and flumped to the floor. She brushed off the dust before setting it on its new shelf.

With an *umph,* she knocked the next one off and caught it behind her head. The third one stubbornly refused to inch forward. She crouched to jump higher.

"What on earth are you doing?" Will stood near her, arms crossed, one eye squinted — a mirror of her father's expression when he'd thought her silly.

"Getting pillows." Eliza glared at the obstinate one and jumped as unladylike as she pleased.

It still didn't budge. What did the pillow have against her?

"You could have asked for help. I'm at least six inches taller than you, and you know we have a ladder, because I've seen you use it — a lot."

She put her hands on her hips. "Why talk about helping me instead of just doing so?"

He rolled his eyes and grabbed the pillow without looking at it.

Rrrriiiiipppppp.

A small shower of feathers floated to her feet.

"Hmmmm." She refused to laugh because he was still so rigidly cold, but her lips quivered in an attempt to keep from smiling.

He batted at the pillow, attempting to pop it off of whatever was hanging it up, but the casing ripped farther, and more down fluffed out. "What is it stuck on?"

"Maybe we should get the —"

Then with a loud rip, a cloud of white poofed, and Will stood frowning with a nearly empty pillow in his hands amidst a fluffy blizzard.

She held a hand over her brows to keep the feathers from catching on her eyelashes and puffed at the ones trying to find shelter in her mouth.

Will sneezed. A rather small sneeze for a man. His hand came up to his nose, and he leaned his head back for another sneeze, sure to be more intense.

Pew! His face contorted as if the mouse squeak he'd let out rivaled musket fire.

Laughter rolled out from the bottom of her gut. She couldn't help it.

He loosed three more petite sneezes in a row, and a tear trickled from one of his eyes. His scowl only made the dam holding back her merriment break wider. He ruffled his hair to extricate the feathers, but his nose wrinkled again, and he let out another pitiful sneeze.

She pressed hard on her abdomen, hoping to stop laughing enough to take a deep breath, lest she faint for lack of air. Her tightly laced corset helped not one bit.

Though a pillow making a grown man cry was mighty funny, she knew she shouldn't laugh. She gulped in some air to stop herself. "I wish I sneezed like you —" She accidentally snorted in an attempt to stay her laugh. "My father would have had one less thing to criticize me for."

"They might not sound like much, but they hurt my diaphragm like the dickens." His voice was clogged with stuffiness. He rubbed at his nose, wiped at his watery eyes, and sneezed again.

She gulped some air and swiped at the feathers on his shirt. "Surely you've got something in your medical box of tricks to take care of the sniffles?"

"I don't normally get attacked by feathers." He glanced down at her hand as she pushed his shoulder to turn him around. "Avoiding them is the best treatment."

She beat the fluffy white bits off his back and then reached up for the ones on the top of his head. Her fingers ruffled through his hair, dislodging the feathers the way she used to remove freshly cut hair from her father's thick mane.

Except Will's hair was much thicker than Pa's. And amazingly fine.

Will's neck tensed, so she dropped her hand to his other shoulder and went back to swiping. She circled around to his front. Her hand brushed along the dark blue of his vest, his chest hard and solid beneath her fingers. Not that she should be noticing such a thing.

Eyes downcast, she kept defeathering him until every last piece of fluff was evicted. "There." Her voice was ragged. Too ragged. She shouldn't have tried to speak. Maybe she could blame her clogged throat on the feathers.

Silence drew her gaze upward. His eyes blinked, but nothing else moved.

She swallowed and reached out for one last feather clinging to the stubble near his cheekbone. "Now, go back to work. I'll clean this up."

William dragged in a rough breath and shooed away a feather floating toward him.

Should she brush off the feather she'd missed on his shirt sleeve?

William put a hand against her face, and she froze. His thumb wiped across her brow and a flicker of white floated away in her peripheral vision. He ran his hand across her hair. Not like she had his — his touch was more a caress than anything else.

His fingers grazed the side of her face, and heaven help her, her whole body shivered. He pulled a large feather away and let it drop, but didn't watch it fall. His eyes flitted to hers for a second — bloodshot . . . and haunted.

Then his gaze slid down to her lips and stilled.

He took a step back, looked at the ground where feathers lay at their feet, and rubbed the back of his neck.

Her chest suddenly filled with air now that he'd moved away. "Are you all right?"

He shook his head but didn't say anything. Didn't look at her. Didn't move.

Was something other than feathers bothering him? Why was he withdrawing from her again? "Will, I —"

"No." He held out his palm before stomping away, muttering something under his breath about casting down imaginations.

Nearly running into the counter, he leaned over it to grab something. "This came for you this morning." He turned half toward her and held out a letter.

The envelope was addressed to her, the handwriting Axel's.

Was this what was bothering Will? She

studied his profile as she tore the envelope's flap.

His jaw twitched. Was he as discombobulated as she was after she'd run her hands all over his chest?

She pulled the letter closer to her waist to read.

Eliza,

I hope you aren't too disappointed I wasn't there to meet you at the station and that I'm not yet back. I trust you got the letter I sent Will, but I wanted to write that my injured leg has kept me here longer than I'd hoped. It seemed doomed to infection but has taken a turn for the better. The doctor wants to keep me, but I'm not going to stay much longer — besides, Will can look after me. I've been off my feet for a while, with both the leg and the dizziness, but as soon as I can sit a horse, I'm leaving. I'm glad Will's been there to help you while I'm gone — you won't find a more decent chap in Salt Flatts.

Watch for me,
Axel

She rubbed her temple. "Axel should be here soon." Did he include himself when he wrote that no other man in Salt Flatts was as decent as Will?

"I suspected as much." He swiped at the feathers still clinging to his trousers. "Excuse me." He disappeared into the back room, returning with a slicker that he buttoned as he passed. "Can you watch the store? I'm going for a walk."

"In the rain?"

"It's letting up." He stalked out the door and into the drizzle.

She didn't stop him.

Perfect. Simply perfect. She still had no idea why he was mad at her, and now she couldn't get the feel of his hair between her fingers out of her mind.

CHAPTER 10

Will sank into the long-stemmed grasses beside the muddy riverbank, careful to keep the slicker beneath him. He selected a small, flat rock and whipped it across the river at a hackberry tree, chipping the bark.

What an awful soldier he'd be in a real battle.

He'd wrestled with his wayward thoughts for a week. Every time he thought of Eliza in any manner beyond a business partner, he'd started dismantling guns in his mind. Trying not to talk to or look at her had also helped.

But when she'd sent word that she was ill, he'd nearly rushed to her side, so he'd summoned every ounce of willpower to stay at the store. Mrs. Lightfoot would've sought help if necessary.

Will blew out a breath as he ran his hands through his hair. His jealousy over Axel finding a woman with such . . . such magnetism was something fierce if he had to ignore a sick person to keep his thoughts pure.

As Everett had said, he was in a war . . . and war was ugly.

Yet a handful of feathers had laid him low.

Her fingers combing through his hair inflamed his bullet-riddled heart. With every swipe of her fingers, he'd frantically searched for a reason to toss his white flag in surrender. But instead of walking away and mentally dismantling that cannon, he'd foolishly touched her. The soft velvet of her brow, the silkiness of her hair, and the smoothness of her cheek had overpowered the battle alarm blaring inside him.

He had been so close to taking her in his arms and kissing her until she forgot to breathe —

No, no, no! What was he thinking? Even here on the riverbank, a half mile from town, he couldn't keep his thoughts in line. They were growing boldly worse. The storm clouds needed to return and drench him; cold water trickling down his collar might cool off his rebellious mind.

A good thing he'd run like Joseph from Potiphar's wife. If not for Axel's letter taunting him from behind the counter, he would've made a very, very bad decision.

He rubbed his eyes with the heels of his hands, then stared at the moist earth between his feet. The smell of wet moss and mud glistening under the sudden-appearing sun should have been calming. But nothing could soothe him at the present.

"Will?"

The familiar feminine voice behind him ran shivers across his exposed neck. What more could go wrong with this day? He turned with a sigh.

The strawberry-blond curls around her face blew gently in the breeze as she collapsed her umbrella. Her smile was tentative. "Surprised to see me?"

Surprised? He'd expected Nancy would visit her parents occasionally, but to seek him out . . . in a muddy meadow? He glanced at the young girl holding her hand. The child, six or seven, couldn't weigh much more than a four-year-old if he wrung the muddy water from her hem. "I thought I'd hear about your return before I saw you."

Nancy nodded solemnly. "I asked Mother to refrain from announcing my arrival until I found you. Though I figured I shouldn't wait more than a day or two in case she couldn't keep from spreading the news."

She took one step forward. "Mind if we join you?"

Of course he minded, but he couldn't say that. He stood, shrugged off his slicker, and laid it atop a thick mound of grass.

She lowered herself onto his coat and tucked the little girl into her lap. "When I saw you walking this way, I figured you might have come looking for plants."

"Not in this rain." He yanked out a nearby yarrow plant, root and all, then wedged himself into the damp, V-shaped trunk of a cottonwood tree. This meadow always held plenty of chamomile, coneflower, plantain, and other plants. He stopped rolling the wet leaves in his hand lest the pungent aroma seep into his skin and stay there.

He looked at the little girl again. Nancy had fallen in love with a widower's children and given up waiting on him to get his life in order. So where was her husband and the rest of his brood? "Who's this?"

"Millicent." She tucked an arm tighter around the pale-faced girl. "Ma says you haven't gone to school yet, but you'll help if someone's desperate enough. Seems you haven't changed." She gave him a flicker of a smile, though at the moment, he didn't feel like smiling with her. "I could use some advice."

He tore off the yarrow's feathery leaf and massacred the smelly thing between his fingers. "You should talk to Forsythe."

"The doctor in Wichita couldn't help, and he was much like Dr. Forsythe."

"You know perfectly well why I shouldn't help anyone until I get proper training." Killing a sister and dooming the other to a life of suffering should make anyone distrust his advice. "I haven't saved enough to get to school yet. I'm trying, but it takes *time.*" Something she hadn't been willing to give him.

She ducked her head and picked at some imaginary thing on her sleeve, the wan little girl trembling on her lap.

He sighed. "Tell me what you want, and I'll do my best."

"A reoccurring fever still gets the best of Millie every now and then." She rested her chin on top of her daughter's head. "She's fine at present, but every few weeks she's in bed with aches and fevers, and each time I think I'm going to lose her all over again."

He wedged himself tighter into the tree and waited.

"My husband and his three boys died from the same fever last year — a month after we wed. Millicent survived, though. My in-laws encouraged me to try every doctor. I've used everything you taught me about wild flowers and such, but . . ."

She turned slightly dewy eyes toward him. "I know now how crippling the pain of losing someone under your care feels. Especially after you lose one after the other . . . after the other . . ." Nancy turned her face away and sniffed.

The little girl's haunted eyes blinked at him.

So desperation had driven them into the rain after him. "I'm truly sorry."

The way Nancy held the girl indicated she'd found some solace . . . and even more hardship.

"I understand you better now, wish I hadn't been so hard on you." Though her head still lay atop her daughter's, her green eyes lifted and fixed on his.

"I've forgiven you, Nancy. Months ago."

She took in a big breath. "Everything I'd rejected you for is something I now admire. This last year I've pondered why you hesitated to doctor and why you wouldn't marry me before you went to school, and well . . ." She shrugged. "Without a husband and my savings depleted trying to cure Millie, I've run out of options. So I'm here permanently."

She licked her lips and swallowed. "Maybe

we could become friends again?" Her darting eyes indicated she was embarrassed to say more.

Unlike Eliza, who spoke her mind.

He knew what Nancy was thinking. How could he not after growing up with her and courting her for five years?

A destitute widow with residual feelings for him and a sick child who needed more care than a doting mother could give. They needed one thing more than any other — a protector and provider.

But he couldn't promise anything — not yet. . . .

He stood and brushed the crushed leaves off his pants. "Let me walk you home." He held out his hand to his former fiancée to help her up. "You can tell me about Millie's problems on the way, and I'll think about things you can try." He looked Nancy in the eye. "As to anything else, give me some time."

"Thank you." She let her gaze drop from his. "Your thinking about it is more than I deserve."

Eliza sat in the back of the store, not feeling like rearranging merchandise or analyzing inventory for the first time in her life. She'd just sit here as long as the gray weather kept customers away.

She picked up some gun part Will had left on the counter and rolled it between her fingers. Why had his hand grazing her cheek to swipe off a feather — and his silence — bothered her so much?

Bothered her more than an engaged woman ought to be bothered.

The ledger near her called to her restless fingers. Will hadn't wanted her to look, but she shouldn't be left in the dark about anything regarding the store. Axel had told her they needed help, and help she would — filling her head with numbers should easily crowd out the troubling thoughts occupying her mind.

After a half hour of scanning columns, she ended on the last page's negative balance.

It was only a matter of time before these men failed or had to sell.

The math was done properly, but some entries seemed to be entered double or triple times. She hadn't touched everything as she'd rearranged shelves, but sixty-five hurricane lamps? Maybe they were tucked away in the corner of the stock room, but who'd thought ordering so many was a good idea?

She flipped the book back to where Will had left it open. He'd insisted she not look in the ledgers. Either Will made awful financial decisions or he was pocketing money. . . .

No, she couldn't believe Will capable of such a thing.

She flipped back a page. Some sections looked as if he'd simply crossed off customer debts. Did the townsfolk invent sob stories knowing Will caved easily? He failed to refuse needy patients despite his resolve not to practice. And he'd sold Mr. Harbuckle those cigars for a nickel off, just because he'd pitied the man.

Charity write-offs had to be a planned thing — otherwise both men would be needing handouts soon.

Eliza gnawed on her inner cheek. She shouldn't jump to conclusions based on her stolen minutes with the ledgers. She needed more time — and better yet, an outsider's opinion.

She shoved away from the desk, needing to focus on something else. Unfortunately the afternoon had been slow, despite the rain stopping. Perhaps the lingering silver-gray clouds were keeping people home. If only her future didn't look as gloomy as the sky.

If she couldn't get these men to follow her advice and had to fight them to change their business practices, would she be living above the store forever? If she couldn't save the store, where would they end up?

The front door bell jangled. She left the books to attend to a heavyset man who limped in. How long did Will intend to be gone on his walk? "Good afternoon, sir."

"Ma'am." The customer stopped to wipe his brow, then charged right past her toward the back.

She followed. "Can I help you?"

He didn't even look at her as he stomped toward the back counter. "Stanton?" he called.

"I'm afraid Mr. Stanton is out at the moment. Since I haven't seen you before, you may not know I'm working here and can —"

"You're working as a clerk?" The man turned and gave her the eye.

Did he find something wrong with that? "Yes, sir."

"Then you can't help me." He set his satchel on the counter and drummed his fingers on the well-worn wood. "When will Stanton return?"

"I don't know."

"Do you know where he is?"

She had no idea where either of the men who'd muddled her life in the last weeks were. "No, but I'm sure he'll return soon."

"Look, I need Stanton to give me some of those weeds he grinds up for Mrs. Graves. She insists he's cleared up her . . . afflictions, and I've got two others demanding I give them Stanton's treatment." He pulled out his handkerchief again and wiped his sweaty brow. Either the muggy afternoon was affecting him adversely, or he'd run the whole way there. "Tell him I'll be at the barber's."

"You're Dr. Forsythe?"

"Yes." He glared at her from under bushy eyebrows. "What of it?"

Clearly Will had told the truth regarding the doctor's poor bedside manner. The heat of the man's glare and the pinch in his voice made her want to quit talking and send him on his way. "Only that I've heard much about you." She swallowed before plunging on, hoping she would hold up under his wilting look. "I'd like your opinion on something."

"If you're a friend of Stanton's, ask *him* if you want free medical advice. I charge."

She cleared her throat. "Of course, and he should too."

Dr. Forsythe rolled his eyes. "He needs a backbone more than he needs school."

"Actually, that's what I was going to ask

about. Do you think he'd make a good doctor?"

The man rolled his big head around, as if the words in his gullet needed coercion to leave his mouth. "The boy's got a sixth sense. He knows which Indian trickery herbs actually work — either that or people believe whatever he prescribes will help. Mind tricks can be effective, I suppose.

"It's not that I won't try new methods if I have no luck, but I don't like being forced to provide one." He snatched up his satchel and dipped his head. "I haven't any more time to chitchat. I need a haircut before I'm summoned by some dirt-poor farmer expecting me to save his children from the diseases they get from refusing to purge themselves periodically."

He brushed past her, muttering under his breath.

"I'll let Mr. Stanton know you're looking for him."

The man waved at her dismissively without even turning around.

This was the man people hoped would care for them on their sickbed? No wonder Will had a line of customers he didn't want. Grumpy Will was a lark compared to Dr. Forsythe.

The doctor stopped on the porch to talk

170

to some poor drenched man. She busied herself with emptying one of the front shelves so she could move it. If she made room up front for a counter, Will shouldn't oppose having one made.

But with what funds? Maybe that had been more his concern than not wanting to follow her advice.

The animated conversation on the porch grew louder. Dr. Forsythe didn't seem happy about being stopped by the tall blond keeping him from his precious haircut.

She'd never before seen the other man either, thin and fair-haired, with sideburns and a mustache. Hadn't that been how Will had described Axel? He'd said he favored his mother.

As she moved closer to the window, the movement must have caught the blond's eye, because the man glanced toward her in the middle of his conversation. He patted Dr. Forsythe on the back, and the doctor looked none too pleased about the affront to his person. They parted ways, and the blond stranger opened the door with a big smile on his face.

Her heart pounded, and her mouth turned salty. She needed water.

The man pulled off his waterlogged hat and looked right at her, but his smile stuck.

His gaze dropped to her cheek, tempting her to cover the scar that itched under his perusal.

He cocked his jaw and replaced his hat. "Silly me, I meant to hit the post office first." Then he turned on his heel.

"Wait, are you . . ."

His back tensed, but his hand rested on the doorknob instead of turning it.

"Axel Langston?"

His shoulders fell limp, and his hand dropped. Had he heard her? But if he hadn't, why was he still standing there?

He turned around slowly, his hat against his chest. "You know me?" His eyes jumped to her scar again and then scanned her entire body.

"Sort of." If she'd had a shawl, she'd have tucked it around her tighter. Axel had every right to look her over, but the scrutinizing he gave her wasn't a man looking at her with admiration or loathing, more like assessing a cow or a horse at an auction. "I'm Eliza."

"Naw." Instead of smiling again, he blinked and cocked his head.

"I assure you, I am."

"You're Eliza? Cantrell?" He took a step toward her. "What are the odds that . . . that you . . . look like you do?"

Was that a bad thing or a good thing? "I

guess I don't meet expectations."

"It's just that you look exactly like the woman I've envisioned for the past few weeks." Axel squinted and ran his tongue around his mouth. "Dreamt about you lots."

She released the breath she'd been holding, and her shoulders relaxed. Was that true or was he trying to be sweet? "For some reason I thought you'd be disappointed with me. I know I'm not the fairest of face, and this scar doesn't help."

He rubbed the back of his neck. "Sorry for staring, but it's . . . unexpected. The scar looks recent."

"I got it two weeks ago on the train."

"You were supposed to come in last week."

"Yes, but I got impatient."

The lazy smile he threw at her made her feel a bit better.

"The train was robbed and one of the men didn't take too kindly to me hiding my money."

His smile couldn't melt the fear that her next words might have on her future. "He hit me with the side of his pistol and stole everything I had."

His eyebrows raised. "All your savings?"

She nodded, waiting for him to process her penniless state.

He looked at the ceiling, his eyes and jaw

working as if calculating.

And she'd thought trying to ascertain Will's feelings this morning had been impossible.

"That isn't the best news, but I've set up more business partnerships while I've been away, and —"

"For your mother? That's wonderful."

He narrowed his eyes at her. "How do you know about my mother? I told you to wait." His abrasive tone made her skin prickle.

"I . . ." She couldn't lie, since she'd received his letter before visiting Mrs. Langston. "I had no choice. Your father figured out who I was when he delivered your letter to Will. Since he knew about me, I figured he'd tell your mother."

"I'm sure you found out that didn't happen."

"Yes." Whatever had torn his parents apart might affect their own marriage. "Can you tell me why they're separated?"

"No one in this town knows why."

"But as your soon-to-be wife . . ."

He loosened up a bit. Had he believed she'd not have him? Though grilling him the second he walked through the door wasn't exactly welcoming. Oh, to be able to start all over.

"Unfortunately, it's a family secret. I'll tell

you, but I'd like you to be family first." He smiled. Not as nice as Will's, but he was quite handsome. He certainly took after his mother — a good thing, since Jedidiah's brooding looks made her feel uneasy. "So how about tomorrow?"

"What about tomorrow?" Did she miss something?

"Becoming family?"

"Oh." She smashed a hand against the sudden upturn of her heart. She'd intended to marry him the day she arrived, but the weeks of waiting had lulled her into thinking she had time. "But you just got into town and learned I've lost all my money and —"

"Where's Will?"

She glanced behind her because Axel was looking in that direction, though she knew she'd see no one. "Gone somewhere."

"He left you alone to tend the shop?"

She nodded curtly. "I can handle the store just fine."

He bobbed his head as he took in that information. "If Will already trusts you with the store, then that will help immensely when I have to go out on business."

"What kind of business?"

His lip twitched, and he sucked in a breath. "I've got a leather worker near

175

Atchison who gave me exclusive rights to sell his wares for this area, and the rancher I stayed with has a ton of bees, and there are . . . other opportunities."

"Surely there can't be enough business opportunities to justify gallivanting about the county."

He blinked at her. Seemed she'd quickly learn if her future husband could tolerate her mouth's runaway opinions.

"I'll get the suppliers, Eliza — you'll sell the wares."

While playing sick at the boardinghouse, she'd pondered the most likely reasons a man would disappear for days without telling people where he was. And one of the scenarios she'd feared the most involved the facts that Kansas had recently become a dry state and Will said Axel drank. She pulled in a breath to fortify her nerves. "Are you arranging to sell alcohol?"

His eyes narrowed. "And if I am?"

She tapped her foot. "It's illegal now."

"Unrightly so."

"Axel, I know it's an easy way to make money, and I'm all for making money . . ."

He shrugged as if he expected her to agree with his running booze.

"But I just went over the books," she told him, "and we can improve the store's profits.

Let's focus on this business. I promise that with my idea to copy Mr. Woolworth's practices from back home, if we can get Will to accept some changes, we'll be profitable. We don't need ill-gotten gain."

He didn't look convinced.

"Look, I know alcohol is controversial — my own father would've been upset if Pennsylvania passed a similar law — but if I'm going to be your wife, I want to be certain you stay alive and out of jail." And following the law.

She fiddled with her hands. He'd have to promise not to run liquor if she married him. Marrying a perfect person wasn't her goal, but she wanted someone she could talk to and make decisions with. And unless Axel was very different than his letters suggested, he'd listen to her. Hadn't he set up the displays exactly as she'd imagined?

He leaned against the shelves. "We won't make near enough that way."

"We'll make enough to cover our expenses."

"My mother, she's . . . going to need financial help."

"I understand." She put her hand on his arm but quickly pulled away when someone stomped across the porch. "We'll talk about how to help her. Promise me we'll talk about everything." Hadn't that been Julia's sole advice?

He shook his head slowly. "I can't abandon my contacts in the middle of an agreement." He pulled at his collar. "I just started. You don't abandon people like that without risking your neck. I'll have to fulfill my obligations first."

She could well imagine the kind of men orchestrating the running of liquor. "But you *will* stop?"

"I only thought to make some quick money, seeing we need it. . . ." He glanced toward the back, as if he'd find Will poring over their terrible ledgers. "But yes, when possible."

"All right." She reached out and squeezed his forearm. Wanting to impress his wife and care for his mother could send many a man into dubious dealings.

She dropped her hand when the front door swung open.

"I'm sorry. Am I interrupting something?" Lynville Tate's leveled glare might have toppled over a smaller man.

Axel turned to him and frowned. "What did you come in for?"

The shorter man's thumbs firmly grasped his belt. His eyes spit fire. "I came in for assistance." He turned to her and smiled.

"Mind helping me pick out a new hacksaw?"

"Why would you ask my fiancée to help you find a saw instead of me?"

"Fiancée?" Lynville sputtered.

Eliza grimaced at her shoes and pinched the bridge of her nose. Maybe she shouldn't have let Lynville believe her available as long as his pockets seemed bottomless. He'd probably never cross the threshold of the Men's Emporium again.

"Yes, Eliza and I'll be married tomorrow."

She swiped at the dust on her bodice to disguise her hands' trembling. Tomorrow. But that's what mail-order brides did — they married the day they arrived. Of course they'd not wait.

"What if another man would like a shot at her?"

Oh no. She couldn't do this. She gave him the best smile she could muster. "Lynville, I'm flattered you'd think another man would want to marry me, but I've been engaged to Axel for over two months now. It's a little late for competition." Would Will have wanted to throw his hat in the ring too if he'd not known she was engaged?

Why did she care about that answer? Besides it was highly unlikely, since he'd run away from her that morning.

"Right." Lynville threw back his shoulders

and thrust out his chin. "I still need a saw."

Letting out her breath, she smiled at both of them. "I do believe Axel is right. He'd be a much better adviser than I."

She turned and hastened to the back room and sank onto a crate. How could a few weeks change her eagerness to wed so much? Axel still wanted to marry her despite her poverty. He'd just now listened to her — as he had in their letters — and she'd seen how much he cared for his mother. Not to mention he was a rather handsome man.

So why did her heart sink a little when she compared his looks to Will's and found them wanting?

What a shallow woman she'd become if she felt disappointment over a mere bout of attraction. She was not nearly as handsome as either of them, and she'd never have caught their eye back in Pennsylvania.

The awkwardness of her first meeting with Axel must have jumbled her feelings. But their next conversation didn't have to be so clumsy. She sucked up her breath and stood. Once Lynville left, she'd go out and discuss wedding plans.

CHAPTER 11

"Thank you for coming in today." Eliza wrapped an elderly man's items, but her smile wavered. Axel stood behind her, as he had most of the afternoon, watching her every move.

"Come again."

"Will do, little lady." The man actually saluted her and walked out whistling.

The sound of soft clapping made her turn, her neck warm with her fiancé's adulation.

Axel's grin was huge. "No wonder Will left the store under your care. We certainly don't have the talent to unearth a customer's need *he* doesn't even know about." He pulled out his timepiece and happily sighed. "Ah, quitting time."

As he ambled down the center aisle to the front, she wilted against the counter. Had she ever had a longer day? That morning, with the strange tension she'd felt during the feather incident before Will ran off, and then Axel watching her like a hawk scrutinizing a field of prairie grasses.

She opened the cashbox and started counting pennies — something soothing, something normal.

At the scrape of the front door's metal bolt being thrown, the gooseflesh she'd had the moment she'd met Axel returned.

Alone . . . together.

Axel had done nothing but admire her for the past three hours. A strange sensation that. What man had truly admired her before? Well, besides Lynville, but his scrutiny hadn't felt as . . . deep. Axel should have quit staring and gotten to work, but how many men had to come to grips with marrying a woman they'd only seen for a few hours? And one who wasn't a stunner. The trembling in her stomach grew.

Tomorrow. She'd agreed to marry him tomorrow. He'd left for half an hour to talk with the reverend, but what else needed doing? She tried to draw in a deep breath, but her lungs refused to work.

How would Will take their sudden news? Would working with him go smoother now that Axel had returned? Or would Will scowl all the more?

"You look out of sorts, darling." Axel came up behind her, lightly pressing his hand to the small of her back.

She put a hand to her throat and swallowed. "Now that the store's closed, I realized how much I have to finish before tomorrow." She began counting the nickels to take her mind off the heat from his palm traveling up to warm her cheeks.

Axel reached around to close the cashbox's lid. "I'll count the money later. We don't have to get everything done tonight, since we're closing the shop tomorrow for the wedding."

Her fingers itched to continue counting. How could someone just stop in the middle? Axel's hands enveloped hers, and he leaned against the counter propped on an elbow. His eyes drooped lazily, and his alluring smile spurred her heart into a gallop.

Every time he caught her eye, she wanted to burst into silly giggles to distract him from watching the heat rush into her face. A man who could turn her into an uncomfortable knot of girlishness must have had lots of practice provoking women to blush. How many other women had he flirted with? Because he was mighty good at it.

She worked to relax her hands in his. Marriage to a stranger had been less alarming before he'd touched her.

"Don't tremble." He turned over her hand

and brought it up to press a kiss into her palm, then winked at her. "This will work."

She pulled her hand from his. To hide the impulsive reflex, she wiped both hands on her apron. They *were* clammy. "I know we'd intended to marry the day I arrived, but living with Mrs. Lightfoot for the past couple weeks . . . I'll have to explain to her first, and then pack, and . . . and eat, of course."

"We can eat at the hotel."

She pressed a hand to her stomach. "I'm not hungry quite yet."

"Well then, how about you give your good news to the circus lady, then get dressed up. I'll come over at six."

Circus lady? Irena was so much more than that. But the moniker probably wouldn't disturb her, being she had indeed been a circus lady. And people surely called the poor woman worse. "All right, but what about Will?"

Axel's brow rose. "What about *Will*?"

Yes, Will. Or perhaps she should have called him Mr. Stanton? At least William. Far more professional. When had she started calling him Will, anyway? And why was she thinking about him while her fiancé stood in front of her, his mesmerizing blue eyes taking in every inch of her face? "Um . . . when William returns, he'll think I've neglected my duties."

Axel pushed the cashbox against the wall. "He'll figure it out when I tell him tonight."

"But" — she glanced at the ledger — "maybe I should do the math. I reviewed the books earlier today and wondered if I shouldn't clean up his numbers."

"Naw." Axel's hand cupped her cheek, bringing her gaze back to him. "Will struggles with numbers and reading, sure, but if something doesn't add up, he brings it to me to fix. A penny off here or there doesn't matter. But if you want, I'll do the books instead of him — we need to save you for the customers."

The heat in her cheeks turned into a more comfortable sort. Her sigh welled up from deep down in her stomach. This man believed in her. Everything would be fine. She smiled. "Well, all right. But besides his gunsmithing, I wish I could figure out where William best fits in this business."

Her eyes widened. Her tongue! Could she ever control it? "I mean, he's a fine worker, but I wonder if we should . . . buy him out — for the price of his medical tuition, that is." He needed to go to school, and since he'd hardly looked at or spoken to her over the past week, maybe it'd be best.

Of course, that was *before* the feather

incident.

Not that she or Will would act upon anything they only *thought* they were feeling.

The warmth in her cheeks ratcheted back up to searing heights. She picked up an extra piece of paper to fan herself — her blushing was getting out of hand.

Axel cocked his head. "Unfortunately, we don't have the money, and if you really want me to quit running liquor, building up a cash reserve will take time. Unless you want me to continue in order to —"

"No, I want you to quit." Though the idea of Will staying around for years agitated her innards. "Too bad the sheriff only recovered ten dollars of my money. Not that my savings were likely enough —"

"Oh?" Axel straightened. "Did he catch the robbers already?"

"Yes." She scowled in the direction of the jail, even though she'd heard word around town that they were no longer there.

"All of them?"

She nodded. "They only had a few of the stolen items on them, and they refused to tell the sheriff where the rest was. . . ." She looked down. "I'm sorry about the money, Axel. I know I promised I'd have some when I came, but the sheriff doesn't hold much hope of recovering any more."

"They probably already spent it."

"How could they spend so much so quickly?"

Axel shrugged. "I imagine criminals are often in debt to other criminals — gambling, and all that."

Right now, her fiancé was a criminal. Running liquor was against the law, not simply a mistake. Did he have criminal debts to clear up as well as those of the store? She swallowed against the foreboding in her chest. Something in the tone of his voice made her think he wasn't telling her everything. He'd said his parents had a secret. Could that revelation affect her in any way?

She'd not thought this arrangement through enough. Could she jilt him after she'd just agreed to marry him tomorrow?

"So what happened to the man who hurt you?" Axel was staring at her scar again.

She hoped Will was right about the pink color fading. "I think the sheriff escorted them all to a prison . . . or maybe they met up with a judge somewhere. I don't know. The less I think about the whole thing the better. When I replay that day, all I do is get aggravated over how I lost my savings, and then I —"

"Shh." He shook his head, his mouth

pursed sympathetically. "Don't dwell on it anymore, sweetheart. No need to relive the nightmare again."

No, she didn't want to relive that day, but her stolen money affected them regardless. "Maybe we should get a loan to buy William out. He's . . . not as interested in my ideas as you are."

"He's not?" Axel frowned.

"I mean, he's a genial fellow, but he doesn't have an eye for business and seems averse to change, even though the store's not doing well." She should stop talking before she insulted Axel as well as Will. Why had she brought up getting rid of his friend again? "And everyone thinks he'd make a good doctor."

How could she work with two men who caused her insides to tremble, each in a different way? No, she was being ridiculous. Once she became Axel's wife in every sense tomorrow . . .

She closed her eyes, reluctant to think farther down that road. Only a few hours to keep her thoughts from wandering . . . worrying . . . and then that night would be behind her.

And then she'd face the rest of her life. What exactly would that look like married to this stranger?

"I can't just fire my friend."

Her eyes snapped open. "I didn't mean that."

"Like you said, he should be a doctor. And with your retail know-how, we'll get his savings built up fast enough, and he'll be gone before you know it." He caressed her hand. "Plus, he'll be helpful in the meantime. You'll need someone to assist you while I'm obligated to travel for a while."

With his gaze so intense, she could barely keep eye contact. Since Axel seemed so captivated by her, maybe she wouldn't have a hard time keeping her focus off Will. But how long would she and Will have to work together without Axel around? How would they pretend the feather thing hadn't happened?

"How long until you think you can get out of your . . . obligations?"

"A few months, maybe, though I'll start to taper them off as soon as possible. They'll understand when I say my new wife wants me home." He smiled, the nearly translucent mustache above his lip glinting in the sunlight.

Would it tickle when they kissed?

"And I'll want to be home as often as I can." He dropped her hand, sliding both of his around her waist, and licked his lips, suddenly fascinated with hers.

Her pulse thumped hard against every inch of her skin. Had he read her thoughts about his mustache? Would he kiss her right here, right now?

Her knees went soft, but he braced her back as he drew her closer.

She locked her legs and made herself look into his eyes. She wouldn't become some fainting ninny just because her fiancé was going to kiss her. The man would be her husband within hours, for goodness' sake.

"Starting tomorrow, you and I . . . well . . . we'll be inseparable."

His mouth hit hers hard, making her grab ahold of his shirt to keep herself upright.

His mustache was not as soft as she'd imagined. It was abrasive, scuffing the tender skin under her nose. He held her lips ensnared for a moment, then moved across them again with an intensity she couldn't keep up with. And then his lips sought to part hers.

She attempted to break away, but his arms tightened around her. Was she supposed to let him do that? She tried to comply, but her lips wouldn't cooperate.

Would Will's embrace have been so demanding? Somehow she didn't think so. He always seemed so quiet, attentive. Not at all the type to yank her against him and —

A hard cough behind her sent a spiral of heat up her spine and into her neck. She immediately let go of Axel's shirt. Thankfully, his arms were still around her or she'd have fallen.

Without removing his hands, Axel looked over her shoulder. "You all right, Will? We didn't see you there."

She forced her head to turn just enough to see him entering through the back room. She tried to step away from Axel, but he didn't loosen his arms.

Maybe that was for the best. She couldn't pretend she belonged in Will's arms just because she'd imagined how they'd feel around her for a second. She'd come to Salt Flatts for Axel Langston, not William Stanton.

And yet she'd thought about another man during her fiancé's kiss. She tried to pull away from Axel's embrace again, but one of his arms remained locked around her waist.

She'd have to work extra hard so they could earn enough to send Will to school as soon as possible. For how could she live with herself if she couldn't stop thinking about Will whenever she was with Axel?

Will coughed again, but the lump in his

throat rivaled the knot in his stomach and refused to budge. "I think I accidentally inhaled something." Something sour and bitter that stopped a man from breathing and his heart from beating — the obliterated hope that Axel and Eliza would find each other unsuitable.

As Axel's obvious best man, he'd expected he'd have to endure their wedding kiss. But what he'd walked in on was no simple kiss. How could a woman who couldn't have been with a man for more than a few hours be so entangled in his arms already?

He rubbed his neck and blinked his eyes, as itchy as if sand had lodged there, along with the gravel in his throat. "Must have been a gnat or something." He took a big breath, trying not to look at Eliza. Except he couldn't help but stare at Axel's hand possessively grasping her waist. "I came back to help Eliza close the shop, though I'm obviously not needed."

"Nice to see you too, buddy."

Will shook himself. "Sorry, it's not every day I walk in on —" He waved his hand absently in their direction but stopped his tongue before he gave away any more of his feelings. "Glad you're back."

And thankfully, when Eliza tried to take another step away, Axel finally let go. Once out of his arms, she turned, flipped open the cashbox, and started counting the bills — but that didn't hide the blush coloring the back of her neck. Had she been miffed he'd cut Axel's embrace short — as maddeningly short as those few seconds her hands had run all over him removing feathers only hours ago?

Axel crossed his arms.

Will shifted his gaze off Eliza and squarely onto Axel's overly bright eyes. "What did the doctor say?" He pointed at his friend's leg, desperate for something to talk about that didn't involve his partner's fiancée.

Axel rubbed the back of his neck. "If I felt dizzy riding, I was supposed to stop, but that didn't happen."

"Good." Though if Axel had fallen off his horse on the way over, maybe he wouldn't have been able to kiss — *No, stop.* How could he wish his friend had injured himself?

Capture every thought.

He'd have to add wishing his friend ill onto his list of things forbidden to dwell on.

"Luckily I didn't break my leg, but the stitches are out, so no more worries about infection."

Will sneaked a glance at Eliza counting the cash and looked away again. "When did you get into town?"

"A few hours ago. I was surprised to find you gone."

Not that Axel had been worried, considering the kiss he'd interrupted. "I assume you've observed Eliza's superior business skills."

"Yes, but it's not like you to leave work unless you're sick or attending someone."

"I *was* feeling ill, but the fresh air helped." Of course, he'd lost whatever good the outdoors had done him by stumbling in on a scene more stomach churning than his earlier discomfort. "Let's get to closing the shop, then, shall we?" The less time he spent with them, the better. He'd thought Axel's return would be ideal — but he hadn't counted on the indescribable longing to beat the tar out of him.

"Actually, Eliza was just heading to Mrs. Lightfoot's to get ready for dinner. Right, sweetheart?" Axel stayed her counting hand, and she blinked like a confused kitten, though she laid down the money.

"Right." She tugged at her apron strings and, without looking at Will, brushed past him.

A good thing she didn't look too closely. He closed his eyes lest Axel see the ache stuck in his very soul.

"I'll see you tomorrow, William," Eliza

called from the front of the store.

"Yes, tomorrow," he whispered to no one but himself.

The second she left the store, Axel put on the widest grin he'd ever seen. "I've got some good moonshine hidden upstairs. I'll break it out after I return from dinner. Might as well ring out my last day of freedom with a drink or two, eh?"

Will only shook his head. Axel knew he didn't drink, but he always wanted someone to blabber to while he guzzled. "Last day?"

"Getting married tomorrow."

All Will could muster was a nod. Kissing after a few hours, wed within a day. He'd been kidding himself that he'd had any hope of changing their plans.

But was Axel really ready to wed Eliza if he compared it to a loss of freedom? "Are you certain you want to rush into marriage?"

Axel's face puckered. "I know I didn't tell you about her — I guess I wasn't sure it would really happen — but you're the one who talked me into a mail-order bride. Surely you aren't advocating I jilt the woman."

"Waiting isn't jilting."

"Why wait?"

To give her time to realize she'd rather have

me. William pulled at the hair on the back of his neck. "I suppose that's not how mail-ordering women goes. I'm just surprised you're so . . . eager."

Way too eager, by the looks of it.

"Despite being good with the ladies, I always get passed over." Axel scowled. "Too many men to choose from out here."

Too many men who — unlike Axel — weren't known for trying to kiss every girl in town. William fisted his hands. Axel had never touched Nancy but had often invited girls he hardly knew to rendezvous at the creek for necking — and returned puffed up like a dust-bathing bird, boasting about how easy it'd been to steal a kiss.

"I know I'm not the best husband material. I mean, Sarah is the only unmarried girl our age left in town, and she'll not give me the time of day." He spun a quarter on the countertop. "I knew Pa would want to strangle me for ordering a bride, but I got to thinking you were right. I need a woman, but everyone around here knows I'm not a saint."

Did he have to listen to the man admit he wasn't worthy of Eliza? He could help Axel list his faults, give him plenty of reasons he shouldn't drag Eliza down by —

"But I have to change. As much as Ma

gives me somewhat of a reason not to get into trouble, I need more sanity. Eliza could be that sanity."

Could be? Will sucked air through his teeth.

She didn't make a man sane — no, she drove him crazy. One minute he wanted to stare her down until she gave up her newest fool-brained business idea, and the next he wanted to sell everything he owned to buy her whatever she set her heart on. And the way her face tilted when she was about to tell him her thoughts, no gut punches reserved? The numerous times he'd restrained himself from clasping her defiant chin and kissing her until she could no longer stand?

She was madness.

"I can't let her get away."

Will licked his lips. His friend was actually considering marriage a good thing? "But are you worthy of her?"

"No, but what better reason to try to be?" His mustache wiggled with his smile. "And you've been suggesting I get shackled for more than a year now."

Will closed his eyes, his skin prickling in defeat. He'd often prayed something or someone would help Axel grow into the man he needed to be. He'd just not realized how much he'd want to arm wrestle Axel for the answer to prayer God had finally given him. "Don't botch this."

CHAPTER 12

"For the hundredth time, stop messing with your hair." Irena hobbled toward Eliza and pushed the pin behind her ear back in place. The lock of hair slipped right back out, as if protesting being put up for the upcoming wedding.

Eliza glanced at the clock in the foyer, where she'd been pacing for the last half hour. If she didn't start walking to the church in five minutes, she'd miss her wedding. Why was Irena being so stubborn? If she wanted anyone to stand beside her, it was Irena. "You won't change your mind?"

Irena shook her head, and Eliza imagined a frown behind the woman's scarf.

"After my first husband died, I remarried and chose poorly because I'd decided emotions were expendable — they're not. I won't witness you making the same mistake."

She hadn't pried into Irena's love life, but

Eliza's mother had made poor decisions by following passionate whims. "You forget. I want to marry Axel." At least she had before feelings came into play. To avoid imitating her mother, she needed to rein in her fickle emotions.

But all night she'd dreamed about yesterday's kiss — but instead of Axel's arms encircling her, she'd been in Will's.

"By the way you've talked about William, I know that whatever's going on up in there" — she tapped Eliza's forehead — "should be giving you more pause."

Could Irena read her thoughts? But her dreams were just that — dreams.

"I had weeks of pause." She grabbed the hodgepodge of flowers she'd picked that morning and stared at the limp bundle. Afraid Axel might hand her a bouquet Will had picked for the store, she'd gathered her own in a meadow outside of town. The flowering weeds would have to do, though one in particular stank. "I'm not a young girl anymore, and I've never been a beautiful one. My dream is in front of me, and I mean to grab it."

"I suppose you're talking about the store and not the man."

Eliza jammed her hand on her hip. "Your dream was to retire from the circus, and you've remained here despite your husband choosing otherwise."

Irena drew up, her scarf fluttering with a huff. "Men can disappoint."

"Exactly. You chose your dream over a man: setting up a boardinghouse so people no longer stared at you for money."

"Yes, I let them gawk for free now."

Eliza couldn't keep a sad giggle from escaping.

Irena chuckled too and shrugged. "I still don't want to sign your marriage certificate. When it turns out badly —"

"*If* it turns out badly. But I can make the best of any situation." Her mother's abandonment to pursue theater, her father's death, her brother's incapacity to see he needed her . . . She'd chosen none of those. At least she had a say in this. Perhaps Axel wasn't the best worker, but she'd have her store. Without Axel, she'd own no store.

"All right, *if* it turns out badly, I'll be happier that I didn't help."

"And if Axel's the best thing that ever happened to me?"

"Then I'll rejoice that God gave you favor."

"I don't see why He wouldn't." Though not being on speaking terms with God could be a problem. "And a decent marriage isn't based on butterflies a man gives a woman upon first meeting. It's because they're in agreement on what to do in life."

Her parents' infatuation hadn't lasted. Just because Will's glance made her stomach churn more than Axel's probing gaze didn't mean she'd avoid her mother's fate once those butterflies flew away.

She'd not relinquish her dream of a store because of flutters and hesitation. Marrying Axel meant she'd get her dream, and she wouldn't have any reason to leave him a decade and two children later to chase it. "I have to go now."

"I do want to give you something before you leave." From the carved box she'd brought downstairs, Irena pulled out a strand of pearls. "I wore them when I married my first husband. They're yours — for the wedding and for good."

Eliza put a hand to her mouth. "I can't take those."

Irena opened the clasp. "I'll never have a daughter to pass them to, and I've never had a friend treat me so normally, who sometimes makes me forget what I am." Irena slipped behind her, most likely to hide her tears, since her voice sounded clogged. "Please."

"All right," she whispered. In the hallway

mirror, she watched Irena's beads slip a little beneath the modest V-neckline of her cream wedding dress. With her grandmother's hair comb tucked into her pile of curls, she almost felt beautiful — if not for the pink scar marring her cheek. The swollenness was no longer noticeable, but her scar still felt puffy.

Irena squeezed both her shoulders, looking at her in the mirror. "Let me put some stage makeup on that. Just for today. You should feel as beautiful as you can."

She nodded her head, continuing to rub her fingers against her cheek. Why had she been so impatient? If she hadn't come early, not only would she have avoided being robbed of both her money and what little good looks she possessed, but she'd not have spent extra time with Will.

Picking at the big ruffled neckline almost covering her entire chest and smoothing the silk ribbon bow trailing down her front, Eliza tried not to think about running upstairs and hiding.

"Here we are." Irena put a few pots on the mirror table and held up a brush. "I brought a little rouge too."

"Oh, no." She didn't want to look like a bawdy-house woman.

"I won't put on more than a subtle dab

— but you, my friend, are paler than P. T. Barnum's albinos. If I put on more than you like, you can take it off."

True to her word, Irena applied only a soft touch of pink to her cheeks, but used a lot of the skin-colored powder to cover the scar. The coloring didn't look natural, but neither did the scar. "Thank you. It helps a little."

"Now, go on. You're late."

After grabbing a quick hug, knowing she'd never spend a quiet evening alone with Irena again, Eliza collected her matching parasol and headed to the church three blocks away. Thankfully, the light wind meant she wouldn't have to redo her hair before walking down the aisle. She pushed herself to put one foot in front of the other.

Outside the large sandstone church on the edge of town, Will paced the bottom step, his feet twenty times more lively than hers. He glanced up for a second and briefly met her gaze before returning to his pacing.

She closed her parasol and let herself in through the churchyard gate, unsure if she should wait for him to finish pacing or push past him into the sanctuary.

But she wanted to wait. To talk to him one last time, alone and unmarried.

He glanced at her again, but this time stopped his frantic walk. "Eliza?"

Her lips twitched. She'd known she looked different, but he appeared incredulous. Did he find her as attractive as Axel seemed to — despite the makeup-caked scar? "Yes?"

"So, that's . . . that's a dress."

She smothered a smile with her hand. "Yes, I do tend to wear those every day."

"I mean, it's just better than . . . I mean . . ."

"I'll accept the compliment. Thank you." She pulled at the sleeves that didn't quite reach her wrists and joined him. "Is Axel inside?"

Will nodded and looked behind her. "Where's Mrs. Lightfoot?"

Eliza sighed. "She chose not to come." She'd not think of Irena's reluctance as an omen of any sort. "I was hoping the pastor's wife would be my witness."

"I'm sure she will." Will turned to face her, his hands behind his back. "Axel's a lucky man."

But was she a lucky woman? Was a store enough to make this worthwhile? She'd argued with Irena, but with Will in front of her . . . She twisted the parasol's handle in her palm. "Maybe. That is . . . I mean, un-less . . ." She sighed. "Can you give me *any* reason I shouldn't marry Axel?" When they'd visited Mrs. Langston, Will had informed her of nothing she hadn't observed for herself yesterday: Axel drank sometimes and wasn't the hardest worker.

Did Will *want* her to go through with this? Yesterday when he'd caught them kissing, he seemed like he wanted to intervene. And that look in his eyes when she'd been covered in feathers . . . and now . . .

She dropped her gaze to the ground. Just because Will seemed attracted, just because her mind refused to relive Axel's kiss in favor of imagining kissing his friend, didn't mean Will would give up his friendship for her — not after only three weeks of knowing each other. She'd watched him with patients — he always chose to do the right thing, no matter how much it cost him.

Eliza forced her eyes to meet him square. Even if he did drop onto a knee and make her an offer, she would refuse. Hadn't she told Irena that feelings could lead people astray? But with him staring at her like that . . .

Will turned to look toward the horizon. He licked his lips and gave a slight nod. Then he turned to look straight at her and blinked hard. "I can't."

She looked at her hands strangling her parasol's handle. Her heart started beating again. "Then good." It was good. It was right. It was moral. "Maybe with my help in the store we can get you to school very soon."

He huffed and ran his hand through his hair, mussing whatever he'd used to make it lie flat. "That won't be necessary. I've talked to a friend this morning whose great-uncle needs someone to take over his broom business, and I think — considering everything — I'll buy him out."

She tried to swallow a breath, but her lungs wouldn't inflate. "You're leaving?"

"Yes."

She forced her mouth shut and stared at his feet. What he did or where he went didn't matter. Or rather, it shouldn't matter. Working alone together after getting married would have been awkward and uncomfortable and all kinds of wrong, but she'd have endured until everything felt normal.

But he didn't plan to be around at all.

"Are you all right?" Will ducked his head to look at her.

She glared at him. "But that's nonsense. You don't have the money. If you did, you'd go to medical school. Neither Axel nor I have enough money to buy you out yet."

"I don't expect you to." Will cleared his throat. "Consider my part of the store a wedding gift."

She blinked. He was giving up his share in the store? She'd known he didn't make great business decisions, but this . . . ?

He grabbed at his hair again but quickly dropped his hand. "The man's going to pay me to work and learn the trade for the next six months. If I decide I want the business, I'll take over and make payments."

That sounded like a fair deal. She jabbed her parasol's tip into a crack in the stair. "But if you agree, you'll spend years buying a broom business."

"Yes."

She swallowed, a harder process than normal. "What about medical school?"

"Some dreams die a slow death. Others . . ." He clamped his jaw and looked away. "Others are ripped away before they begin."

Her heart *kathump*ed harder than when she'd contemplated tonight with Axel. The infernal organ was far more attached to this man than the man awaiting her at the front of the church.

But an infatuation was not worth bailing on a commitment. What kind of wife would she be if she couldn't keep her promises and her head turned at the sight of a handsome man? What kind of store owner would she be if she made business plans but changed her course with every new idea? What kind of pride had she, desiring to grab Will's coat and beg him to reconsider when accepting the broom business offer was what he ought to do?

When he finally turned back to her, the look in his eyes was far more haunted than yesterday.

Was this truly good-bye? For a broom business? "Why are you really leaving, Will?"

The door opened and a balding man stuck his head out the door. "Ah, I thought I heard voices." He smiled at her, seemingly unfazed by the scowl she turned on him. "Where's Mrs. Lightfoot?"

Will cleared his throat. "She couldn't come, but Eliza hoped your wife would stand in for her."

She nodded, though she felt more like screaming at the pastor for interrupting their conversation.

Axel peered out from behind Reverend Finch. "Of course she will." He bit the side of his lip and a toothy smile shone as Axel took in every inch of her. "You're breathtaking, Eliza." He held out his hand, but the pastor stepped in front of him.

"If you're going to have my wife witness, she'll want you to do the ceremony thing proper." He turned Axel by the shoulders and pushed him inside. "Bride coming down the aisle and all the rest." The pastor opened the door wider. "William, join him up front. Tillie, start the music!"

Eliza took a step forward to cut off Will's retreat. "Are you going to answer me?"

He shook his head, his jaw tense, his eyes a touch wild. "You deserve nothing but the best, Eliza. The *best.*" He took the stairs two at a time and followed the pastor inside.

Alone on the doorstep, Eliza closed her eyes as chords from an ill-tuned piano grated the air.

She had to push one foot in front of the other again, stand on her convictions, chase her dream — a dream that did not involve brooms, kissing would-be medical doctors, or denying herself the store she'd wanted for as long as she could remember . . . despite the misgivings wreaking havoc with her soul.

Will stomped up the aisle sprinkled with wild flowers. Mrs. Finch found this whole mail-order bride thing way more romantic than he did. He shoved his hands into his pockets and kept his eyes on the floor as he crushed every pretty flower he came across.

He glanced over his shoulder at Eliza in

the doorway, decked in fancy eastern finery, curls piled on her head. To think he'd once thought her plain. In a dress meant for a fine woman, her waist seemed overly delicate, and those pearls accentuated the pink in her cheeks, which in turn warmed her brown eyes.

And he'd just told her to marry Axel.

Which was the right thing to say. No matter how much his stomach had revolted at saying so.

He stomped up to where Reverend Finch pointed for him to stand and glared at the back of Axel's suit jacket.

He worked to keep his heavy eyelids parted. He hadn't slept a wink last night as he'd tried to figure out how he might encourage the two of them to push back the wedding — and figure out why he wanted it delayed so badly. Did he truly want to be in the groom's shoes this morning?

If he stole his friend's bride at the altar, there was no way they could continue working together. If he persuaded Eliza to jilt Axel, he wouldn't be able to provide her with a store, or obtain a medical degree for himself. Together, they'd have nothing. And like Nancy, Eliza wanted him to be a doctor. Losing his only source of income would push school that much further from his reach. She'd have to follow him into the broom business, and she probably wanted to fabricate brooms as much as he did.

A woman with Eliza's dreams would never be content with him. Any romantic attraction they might have would sour the longer she couldn't rub two pennies together.

So he'd gift her with his share of the store — the best present he could give such a woman. She deserved to be blissfully happy, and Axel was her best opportunity.

So he would wish them well, and then disappear. Being stuck making brooms for years would give him enough time to forget her, and once he made enough money to sell the business — perhaps decades from now — he'd stop by and let her know he was finally headed to medical school. She'd be happy about that.

Eliza's shuffling steps caused him to look up. Her gaze was pinned on him instead of her groom, a befuddled look in her eye. He tried to smile, hoping she'd not see the watery sheen obscuring his vision, nor the tension in his every muscle. He nodded to encourage her when she seemed to slow.

Axel held out his hand, and Mrs. Finch abruptly stopped the music.

"Come on over, Tillie. You're to stand up with Miss Cantrell."

The older woman popped off her bench, smiling as if nothing could give her more pleasure than to witness these two becoming one.

At least one witness was glad to be there.

No longer able to see Eliza, Will paced to the left but still couldn't see her over Axel's shoulder, so he tried from the right. Her jaw was set, her blushing neck exposed. Maybe he shouldn't look at her anymore, but he wanted to, despite the overwhelming smell of flowers messing with his sinuses and blurring his vision.

He paced back to the left and tried to stand still as the pastor read from his book. When he fidgeted again to the right, Mrs. Finch gave him a frown meant for a wayward child. Sure he wasn't acting right, but how could he?

He focused on nodding his head in rhythm with the pastor's rote reading of the wedding ceremony. But Will couldn't hear anything but the litany he chanted in his head to keep his mouth shut until the inevitable was over.

It's not about what I want.

A patient's needs come first.

Do unto others as you would have them do unto you.

Better a bit of pain now than a lifetime of

unhealthiness.

This might sting, but it's for the best.

Then the wedding kiss he'd dreaded happened. A stilted peck on the lips. Yet the memory of the kiss he'd witnessed yesterday weaseled its way into his brain and threatened to cut off his air supply.

Reverend Finch smiled brightly and held out his hand toward the communion table. "Now, all we need is everyone's signature, and you two newlyweds can be on your way."

On their way. She was now forever out of his reach.

The end of the story.

Axel leaned down to whisper into Eliza's ear. The low rumble of his voice made Will want to gag. The blush he'd expected to flare up Eliza's neck at whatever ghastly inappropriate thing he'd said while standing in the house of God didn't happen.

Instead, her face paled.

Perhaps Axel had said something extremely vulgar. Will fisted his hands and waited for her to look at him. The slightest hint of indignation on her face and he'd pummel her groom. He positively itched to punch something.

Axel smiled at her and pulled her forward, reaching for the ink pen the pastor offered him. "Where do I sign?"

Eliza's gaze fixed on Axel's hand as he took his time signing all four of his names. *Axel Reid Jedidiah Langston.*

Eliza's face was unworldly white.

Will looked to Mrs. Finch. Did the woman notice Eliza was surely about to faint? But the pastor's wife had laced her arm into her husband's, smiling as if she were about to sign her name on the bride's line instead of the witness's.

Stepping behind Axel, Will moved closer to Eliza. He could keep her from falling to the floor with a thump at least. He shot a glance at Axel. His friend needed to pay attention to his bride, because if she fainted, Will didn't want her in his arms. The memory of her hair between his fingers and her thumb brushing a feather off his face was plenty enough touching to erase from his mind.

Axel turned with a smile and held the pen out for Eliza, but she didn't take it.

"Eliza?"

Her hand crept up to her neck, and she shook her head slightly. Her eyes were transfixed on his hand. "You knew." Her voice was so raspy, Will couldn't be sure what she'd said.

He leaned closer and tried to catch her

gaze. Though the entire walk down the aisle she'd looked at him more than her groom, her eyes weren't on him now, but narrowed on Axel.

Axel's smile fell, but not his pen. "Here."

"No."

The pastor finally tore his focus off his wife, and his face drooped. "Do we have a problem?"

Axel spoke through his clamped jaw. "Darling, I —"

"Don't," she spit through gritted teeth, her eyes narrowing. She turned to the Finches. "I can't marry him."

The pastor's wife put a placating hand on her shoulder. "You already did, sweetie."

Eliza pointed to the ink pen still hovering between them. "That scar."

Will looked to where she pointed. "The one on his hand? He got that the summer we were fourteen and sixteen. My first stitching job." He'd sutured atrociously, not realizing how strange sewing through flesh would feel. He'd been proud his friend had enough confidence in him to let him try.

Axel dropped his hand and took a step back.

She turned to Will, her eyes as big as last night's low-hanging moon. "I wanted to bite that scar."

"What?" Had she taken leave of her senses?

"On the train. A perfect half circle that would fit my teeth . . . blond scruffy sideburns." She took a step toward Axel like a guard dog threatening an unwelcome visitor. "And blue eyes. Light blue. When he whispered to me just now, I felt as if I'd heard that low, rumbly voice before."

"What's this?" The pastor dropped his wife's arm and moved closer.

"He robbed me. On the train." She pressed her hand against her cheek. "He hit me."

Axel set the pen down, shaking his head. "You're mistaken. You said they caught all three thieves."

Eliza took a step back. "I never told you there were three."

"Everyone in town knows there were three." He took a step back and licked his lips. "I'm sorry my scar reminds you of somebody, but it's not me."

Will narrowed his eyes at his friend. Eliza wouldn't forget that scar if she'd gotten a good look. The semicircle might not be very noticeable anymore, but it was definitely crooked with a divot in the curve where the dog's teeth had torn the skin. He'd not known the best way to sew around a missing piece of flesh back then.

Eliza's mouth was slightly agape and her eyes roved around as if they were searching for something in the air. "The moment you first saw me at the Emporium, you stepped back out the door. You recognized me, knew you'd taken my money, knew you'd split my cheek with the butt of your pistol while threatening to make an example out of me in front of everybody. Yet you just signed your name to that paper."

Axel ran his fingers along his mustache. "Now, hold on. We can settle this. I'll go get the sheriff, and we'll get this straightened out." He turned his eyes on Will but couldn't hold his gaze long. He backed out the door. "I'll be back."

Eliza sidestepped, as if she were about to crumple. Will snaked a steadying arm under her shoulder. Her fingers clawed into his bicep. He looked over his shoulder toward the open front door, then at Mrs. Finch. "Take care of her." He helped her into the nearest chair, then ran outside. Where'd Axel go?

The sound of Axel signaling to a horse sounded to the left of the church. Will rounded the corner as Axel jumped onto his gelding, which he must have just unhitched from the livery's buggy.

"Stop where you are." He had no horse,

no gun. How could he enforce his command? "I'm going with you."

Axel turned his paint and steered a wide arc around Will. "I'll be back with the sheriff." And he kicked his horse into a trot toward town.

The Finches didn't own a horse, but did any of the neighbors?

Axel turned onto Main Street, a cloud of dust billowing behind him. Was the man honestly going to get the sheriff? How could his childhood friend actually be a train robber — a man who could point guns at children and ruin a woman's face? Will raked a hand through his hair. Axel had given up defending himself too easily — he was lying. He had to be. Which meant he wouldn't be headed to the sheriff but out of town.

Will took the stairs back inside two at a time. Was there a way he could stop him without a horse?

"I married a thief," Eliza said, her voice cracking. She took Mrs. Finch's offered handkerchief.

"No you didn't." Will pointed at the certificate, slightly out of breath. "Axel's signature is the only one on that document."

Reverend Finch's jaw worked from side to side, his fingers rubbing against his stubble.

"I . . . I suppose that's true, in the sight of the courts, anyway, but in the sight of God? I'm not sure. They did say vows."

Eliza slumped in her chair.

Will blinked at the pastor. Did he really think God would approve of such a union?

Mrs. Finch bristled as if she had the feathers that went along with her surname. "A marriage under false pretense is no marriage God would want for Eliza."

Exactly. Will walked toward the desk. "We'll tear up the paper."

"Now, wait a minute." Reverend Finch's long stride caught up with him, and he grabbed the document. "We'll wait to see what the sheriff says first. That way, if Mrs. Langston here —"

"Miss Cantrell," Will said through clenched teeth.

"Anyway, if Eliza realizes she's mistaken in her accusations, we can simply finish putting on the signatures so I don't have to go through the hassle of getting a new paper." He looked to his wife, but her eyes held no sympathy. He shrugged. "I wouldn't know how to explain how I'd been so careless as to let one of my witnesses destroy an official document. And how would that look for the couple?"

Strangling a man of God inside a church

was surely something the Lord would frown upon, even if the pastor needed a good choking to set his priorities back in order. "I think paperwork is the least of our worries." Will shook his head. How could he have missed all the signs? "Axel can't be telling the truth. Not with Eliza recognizing that scar. And his disappearances . . ." He looked at Eliza, pale except for an unnatural blush in her cheeks. Her scar stood out against her skin like a lightning bolt.

His vile friend needed to be caught and held accountable. "Do any of your neighbors keep a horse?"

The pastor frowned. "Everyone walks besides Mr. Morton, and he'd be working. Which direction did Axel go?"

"Into town." Will ran a hand through his hair and stifled the urge to curse. Even if he had a horse, Axel could outrace him any day.

"See, my dear." The pastor clamped a hand onto Eliza's shoulder. "He's going to the sheriff."

"He's not at the sheriff's." Eliza's face was so blank, she looked like the woman down on Turkey Creek who sat in her rocker all day staring at a knot in the porch beam.

Will knelt beside her, and she looked at him as if he were enveloped in a fog, tears filling her eyes. "You have to catch him," she said.

Will pulled her hand into his and resisted the overwhelming temptation to kiss the tops of her knuckles. "I can't ride after a criminal with no gun and no posse."

"Then get a gun and gather a posse." Her hand trembled in his. "My money. Mr. Hampden's grandfather's pocket watch. Everyone's things might be recovered. I can't believe I married him, because I really wanted . . . I wanted . . ."

Will's breath caught. Would those perfectly bowed lips utter his name?

"I wanted that store so badly."

His chest deflated like a pin-popped bubble.

Nothing had changed. She might not end up married to his friend, but unless he gave up his doctoring for the Men's Emporium, there still would be no future for them.

He pulled her up from the chair. "Come on, Eliza." He glanced over her head at the Finches, who were clinging to each other, though no longer radiating the happiness of reliving their own nuptials. "We all ought to head for the sheriff's."

"Let's pray Axel's already there clearing this up." Mrs. Finch pulled at a button on her high collar.

"You do that, Mrs. Finch." Will couldn't deny the older woman the desire to pray for a boy she'd taught for years in Sunday school. She'd poured so many prayers into the young ones of Salt Flatts, something like this must devastate her.

He should pray too. Except he didn't want to. He much preferred the idea of wrapping his hands around Axel's neck. How could his friend treat Eliza — or any woman — in such a manner?

He'd thought his decision that morning would give Eliza the happiness she desired, and he'd believed Axel was her ticket there.

If he was wrong about that, could he be wrong about everything concerning the woman slumped against his arm?

CHAPTER 13

Eliza released the last petal from one of Irena's yellow roses. It danced in the wind and caught in a thorn bush. She yanked off another flower. How many roses had she torn apart in the last four days?

A heavy hand dropped onto her shoulder. She didn't need to look up. Mrs. Lightfoot's footsteps did not match her surname. Did her husband's? She'd never ask though. She could only imagine Irena's misery over being abandoned by a no-good husband.

At least she'd discovered who Axel was before he'd anchored her to him forever. How many months would have passed until he left her? He could have been killed in a shootout or any number of brawls with the criminals he associated with. Maybe he would have just plain abandoned her. Criminals certainly wouldn't consider the bonds of matrimony worth preserving if they didn't respect the law.

How long might it have been until she would have realized he'd been the train robber who'd sliced open her face? The next time he slapped her, perhaps?

A shudder traveled up her arms and took over her body. How could she have been so stupid? She flicked away a petal clinging to her fingers.

"Dear, you need to stop tearing off my roses. I'll have none left."

"Sorry." Eliza tried a smile, the first one since her wedding disaster. The expression didn't sit well.

Irena walked around the bench to sit beside her. "You can't hide in my garden for the rest of your life."

Why not? She wiped the spent flowers off her lap. "I suppose I need to find a job to pay for my room and board now."

"I'd like to slap you silly sometimes. I don't care about the money."

"You should." Why were these western business owners so unconcerned about making a decent living?

"I care about my friend, the one moping as if the whole world has burned to ashes."

"Can't I grieve for at least a full week before you tell me to get over this?" She couldn't look at Irena anymore. The ink on the annulment papers she'd signed this morning was probably still wet enough to smear. "I suppose when I was little and my cat died, you'd have said wearing black for a pet was silly."

"You *should* be upset, Eliza, but this turn of events saved you."

"Right. I'm not married to a lying, cheating thief." She flopped against the bench and huffed.

"That's not a good thing?" Irena's eyes registered confusion.

"Of course it's a good thing, but my dreams?" She stared at the soft blue, empty sky. "Gone."

"Owning that store, I suppose?"

"Any store. Axel stole my dream in more ways than one. A dumb dream I never should have pursued." Eliza leaned forward and stared at the ground. "My brother was right. He said wanting anything besides sitting at home and rocking babies would get me in trouble . . . and did it ever."

"So you're giving up, just like that?"

"Yeah." She swiped the last pale yellow petal off the bench. "Like that."

"You're not the girl I thought you were."

Eliza rubbed her eyes. Good, she was done being a foolish chit. One who would've married a criminal and then watched him siphon every profit she made for ill-gotten gain. She sighed and stood. "I can't start a store with no money, so I'll have to find something more sensible to do."

"Why don't you talk with William? Maybe you can work together."

Eliza scratched at her hairline. The odd emotions she'd experienced the day of the wedding made everything more confusing. "I don't . . . trust him."

Irena stood and put her hands on her ample hips. "Don't tell me you believe he's in cahoots with Axel, like the other people in town. That boy hasn't a bad bone in his body."

Oh no? Would a man of integrity make sneaky changes in the store's ledgers? Axel had mentioned fixing Will's math. . . .

She smacked a hand against her forehead.

Of course. Why should she believe Axel about anything? *He* had most likely doctored the books.

But how could she be certain Will was innocent? The man *had* worked with Axel for years — they were good friends.

Maybe he was as innocent as Mrs. Lightfoot suggested, but she wouldn't ramble down stupid lane again. Though her accusatory thoughts against Will were probably unfounded, she'd engaged herself to not one but two reprobates — she couldn't trust herself to make good decisions when it came to men. "Perhaps he's never intentionally done as much as squashed a bug, but how would attaching myself to someone under suspicion a week after being abandoned by a train robber help my reputation?"

Irena sat. "And that reputation would affect future store profits, I suppose."

She gave her a sad smile. "No. No store. I give up."

Irena snorted. "You can't change who you are."

Enough with the interrogation. "I'm going to start housekeeping." She softened her face, knowing how her next words might affect her prideful friend. "I've noticed how difficult it is for you to clean and cook with your joint pain, and your breathing gets labored when —"

"You think me an invalid?" Irena's eyebrows lowered.

"No. I only want to clean and cook for you to earn my board. I'll look for other housecleaning positions with a few other wealthy families to —"

"You'll not earn enough money to live on."

She shrugged. "If I'm boarding with you, I only need money for clothing and perhaps a bit of entertainment. Unless . . ." Was

Irena angry enough to end their friendship over her distrust of Will and giving up on the store? "Unless you require money for me to remain here."

Irena huffed and stared out over her bushes toward the haze billowing off the dirt road as a team of oxen shuffled into town.

O God, let her say I can stay. I'd rather dust Irena's strange knickknacks than return to my brother in such shame.

"I guess you can stay in exchange for housecleaning. My feet and hands would thank you."

"Wonderful." She gave her a hug.

Irena halfheartedly patted her. "There aren't many wealthy families in Salt Flatts. Even if a few women hired you for odd jobs, you wouldn't make enough to save anything."

"Well then, I'll live out my spinsterhood with you. Volunteer at the church, maybe." A twinge twisted her insides. How long since she'd done anything charitable? Been to church?

Irena huffed again. "You live in a town full of bachelors. You won't remain a spinster."

"I'm not considering marriage right now — maybe not for years, and then I'll be too old for anyone to want." Eliza looked in the direction of Main Street, hugging her arms, and envisioned the Men's Emporium. "One thing's for certain. I'm going to know a man's coming and goings, his past and present dealings, better than I know myself before I commit to anyone again."

"I suppose that's wise." Irena rubbed at her knuckles.

If Irena agreed, all the better.

A man turned the corner down the street, his gait familiar.

Will.

Had they caught Axel? Would he be the one to tell her? What if he'd decided to visit her just to . . . visit? Please no, she wasn't ready to talk to him yet. "Did you ask Will over?"

Irena turned on the bench with a little groan. "No, but I sure wouldn't mind him looking at my foot again."

Will spotted them from the porch before reaching the front door. He pulled off his hat and walked into the side yard. "Good evening, ladies."

"Are you scrounging around for someone to feed you, boy?"

Will smiled at Irena. "Not many men will turn down food."

Irena rolled her eyes, though a twinkle

enlivened them. How could her husband and son have left a woman who found such pleasure in filling stomachs? "Then I'll check the ham and add an extra place setting." She hobbled off without another word.

Eliza hugged herself harder. She'd not seen Will since he'd walked her home in a daze after they'd found the sheriff — whom Axel had not visited as the Finches had hoped.

Will's eyes were as focused on her now as they'd ever been.

She couldn't stop her stomach's fluttering, but she'd refuse to heed it. "I doubt you came to mooch." She spread her feet, planting her bootheels in the grass to steady herself if he was going to deliver news of Axel's capture and upcoming trial. She half wished her former fiancé would escape so she would never have to face him. Then again, she wanted her money. "Did they catch him?"

Will shook his head. When she sighed, his mouth puckered. "You seem relieved."

He'd probably think her insane if she admitted why. "Has it gotten out that we . . . that he and I . . . almost wed?"

"Unfortunately, you're the talk of the town." He played with the hat in his hand.

"But more so, I think, because you've stayed hidden away." He looked at her with pity-filled eyes. "They think you're devastated."

"What woman wouldn't be?" Not that she was distraught over the loss of Axel himself, but what he'd promised her.

"Of course." He dug his toe in the dirt and flicked up a pebble. "So . . . why haven't you been to the store?"

She narrowed her eyes at him. "What would I need at the Men's Emporium?"

He furrowed his brow right back at her. "Work."

"You can't afford to pay me."

Well, that shut him up. He stared off at the clouds on the horizon.

Had he thought she'd work for nothing? Even if she wanted to work with Will, he'd be going to medical school sometime. And what if pesky emotions got the better of her again before he left? It was best to start housekeeping now.

He ran his hands through his hair as he always did when tongue-tied.

What else was there to say? It was the end of their time together. Might as well end the conversation . . . drift apart . . .

"Dinner's ready!" Irena called out the front door.

Eliza started toward the house.

"I know I can't pay you much, but surely —"

She held out her hand to stop him. "Don't worry about me. I'll be fine working for Irena as her housekeeper, and I'll seek similar jobs."

"You're giving up owning a store?" he sputtered.

She steeled her back. "I haven't much choice."

He grabbed at the back of his neck, but she wouldn't stand around for him to argue with her.

"As you said, Will, sometimes dreams die."

"Sometimes dreams die."

Will put the last repaired firearm under the counter and drummed his fingers, surveying his empty shop. From the front.

The pungent smell of new lumber and sawdust blanketed him like a pile of suffocating quilts. What good would come from having this counter built if no customers came and Eliza wasn't there to appreciate his efforts?

For the first time in months, he'd finished all his gunsmithing jobs and no one needed assistance. He should restock or something.

Surely his customers would return once the shock of one of their own belonging to a bunch of train robbers wore off. Then they'd realize he couldn't have been involved. Not a boy who'd bandaged wounded animals, not the man who cared for them when Dr. Forsythe gave up. What kind of criminal spent an entire night holding a widow's hand until she met her Maker? They'd remember who he was soon enough and return.

They had to.

How often had he raided his nest egg to buy medicine for people who offered only a lump of butter or a handful of eggs for his visits?

And this was how they repaid him?

Boot stomps on the porch made him shake his head at himself. He needn't have fretted so — the townsfolk just needed time. Or so he hoped.

Lynville Tate stepped in and dragged off his hat.

"Good afternoon."

Lynville jumped and turned to face him. "Whatcha doing there?"

"Miss Cantrell suggested I sit up front to greet the customers." He walked around the L-shaped counter. "What can I do you for?"

"Um . . ." He licked his lips, and his gaze darted around the store. "I'd hoped Miss Cantrell might assist me."

Really? The man was back to flirt already? Will crossed his arms. "She no longer works here."

Lynville spun on him, his hat smashed against his hip. "You fired her just because she almost married your no-good friend?"

"You know me better than that." Will fought to keep from rolling his eyes. "She's chosen not to return." Which meant he probably had as much chance at winning her as Lynville.

"Ah." Lynville relaxed and glanced out the window. "So where can I find her?"

"Leave her alone, Lynville."

He sized him up. "You got your eye on her?"

Even if he'd admit it to someone other than himself — he wouldn't fight Lynville over a woman so grieved over her attachment to a train robber going sour that she was giving up her long-held dreams. She'd not refuted the town's gossipers when he'd visited her at Irena's. She *was* devastated over losing Axel.

He'd assumed she'd be happy to have escaped a marriage to a criminal, but evidently he'd imagined her attachment to the Axel she'd fallen for through letters to be far weaker than it truly was. "I'd think you'd be gentlemanly enough not to swoop down on her like a turkey buzzard."

"I would do no such thing." Lynville flipped his hat onto his head. "A woman all alone in town needs someone to cheer her up after such an incident."

"You don't think Mrs. Lightfoot is adequate?"

"The bearded lady?"

"I don't understand how facial hair signifies she's inadequate." He eyed the man's pitiful mustache. "Unless you're saying something about yourself."

Lynville scrunched his nose. "All I'm saying is a girl who's been heartbroken needs a distraction."

Ah, that was the strategy. "She's not that fragile. A decent man would wait until she healed before —" Will stopped short. Surely she'd never choose to be a farmer's wife once retailing got back into her blood.

But then, he needn't give Lynville helpful advice either. "Do you need something from my store?"

"Not really. I think I've bought plenty here lately."

Will couldn't help the smirk. "I believe you have."

"I'll bid you good day, then." Lynville pushed up the brim of his hat a touch before leaving.

236

How he wanted to stick his head out the door and holler *Leave Eliza alone!* Instead, he tromped to the back for his feather duster. He sighed and yanked the duster off its nail.

He wouldn't believe Eliza could give up her dream of running a store so easily. Yes, he *had* once told her that dreams sometimes died, but he hadn't thrown his school dream onto a garbage heap to rot — it simply refused to live no matter how often he attempted resuscitation. Hadn't he offered her the work she needed? Her refusing the position made it clear she wanted nothing to do with him.

However, Eliza wouldn't be content cleaning houses for long. She'd find some way to become competition before he was ready.

Ugh, competition. Not what he needed.

The bell tinkled up front.

Customers were what he needed. He walked over an aisle to see the door. "May —"

And of course Eliza stood there beside an empty counter, not greeted the moment she stepped inside. He groaned at his failure and walked toward her. "I suppose you don't need help finding a razor strop or a bucket of nails."

"What's this?" She pointed at the counter,

her eyebrows high.

"A counter, up front, as you suggested."

She blinked, her eyes as big and luminous as ever. "You said you had no money for this."

He didn't know what to do with the duster in his hand, so he tucked it under his armpit. "A patient built it as payment for helping his sick child last year. He's good at carpentry and had a pile of salvaged lumber." He waited until she looked at him. "I thought I'd surprise you."

"Well, you did." She shrugged as if the counter didn't mean anything.

He'd meant the counter as sort of a gift since he could no longer hand her and Axel his part of the store, but her nonchalance felt as if she'd tossed his handpicked flowers in the trash.

Her eyes roved the store. "No one's here?"

"Business has been poor."

"Because of Axel?"

"They'll get over it." And he'd tell himself that over and over again until it became true. Because how would the store stay afloat if they didn't? "I need your help, Eliza. I'm not going to be able to get this store to make a profit without you."

She tipped her head. "You haven't taken any of my advice before."

He looked pointedly at the front counter.

Her gaze followed his. "You can't afford me."

"That's the second time you've mentioned that. Are you going to demand an exorbitant hourly wage?"

"I've seen your books, Will."

He rubbed his temple and swallowed. Did she think less of him because he couldn't balance the ledger? Did she know how hard he struggled with figures? "You mean you looked at them after I told you there was no need."

"No need, eh?" Her hard glare almost knocked him over. "What *are* you hiding from me?"

The daggers she threw at him from her big brown eyes made his lungs deflate. "You think I'm as shady as Axel."

"Your ledgers don't balance, and —"

"That's exactly why I didn't want you looking at them. I need more time to figure out what I miscalculated." Maybe he ought to poke a pin in his pride and take the books home to Ma. She was a math enthusiast, but no grown man took things home for his mother to patch up unless absolutely necessary.

"Even if you correct the books" — Eliza shrugged — "you're still too far in debt to hire someone."

He held out his hands, palms up. "Unfortunately, that's so, but what about splitting any profits?"

She looked askance and shook her head. "This isn't the kind of store I want to run anyway. If I ever run one, it'll be my way. A setup just like F. W. Woolworth's."

A small flame of stubbornness and yearning still flickered in her eyes. Good. She'd get over this need to do something else faster than Axel ran out of town. "Can't you work with whatever's already here?"

"No. The inventory is all wrong." She frowned a little and sighed. "I won't even entertain the idea. I came here for recommendations. You make house calls when someone needs doctoring, yes?"

He nodded. Was there any other way to entice her to work for him?

No. He had nothing, and she knew it.

"I figured you'd know who has money to pay their medical bills and who might have houses in need of help. I'd also be willing to help nurse invalids or the bedridden."

So he'd be the storekeeper, and she'd be the medical professional? Could the world turn any more topsy-turvy? "Mrs. Graves might like the prestige of another maid. But she'll not pay you well." And did he really want her working in the same house with Nancy? "Maybe Mrs. Raymond, the banker's wife, but I think Señora Nogales's girls work for her. I'd hope you wouldn't want to underbid the girls — the Nogaleses really need the money."

Eliza's shoulders slumped.

"Instead of focusing on families, maybe you should approach businesses?" He held up his duster. "I wouldn't mind if you cleaned all this sawdust instead of me."

A twitch of amusement played at the corner of her mouth. "How are you going to pay me again?"

"How about the same way my patients do? Bartering. Goods." He picked up a pair of suspenders. "How about these? They'd look good with that plain button-up shirt of yours."

She pulled at her collar but didn't smile back. "I think I'll pass. I'm afraid you'd quickly run out of things I'd want from your shelves."

"How about a top hat you could glue some lace to?" He scanned her unadorned shirtwaist and dull navy skirt and couldn't keep the question in any longer. "Why do you dress so plainly anyway?"

"If I don't draw attention to my femininity, male customers are more likely to bypass flirting and get on with business."

He scratched the side of his face. "So you think Lynville hasn't been buying an awful lot because —"

"Maybe the strategy hasn't worked here as well as it did in Pennsylvania." She scrunched her lips.

He couldn't keep from smiling at a woman who found polite male deference less than chivalrous.

"There were plenty of frilly ladies to distract a man's attention there. Here . . . well, fewer ladies are gussied up in feathers and ruffles and fringe like back home."

"So why not wear something more becoming now?" He'd tried banishing the vision of Eliza in the churchyard in her silk dress for days.

"I'm not comfortable in fancy dresses."

"But you were breathtaking in your wedding dress — with those ruffles and all that . . ." He stopped talking when her face fell.

His palms hovered in midair, where he'd unconsciously undulated his hands, mimicking her curvy form. He dropped his arms, but she'd already retreated toward the door.

"I believe I'll visit Mrs. Graves now, and while your insight to offer my services to businesses is a good one, I shouldn't work for you." She backed away, bumping against the door, then turned the doorknob behind her. "I'm very sorry. Good day."

He kicked the counter once she disappeared from sight. What an idiot. That's what he got for letting himself fall asleep the last few nights imagining her in that gown.

Walking toward him.

But if she didn't walk toward *him,* how long until another man met her beside the pulpit? Single women were rare in Salt Flatts — too many men needed a wife, and Eliza would break under the constant assault of wooing and the empty pockets housekeeping jobs wouldn't fill.

Could he, or rather should he, try to win her? Was that what all his wayward thoughts were leading to? Matrimony?

He wouldn't consider offering his hand or the store until Axel was caught and convicted. For how could he woo Eliza if his friend might return with evidence to prove his innocence — as unlikely as that would be? How would Axel's criminal activities affect the store once caught? She'd said she didn't want this store anymore — he couldn't blame her after what happened — but maybe with time she'd change her mind.

Yet all the reasons that had kept him from

stopping her wedding were still valid. And even if she were willing to completely give up owning a store, he'd postponed marrying Nancy until after he'd gone to school — for how could he provide and care for a wife while spending every waking minute trying to read and keep up with his studies?

Will turned at the sound of boot steps on the front porch. He saw the sheriff walk up to the door and then stop. Will beckoned him in.

Once inside, Sheriff Quade cleared his throat and scratched at the back of his head. "Good afternoon, William."

Will sat on the counter, shoulders slumped. "I suppose you aren't here to buy anything either?"

"Business that bad?"

"Afraid so."

The man grimaced. "I feel like scum coming here while you're struggling, but I've got to do my duty."

His duty? Could the week get any worse?

"I need to forewarn you."

"Axel's been caught?" Wouldn't that be a good thing?

He shook his head. "I've talked to the lawmen in the surrounding counties, and Axel's description fits a man who's been aiding the Waller gang recently. Axel's mother's assertion that Miss Cantrell is mistaken doesn't appear to hold water."

Will licked his lips. "I've been mulling over the changes in him over the past several months. His disappearances and preoccupations . . . Illegal activity makes perfect sense. I'm a fool for not seeing it earlier."

"Well," the man said, his jaw working, "I'm afraid you might not feel any smarter once I tell you why I've come." He put his hands behind his back and looked him square in the eye. "Did you hire a lawyer when you started this business?"

What did that have to do with anything? "No. Axel already had the store running. I just joined in."

"Nothing written?"

"No." William's heart threatened to leave his chest.

"That's what I was afraid of. Unless you have a good contract drawn up protecting your assets in the company, once I find Axel and the judge hands down a conviction, if he can't produce the goods the gang stole, they'll require restitution."

"But we've rarely made a profit — we don't have much."

"And so, the judge will ask me to liquidate his assets." He gave Will the look people gave widows at funerals. "Any profit from the sale of this store would be used to cover what the Waller gang has stolen."

"He shouldn't be responsible for the entire gang's thefts."

"Maybe so, but people are mad. So the judge ain't going to be too particular about that. He'll want to return as much of the victims' money as possible."

"What about me?" His arms went numb.

"Off the record, I'd put what money I could in your personal bank account, which I couldn't touch. Hire a lawyer to see if there's some way to sue Axel for the store. Though if you have no written agreement . . . and if the judge suspects you might be in cahoots with Axel, like some others in town, he might put an injunction on any auction or sale you might attempt anyway. . . ." The sheriff frowned. "Well, I'm sure a lawyer could help you figure things out better than I could."

Right, a lawyer who'd want money. Of which he had none. Will rubbed his temples.

Sheriff Quade slipped his hat up an inch to scratch at his hairline. "I hope for your sake Axel gives up the stolen goods — if any's left. Otherwise, I'm afraid the Waller gang's victims won't be the only ones mourning what Axel's stolen from them."

Will couldn't muster a good-bye as the

sheriff took his leave.

Sometimes dreams didn't just die. Sometimes they were annihilated.

CHAPTER 14

The morning sunlight pierced through Will's eyelids, and he moaned, pulling at the covers to burrow deeper. The sound of paper sloughing onto the floor jolted him awake. He slapped his hand onto the pile spread atop his blanket, but most of the pages fanned out across the floor anyway.

Hoping to disperse the fuzziness in his head, he rubbed his temples. But reading all night, especially when words danced in dim candlelight, hadn't helped the headache the sheriff had left him with. Will had searched through Axel's papers for anything he might have written that could prove Will was a partner and not an employee, and then he'd stumbled across Eliza's letters to Axel.

He should have retied the bundle to give to Eliza, but he figured he might find some clues to Axel's whereabouts.

An excuse, of course. But still, he hoped

he might find something.

And he had. Every single business idea Axel had passed off as his own was hers, though that shouldn't have surprised him. Her ideas to improve the business went beyond what Axel had tried to implement.

After telling him she didn't want a men's store yesterday, she'd mentioned somebody named Woolworth. Hadn't she said that name the day he'd stitched her cheek? Eliza would run an amazing store if given a clean slate.

He scratched his scalp and yawned. Since the sun was so bright in the solitary window, he should've already flipped over the Open sign, but why bother? He had to carry on, of course, but the futility reminded him of holding his dead little sister and later watching her twin struggle to crawl and walk.

Leaning forward on his narrow tick bed, he held his head in his hands and rubbed the sleepiness from his eyes.

When he'd gone to the bank for a loan three years ago, Mr. Raymond had told him their venture would end badly. At the time, Will hadn't believed the banker could judge his capabilities from a fifteen-minute interview, but the man had been right to deny them a loan — he and Axel hadn't had a business plan nearly as well thought out as what Eliza had hastily penned in her letters.

If Eliza had petitioned Mr. Raymond on their behalf, she might have convinced the tight-fisted banker to believe in them. *Her* business plans would have won him over, and —

Will slapped his knees. Mr. Raymond would surely help her. Will rushed to the water basin, washed, and put on his least wrinkled coat. As he exited the front of the store, he wasn't surprised that no one waited outside the door. After locking the door and stepping onto Main Street, he tipped his hat at a few early-morning pedestrians and forced himself to smile at those who'd shunned his store since Axel's disappearance.

His steps slowed before he entered Salt Flatts Savings and Loans after crossing Main. Admitting that Mr. Raymond had been right would be easy, considering the mess the store was in. He'd have to be full of himself to believe otherwise. Though if Mr. Raymond agreed to his proposal, he'd be shooting himself in the foot.

He rested his hand on the door handle but didn't push the lever. This wouldn't hurt much more than waiting for some judge to strip the store away from him. Forging into the dry air of the bank foyer, he glanced toward the caged-in teller counter, but no one stood behind the bars.

"I'll be there in a moment!" Mr. Raymond's voice called from his office, followed by the sound of shuffling papers and a chair scraping across the floor.

Will walked straight over. They ought to discuss this in the office anyway. "I'll come to you."

Hugh Raymond looked over his glasses as Will stepped inside the handsomely furnished office. "Ah, Mr. Stanton. I figured I might see you after my conversation with the sheriff yesterday."

Will held his palms out. "Can you do anything to help?"

"I'm afraid I wouldn't touch you or anything you owned with a ten-foot pole right now." The older man's upper lip twitched. "Probably not what you wanted to hear, but beating about the bush wastes time."

"I don't expect anything less from you, Mr. Raymond." How many times had he seethed over the banker's prediction that they would fail? Yet he'd barreled headlong into trouble with Axel in an attempt to prove the man wrong. "Hopefully, I've matured enough these past three years for you to hear me out, though."

Hugh pointed to a fancy leather seat and

waited until Will sat before returning to his chair behind his massive mahogany desk. "I don't turn people away before they've spoken. I may not run a charity, as so many of you young'uns think I do, but I'm respectful enough to listen."

"I didn't doubt that, sir." Will tried to settle into the seat, but the cushion proved stiffer than it looked. He gave up being comfortable and scooted to the edge, closing the gap between them. "I suppose the sheriff told you everything."

Hugh shrugged and nodded at the same time. "Most likely."

"And I assume Axel's savings are in this bank."

"Yes."

"Could you tell me whether or not there's enough in his account to save the business if indeed he's caught and convicted?"

"I'm afraid I can't disclose that information." Hugh shook his head longer than necessary, keeping his gaze firmly on Will.

So that was a no.

He tried not to slump. He'd suspected as much. "I see."

"Look, son. I'd suggest you hire a lawyer, because unless you've invented an instrument every doctor around the nation will salivate over, I doubt you've got anything with which I'll want to involve myself. Your business will likely be swallowed up upon Axel's probable conviction."

"I'm afraid my herbal remedies won't tempt anyone except midwives and country doctors."

He'd have to consult a lawyer, but did he have enough money? Was an auction worth the effort? And if he started whatever litigation a lawyer recommended and lost . . . how could he cover the expense?

Hugh leaned back in his chair and placed an ankle on his knee. "When you cured my brother's fever after Dr. Forsythe hadn't any luck, I told my wife you should forget clerking and go to school —"

"Yet you didn't offer to sponsor me."

The man shrugged one shoulder. "Life is tough."

The townsfolk often said clay clogged the banker's veins. Seems he'd have to agree. "You offer no charity, yet you advise me to enter a profession where charity is expected. What kind of doctor wouldn't help a man on his deathbed despite his empty pockets? Dr. Forsythe usually insists on cash, yet even he will accept a half a hog or a pail of stew if that's all his patients have."

"That only proves you two are a different breed than I."

x

253

Will scowled. "Dr. Forsythe and I are nowhere near the same kind of man."

"No, you're better." Hugh scooted closer to his desk, grabbed a pen, and laid a hand on a stack of papers, signaling an end to the conversation.

But Will wasn't there for himself. "Thanks, but I haven't told you why I'm here yet."

"If you came for financial advice regarding Mr. Langston — I hope you caught my hint about his assets."

"I did, but I'm here on behalf of another."

"Why isn't he here, then?"

"Because if *she's* heard anything about you, I doubt she'd bother."

And because she wasn't in her right mind at the moment, though he wouldn't share that with the banker.

"A woman? What could she want from me?"

"What any man would. A chance for her ideas to be judged on their merit rather than her lack of connections, capital, or how she looks. I have no doubt if you listened to her business plans without prejudice —"

"I'm sorry, son —" he held out his hand, a sigh escaping — "but how would you know what makes a business plan good or bad?"

"Oh, I balked at some of her ideas, because you're right, I don't know a good plan when I see one. But I just learned every idea Axel implemented that gave us any success came from her. She's had years of experience, and her last store appraised for forty thousand dollars."

The man's eyebrows raised, and he leaned against his chair, steepling his hands. "What does a woman with forty thousand dollars need with my assistance?"

"Unfortunately, her father gave the store to her brother, who'd never done much more than sweep, and her fiancé robbed her on the train here."

"Mr. Langston's almost bride?" The man sneered. "A woman with judgment that poor doesn't generate esteem."

He wouldn't let Hugh sidetrack him. "Look, has Eliza Cantrell come to talk to you about cleaning the bank?"

"Not that I know of."

"When she does, would you mind asking about her original plans when she came to town? Get her talking about her dream of store ownership and see if you aren't impressed yourself. You said you're willing to hear people out, and that's all I ask."

"But if that's not why she's come —"

"I won't charge you for your next doctor's visit — as long as you don't tell her I put you up to it."

"All I have to do is weasel out her store ideas and not mention you?" He chewed on the end of his pen. "And if her business plans don't impress me?"

"Then they don't."

He smiled around his pen. "Seems an easy way to get a free house call. If she comes by, I'll entertain myself."

So easily enticed by a free visit. The wealthy man's avarice was amusing. "Thank you, sir." He leaned across the desk to shake the man's hand. "She'll impress you."

Even if she didn't, he had tried to help her be the woman she wanted to be, the woman he might just be falling for.

Steeling herself for another no, Eliza straightened her back and shoved into the bank, putting on her brightest smile for the teller without a customer. "Good morning."

The man glanced up from counting coins and held up a finger for her to wait. He finished forming a stack and slid the coins to the side. "What can I do for you? Need to open an account?"

Wouldn't having enough money for that be nice? "Perhaps later. I'd like to see whoever is responsible for hiring."

The man behind the counter frowned. "I

don't know of any job positions for . . ."

A lady. Of course not. "That's all right. Where can I wait to talk to someone in charge?"

"I'm fairly certain we're not hiring."

No, nobody was, but she'd wait until the person who actually made decisions denied her. Yesterday, she'd tried to convince the six households Irena and Will had suggested that she was a luxury worth having.

She'd received no job offers, not even for once-a-month cleaning.

However, she had garnered three marriage proposals from businessmen this morning. Wouldn't Lynville Tate be jealous? Would Will? She sighed. "I'd still prefer to talk to someone in charge, if you would announce me."

She walked to the wooden bench beside an impressive grandfather clock, dust free and polished. She tried not to hang her head. No cobwebs, no grime, no smudges anywhere in the foyer. This interview would be a waste of time, but she kept her feet firmly planted on the floor. She'd decided this morning to start at one end of Main Street and not go home until she'd offered her services to every owner on the north side of the road, which numbered about twenty. Tomorrow she'd inquire along the south.

She'd follow her plan to its bitter end.

Pulling aside the blind, she could just see the left side of the Men's Emporium across the street a few blocks down. Maybe she should clean for Will without compensation. That way, she could determine whether or not her gut was right about Will's innocence. Surely Irena was right about Will having nothing to do with Axel's deception.

And *if* she decided to let her emotions have free rein again, no moral misgivings would bar her from spending time with him.

"Miss Cantrell?" A man, probably in his early fifties, with golden spectacles atop his nose and gray streaking his temples, stood in a doorway.

"Yes?" How did he know her name?

"Do come in." He waved his hand for her to precede him. Each bookshelf in his office gleamed, as did his immaculate desk. Even his papers lay in meticulous piles.

Her quest seemed hopeless here.

"I'm Mr. Raymond, the president of Salt Flatts Savings and Loans."

"Pleased to meet you, sir, and thank you for seeing me."

He waited for her to be seated before sitting behind his desk. For some reason, he leaned forward, grinning — as if he anticipated something amusing.

What had the teller told him? She quickly scanned her clothing. Nothing amiss, plain as usual.

"What can I do for you?"

"I'm here to see if I might be of assistance." She forced herself not to take another look at his pristine bookshelves. "I'm looking for cleaning work. No position is too small. I can clean after business hours, a certain number of days a week, or once a month."

"How long have you had this cleaning business?" His amused grin was disconcerting.

She wouldn't slump. "The business is new. Little start-up cost, meeting a need that never goes away."

"I see." His smile only got bigger. "And what have you done prior to this?"

Why did he want to know that? Her past work had nothing to do with cleaning. "I . . . um . . . co-ran a store for the last five years."

"What kind of store?"

His incredulous face irked her. "A general store — a family business. In a city ten times larger than Salt Flatts." He didn't need to know her father hadn't left the mercantile to her. She closed her eyes and inhaled to keep out the negative thoughts. She had to believe her father had loved her, despite his decision that had caused her to end up alone, throwing herself at the mercy of strangers to provide for herself. Otherwise, she'd have to admit that no one had ever loved her. . . .

"So why do you want to clean my bank?"

She closed her eyes briefly. Was he mocking her? Surely a bank president would consider cleaning an appropriate venture for a female. Would he regale his dinner companions tonight with stories about a silly woman in town begging for a cleaning job yet thinking herself capable of running a mercantile? "Because I need money to start my own store someday." There, she'd admitted it. She couldn't truly give up the thought of having a store.

"You think housekeeping will provide enough capital?"

"Years from now." He knew as well as she did she was fooling herself. But how else could a woman with no money and no connections start over?

"You're certain that's a worthy goal?" He smoothed his mustache and cocked his head. "Why not marry, like most young ladies? I have a feeling at least one man in town is already smitten."

If he'd seen Lynville Tate near her, he'd have been blind not to have noticed his regard. "I would be happy to marry, but unless that man's dreams line up with my own, why should I settle?" She crossed her arms, tempted to leave. "I'm not here to be interrogated; I'm here to inquire about a cleaning arrangement. What will convince you that you need my help?"

He smiled and leaned back. "Tell me, what kind of store would you set up? We already have three in town."

She crossed her arms and huffed.

"Humor me, Miss Cantrell, and I'll allow you to speak of your cleaning abilities for as long as you wish."

Fine, anything to get him back on topic. "Have you heard of Woolworth's?"

He shook his head, but lifted his hand, inviting her to continue.

"In Scranton, Pennsylvania — where I'm from — F. W. Woolworth and his brother set up what he calls a five-and-dime store not even a year ago. He's owned a few others elsewhere. It's a novel concept, with low-cost goods and clearly marked prices, promising not to empty a customer's pockets."

She smiled, recalling walking into his store for the first time, feeling like a spy. "Knowing prices without having to ask is comforting for customers. I am not sure if you are aware, but I worked for a time at the Men's Emporium. I tried to get Will Stanton to understand the need to label merchandise, but he wouldn't listen. A customer might assume an item is beyond their budget and not even pick it up if they don't know the price. But once they hold it, set their heart upon it —"

"But with such inexpensive pricing —"

"Oh, but when the thing in your hand only costs a small stack of pennies, customers aren't as reluctant to spend a few more . . . and a few more after that. And just because the majority are five or ten cents doesn't mean you can't include higher priced items as well."

"What else did you learn from the practices of this Woolworth fellow?"

"He also worked the floor, as I'd wanted my father to do, but sixty-year-old men are often set in their ways."

"What do you mean by 'worked the floor'?"

"An owner should be accessible. Out on the floor, talking to customers and employees. Keeping the place clean and tidy. Paying attention to where people look and putting whatever's interesting or colorful there. No need to use that space for pencil lead or soap — they'll ask for those things when they need them. Woolworth also partnered with stores in other towns to buy big lots of inventory for better price margins. His ideas are very promising. I'm betting lots of people will adopt his business model once they hear of it."

"You think you'd make enough profit to compete with the other stores in town?"

"The first few years would be tight, but I wouldn't directly compete with anyone. The Hampdens have a general store, and Lowerys' is mostly a feed store." She licked her lips in hesitation. To be honest or diplomatic? What did it matter?

"And Will and Axel chose poorly. They targeted a particular consumer, narrowing themselves mostly to items the other stores stocked as well. They relied on their connections and return customers for sales, but most men won't go to the Men's Emporium when they have other stores where they can get all their shopping done at the same time. To be worth visiting, they should have focused on making it a place for gentlemen to gather — perhaps a checker-and-chess board always ready, a wall of business news and wheat prices, etc."

At least Mr. Raymond's face no longer

looked so amused — his smile had flipped into a frown. "Aren't you doing the same thing with this five-and-dime? The other two stores have items that fall within that price range."

"Ah, but mixed in with everything else, unpriced, and not in huge batches. I'll have more variety and whimsy. You'd be surprised what people buy if the item only costs five cents — even knowing the quality might be lacking. Of course, I wouldn't purposely stock my store with poorly manufactured wares, but I would favor mass-produced items."

She picked at the lint on her skirt. "I can't copy everything Woolworth did in Scranton, but I can run a good store. Even before I recognized Woolworth's innovations, in five years I doubled the equity of my father's store, after he'd owned the property for thirty years prior to my stepping into management."

"If you were so successful, why, pray tell, did you come here to marry a stranger?"

Yes, that question. "Engaging yourself to a longtime friend can be as idiotic as engaging yourself to a stranger." She pressed a hand to her throat to help her swallow the lump caught there. "I was engaged to marry back in Pennsylvania. My first fiancé had more interest in taking advantage of my store's sudden profit than in marrying me — though he made certain to woo me enough to keep my head in the clouds."

She closed her eyes, feeling the color rise in her face. "He sabotaged me, convincing many of my suppliers to supply his father's businesses exclusively. *My* father was obviously disappointed and changed his will, making my brother the sole owner. I was to work for him, but he's always been jealous and never listened to anything I've said. So I decided to find a place a woman business owner might find respect."

That place probably didn't exist in Salt Flatts — probably didn't exist anywhere but in her dreams.

"You seem like a smart woman." Mr. Raymond stared out the window, tapping his pen on the side of his shoe, where his foot lay anchored on his knee.

If she let it, the compliment might puff her chest, but what good would it do?

"But without capital, you've got nothing to lose if someone backed you." He frowned at the ceiling.

"Yes. Well, that's what happens when your *second* fiancé robs you of said capital on the train into town. I *had* money when I left Pennsylvania." Not a lot, but enough to invest in a start-up of something . . .

Why was Mr. Raymond lecturing her on things she already knew? She'd held up her end of the bargain, prattling off about a dream she'd likely never achieve. "So . . . I'm here for a cleaning job. How about once a month? I see someone does a great job of keeping things tidy, but I'll do the deep cleaning, the corners and under furniture." She looked him in the eyes. "Let's agree to the first Monday of the month for the entire day. Five dollars seems reasonable for the heavy lifting I'll be doing, and —"

His laughter stopped her, though it wasn't exactly derisive. "I do believe you'll get what you want come hell or high water." He leaned forward. "But how are you going to survive on a handful of cleaning jobs? And they aren't about to earn you five dollars a day, by the way."

She frowned. "Mrs. Lightfoot has been exceedingly kind and is letting me clean for room and board, so my essential needs will be sufficiently met. What I'm here for is —"

"Mrs. Lightfoot, eh?" The man leaned back, tapping his chin as if recalling something pleasant. Could a man like him be interested in a bearded lady?

No, he was married. She narrowed her eyes at him. What kind of man was he?

"I'm interested in your business strate-gies, Miss Cantrell." He leaned forward, his teeth pulling at his lower lip, his eyes bright. "I bet you didn't hand over your money without a fight."

She turned her head so he could see the pink skin she'd unconsciously turned away from him upon entering his office and shrugged. "I didn't get a face-disfiguring scar for no reason." But what did that mat-ter? Unless . . . "Are you interested in part-nering with me, Mr. Raymond? If you're interested —"

"As I said" — he held up his hand — "you have no capital to share in the risk, but let me look into something. Come back tomor-row after noon."

She stood and smoothed her suddenly sweaty palms against her skirt. "I suppose you're turning me down for the cleaning job?"

"Right, no job." He stood and smiled wide. "But I find your persistence com-mendable."

Whatever that meant. But she would listen to any offer; flexibility often brought reward. "What do I need to bring with me tomor-row?"

"Whatever you need to face disappoint-ment."

That wasn't exactly promising, but she refused to drop her smile. "I'll see you tomorrow, then."

And she'd do her utmost not to expect anything to come of the meeting — but that didn't stop the hope.

CHAPTER 15

Mr. Raymond was pacing the sidewalk in front of the bank as if bars surrounded him rather than the dust swirling around him as wagons drove by. A block away, Eliza glanced at the seamstress shop behind her and then the clock above the bank: 12:15.

Had Mr. Raymond meant she should meet him *precisely* after noon? Was he waiting for her?

The thought of Mr. Raymond impatiently waiting would distract her from the conversation she hoped to have with the seamstress. She couldn't afford to make a poor impression — she needed every job she could get. She'd only managed to snag a two-dollar weekly cleaning position at the butcher's. She tried not to think about what such a cleaning job would entail, but for the first time, going home and asking her brother for a job and becoming the crazy old aunt who lives in the attic sounded like a viable option.

No, she preferred Irena's company to her brother's, so she'd deal with the butcher shop's floor.

She squared her shoulders. Visiting the seamstress could wait until after her meeting with Mr. Raymond. After a buggy passed, Eliza quick-stepped across the pitted dirt street.

On one of Mr. Raymond's quick about-faces, he caught a glimpse of her, and his countenance brightened. With his hands still behind his back, he met her at the edge of the road. "Good afternoon, Miss Cantrell. I'm glad you're early."

Good thing she'd seen him pacing. "Well, I hate being tardy."

"Follow me." Without waiting, the man barreled down the sidewalk toward the center of town. His unusual manner put a twinge in her abdomen, and she tried not to fret over their destination.

Mr. Raymond stopped in front of an empty two-story storefront in a brick building between the bakery and the confectioner's. She'd tried to get a cleaning job at both places yesterday. Considering the amount of flour and sugar dusting innumerable surfaces, her offer should have enticed them, but she'd been denied.

The building's beautiful stonework had drawn her attention the day she'd arrived. Sweet and yeasty smells escaped every time customers opened the doors, adding to the allure. Pigeons cooed in the intricate stone-columned balcony that spanned the entirety of the upper stories. The owners should have at least paid her to clean the birds' mess.

The jangle of keys returned her gaze to ground level.

"Let's go inside and have a look." He shoved his keys into the fancy escutcheon and turned the patterned brass doorknob.

Should she follow him in? This building wasn't for her. He was just . . . What *were* they doing?

"Beautiful building, isn't it?" He ran his hand over the granite rock work surrounding the front door. Two tall glass displays formed a hallway that angled in toward the front door, creating an almost triangular entryway.

She followed him inside. The interior was empty except for dust and some massive furnishings. The carved floor-to-ceiling cabinetry led up to embossed tin ceiling tiles, and counters on top of the glass display cases lined the left side of the store. At the back, a magnificent staircase worthy of a fairytale's castle swooped up from a wide base and narrowed onto an open balcony, creating a second floor over the back quarter of the room.

His heels tapped on the varnished wood floor, his footprints disturbing the dust. "What do you think?"

What was there to think? The glass displays would keep china out of reach of little hands. The open cabinetry with its scrollwork would make a shelf of five-cent oil lamps look worth a dollar. The staircase alone would cause a customer to believe whatever lay above was worth more than a week's salary. "I never saw a lovelier store in Pennsylvania. What was it used for?"

"A jeweler. A very good jeweler whose wife was also quite the seamstress." He ran his fingers through the powder blanketing the counter. "Their only child moved here a decade ago, and his mother couldn't bear to be parted from him, so they set up shop like the one they'd owned in New York without thinking things through. When the wife died and the son moved farther west, the man left this place empty." He clucked his tongue, stared at the high ceiling, and smiled. "I've wanted it ever since."

Counters filled with diamonds and sapphires. Fitting. "So what keeps you from owning it?"

He scrunched his face. "A mere five minutes. The bill of sale was signed by the time I approached him. It was the closest I've ever come to weeping in public."

"What good is a fancy store to you? Surely no merchandise could garner the profit needed to succeed in this place."

"Ah, but the rent I could charge. We're fast becoming one of the largest towns in south-central Kansas, thanks to the railroad. The jeweler would have likely succeeded if he'd started now and expanded his wares a bit more."

High rent and a five-and-dime store were not a match made in heaven. She clasped her hands. Time to get back to business. "So I guess you've finally bought the place and need me to clean it? That won't be too difficult considering it's mostly street dust on an empty floor. How about fifteen dollars?"

He snorted. "Again, you start too high."

"You would start too low."

He shrugged, the smile staying on his lips. "I won't pay you to clean it, but you'll want to clean the place nonetheless."

She was done with the banker's riddles. She couldn't afford to get her hopes up over something that would never be. The longer she stood there, the harder it would be not to imagine tables filled with toys, knick-knacks, and everything else she'd seen at the Scranton Woolworth's store. "Speak plainly, Mr. Raymond, if you would. I have other businesses to visit before the day is done."

"No you don't. Your search stops here."

She shook her head. "You and I both know I cannot afford the huge rental fee. And there is no way I can afford the amount of inventory I'd have to order, and —"

"It's offered rent free. I'll finance the inventory, which you will need to pay back, and my investment will be the other start-up costs."

They stood in silence until Eliza couldn't help but blink. "I don't follow. You told me you don't make foolish business decisions."

"I don't. Without capital you'll need a business partner, silent though I may be. Sixty percent for me and forty for you seems fair."

So he thought her ideas strong enough for him to back her? Eliza pulled at her collar. "It's quite unfair of you to bring me in here, to let me see it — set my heart upon it — just for you to get me to sign something I'd never in my right mind agree to if I hadn't fallen in love with the place." And boy had she. "I'll not be taken."

"I may be hard-nosed and penny-pinching, but that doesn't mean I'm a cheat."

"I didn't mean to insinuate such, but men often believe they can give a woman worse terms, assured she'll accept any offer, ecstatic that someone chose to do business with her."

"Be assured I have no intention of getting more than my fair share."

"And if I buy you out within the year?"

He frowned. "That may have worked for the blokes you talked about in Pennsylvania, but I'm not sure that will be possible in Kansas. So I guess I'll have to include one stipulation: you'll have to stay in this location for at least five years."

"Why's that?"

"I'm not the property's owner — otherwise you'd indeed be paying me rent." He held out his arms. "I've set up a deal with the owner that, if I loan you the money for inventory and pay all the other start-up costs, I get the option to buy the building . . . after five years. The owner's been a fool to let this place sit and collect dust." He smiled. "But just because someone else makes foolish business decisions doesn't mean I can't take advantage of them."

"And if I wish to be sole owner after five years?"

"I don't care once my name is on the deed. The inventory loan should be paid by then, but you'd have to buy out the partnership. I'll own the building and start collecting rent either way."

Her heart raced. This plan might get her a store within a month instead of a decade. She worked to keep her voice businesslike. "How involved do you plan to be?"

"I don't have time to play retailer. I'll leave that to you, though I'll peruse the books regularly — and you should also pass large decisions by me first."

With free rent, she'd quickly stack up profits. To keep from squirming, she clasped her hands tightly behind her back. She needed to think this through. "I'm afraid I can't decide today. I'll need to talk to a lawyer first." Perhaps he'd know who owned this store. What could this mysterious benefactor possibly gain from the rent-free offer?

"Of course. There are two in town, both on Eighth Street."

"Which is your lawyer?"

"Mr. Gerard."

"And the other?"

"Mr. Scottsmore."

"Then I'll be talking with Scottsmore."

He smiled. "We'll work beautifully together, Miss Cantrell. Why don't we meet in four days' time? I'll have a contract drawn up for consideration, and I'll want to see a business plan. We can decide then."

Good, she needed time. "We're in agreement so far. But make sure your contract lays out clear purchase options for when I want to buy the rest of the business from you. And I want fifty percent equity, and you take fifty — equal partners. I will, after all, be doing the most work." She held out her hand, giving him a firm grip when he reached out. "Perhaps we'll be working together sooner rather than later."

He nodded — "I hope so, Miss Cantrell" — and placed the keys into her palm. "Look around and return the keys before the bank closes. This is the best possible arrangement for you in your particular predicament. You're smart enough to be working with me soon." He tipped his hat. "Good day."

She stood perfectly still as he walked toward the exit. Once he shut the door, she moved slowly to the staircase and ran her hand along the smooth banister, climbing halfway to the top before turning and sitting on the dusty wooden stairs.

"Perfect." She pursed her lips and exhaled

through her nose. Beyond perfect.

But she'd thought Axel was a perfect solution as well. She'd have to ask Irena for her opinion — maybe she'd know who owned the place and whether Mr. Raymond could be trusted. Eliza would give serious consideration to any reservations Irena voiced.

And prayer.

She stared at the keys to the spacious store she could have only dreamed of obtaining.

Lord, in the past I've been too quick to follow the first promising door that opened. I need your guidance. As much as this sounds like a present from heaven plopped in my lap, I don't want to barrel forward because of the pretty architecture, the good terms, and the fact that I wouldn't have to wait years to prove myself.

Had God given her the desire of her heart despite her shortcomings?

Will peeped outside to make sure no one was heading toward the store. Of course, no one even looked his way. What did it matter if he snagged one more customer today? A third patron wouldn't buy enough to make keeping the store open worthwhile anyway.

He turned the key and checked that the door was securely bolted.

Surely he was overreacting. No one would

have stolen from him; he'd simply misplaced his savings, but he didn't want to take a chance.

Shoving his hands into his pockets, he shuffled down the sidewalk toward Mr. Arnett's livery. Yesterday Will had treated the man's infected rope burn but couldn't for the life of him remember if his leather coin purse had sat in its usual spot next to the ointment and bandages.

Before opening the store this morning, he'd visited Nancy's mother to check on her condition, but he couldn't recall if he'd had his money then either.

He prayed Mr. Arnett had seen his change purse. Will couldn't endure another visit with Mrs. Graves pointedly looking at him and then at Nancy. He wasn't ready to think in that direction. Now that Eliza had been freed from Axel, would she consider him? Not if she wanted a fancy store . . . which she would gain in time, and he'd never be able to provide.

Maybe he'd check Christenson's little shack on the edge of town before visiting the Graves family — but if he'd lost his savings there, Mr. Christenson likely wouldn't admit to finding it. Even though his seven children hadn't enough to eat, the drunk would have taken the money to the closest still.

If only he could remember the last time he'd seen his coin purse. The longer it'd been gone, the more likely his money had fallen into the wrong hands. He'd have to start saving all over again — while running a failing store that might earn him nothing if the sheriff caught Axel and auctioned off their business.

Maybe he should just board up the doors, travel to Atchison, and beg his friend's great-uncle to start the broom-making apprenticeship immediately. Even if he could successfully sue for the rights to the entire store and auction it off, would that be fair to Axel's victims or the Langstons?

He hadn't sympathized enough with Eliza when her savings was stolen. His eighty-four dollars was measly compared to the hundreds she must have lost.

A groan and unladylike mutter sounded just ahead. Will hastened his pace. He recognized the sound of someone getting sick, yet no woman was standing on the sidewalk ahead or slumping against a building. The groan echoed again. Down the next alley, a girl, doubled over, held herself upright with a mop while clutching her stomach.

He rushed down the alley. "Are you all right?"

Eliza looked up at him, pale and disheveled. "I will be."

He couldn't help but push back the damp hair from her forehead and check her temperature. "You don't feel hot, but you look sweaty and flushed."

"I'm not used to carting around entrails and cow parts that swish . . ." She closed her eyes and swallowed. "I have to stop looking at whatever's floating in my mop bucket." She put her hand to her mouth.

"And you better stop imagining it as well."

She nodded and took a deep breath.

"What're you doing?"

She dumped her water, letting the nastiness drain down the alley. "As you suggested, I found a business that needed my help. I promised to start working today."

He wrinkled his nose at the smell finally entering his consciousness. "This wasn't exactly what I meant."

Shaking her head, she dropped onto the side steps of the butcher's store. Had he ever seen her sit while working?

"I asked every business on Main Street, Maple, Fourth, and Fifth, but the butcher was the only one willing to hire me."

Mr. Raymond hadn't offered her anything?

Will rubbed the back of his neck. The banker must have judged her by her gender rather than her acumen.

Will sighed. It had been worth a try.

She grabbed the stair railing and peered up at him through the bars. "Its all right. Things are going to get better soon."

He squatted to eye level. "You shame me."

"How's that? As a doctor, you've probably seen nastier things than floating pig entrails. On the farm, you've probably even been covered in them."

"That's not what I was talking about." He moved to sit beside her, the narrow stairs forcing him to push aside her skirt. "I'm leaving work early because I don't feel like doing my job, whereas you're doing work that turns your stomach. I do believe I have more of Axel in me than I care for."

She leaned away from him. "How's that?"

"I'm lazy."

Her chuckle added some color to her face. "I've seen you work at the shop all day, then lug your medical box out to help someone before the sun goes down."

He ground his bootheel into the dirt. "Nevertheless, I should be working instead of pining for my hardships to go away."

She shrugged. "Well, I now know one thing." She grinned at him. "I might be able to force myself through a week or two of this" — she gestured toward the mop bucket — "but not a lifetime. So I can cross off marrying the butcher's son as the way for me to escape my troubles."

Her lopsided smile did not elicit the chuckle she'd likely expected from him, but rather a jab to his middle. "No, I don't advise marrying a butcher's son." Heaven help him if she met the butcher's eldest. Micah was an adventurous land surveyor with a ready smile and flippant charm.

"Doctor's orders?"

Oh, if only she'd let him write a prescription to ban her from all men but himself.

She blinked but didn't lose eye contact. Her grin faded. "Will?"

He swallowed hard but didn't look away. Who was he kidding? He couldn't fabricate brooms or believe himself capable of reattaching himself to Nancy. Sitting next to Eliza with her apron covered in slop and a smear of something unidentifiable across her cheek didn't dampen his desire to pull her into an embrace.

And test out those lips.

How on earth could he have continued to live in Salt Flatts with Mrs. Eliza Langston? He'd have been besotted with a married woman.

She cleared her throat. "Now it's my turn to ask if you're all right. You look a bit . . . peaked."

"Just distracted by what's on your face." He pulled out his handkerchief and reached for her cheek. How he longed to touch her face without the hindrance of a cloth, but he hadn't the right.

"Oh." She frowned as he rubbed, pulling her skin taut and leaving her cheek rosier. Though he'd successfully wiped the smear off her face, he didn't take his hand away. This close, he could see the golden flecks hidden in her brown irises, the minuscule freckles across the bridge of her nose, the slightly off-center philtrum above her mouth. No wonder the term meant love charm — he couldn't take his eyes off the little indentation above her top lip.

But the alley was too smelly for courting, the timing all wrong. He needed to stop touching her before he kissed her amidst the muck — where any passerby could see. He stuffed his handkerchief into his pocket. "I plan to stay in town."

She scrunched her eyebrows.

"Instead of becoming a broom maker."

"Right. I figured with Axel not being around, you'd have to stay . . . for the store."

"For a while, anyway." He'd need to find

a way to get to medical school before everything fell apart. How long until she was over her wedding mishap and might welcome his court? How many weeks needed to pass before declaring his intent wouldn't make him seem like an impatient buzzard? "I'll be around."

He'd not steal kisses in an alley now. Nor hover like Lynville.

"Miss Cantrell?" The butcher's voice boomed from the interior, and they both startled.

How long had they been sitting staring at each other?

Eliza struggled to stand, so he reached down to help her. His fingers locked on to her elbows, and he pulled her up, but his hands refused to let go.

She tugged a little, then stilled. "I'd better get back to work. I've never taken a break this long in my life."

"Right." He still didn't release her.

"Will?" The whisper of his name sent chills along his arms.

He squeezed her a bit more. "Promise me you won't marry any of the butcher's sons."

"I won't." She swallowed, her eyes locking on his. "Anything else?"

Promise not to think of anyone but me. "No, nothing else for now."

"I'll see you later, then?"

"Sooner."

The moment she disappeared into the butcher shop, he strode out of the alley. The first thing he had to do was find his eighty-four dollars, then figure out how to get the store running so well he could pay a lawyer to help him figure out what he could do with the store that might help his coffers.

What else would he need to do to make Eliza find a life with him more appealing than owning a store?

Thinking about kissing would definitely have to wait until after he got his life together enough to keep Eliza from running away from the disaster he was at the moment.

CHAPTER 16

Will glanced at the clock. Quarter to five. He walked past the aisles to see if he'd missed a customer, but the store was still empty, as it'd been for the last two hours.

He hung his hammer on the storage room wall. The people in this town should be done shunning him because of Axel. If he'd been implicated in his friend's shenanigans, the sheriff would have hauled him in already.

But no matter how much he berated the townsfolk in his mind, they didn't listen.

Though there was one good thing about being spurned: he could close the store early every day and look for Eliza. He'd walked past the butcher every afternoon since first seeing her there — hoping to catch her dumping her mop bucket.

He wasn't about to court her on the butcher's stairs, but was hoping to talk to her for a minute or two so bad?

He'd only caught her twice. Both days had

287

been Thursdays, and today was Thursday again. But if he didn't find her, he ought to go see Silas Jonesey. Will hadn't been invited back to his farm, but the man needed some human conversation and perhaps a game of chess to keep his spirits up. Jonesey spent entirely too much time alone.

The front door opened, tripping the little bell.

He closed his eyes and let out a tiny groan. A chance to see Eliza or a chance to sell something? Other than the store's selection of canned goods, he was frightfully close to going without food. Of course, finding his missing savings would help buy groceries, but he had yet to find his change purse. He needed a coin or two in his pocket more than he needed to see Eliza.

At least that's what his stomach told him.

He dragged himself up front.

"Good afternoon, William." The sheriff pulled off his hat.

Will slowed. Did the man bring good or bad news this time? The best news would be that he'd caught Axel sitting atop a pile of loot. "Did you find Axel?"

"The sheriff's deputies up in Atchison have taken over the search since that's where we caught the Wallers."

Will pressed a hand against his hollow

stomach. "What can I do you for, then?"

"Several businesses have reported missing merchandise. Have you noticed anything amiss? Seen anyone lurking around or have something unaccounted for?"

"I am missing something, but I thought I'd misplaced it. Has anyone turned in a circular leather pouch containing eighty-four dollars?"

The sheriff whistled. "That's a lot to misplace."

"Don't I know it." Though the money wasn't near enough to go to school. "I can't recall seeing anyone doing anything suspicious or unusual."

The sheriff pinned him with a narrow-eyed gaze. "I have to ask this, Will — why have been you walking down Main Street aimlessly peering into windows?"

Huh? Certainly the sheriff didn't think he —

"When I've asked others about suspicious activity, three people pointed fingers at you. Now I've known you for a long time, but I've known Axel about that long too. . . ." The sheriff scratched at his chin. "This ain't the time for acting suspicious. I'm a mite concerned you're still helping the man."

"Uh . . ." He squirmed a bit under the sheriff's intense glare. "The townsfolk are looking for someone to blame. I'm not checking out anyone's property or wandering . . ." All right, so pacing near the butcher's in the afternoons was happening a lot lately.

He tugged at his tie. "I, uh, have been walking the street lately, but not for that purpose. I've been . . . agitated, but I'm not your thief."

If he'd been alone, he would have smacked himself. How would he regain customers hoofing around town like a madman so he could *accidentally* cross Eliza's path to ask her nothing more than how she was doing? He should just stand at the end of the alley and wait for her. Let her know he'd come to see her.

The door swung open so quickly, the sheriff barely jumped out of the way before being smacked in the shoulder.

The banker's eyes roved like a panicked calf cornered in a stall. Hugh's gaze fastened onto Will. "I need you. You owe me a medical visit."

"Of course, Mr. Raymond, but the sheriff and I —"

Hugh turned to face the sheriff. "I apologize for interrupting, but my wife is ill. When I left her this morning, I thought it was nothing. The Nogales girl came a few hours ago, but I barely understood what she said with her Spanish mixed in, and fool that I am, I decided to finish a transaction, and then got sidetracked . . ." He swung his gaze back to Will and grabbed his arm. "Come."

The sheriff ducked his head in dismissal as he followed them outside.

Will sighed and locked the door. Eliza was right. He kept plenty busy — doing things that earned him no money. He'd never realized how unrelenting the demand for a doctor could be — and he wasn't even trying to be one at the moment. "What's wrong with your wife?"

Hugh ran around his buggy and jumped into the driver's seat. "I don't know. That's your job to figure out."

Will climbed up beside him and almost bounced back off the seat as Hugh smacked his horses and they shot off.

When they careened around a slow, plodding donkey cart, Will grabbed for a second handhold. "I mean, what are her symptoms?" He glanced toward the butcher's alley as they raced by. A fleeting glimpse of Eliza and her mop bucket made him wish he could wave at her, but he couldn't let go of his seat.

Even if he did, they had already sped past

the alley.

"I'd figured it's what always bothers her in the spring." Hugh hollered at a man to make way before smacking his poor horse again.

He'd never seen Hugh this agitated. "And the Nogales girl said . . . ?"

"That Deborah was sick and I should go home early. That's all I understood!" He jerked his hands, strangling the reins, but the moment his horses slowed to a trot, he none too gently prodded them faster. "How was I supposed to know she was emptying her stomach every hour and paler than a ghost?"

So vomiting, pale, and symptoms of a catarrh. Hopefully nothing more than something she ate. Hugh took a turn too fast, and the buggy leaned dangerously onto its two right wheels. Will clamped onto the man's arm. "Reaching your wife five minutes faster is not worth killing us both. Slow down. She'll not get any help if you've broken both our necks."

The man pulled back slightly on the reins, but his jaw clamped. "Just a little."

Will swallowed and nodded his approval.

Hugh's wife might very well be on her way to eternity, but they didn't have to take Salt Flatts' pedestrians and themselves along with her on the journey.

Eliza tipped over her mop bucket, watching the murky water spill into the alley. She'd stood on the steps for ten minutes trying to look busy, hoping Will would visit, but he'd just flown by on a buggy at such a ridiculous speed it sent a stray dog scurrying.

Where was Will going in such a hurry? She trailed her fingers along her cheek and down her jaw, the same path his thumb had followed the day he'd destroyed a pillow.

Certainly he felt something, with the way he'd looked at her since the wedding . . . and even before. What kept him from saying something?

Too bad she hadn't more chores at the butcher's in case Will planned to return. How silly was that? Wishing for more dead animal parts to clean up!

Last week when he'd dropped by, he'd babbled about the weather, but at least he'd come by. Besides Irena, he was the only person she wanted to talk to about the agreement she was about to finalize with Mr. Raymond. But could Will be objective, since her business could easily hurt his? — not that his store wasn't already in trouble.

Maybe she shouldn't discuss the business deal with Will. She didn't need his business advice, but what about hinting at wanting to see him more often? However, wouldn't that essentially be asking him to court her?

Did she want to give him that impression?

She wrung the mop head until no more water dripped from its nasty cotton fibers. Why were relationships with men so complicated?

After weeks of negotiation between the lawyers and delays of one kind or another, Mr. Raymond said he would make a few final changes. Assuming she was satisfied, she planned to sign his revised contract tomorrow morning. With a store of her own, she wouldn't need a man to feel secure. She would be free to court whomever, free to break off a relationship if things felt wrong.

But if she and Will became more attached, what would she do when he left for school? Maybe she should wait to drop courting hints until he returned. But how long would that be?

No matter what Will did, she had to decide what was best for her today, and her heart skipped beats every time she contemplated this final meeting with Mr. Raymond. She'd imagined signing her name; she'd imagined walking away. Both scenarios made her palms sweaty. Months ago, she'd have jumped at this chance without a second thought, but supposedly perfect opportunities often came bundled with problems, as she'd learned since arriving in Salt Flatts.

God, did you give me this opportunity or are you testing me somehow?

As much as she wished the audible voice of God would echo down the alleyway, no answer came. She'd been praying every night since the opportunity had presented itself but still wasn't completely assured that He'd approve one way or the other. She dragged the mop bucket inside and untied her apron. Mr. Otting came out from the back carrying some paper-wrapped meat. A redheaded woman attired in a brilliant blue day dress held the hand of a willowy young girl as they waited at the counter.

Mr. Otting glanced toward Eliza and frowned. "You haven't left already?"

She grinned. "Did you think I'd leave without pay?"

He snorted, then handed the meat to his customer. "Seventy-five cents please."

The woman handed over her coins and smiled at Eliza. "I'm afraid we haven't met."

Eliza tried to hide her soiled hands amidst the folds of her skirt. She normally paled in comparison to the women around her, but right now, she might as well be a pig farmer standing next to a lady at court. The woman's smile seemed genuine though.

"I'm Eliza Cantrell."

"I'm Nancy Wells." She smiled and clasped the shoulder of the young lady beside her. "This is my daughter, Millicent."

Might this be Will's Nancy? Was she back in town for good or only for a visit? Eliza worked to keep a pleasant expression, but when the little girl peeped up at her with bashful misty-gray eyes, an easy smile relaxed her face.

"How long have you lived here? I'm afraid the town's grown so large in just a year I hardly recognize more than a handful of people."

Eliza swallowed hard and rubbed her scar. If this attractive woman was Will's ex-fiancée, no wonder he'd been devastated. "About two months."

"I've started a ladies' Bible study group on Tuesday mornings at the little white church past the sawmill." A beautiful smile flashed across Nancy's flawless face. The woman's hair might be a bit too frizzy, but who would notice with her porcelain skin? "I'd love to have you come."

Eliza glanced at her feet. As much as she should start reading her Bible more, and a Bible study would definitely encourage her to do so, could she sit across from this woman weekly, comparing herself to Will's former fiancée?

If she took Mr. Raymond's offer, she definitely couldn't attend — she wouldn't have time.

She glanced at Mr. Otting. Since she hadn't yet seen Mr. Raymond's last offer, she didn't want the butcher thinking she was quitting, in case she decided not to sign the contract. If things fell through, she needed the money from this job. "I might be working Tuesday mornings soon, but if not, I'll consider coming."

"If it's possible, please do — I'd love more ladies my age joining us." Nancy smiled and took the girl's hand again. "But I won't keep you any longer. Good-bye."

Mr. Otting wiped his hands on his bloody apron until the door closed behind Nancy. "She's such a sweet young lady. Sad that she's a widow already, but her mother thinks she and William Stanton will get back together. I'd hoped she'd consider one of my boys, but her late husband's little girl needs lots of medical attention, so it's probably best Mr. Stanton marries her anyway."

Widowed? Available to court? Will must've known she was back in Salt Flatts, since he mentioned visiting Mrs. Graves last week.

Was he forgiving enough to take Nancy back?

Of course Will was; he'd forgive his own murderer.

Eliza stared at what looked like the evidence of a massacre smeared across Mr. Otting's chest. Had she been wrong about Will's feelings toward her?

It wouldn't be the first time she'd misjudged a man's affections.

What man would choose her over a beautiful woman like Nancy? He had to still feel something for her, though the woman had jilted him. One didn't just turn off emotions like one blew out a lamp. And with a sickly little girl in need of medical care . . . how could Will not be drawn to her?

Eliza closed her eyes and clenched her fists. Tomorrow she'd sign the papers Mr. Raymond had drawn up, even if there were some less than ideal terms — anything else in her future would have to be worked around her store, otherwise she'd regret not signing for the rest of her life.

"Miss Cantrell?" Mr. Otting scratched the hair behind his ear, his frown hanging heavy on his face as he peered at his cashbox.

"Yes?"

"Do you mind if I send you home today with ribs or maybe a roast instead of cash? I don't exactly have enough this week, not with the bills I had to pay."

She fought against a frown. "That's all right, Mr. Otting. Mrs. Lightfoot and I would enjoy a roast."

He brightened. "Great." Then he disappeared into the back.

She quickly swept the floor a second time to make up for wasting time earlier.

"Here you are. And since you do such a fine job, here's some fresh side pork as well."

A fine job? He definitely hadn't seen her dallying in the alley, then. "Thank you."

Outside, she strolled down the street and stopped in front of the store she would start filling with merchandise within the month. Her heart lifted at the sight of the magnificent stone building, the spiraling rockwork at the top piercing the heavens.

Lord, if this isn't the best thing for me, let me know. But it feels right.

The cold meat under her arm propelled her to leave the heartwarming sight behind and return to Irena, who'd taken to her bed yesterday and hadn't come downstairs for breakfast.

At the boardinghouse, Eliza put the meat in the little wooden icebox, then tiptoed upstairs. She cracked open her friend's door and peered inside the dim room.

The bed creaked. "Come in."

Eliza crossed to the bedstead and frowned at the uneaten food on the dresser. "Still not hungry?"

"I ate a little."

An inchworm would have eaten more. She bent over to feel her forehead.

"Can't an old woman lie in peace?" Irena moved away from Eliza's hand, struggling to sit up. "You'd think you wanted to doctor instead of run a store with all your fussing." A cough racked her body.

"Would you like Will to look in on you?"

Irena waved her hand for a split second before returning it to her mouth to cover another cough.

"Maybe I shouldn't bother with your permission. You should be looked at." If only she knew where Will had gone.

"Your hands on your hips don't threaten me, missy." Irena closed her eyes and leaned against the headboard. "When you get old, it's hard to get over illnesses. My joints already ached before this fever."

She reached out a hand again. Irena sighed but endured the probing.

"I've got the pain powders William gives me for my joints and plenty of his crushed yarrow for the tea he makes me, so don't bother him." She pulled her blanket to her chest. "Though I feel as if the fever's returning. Perhaps you should make some of that tea."

"You're a little warm, but nothing like last night." She dropped her hand. "What about for dinner?" She frowned at the uneaten cheese and crackers on the bedside table. "I want to bring you something you'll eat."

"Broth sounds good."

"Do you mind if I ask a question before I leave?" The haze marring Mrs. Lightfoot's normally twinkly blue eyes gave Eliza pause, but would she have time to talk to her in the morning?

She gave her a wavering smile. "All I'm good for is listening right now."

"Do you think I can do this store thing alone?"

Irena rolled her eyes and shifted to open the end table's drawer. She pulled out a thick book and tossed it toward Eliza. "You're not alone. Mr. Raymond is supporting you — and I believe in you too."

Turning over the book, Eliza grinned at the merchandise catalog. "You must have ordered this the first day I returned from the bank."

"You're meant to run a store. You'll do just fine. Maybe things won't work out as you've planned, but you'll readjust and improve." Irena's eyelids fluttered.

Eliza rose from the bed. She'd have to eat dinner by herself again tonight. If Irena didn't recover soon, Eliza would have no one to celebrate with over the papers she'd sign tomorrow. Will or Kathleen wouldn't appreciate a dinner invitation to celebrate their newest business competition.

"I'll bring your meal up in an hour or so."

Irena muttered her thanks. She'd most likely be asleep within minutes.

Eliza paused on the stair to look through the narrow window on the landing. Would Will be upset she'd chosen her own store instead of helping him as he'd asked?

She had to make good business decisions, not emotional ones.

He'd be fine; she shouldn't worry.

Will slumped against the hard bedroom chair, trying to get comfortable for the long night ahead of him at Mrs. Raymond's side. He didn't know what else to do besides pray her through.

The door behind him cracked open, letting a sliver of light brighten the dark room.

Mrs. Raymond lay writhing on the bed, her painful groaning uninterrupted by her husband's entrance.

"Can I convince you to retire to the guest

room?" Hugh, dressed in striped pajamas fancier than Will's Sunday suit, shuffled in, wringing his hands.

Will pulled the other chair closer and gestured for the man to sit. "You're the one who needs rest. I'll have few customers disappointed to see my Closed sign tomorrow, whereas you said you have several meetings."

Hugh hovered on the edge of the seat, as if uncertain sitting was a good idea. He stared at his wife rather than turning to Will. "Maybe I should cancel." He scooted back against his chair but a second later perched on the front edge and turned, his eyes as wide as they were hours ago. "Are you sure?"

Will couldn't help but smile. How long until the shock wore off? "Yes, I'm positive."

"But she's forty-two, and I'm fifty."

"*Your* age has nothing to do with it."

"But she said . . ." He pulled on the lapel of his pajamas as if the cloth were a tight cravat instead of a loosely tailored collar. "She said that her courses were over."

"Evidently not long enough." Will folded his hands between his knees. "She's not dying of a tumor as she feared — there's a baby, sure enough — the fever, well, that's something else. They need to be nursed through this."

"They? The fever could affect the baby?"

Will nodded, his smile drooping. "It might've already."

"She's wanted another child for so long. Can't you do something?"

"I'm not certain what's causing her fever. I can fetch Dr. Forsythe in the morning, if you'd like. A second opinion won't make me feel as if you're slighting me." In fact, with another baby at risk to his medical inexperience, maybe that would be best.

Not that Dr. Forsythe would try diagnosing much. He'd most likely just give her calomel to clean out her system.

Putting a writhing woman through such treatment seemed cruel. But maybe he shouldn't favor the patient's comfort over the accepted way of dealing with ill humors.

"No, absolutely not." Hugh grew rigid in his seat. "Not after the way the man treated her last time. She'd rather me let her die."

"Come now. If she were dying, you'd do anything to save her, wouldn't you?"

"Is she dying?"

Will ran a hand through his hair. What if he was wrong? How could he face Hugh again? He'd had enough difficulty accepting his parents' forgiveness after his arrogance resulted in his baby sister's death and

Nettie's disability. They shouldn't have forgiven him so easily.

However, he still needed to say what he thought correct. "Anything can turn worse unexpectedly. But right now, I figure she's all right. But you might not want to trust my say-so since —"

"Forsythe's being here won't help. You've soothed her better in the last hour than either I or the maid."

"Then I'll stay and keep an eye on her."

Hugh fidgeted.

"Unless you want me to leave?"

"No." He held up his hand. "I was only concerned about you. Why don't you hire a lawyer, sell that millstone of a store, and head to school?"

Will sighed. "Even if I retained a lawyer, I can't profit one hundred percent from a store when Axel might have some debts that need to be paid."

"But if he's convicted, your percentage could be compromised too."

Will rubbed his brow. "I know. I've already talked to a lawyer. The judge will most likely place an injunction on an auction until Axel is caught, so I can't sell now. Even if I could pay a lawyer to try to win me full ownership, I have no money, just a failing store — and if he couldn't win on my behalf . . .

how would I pay him?" Will clasped his hands together. "I hope to make the store profitable enough to exit with the clothes on my back when Axel is caught and the place is sold. . . ."

Hugh grimaced and shook his head. "You wouldn't be in this mess if you'd listened to me years ago."

No doubt. But he'd not dwell on the *what ifs* — better to focus on what he could do now.

Considering the poor choices he'd made, he deserved to lose everything. But now that he'd set the store to rights following Eliza's suggestions, maybe he could earn enough to cover his school fees and pay for Axel's misdeeds.

If he had enough time. "I'm making improvements to the store, and pray —"

"I'm sorry, but if one more store comes into town, you'll be sunk." Hugh shook his head. "I'm afraid —"

"Water?" Mrs. Raymond twitched, and her hand snaked out to the edge of the bed.

Will grabbed the porcelain cup beside her, but Hugh stopped him.

"I know you said I shouldn't sleep near her, but can't I do this?"

"Of course." Will's heart twisted at the sight of the hard-nosed businessman sliding next to his wife's sweaty form, pulling her into his arms, and kissing her bed-mussed hair. He'd seen heartfelt affection between his parents, but the longing to embrace a woman of his own consumed him as he turned his head away from the Raymonds.

Because the woman he envisioned in his arms was Eliza — a dream as far out of reach as his medical degree.

"Why don't you go down the hall and get yourself bedding from the linen closet?" Hugh tipped his head toward Will. "I've sat in that chair. Deborah chooses furnishings because of their beauty, not their practicality."

And that's what his love for Eliza was. A love for a masterpiece, but an impractical relationship at best. She was too smart to marry a man who was as penniless as the day he was born.

Maybe the judge would allow him to sell the Men's Emporium to Eliza, then he could go to school and come back for her. But she'd have to clean the butcher's floor for many years before she had enough money to buy the store.

Why couldn't Hugh have done something for her? Will's shoulders slumped as he trudged from the room.

There was no reason to make her a partner, because she'd lose everything to Axel's crimes as easily as he. She'd been hurt enough. He'd not set her up to fall victim to Axel again.

CHAPTER 17

Eliza rubbed the last streak off the glass display encasing her store's stacks of patterned china. If she'd been anywhere close to heaven, it was here, standing in a gleaming showroom filled with goods of her choosing, arranged to her satisfaction.

Of course, she needed more merchandise and tables, but the rest of what she'd ordered would arrive soon. With no savings to help her recover if she had a month of poor sales, everything had to go as planned. Thankfully, Mr. Raymond had allowed her six months before her first payment on the inventory loan was due.

Leaving her apron behind, she stretched before heading out into the afternoon sunshine and end-of-day bustle. She breathed in the sudden gust of wind shooting in from the prairie and momentarily erasing the smell of horses and dank alleys.

Catty-corner across Main Street, Will

passed near the butcher's. Her heart pumped a bit harder at the sight of him. Since she'd skipped church the last two weeks while cleaning and preparing, she'd missed seeing him.

Surely God would forgive her for not attending church to be a good steward of the chance He'd given her.

Will about-faced past the butcher shop and then headed back in the direction he'd come from.

She waved. "Will!"

The woman passing by on the street looked up at her with a scowl.

Eliza lowered her arm and shrugged.

Will glanced over his shoulder before turning in to the butcher's alley. Was he looking for her? It wasn't Thursday. She'd hoped to have caught him last Thursday, but had gotten caught up polishing her store's staircase spindles until her stomach insisted she go home to eat.

After locking the door behind her, she raced across the busy street but stopped short of the butcher's alley to catch her breath. Using a window to redo her hair, she reined in her misbehaving tendrils, the pink scar taunting her. Had Will been wrong to promise it would fade with time?

She rushed around the corner and

bumped into Will, their heads knocking together.

"Ugh." Will winced and put a hand to his jaw. She pressed the heel of her hand against the throbbing in her brow.

"And I thought I liked your being tall for a woman."

"Sorry." But at least she'd caught him. By the chin no less. "Were you looking for me?"

"Um, well, just passing by." He colored and rubbed his red neck. "How's your head? I could escort you home and measure out something for the pain."

"No need to bother. It'll go away in a moment."

"Oh." He looked positively depressed that she hadn't a headache.

So what if she'd decided weeks ago not to ask him to visit her more often? Why couldn't she spend a little time with him before he found out she'd likely ruined his chances of getting to medical school anytime soon? "Perhaps you could check on Irena though? She hasn't been feeling well." Her own stomach churned — but more from what she was keeping from him than any sickness she might have caught. "She felt well enough to get out of bed for a handful of days, but she retired to her room again this morning."

"What's her ailment?"

"She has a cold." Eliza shook her head. "But she tells me it's nothing but old age."

"I'd have guessed with her joint pain she wouldn't want to stay in bed too long."

Exactly. "However, she doesn't want you to come."

He frowned, and she bit the inside of her cheek. Had that upset him? He claimed he didn't want to be called on as a doctor yet, but maybe he had some doctoring pride after all.

"But if you walked me home and she didn't greet you, that would naturally cause you enough concern to check on her, yes?"

"Yes, I believe so." He smiled at her and held out the arm not carrying his medical box. "Shall we?"

She glanced back at her shop, not certain she should take his arm. Would Irena mention her store to him? Oh, the indecision . . . the indigestion. She tightened her stomach. Should she tell him? Would that make the inner roiling settle? It's not like anything would change if she didn't tell him — he'd just realize a few days later that she'd chosen to hurt him in order to help herself.

But a man could pick up and do whatever he wanted with no worry about his place in society, his ability to provide for and protect himself. Unlike a woman. How often did a lady alone, abandoned, without any family or nest egg to depend upon, get a chance to actually pull herself out of poverty without throwing herself at the marriage altar to anyone who'd have her?

And why did it bother her so much that she'd made the decision to chase her dream, so much that she feared telling him? This was a business decision — nothing more, nothing less.

The arm Will held out slumped. Eliza grabbed for his elbow before her hesitation made him pull it back. Would he enjoy having her on his arm if he learned her secret? "Yes, let's go now."

Keeping her gaze off the store as they passed, Eliza pressed a hand against the internal unease. No reason to cause Kathleen and Will extra days of worry — because nothing could be done to ease what she'd set in motion. She'd not announce the opening of the five-and-dime until it was perfect and ready for business. Will and Kathleen would find out about her venture along with everyone else in town.

But owning her dream store felt less wonderful each time she reined in her impulse to visit the Men's Emporium and tell Will everything before opening day. If

Will felt anything for an unattractive spinster like her, her owning a business that would kill his profits would douse any interest he had. Why not enjoy his polite attentions for a few more days?

"I haven't seen you in church lately."

She swallowed and forced herself to look up at him. "Busy cleaning."

He tipped her a smile. "You've gotten that much work?"

She nodded and dropped her chin. "I'm glad you have the time to check on Irena."

"You should know you can call on me any time." His voice sounded slightly desperate, as if he wanted her to call on him every day. That couldn't be true, could it?

Did he know his thumb was rubbing a lazy circle on her arm?

Will cleared his throat. "I've been meaning to talk to you."

When a minute of silence passed, she looked up at him again. His eyes were closed though he was still walking.

"About what?"

"Do you think I should go to school . . . no matter what I need to do to get there or how long it takes? Or do you . . . or would you rather I . . ." He huffed.

What was making him so tongue-tied? They'd discussed this plenty of times before.

"Of course you should go to school. It's where you're meant to be." Though her heart slowed at the contemplation of how long he'd be gone . . . and how long it would likely take him to get there now. "How many years is school?"

"Two or more. Longer if I have to work at the same time. And I don't know when I'll get there, since I decided it's only fair to make sure Axel's debts have been covered first."

"How are Axel's debts your responsibility?" If anyone shady knew how easily Will felt responsible for someone else's problems, he'd get swindled more often than he already was.

"Considering you've been his victim, wouldn't you be cross if I didn't —" He jerked to a halt.

She faltered. "What's wrong?"

He stared at the cedar shingle hanging on metal hooks beside the door of a white false-fronted building. *Doctor J. J. Benning* in hammered metal letters glinted in the sun.

How long did Will plan to stand there and stare? "Did no one tell you about the new doctor?"

"This changes everything." His mouth went slack, and his shoulders fell. Pulling away, he clomped down the sidewalk as fast

315

as the horse pulling a buggy beside them.

Though she was tall, the sea of petticoats around her legs nearly kept her from matching his stride. "Will?"

He didn't seem to hear.

"Will, please slow down."

Without breaking his pace, he raked the mess of hair from his eyes, yet his bangs flopped back once he let go. "He told me I'd have competition."

"Who told you?"

He sped up again. "If I leave, I can't come back."

Her heart plummeted. He was leaving? Stupid heart, of course he was. And she wanted him to. At least she should, no matter how she felt. "Don't tell me you're giving up on school because there's another doctor in town."

"I hadn't figured on another doctor . . . or even more." He stopped and pinched the bridge of his nose. "No wonder I get nowhere in business — I can't think past today."

She put her hands on her hips. "You're not making any sense."

"Of course I am." He gestured toward her with his medical box. "You're a smart businesswoman. You tell me what a new doctor in town means for me."

Though the compliment should have warmed her, his scowl kept any blushing at bay. She put a hand to her chin, her thumb rubbing against the puffiness across her cheek. "Well, a new doctor would mean competition."

"And if I left for two years . . . ?"

"He'd probably care for your patients." She glanced back down the road toward the offending professional. She worked at the lump in her throat. "But you can't predict everything. The population might grow more than expected."

"No, don't try to sugarcoat this. If I leave, I'm unlikely to find enough patients to keep me from needing a second job when I return — too much competition. And we both know how well I do at running a business."

She quit biting her little pinkie nail. "Maybe Dr. Benning won't last."

"I can't pin my hopes on somebody's failure." Will's mouth twitched. "If he's degreed, I'll lose all my current patients to him, except family and friends."

"Maybe he's as arrogant as Dr. Forsythe."

He pursed his lips. "Highly unlikely. Even so, what would keep another doctor from moving here to take his place while I'm gone?"

"So when you finish school — if Salt Flatts couldn't handle another doctor — you'd not return? Even though your parents live here?" She'd never see him again? She pulled at her lip with her teeth.

Never again . . . Maybe he'd be interested in a second job under her employ? Surely she'd be profitable enough to hire on several people within a few years. But what man wanted to be beholden to a woman?

"How could I justify the cost of schooling only to return and make no money doctoring? I'm already doing that." He stared down the road leading out of town. "I'd have to go farther west to find work."

Go farther west. Growing towns in Colorado or Nevada probably needed stores. . . . Maybe not stores like the one she was stocking in Salt Flatts, but stores.

The contract she'd signed promised Mr. Raymond five years, and by then she'd be more than prosperous if nothing unexpected happened. How could she abandon a thriving dream?

She closed her eyes, trying to envision walking away from her beautiful store to go with him years from now — if he ever did feel for her enough to propose, and if she ever did feel enough for him to say yes.

She bit her lip. She couldn't imagine leaving the store she'd just gained.

Backing out of the printer's into the sunshine, Will held tight to his stack of papers lest they blow away, though the wind-blown hair in his eyes annoyed him. He'd have to visit his mother soon; he couldn't afford the barber.

Now, where was the depot manager's son? Oliver would jump at the chance to distribute these flyers for a quarter.

Will read the words one last time to make certain he could do what they promised. *FREE medical examination with $15 purchase at the Men's Emporium.*

He refused to look toward Dr. Benning's office. Once word of the new doctor got around, Will might not find anyone wanting to pay for his medical attention, but free would tempt people.

He'd started visiting people last week, asking them to pay as much as possible on their store account and to attempt to pay for past medical services. A few had already paid down their debt, and with these coupons, hopefully he'd regain enough business to deposit some profit into his personal account before Axel was caught and the store was sold. If he could just get enough to travel to school, pay for the first lecture series, and find somewhere cheap to live, he'd go.

He couldn't sit around Salt Flatts watching Dr. Benning take his patients away one by one — he was close enough to giving up on his dream already. He'd have to find work to fit around his school schedule and pay as he went. Getting through school would take longer that way, but trying to earn enough up front obviously wasn't working.

"Good morning, Will." Nancy stepped in front of him, her eyes twinkling above her sunshiny smile. The sun made the red highlights in her frizzy hair more fiery than normal.

Will glanced at his coupons, again hoping they'd bring him the business he desperately needed — especially since he'd heard rumors that Eliza had recently gained a store. Why hadn't she told him about it? "Good morning." He thought of handing Nancy a coupon, but what would she purchase from him? She was as penniless as he.

"Would you like to come to dinner tonight, Will?"

He wedged the stack of papers under his arm in order to rub at the back of his neck. How could he excuse himself politely? A crowded sidewalk was no place to inform her he hadn't the heart to pursue a woman when he loved another. Even if he had more chance of winning Nancy than Eliza. But she had to be told he'd decided against her. "Maybe another night."

Mrs. Graves walked up behind her daughter. "What have you got there?"

Ah, his first taker. "A coupon." He handed her one.

She read the flyer and perked up. "Do you have bedding?"

"Sheets and blankets and pillows." One less after the pillow that died on a nail the day he'd touched Eliza for what he'd thought was the last time.

Mrs. Graves' head cocked to the side. "Well then, are you returning to your store? Millie's bedroom needs a few things."

"I'm heading that direction." Would Mrs. Graves expect something fancy? The Men's Emporium wasn't stocked with patchwork quilts and embroidered pillowcases. "Excuse me, but I see the boy I've been looking for." He stepped around Mrs. Graves and ignored Nancy's frown, leaving them both behind so he could flag down the depot manager's son. "Oliver!"

The skinny nine-year-old turned midleap over a puddle and ran straight toward him. "Yes, sir?"

"I've got a quarter for you if you'll hand out these flyers."

"Yes, sir, Mr. Stanton!" The lad grabbed the papers and ran off, shoving the first coupon into Mr. Raymond's hands. The banker glanced at his paper, but instead of the pleased look Will expected, Hugh frowned.

Why wasn't he as eager for a free exam as last time? Though his wife had recovered from her fever, he'd surely want her examined when the baby came.

Hugh strode up, his eyes narrowed. "Where'd you get this idea?"

Will refused to look contrite. "Eliza said we should offer deals to entice customers when business is slow."

He glared up the street. "*She* told you to do this?"

What was he glaring at? Will looked behind him. Eliza was nowhere in the crowd. Too bad. He hadn't seen her all week.

"Well, yes."

"Excuse me, then." Hugh charged past him.

Will waved at the man's back. "Good day to you too, sir." He'd better return to the store so Mrs. Graves and anyone else could spend their fifteen dollars as soon as possible. If Eliza was about to give him business competition, he hoped these coupons worked and got his business moving before her shop opened. How long might that be?

Last week he'd gone by the storefront where Lynville had told him he'd seen Eliza ushering in a shipment of crates and boxes, but he hadn't been able to see much inside. Maybe she wasn't selling anything that would hurt his sales. . . . Maybe it wasn't even her store, but someone's she worked for. No one seemed to know for certain, and Eliza had practically disappeared.

But she'd tell him what she was up to soon, surely. Maybe she was too busy — and he definitely hadn't been around to catch for chitchat. He'd been out every night for the last week and a half helping somebody with some ailment.

"Hello there." The garbled speech behind Will increased his concerns. He turned to face Silas Jonesey, hoping he'd imagined the slur.

His friend stepped forward with a little lurch to the left, though he appeared bright-eyed and congenial. "Can't greet me back?"

Will forced himself not to growl. "You told me you weren't drinking anymore."

"I haven't touched a lick of alcohol." He shook his finger. "You told me medicines wouldn't help, but I found a new tonic. And it works."

"It doesn't work, Jonesey." Will rubbed a hand down his face. "It makes things worse."

"No it doesn't."

"Are you following the tonic's dosages?"

"Of course. It says take as needed." He pulled out a square bottle. "See — right here."

Will took the tonic from him. *Mr. Miracle's Elixir.* "No ingredients are listed."

"Why does that matter?"

"It matters." Will gripped the man's shoulder. "You need to go to the Lord for your problems, not a bottle."

"I am. I was only trying to lighten my disposition." Jonesey smiled as if he'd shared a great joke.

"This medicine isn't good for you."

Jonesey blinked as if he was having difficulty thinking, though most wouldn't notice his behavior. "But it tastes like fruit. That can't be bad. And I feel better."

"Are you needing more of this stuff to feel better when the tonic wears off?"

"Well, I guess so." He held out his hand, expecting Will to return the bottle.

Will slipped the elixir into his pocket despite his friend's scowl. "If you knew how you were acting, you wouldn't want this back. Where'd you get it?"

He jammed his hands on his hips. "Hampdens'."

Will ducked his head a little to look into Jonesey's dilated, empty pupils. "Go home and sleep. I'll come by tonight."

"What about my medicine?"

"It's no better than the other tonics I told you to stay away from."

Jonesey ran his hand across his stomach. "But I've felt better — like it says."

"Trust me — sleep it off. I'll get you something for the headache you'll wake up with."

"Can't. I've got chores."

"Then sleep as soon as possible. Do you have more of this stuff?"

"I just bought two more." Jonesey pulled out the other bottles, his gaze pinned to the tonic. "Are you sure about this?"

"I'm sure."

He frowned and thrust the elixir toward Will. "Then bring me something better. I don't want to mess myself up again, but I swear this helps — the doctor in the advertisement said it cured everything from melancholia to liver —"

"I believe you, Jonesey, but this isn't good for *you*." Not anybody else either, but he'd not argue that now.

Jonesey shrugged. "See you later, then." He turned, waving at people as he sauntered back to his wagon.

Hopefully his friend would get home safely. At least he was walking fairly straight. Will marched to the Hampdens' store and went straight for their medicinal shelf. Twenty or more dark blue bottles of Mr. Miracle's Elixir stood at attention beside an advertisement listing all the benefits of imbibing the newest scientific cure. "Carl!"

"Whatcha yelling for?" The man's voice spiraled down from above, where he was perched high on a ladder rearranging boxes.

"I thought you said you'd get rid of the tonics." Will held out the offending bottle.

"But that's a new one, and the testimonials —"

"Are misleading. Most likely fabrications rather than true stories."

"Mr. Jonesey and Mrs. Lafferty say it helps. And the label says it's effective for all kinds of maladies."

Will narrowed his eyes at Carl.

"Not everyone can afford doctoring whenever they feel a little down in the mouth."

Will simply stared. He'd already been through this with Carl.

"All right." Carl flung up his hands. "I won't buy any more."

"What about these twenty bottles?"

"They're ten cents apiece. I'm not going to dump them down the drain."

Kathleen waddled out from the storeroom, her large pregnant belly stretching her checked brown gingham dress taut. "Good afternoon, William. Is there a problem?" She eyed her husband on the ladder.

Only for Jonesey and the other poor souls seeking relief from serious illnesses . . . or bitterness and lack of forgiveness.

Will dug out two dollars in change and placed them on the counter, leaving him with seventy-five cents. If he wanted a haircut and something to eat besides another can of beans or a jar of peaches, he had to go home Sunday. "I'm buying all of your magic elixirs."

Kathleen eyed him but scooped the money toward her. "Are you sure?"

If he was to help Jonesey resist temptation, he had little choice. But Carl could easily order another batch. "Replace them with Dr. Ruskin's Homeopathic Medicine, if you feel you must sell something instead of advising your customers to talk to a doctor. But nothing that says *cure-all* or you might as well sell whiskey."

"Are you suggesting I sell liquor?" Carl gawked from above as if appalled, though if not for prohibition, the man would be stocking cases just like he had before.

"No, but why don't you buy a few boxes of Stop Drinking: European Cure for the Liquor Habit? If you're going to carry medicine, why not that?"

The shopkeeper scratched his head as if considering a counter-argument. Tonics made for repeat customers — his friend wasn't dense. "I guess it won't hurt to try."

Will turned back to Kathleen. "If Silas Jonesey comes in for more, point him toward the Stop Drinking pills your husband is going to order or send him to me."

"I'll make sure he does." Kathleen gave him a little smile while looking askance at her husband.

Will gathered up the flimsy box of bottles Kathleen slid across the counter toward him and frowned. Could he reuse the glass for tinctures? "Thanks. And please inform me or one of the midwives of any labor signs you have. Don't want Junior or Gretchen having to deliver their newest sibling." He returned Kathleen's playful smirk and turned for the door. He had to return to the Men's Emporium before his closed doors ruined his coupon scheme.

O Lord, please bring me customers. I need to pay on the lumber I bought for the new tables. And I need to be able to eat.

The glass bottles clinked together as he walked, making him want to ring Jonesey's neck.

Help Jonesey realize the cure for what ails him can't be bought in a bottle. It's your Word and the fellowship of believers that provide the strength to get over the anger of his wife leaving him. I can't imagine losing the woman I loved, but . . .

Actually, he could. Hadn't he been jilted by Nancy and faced losing Eliza on her wedding day?

But he'd not run to God for support then either. He'd walked around in a rage after Nancy left and almost left the county to labor as a broom maker to get far, far away from Eliza.

Swallowing hard at the wonderful sight of three men and Mrs. Graves waiting outside the Men's Emporium, he slowed to give himself a second more to repent.

Lord, no matter what happens with my store, Eliza, or the new doctor, help me remember I'm to seek you above all, to trust in you and nothing else — even when I'm disappointed.

CHAPTER 18

Out of breath from marching down the road faster than the donkey carts, Eliza shoved her way into the Men's Emporium. Sidling past a couple in the aisle, she gritted her teeth to keep from glaring at the crowd that should have been shopping in her store.

She pressed her way toward the back counter. Where was Will?

Right. He'd built a front counter. She whipped around and weaved through the less-congested left aisle.

Will's crazy ruffled hair rose above a young couple in the corner as he climbed a ladder.

Stopping, she attempted to loose some tension by exhaling slowly through pursed lips. Otherwise she might demand he get down that instant.

How many people were in the emporium? She counted ten from where she stood. Good for him, but why today? Why'd he have to do this to her now?

Her sweaty palm dampened the crumpled paper Mr. Raymond had slammed into her hand. She crunched the wad tighter. Medical checkups? His services were of more value than he should have exchanged for fifteen dollars of merchandise. What could she offer remotely close to that? One should ask the redeemer to spend more than the price of a free item. Didn't he understand that?

She glanced sideways and frowned. Where had these shelves come from? Surprisingly, the kitchen items were arranged outside of their boxes in neat rows. She plucked a knife off the second shelf above the floor. Did Will forget about children coming in the store? She grabbed a handful and rearranged the shelving space to put the knives higher. Finished, she moved around the price-tag signs he'd hand-lettered. She glanced down the aisle. Every shelf sported little white signs with printed prices.

"What can I do for you?" Will's voice, lower and more charming than normal, wrapped around her neck and tickled her ear. She lifted her eyes heavenward, wanting to pretend the flyer she held in her hand didn't exist for a second, and . . . and . . . and do what? She wouldn't let the strangely sensuous caress of his breath distract her. She stiffened and turned around.

Ignoring his lopsided, roguish grin, she tilted her head up to meet him eye to eye. "It's not what *can* you do for me. It's what *did* you do to me."

"I don't understand." He pulled back.

That was the voice she knew — a bit lost, authentic. "This." She held up the offending paper ball.

He shook his head, stepping close enough that his trousers disturbed her skirts. "Which is?"

She tried to smooth the flyer, but her angry, jittery hands brushed against his coat, causing them to tremble from another emotion entirely. The paper ripped in two.

Never mind. She smacked the wadded paper into his hand. "Your coupon."

"Isn't it great?" His smile transformed his face.

Her irritation threatened to drain away at his enthusiasm, but she held on tight.

He gestured toward the people walking past the end of the aisle. "Who knew a coupon could bring in so many people?"

Oh, sweetheart, of course they'd come in for this. You gave too much away. She clamped her hand over her mouth.

But his expression remained quizzical, his

gaze as light as normal, his hands casually parked on his hips.

She swallowed and hefted a sigh, thankful she hadn't said that aloud. She refused to ponder why she'd found it so easy to think of him as *sweetheart* — she was mad at him!

"Are you all right?" His face lost its excitement. He lifted the paper coupon ball. "If you're not feeling well, you don't need to buy something from me. I consider you . . ." He poked his tongue into his cheek, his eyes shifting to the side. "I mean, I don't hold out on family or friends who need medical help."

"You don't deny strangers or enemies either."

"Well, no. But I'm a little busy right now . . . unless you feel it's dire."

"I'm not sick."

He rubbed a thumb against her hairline but quickly turned the gesture into feeling her forehead. Was he covering for what felt like his tucking a strand of hair behind her ear? "Good."

"Excuse me, Mr. Stanton. I'm ready to pay." A man in a tattered shirt and mud-caked pants held out a bundle of ready-made clothes and a bar of soap.

Will lifted a finger to signal him to wait. He gripped her upper arm as if he might drag her with him to the cashbox. "Don't go anywhere."

She glanced at the timepiece above the front door. "I don't have much time. I must return —"

"Just wait." The look Will gave her would make a woman promise him her firstborn — perhaps that's how Rumpelstiltskin had wrangled such a commitment.

She swallowed. "All right." Technically, she could stay as long as she wanted; she set her own hours, after all. But a smart shop owner didn't stay closed past lunch hour on opening day — though no more than a handful of people had trickled in this morning.

He placed a hand at the base of her neck, turning her around to guide her down the aisle. She closed her eyes against letting her imagination feel his fingers threading themselves into her hair. Though the longer his hand lay against her neck, the desire to stop imagining ebbed.

He pointed to the right side of the store. "Go look where we used to have hanging pots. I think you'll be impressed." His hand slid down to her shoulder. "I'll be right back."

With that, he left her to be brushed by customers trying to get around her. Another glance at the clock told her to leave now and talk to him later . . . yet she was curious about what he had done to the pots.

She scooted past an elderly couple and turned the corner. On the west wall behind the wood stove, he'd removed an entire section of shelving. The Wanted posters and hand-written advertisements from folks around Salt Flatts were now all pinned neatly onto a series of boards arranged on the wall. Chairs from the upstairs apartment sat arranged for conversation, four of them pushed against two game tables, one with a chessboard, the other checkers. A newspaper and a Montgomery Ward catalog lay atop another small table.

She'd mentioned to Axel in a letter that they ought to make the store somewhere men would congregate — someplace exactly like this. But had she said anything to Will? She ran her index finger along her scar, feeling the now familiar ridges.

No. She couldn't think of a time she'd discussed that idea with him. Maybe the man had some business sense after all.

Jostled from behind, she moved to sit in the rocker. More than twelve customers milled around the aisles — all of them with paper coupons in hand.

Now that Will had broken the townspeople's boycott with the lure of free services, could he keep them there? He needed to make a living, but would loyalty to a shop-keeper who'd grown up in Salt Flatts hurt *her*?

Had she ever seen so many women in this store? If ladies could be lured into a men's store with a free offer, then they'd be the best targets for a campaign of her own.

How could she top this?

"What mischief are you planning?"

She startled at Will's voice. The back of her rocker thumped against the wall when she popped up. "Nothing."

"Do you like how I've changed things?"

Taking another glance around, she saw nothing but perfection. She couldn't have done better herself. "I'm surprised."

"In a good way, I hope?"

"Yes."

"And you came to see me because . . . ?"

Why did his voice sound so elated? He knew what he'd done to her.

"I can't believe you of all people would hand out coupons on a day like today."

He stiffened. "Did I miss someone's funeral or . . . ?"

Why was he playing dumb? "My grand opening."

"Your grand opening?" He squinted.

"My store's grand opening, of course."

He blinked. "So it's already open?"

"Yes. You're passing these out the day I open, and everyone's flocking here."

How could he have missed the sign? Kathleen had come by to congratulate her — though she'd admitted Carl was miffed.

And since Will hadn't stopped in to congratulate her on her opening day, she'd figured he'd needed time to adjust . . . until Mr. Raymond brought in Will's coupon.

She hadn't figured on Will plotting against her.

"Why didn't you tell me about your store?" Will tucked his hands under his arms, his eyes registering . . . sadness?

She forced herself to swallow. "I didn't want you to worry about me stealing your business . . . and . . . and this coupon made me think I'd been a fool to believe you wouldn't do the same to me."

"You thought I'd try to steal your business?" He looked at the ceiling for a second, his mouth disfiguring into a frown. "Do you understand nothing about me, Eliza?"

She took a step back from the glare he aimed at her.

"When have I ever done anything but help you? I found somewhere for you to stay, I gave you your wages from my savings, I never asked you to pay for those stitches, I offered you a job. If I thought you cared enough for me, I'd have offered . . . I was going to offer . . ." He huffed and looked away. The hand that had been running through his hair again dropped to his side. "Why would you assume I was trying to hurt you?"

Thankfully, the customers shopping around them were oblivious to his rambling, or at least pretended to be. She hugged herself. "You didn't see my sign? No one told you?"

He blinked repeatedly — almost as though he were about to cry. But no, a grown man like Will wouldn't cry because she'd opened a store. . . . Could her accusations have hurt him that badly?

"I've been really busy, Eliza. I knew something was going on, but I figured you and I . . . Well, I figured you'd at least share with me before . . ." He shook his head and looked away. "This whole time I've been re-arranging things to your specifications, deal-ing with Mrs. Raymond and some other patients, waiting for you to —"

"Rearranging to my specifications?" She slid a finger along the edge of the chess-board.

"You think these improvements were my

idea?" His face scrunched. "It's clear you think me utterly inept. So much so you won't work for me, help me, talk to me, need me for anything beyond —"

"Excuse me." An older gentleman hobbled over on his cane. "Can I get assistance? My wife wants another cast-iron pan for her birthday." He smiled at Eliza. "But if I lean over that far, I might not get back up."

Eliza forced herself to smile back at the gentleman.

"I'm sorry, Eliza." Will's eyes didn't twinkle like the old man's. "Seems I can't talk for more than a few minutes in a row."

"No need to apologize. My lunch break's over. I can't stay." A grand-opening week held too much potential for her to twiddle her thumbs.

She clasped the apple in her pocket; she'd have to eat on the walk back. Rather unlady-like, but her stomach wouldn't survive until dinner, not with the way it was churning over the mess she'd created.

Of course Will hadn't meant anything by the coupon. She'd let Mr. Raymond's anger incite irrational thoughts.

If Carl had pulled something like this, her reaction would have been warranted — he'd have meant it. When she'd thought Will had worked against her it had stung terribly.

With Carl, she'd have set her sights on outdoing him the next day, but with Will? She'd come down to blast him because he'd hurt her — not the Five and Dime — but *her.*

"I'm sorry, Will. I was wrong to think you'd deliberately ruin my day." Now she felt ill enough to need his doctoring. "Can we talk later?"

Will glanced over his shoulder to the elderly man fidgeting with his cane. "I'll try —"

The man cleared his throat.

She gave the gentleman a tense smile. "Wish your wife a happy birthday for me."

Will strode past her to open the front door. "I'll drop by after work to check on Mrs. Lightfoot."

"I won't be home right after work." She held her fingers to her lips. She couldn't avoid him just because she'd been an idiot. He didn't deserve that — he deserved the opportunity to yell at her for thinking him underhanded. "I'll be there around dinnertime, though."

She couldn't look at him as she stepped out into the bright sunlight. What a disaster. Her dream of people lining up at her store hadn't come true, so she'd lashed out at Will.

She deserved his wrath . . . and she also needed better advertising. The sign evidently hadn't caught enough people's attention.

She swallowed the moisture in her throat. She'd have to be careful not to chastise herself all day for thinking poorly of Will lest she cry in front of a customer.

Feeling light-headed from skipping lunch two days in a row, Will placed a steadying hand on the counter after handing Mr. McManus his change. He fished for the sack of beef jerky he'd traded Mrs. Underwood in exchange for helping her ailing pig last night. Between the sow and his exhaustion, he hadn't been able to check on Mrs. Lightfoot or have dinner with Eliza. Not that he'd wanted to see Eliza — at least not until he'd cooled down some.

How could she have thought he'd intentionally hurt her?

She'd stormed in and bitten his head off without giving him a chance to explain about the coupon — though he hadn't known he needed to explain, since she hadn't seen fit to tell him she was opening a store. He shook his head. He wasn't sure what hurt more: that she'd kept such an accomplishment to herself or that she'd thought he'd set out to harm her.

Why hadn't she told him? Still, he wasn't comfortable with how they'd left things.

A customer slid her purchases toward him, and he started adding the prices without bothering to chat. Too many people in line to slow down his math with small talk.

Did Eliza truly not care about him enough to share her big news? Or maybe she'd felt bad about making a decision that would affect him negatively, despite it making sense for her to do so.

And if she couldn't trust him with such a huge accomplishment, if she thought he'd somehow purposely ruin her business, maybe he didn't know her well at all.

Regardless, he should let Eliza know he was happy for her, but the business he'd gained with the coupons kept him swamped during work hours, and people were scheduling him for after-hours medical exams already.

When a very pregnant woman plopped down tack and a handful of other things onto the counter, Will pressed a hand against his abdomen to attempt to silence a rumble. He had to eat no matter how unprofessional chewing looked while transacting business. He forced a tight smile. "Did you find what you need?"

Her husband shoved a lantern and a watch onto the counter. "As long as this equals fifteen dollars, I'd say yes."

Will sighed. Considering he probably could have charged this couple between ten and twenty-five dollars to deliver their baby, the money he'd pocket from this twenty-dollar purchase wouldn't pay for his time.

Will ripped off a hunk of jerky with his teeth and started adding. "That's $22.25."

"All right." The woman fished in her reticule as Will signed her coupon.

He rubbed the heel of his hand across his brow, where a pounding ache had started an hour ago. "I guess I'll be seeing you in a few weeks?"

She smiled at her husband and sheepishly nodded. She knew how much he was losing on this deal.

Mrs. Leddbetter approached the counter with nothing in her hands, though she'd bought a set of andirons and tongs yesterday.

"Can I help you?"

"When can you check on Granny?"

He blinked and pulled out the datebook he'd started using. "How about Thursday at . . . No, I'm way over at Fossil Creek. How about Friday around dinnertime?"

"That's three days away."

Her whine irritated his headache. If he wasn't careful, he might join in with her bellyaching. He rubbed the bridge of his nose. "That's the soonest I have."

"Fine."

He wrote down her name, then motioned for the next customer in line to come forward, despite the woman beside him tapping her foot impatiently on the other side of the counter. What did she need his help finding, or grabbing, or ordering to get her fifteen dollars' worth?

No need to have a nightmare tonight; he was living one. If he didn't get help soon, he'd collapse. Attending never-ending customers had to be worse than Axel abandoning him to rob a train, hearing Eliza say I do to someone else, Axel's mouth smothering hers . . .

No, he'd choose unrelenting business over watching the woman he cared for nearly marry another man. . . . Cared for? Did he only *care* for her?

No, it was more than that. A whole lot of good that did him since the woman valued property more than a man.

"What's the matter, Will?" Young Clarity Faith leaned her elbows on the counter, her strawberry-blonde head tilted in concern, her bright blue eyes staring up at him rather intently. "You don't look very happy."

He searched the counter to find his beef jerky again and tore off another bite. "I'm just hungry."

"Do you want us to go to the hotel and get a sandwich for you?"

Mrs. Autry came up behind her grand-daughter and squeezed her shoulder. "What are you offering to give somebody now?"

"Good advice — that's what she is offer-ing." Why was he playing the martyr any-way? "Thanks for the offer, Clarity Faith, but I'll go get one myself, since I know what I like." He walked around the corner of his counter and smacked the bell above the door enough times that most of his custom-ers quit shopping and looked to the front.

"If I could have everyone's attention." He waited until a few people from the back moseyed up. "I have to get some lunch. I know it's four o'clock, but I've not eaten and am about to pass out." And possibly strangle some people. "So if you have purchases, please find a place to set them, and when I reopen tomorrow, you can pick up where you left off. I'm sorry, but I've got no help and I need some food."

A few out-of-towners grumbled, but most turned sheepish, as if they'd purposely stolen his time. He nodded to each as they filed out and winked at Clarity Faith. "Thank you for coming in." When the last man exited, Will turned over the sign to Closed.

Somehow his mother forged through the retreating flock of people.

He held the door open for her, but the second her skirts cleared the threshold, he locked them in.

"Why's everyone leaving?" She frowned at the people outside the window. "I haven't seen such a crowd in here, well . . . since ever."

"I've had crowds that big for two days."

"Good for you." She glanced at his Closed sign still swinging against the glass. "But did you just send them away?"

"I haven't eaten lunch the last two days either."

His mother tsked. "That's not good for a growing boy."

"I don't think I'm growing much anymore, Ma."

"Right." She hefted her basket.

Thank you, God. Hopefully, the hamper contained the usual assortment of food, though he'd welcome double the amount at the moment.

He nearly groaned, his mouth salivating before Ma placed any food on the counter.

As she pulled off the tablecloth cover, a paper fluttered, skittering across the counter and toward the floor. She tried to grab it but missed.

He snatched a biscuit before bending over to pick up the little white slip. "What's this?"

A fancy border decorated the paper, and the title, *Five and Dime,* grabbed his attention.

FIVE AND DIME
Grand Opening
With $4 purchase, get a free starter place setting for that fine china set you've always wanted. Offer ends May 31, 1881, or as long as supplies last.

Why hadn't he thought of an expiration date? He smacked his crumb-covered hand against his pant leg. How many of his coupons had Oliver distributed? Could he get any back, or would he be doctoring for free until he died?

Rachel slipped the fancy little paper out of his hand. "Why didn't you tell me Eliza has her own store now? I bought a whole set of towels there this morning and each of the girls found something for a nickel. But I didn't get one of these flyers until I met up with your father at the lumber mill. Since your grandmother refuses to ship my china to me, I shouldn't pass up a free setting." His mother's face glowed like Nettie's when he produced some saltwater taffy from his pockets. "She's got three patterns to choose from, all surprisingly inexpensive. I'll have to budget for the rest, but no reason not to get started."

Free china. He didn't stand a chance of surviving in this town with Dr. Benning and Eliza as competition. He looked at his Closed sign, then let his eyes slide shut. If only he could leave it flipped over permanently.

He grabbed another biscuit and dug into the basket for the salt-cured ham sure to be tucked away inside. He unscrewed a canteen of tea and sat down on the countertop. "I'm glad you came by. Though I'm nearly starved, I don't think I could have stomached another can of beans for supper."

His mother's glare raked the length of him. "Don't tell me you've been eating nothing but canned beans."

He took another huge bite of ham and biscuit rather than answer. He couldn't afford the hotel diner every day . . . though surely he could tonight. *Thank you, Lord, for some money flowing my way.*

"I'll return for the basket." Ma patted his arm. "I'll go back to Eliza's store while you eat."

She was going to Eliza's now? He forced down his mouthful and grabbed another slice of ham. "I'll join you. I haven't yet seen the inside."

Following his mother out, he almost stumbled over his sister Emma sitting on the stair. "How'd you avoid getting trampled out here?"

Her fierce frown turned comical when she added a glare.

"Emma." Ma's face matched her oldest daughter's. "Your attitude is frightfully close to getting you into more trouble. Watch your tongue and come along."

Will followed them down the street. Emma and Ma butted heads all the time now that the eight-year-old had decided they were equals.

At Eliza's Five and Dime, he stepped in front of his mother and sister to catch the swinging beveled-glass door. Several ladies exited, carrying paper-wrapped items and heavy bags. From where he stood, the interior appeared more suited for a fancy hotel. The rough wood walls of his tiny store looked like a railroad shanty in comparison.

How much had this cost her? Where had

she gotten the money? When he was a child, his parents had never taken him inside the jeweler's, and he'd never been curious enough to peer through the windows, but he never imagined a store like this in Salt Flatts.

Emma and his mother bustled inside between customers, leaving him to hold the door for several more ladies. When he found his ma again, she was standing in front of a table of the advertised china with a finger against her mouth.

How smart of Eliza. If a woman started a collection, she'd finish, down to every last matching piece. Her coupon enticed customers to return without any promise of more free items.

He fingered a teacup. The sign in the middle of the table read *Five Cents.* Taking in the little signs on the various tables, he calculated the cost of a set. Eliza would lose thirty-five cents out of a four-dollar expenditure.

He'd given away five to a possible fifteen or more dollars of services for an equivalent purchase, with no enticement to return.

Should he groan over his stupidity or chuckle at Eliza's genius?

Where was she? Hadn't she always harped on him to greet customers at the threshold?

He looked around. Behind the crowd at the main counter, Eliza was wrapping china with a flourish, the brightest smile he'd ever seen plastered on her face.

"Hold this." Ma handed him a painfully delicate white plate bordered with a simple string of blue leaves along the outer edge. Not the fanciest pattern, but then, what did people expect for a dime?

"Now, what to buy for four dollars? There's really nothing I need." She narrowed her eyes at him. "Don't tell your father that."

Will widened his eyes, pretending innocence. "No, ma'am." He scanned the tables of toys, household items, and clothing accessories. "Don't suppose she has food in here."

Emma tugged on his sleeve, making him grip the china harder. He quickly relaxed his hold, lest he crack the plates.

"She has candy."

Candy wouldn't settle his stomach.

"And taffy and gumdrops and stuff I've never seen before!"

Will grimaced. The candy bins wouldn't thrill the confectioner next door.

"All penny candy."

His mother drew up, hands on her hips. "We're not buying four dollars' worth of penny candy. We'd have to eat a piece a day to finish them before half the year —"

"One a day?" Emma's blue eyes lit.

"Not going to happen, young lady. Go pick out ten pieces for yourself and for each of your brothers and sisters."

Emma scurried off, and his mother turned her frown back on the china set in his arms. "Maybe I shouldn't buy this. I'm only wasting money on things I don't need — like candy." She ran a finger along the slightly fluted edge of the teacup.

"Ma, you don't have to use the coupon." Eliza might want to throttle him for pointing this out, but his mother wasn't thinking clearly. Who knew china could turn an intelligent woman's brain into mush? "You can buy the set later. Pa knows you've regretted leaving your china behind when you moved out here, but you were a mite distracted if I recall the story."

Her eyes twinkled and her frown disappeared. "Yes, packing within an hour to run after a wagon train so the preacher could marry us before nightfall made me forget more than just dinnerware."

"A few more months without fancy dishes won't feel like the twenty some years you've gone without."

"Twenty-three." With a little sigh, she collected the dishes from his arms, then slowly replaced them one by one as if saying good-bye to each piece.

He read Eliza's flyer again. "Besides, you've got until the end of the month. If you need something for four dollars before then, you can still use your coupon."

"Only if supplies last, and I like this pattern." She set the plate down and another woman swiped it off the stack.

"I bet Eliza will stock enough of each pattern so she won't miss a sale. But if your pattern isn't here, there's nothing wrong with supporting her by buying at full cost when she restocks."

"Right." She patted his cheek. "Always thinking about what's best for others."

"I got the candy, Ma." Emma held out a paper bag.

His mother's upper lip twitched, making him want to laugh. She'd agreed to buy more candy than he recalled ever having in a year.

Eliza certainly understood what drove customers. He sighed. If only he'd asked her advice about the coupon, he might not be booked until Christmas fixing ingrown toenails and popping boils on the backs of old bachelors.

Will peered into the candy bag full of

black gumdrops. "I don't think John likes these."

"Everyone likes black gumdrops."

"No. I'm pretty sure he hates them."

Emma didn't look contrite. "Well then, I guess I'll have to eat his."

Ma scowled. "Since she's touched them, I suppose it'd be wrong to put the candy back in the bin."

Emma beamed, and Will tried hard not to smile at his sister's underhandedness. He didn't want to encourage her.

"We could buy more, Ma." Emma looked up into the air. "Maybe he'd eat red ones. I like red ones too."

"What color don't you like, young lady?"

Emma stuck out her tongue. "Yellow."

"Get ten yellow ones." Ma watched her trudge away, then turned to him with a frown bigger than Emma's. "Does John like yellow gumdrops?"

Will laughed. "I don't think he likes gumdrops at all, Ma." He walked after Emma, glancing back at his mother. "But I'll pay for them." Six dimes would be worth getting a minute with Eliza. He only wished he could see John's face when he opened up a bagful of the one candy he despised.

Emma had already scooped out the yellow ones, so Will grabbed five sticks of rock candy and threw them in the bag. "These are for John, not you."

His sister rolled her eyes and clamped the bag to her chest as he pushed her into the slow-moving line.

Shadows of fatigue decorated Eliza's face despite the happy crinkles around her eyes. Did this many people normally come into town on Tuesdays, or had he forced all his customers here by closing early?

If only they could have worked together. But the more he wanted her by his side, the less it seemed likely to happen. Once again, all he could offer was himself, and she'd truly find him inadequate now that she had this fancy new store. And she hadn't even trusted him enough to tell him about it.

She'd never want to leave a successful store — and it seemed she didn't want him involved in her life either — not that she needed his advice, considering her store already outshone his. He forced himself to stop clenching his teeth.

When Emma made it to the front of the line, Eliza glanced up at him and then toward the clock. "Did you close early?"

He shrugged. "I needed food."

She put a hand to her stomach. "I think I forgot to eat."

"You've been busy." He pushed the bag of

candy toward her. "And to think, yesterday you thought I'd stolen all your customers."

She grimaced and ducked her head to look in the bag. "I should've known you wouldn't purposely hurt me."

"Never." He reached out his hand, covering hers, waiting for her to look at him. "I'd never do that." He'd forget about a life with her before he hurt her.

The feel of her skin under his hand recalled the sensation of her cheek while removing her stitches, her soft hair between his fingers as he'd plucked away a feather, the warmth of her forehead against his palm in the butcher's alley.

It was hard to be mad at her when she felt so . . . so . . .

"There's sixty gumdrops and five sticks of rock candy in there." Emma leaned against the counter, arms crossed. "Can I eat one now?"

Eliza stared at his hand on hers.

"You have to ask Ma first." He snatched his hand away and pulled out his money clip.

Emma cradled the bag as if they'd take it from her if Ma said no.

"Might you be able to . . . come to dinner after work?" Eliza fingered the dollar he'd pushed toward her. At the sound of a woman's impatient sigh behind him, Eliza's scar stood out sharply against the pink infusing her cheeks. She swiped his money off the counter, dropped it in her box, and counted out change.

He scratched behind his ear. "Unfortunately, I've got dinner plans." After turning down the Graves' last invitation for dinner, he'd realized he really should have accepted, and did so when they came into the store that morning. He had to tell Nancy his affections lay elsewhere, that whatever he'd once felt for her had been surpassed by his feelings for another.

But maybe he was wrong to hold out any hope of winning a woman who couldn't confide in him about the significant changes in her life that would affect him and —

"Ahem." The throat-clearing woman behind him pressed closer. "Excuse me, but I haven't got all day."

Eliza gave him a little smile. "Maybe another time?"

He swallowed. "Perhaps."

Her smile slowly flattened. "All right."

"Come on, William." Emma threaded her hand in his and tugged.

He tipped his head toward Eliza, keeping his gaze on her despite being dragged away by his sister. The phlegm-plagued lady took his place at the counter, obscuring Eliza from sight.

The desire to walk back and tell her he'd cancel his dinner plans with Nancy and her family almost stopped him. Almost.

Despite leaving him, Nancy had never kept anything from him. She'd told him when she'd been upset about how his career goals weren't coming to fruition. She'd told him about her decision to pursue the widower who was in town visiting her brother.

He'd thought Eliza kept nothing to herself, since she'd seemed to be frankness personified. But evidently she wasn't always forthright.

Emma dropped his hand. "We ready to go?"

Ma frowned and touched him lightly on the shoulder. "What did Eliza say to you to put that look on your face?"

"Nothing." Will closed his eyes. "She told me nothing."

CHAPTER 19

Will drummed his fingers. He'd recalculated and recounted. Money was definitely missing from his cashbox — like so many times before.

He'd always figured his poor math skills caused the discrepancies, and Axel had never failed to find the mathematical mistake or recall an unrecorded purchase. He'd always given him that look, subtly blaming Will's trouble with numbers and letters.

Had the discrepancies never been his fault?

What if Axel was still around? What if his trail had gone cold because the posse hadn't thought to check for any evidence that he'd circled back, returning to Salt Flatts?

If Axel was in town, he'd probably steal something he knew Will would never check on — Nancy's engagement ring. Axel had often pushed him to sell the opal and diamond ring belonging to Ma's grandmother and rolled his eyes whenever Will refused.

Will clomped to his room, turned on a lamp, and kneeled beside his cot. He fished for the box containing Nancy's old letters, but only felt cobwebs. He lay flat on the floor and stretched his arm toward the wall. There it was.

He dragged it across the floor and blew off the dust before opening the lid.

No ring.

Of course it was gone. But how long ago had Axel stolen it?

Will leaned back against his bed and let the air rush out of his lungs. He'd been stupid not to think of Axel the moment the sheriff asked about petty thefts. A complete imbecile for ignoring his childhood buddy's waywardness. A hundred times the fool for trusting people so easily.

What would his mother say when she learned someone had stolen it? What would he present to a woman — Eliza, perhaps — if he ever got the chance to get down on one knee again?

He pinched the bridge of his nose until he was able to think straight. What else had Axel stolen? He'd have to talk to the sheriff, but was this an old theft or a new one? If Axel was responsible for the current rounds of thefts, maybe he'd be captured soon.

And if Axel was caught and the store auctioned . . .

Will dropped the box onto his cot. Returning to the front, he walked the aisles, scanning everything of value. The guns on the gunsmithing counter were accounted for. The five plain wedding bands glinted on a velvet cushion under their glass box.

A normal thief would have stolen things in plain sight.

But if it was Axel, why hadn't he pilfered the Waller gang's loot, taken everything out of the Men's Emporium's cashbox, perhaps robbed a bank, and then dashed out of town a long time ago?

Mrs. Langston.

With few friends, she'd most likely hide her son no matter the consequences, and Axel probably wouldn't leave until he felt his mother was taken care of or he convinced her to leave town with him.

How could a man who cherished his mother turn out so badly?

Will grabbed a lantern and closed up. The best time to catch Axel at his mother's would be after visitors were no longer expected. If he saw any sign of his friend, he'd go for the sheriff. If not, he'd get what information he could out of Mrs. Langston.

Because if Axel was still around, he needed to be captured before he caused anybody — especially Eliza — any more harm.

Turning the wick up in her cramped back office, Eliza blinked bleary eyes, trying to focus on the numbers in front of her. If she didn't have this order in the post by tomorrow, the store would soon run out of toys and candy. She ought to put in another order for china too, and inventory the rest of the kitchen section.

Despite the tug to sleep sitting up, she smiled. The throng of customers the past few days had forced her to clean, organize, and tally her sales late into the night.

Business was better than she'd hoped!

God, thank you so much for things going so smoothly. I'm sorry that I didn't trust you to help me for so long, and then you helped me even though I didn't ask.

Leaving Irena alone so many nights in a row didn't sit well, but the woman insisted she'd been alone before and could be so again.

Besides, it would only last a few more months. If business continued this steadily, she could hire a clerk soon.

A whine, seemingly from the street, prickled the hair on her neck. She quit writing and listened.

The ticking of the clock beside her grew louder with each second.

Nothing.

She released the breath she'd been holding and scanned the catalog for new items. What would a child or parent with a little extra change find irresistible?

Boards squeaked overhead, but she refused to pay them any mind. Working in a huge store at night with only the Kansas wind for company would make anyone jumpy.

"Uff."

Eliza froze, but every single nerve twitched in her body. That wasn't the wind. Or a coon, or any other creature she could blame but one.

What she wouldn't give to have Will working behind a gunsmithing counter now.

Lowering the lamp's wick ever so slowly, she looked around for something to use as a weapon. Hadn't she locked up? Maybe the wind had pushed a door open. But that other sound . . .

What to do? Hide, or yell in hopes of scaring the intruder away?

Lord, help me.

She'd never fought anyone in her life, and if she ran, her cumbersome petticoats would make her easy prey.

But she couldn't just sit and wait. A thief would head straight for the office in search of a cashbox. The Jacob's ladders, teacups, and hand towels out front wouldn't interest someone looking for quick cash — and she wouldn't hand her money over to another criminal.

If only she'd made it to the bank before they closed. She unlatched the cashbox as quietly as possible, pulled out the bills, then shoved them under a stack of old papers she'd collected to wrap fragile items.

The unmistakable scuffle of a footstep made her tremble. The trespasser had likely finished traversing the dark maze of tables, leaving only the staircase between him and her.

She grabbed the cashbox and squared her shoulders, clamping her jaw to stop her chattering teeth. With a quick shove, she opened the door and walked forward, searching for a silhouette. "Halt, or I'll shoot!"

A curse called attention to the shadow running toward her. She threw the box at what was likely his face. A dull thud, a groan, and then coins scattered across the floorboards.

"Help! Intruder!"

The silhouette stumbled.

Turning, she took one step toward the back but stopped midstride and ducked between two tables. Without a light, she'd not be able to unlock the back door — and she didn't have the key.

Did anyone live in the apartments above the nearby stores? Would anyone be working this late at night?

Why hadn't the man continued to barrel after her?

Was all the heavy breathing hers alone?

She held her breath, working to hear over the thumping of her heart. Keep silent or scream?

A creak behind the stairwell made her throat clog. She couldn't see the shadowed man's features with the moon behind them both. Could he see her? She should've turned the lamp all the way down and gotten accustomed to the dark before leaving the office.

"Where'd you go?" The man's angry voice floated high above her several feet away. Did she know that voice?

Did he think her stupid enough to answer?

Which of her patrons had decided she'd be easy pickings? Losing money again would be nothing compared to a wicked man catching her in the dark.

"There you are." The merriment infusing the gravelly voice stopped her heart. "And I thought you were going to shoot me."

With all her might, she pushed over a table full of dishware. Ceramic pieces broke and scattered across the floor.

Screaming, she lunged for the irons on the table next to her and lobbed them as hard as she could into the blackness.

Even with no shirt and no covers, Will couldn't sleep in the sweltering heat. He gave up and sat, pressing his palms against his eyelids. Tonight had been beyond frustrating. If Axel had been in town, he surely would've laid low at his mother's. But if Mrs. Langston was keeping him, she was the finest actress in the world. When she figured out Will thought her son was still around, he'd almost had to tie her to a chair to keep her from running outside and screaming for her boy.

So either his suspicions were completely wrong, or Axel — if the thief was Axel — had hid elsewhere. Maybe the ring had been gone long ago.

Or perhaps he had a gift for losing things. He'd look harder for his money and the ring in the morning.

He wiped his sweaty brow. Being this hot

in May, he dreaded August. If only the windows opened so he could sleep.

Groaning, he smacked his forehead, slipped into his trousers, and grabbed his bedding. How stupid to sleep in his tiny cubbyhole when Axel's upstairs apartment could have been his weeks ago. The second story had four windows that opened onto the street.

The smell of sunbaked horse droppings wouldn't disturb him in the least if he had a breeze — and Kansas was rarely without a breeze.

He stumbled up the stairs, eager for a mattress to sprawl across instead of his tiny cot.

After dropping his blankets on the bed, he crossed to the windows and shoved up the stubborn sashes, letting the breeze cool his clammy skin. He leaned against the window frame, his eyes drifting closed.

Crash! The clatter of glass breaking — a massive amount of glass — yanked away sleep.

He gripped the windowsill and leaned out farther. Which direction had the noise come from?

A lady's scream sent him racing down the narrow stairway. He smacked his hip on the pickle barrel at the end of the counter, then ran pell-mell for the front, hitting the front door hard. The lock was its usual stubborn self. He jostled the stupid thing until the bolt turned.

The second he stepped outside in bare feet, he realized he had nothing to fight off a possible attacker. Sprinting back inside, he snatched a local farmer's Sharps he'd fixed yesterday and ran toward the ammunition. The time it would take to find the right bullets in the gloom made him utter a curse he'd only heard others say.

Sorry, Lord, but what if Eliza's in trouble? No woman lives on this street, and I wouldn't put it past Eliza to work sunup to long past sundown.

He shoved some wrong-sized shells aside and grabbed another box. Holding the case up to the moonlight, he could just make out the letters.

Thank you, God.

He snatched a handful and ran outside. Maybe it wasn't Eliza who screamed, but he sprinted toward her store anyway.

I don't want anyone hurt, but please have her cry out again so I know where I'm going.

The slapping of his bare feet against the ground and his heavy breathing hindered his hearing, but he'd not stop to listen until he stood in front of the Five and Dime.

Scanning each alley he passed for a darting figure, he tried to load the rifle without slowing.

That wasn't working. He stopped to shove the stubborn shell into the chamber. A shadowed form appeared in the middle of the road, darting straight for him.

He hoisted the gun to his shoulder, but immediately lowered the rifle — the runner had a bell-shaped figure.

"Stop!" He swung the barrel away from her just in time. The woman ran smack into his chest.

The smell of her this close, in his arms . . .

"Thank goodness!" Eliza squeezed him for a regretfully short second before jumping away. She grabbed his hand and pulled his arm in the direction she'd come from. "Somebody tried to rob me."

He followed her, tightening his hand around hers lest she let go. "Who?"

She picked up her pace. "I don't know."

On her porch, he readied his rifle. "Stay here." He kicked open the door, walked in a pace, then reached back for her. "No, wait. I'm not leaving you outside alone."

Ignoring his hand, she scurried around him and ran ahead. "I'll get some irons."

Huh? What good would that do? "No, light the lamps."

She rushed behind the counter and within seconds had two blazing.

He shut the door behind him and secured the latch. The robber had likely escaped, but he crept toward the back anyway, gun ready.

Dull gray light spilled in through the wide-open back door. He peeked out into the alley. A small shadow scurried low to the ground, but nothing else moved. He shut the door, dismayed to see the intruder had splintered the wood near the lock. How had the thief found this exit? With only the dim glow of Eliza's office lantern, the entire back wall was cast in shadow.

Eliza couldn't stay here late at night ever again.

He jerked the door shut, but the extra upper latch barely kept it closed.

Though certain the robber had fled, Will checked the storage room under the stairs and stalked up to the second story, looking back every few seconds to make sure Eliza remained behind the counter within the circle of lantern light. Her fists were clenched around the handles of two irons.

When the last corner turned up empty, he lowered his firearm and descended the stairs. A few feet away from the counter something sharp stabbed him in the heel, almost eliciting the second curse he'd ever uttered in his life.

Eliza dropped her irons with a thump and left her spot.

He lowered himself to the floor with a groan and felt the item in his heel. A large piece of something glasslike jutted from his foot.

"I'm so sorry. I knocked the dishware over to keep him from getting me." She navigated around the little glimmers of broken dinnerware between them.

He stopped pulling on the piece. "He came after you?"

"He didn't exactly appreciate my throwing the cashbox in his face." She knelt in front of him and took hold of his foot. "Or the irons. But *they* changed his mind at least."

He straightened his leg to let her look at the glass. "Whatever possessed you to throw things at him?"

"I wasn't about to hand over money a second time." She inspected his heel, sucking air between her teeth in sympathy. "And, well, he didn't believe me when I threatened to shoot."

Will frowned. "But why wouldn't you?"

"I didn't have a gun." She put his leg down gingerly. "I need to get a lamp."

Will bent his foot toward himself as she headed back to the counter. He wriggled the shard from his flesh, sucking in air the entire time. The wound could have been worse if the shard had embedded in a softer part of his foot. He looked around for something to staunch the bleeding, but he had no extra clothing. In his haste, he hadn't even thrown on a shirt. He clamped his palm against his heel.

"You pull it already?" She set down a roll of bandages and a small dark bottle next to a lamp.

"Yeah."

She took his foot in her lap again and reached for the bottle.

"You don't have to do that. I'm certainly capable of tending my own injuries." He sighed. "About the only thing I'm good at."

"Nonsense." She peered at the gash, then frowned. "What if a piece broke off in there?"

He grimaced as he pulled his foot back and probed the wound for the telltale feel of something hard and sharp. "Not that I can tell."

She popped the little cork off the bottle and wet the end of the bandaging material.

"Where did you learn to doctor?"

"I don't consider cleaning a cut with

iodine doctoring." She paused and stared at his heel. "You don't need stitches, do you?"

And for some reason, he wished he'd cut himself worse. How would she handle sewing flesh? Carl Hampden couldn't even watch him put in sutures, but Eliza would likely shine in a medical emergency. "A tight bandage will be enough."

"Why were you running without shoes anyway?" She glanced up, and her gaze locked on his chest. She looked down, quickly returning her focus to his foot.

Will pushed himself more upright. "Where were you going when you ran into me on the street?"

She reached for the iodine. "To you."

"Not the sheriff?"

When she shook her head, he smiled. Propping himself up with his hands, he leaned back as if enjoying a relaxing massage, the bite of iodine barely noticeable. She'd run to him for protection rather than the law — that had to mean something. "I'll have to inform Sheriff Quade about the break-in. Did you see the robber? Was it Axel?"

"Why would you think it was Axel?" She blew on his wound like his mother used to. "Surely he's long gone."

"Or he's returned."

"But why would he?" She kept her eyes pinned to his foot instead of looking at him. "How could he slink around his hometown and not be noticed?"

"He'd know every hiding spot, where the back door to your store was, where my cashbox's stashed, when the butcher leaves for lunch, who lives above which stores, where the sheriff walks at night . . ."

Her fingers absently played with his bandage's knot. Though she no longer needed to cradle his foot in her lap, he wouldn't tell her to let go.

She looked toward the back. "Since I'm the one who unmasked him, the one who forced him into hiding, if he found me alone . . ." She reached for her throat.

Axel couldn't . . . wouldn't.

Then again, he'd never suspected his childhood friend would join a gang, rob a train, or bust a woman's face either. He'd be a fool to rule out anything as too evil for Axel.

"I'll go to the sheriff's." She released his foot.

"We'll walk there together."

"You can't. You don't have any shoes."

"That didn't stop me from running to you."

She glanced up for a short second. "You're

shirtless too. If anyone sees us, they'll gossip first and ask questions later."

"Then we'll go to my store so I can get a shirt, but I'm not leaving you here alone."

She shook her head. "We'd create just as many rumors if I was seen outside your door at this time of night."

"It's no worse than us being together now."

She scowled. "But I was robbed."

"Gossip first, questions later. Remember?"

She collected her medical supplies and handed him the lamp. "Then perhaps we should leave separately."

"Not going to happen." She might be the bravest woman in Salt Flatts, but that wouldn't keep him from protecting her if he had the power to do so. "I can find something to wear here."

"I don't carry men's clothing."

He scanned her tables. "What about an apron or a skirt?"

The ridge between her eyebrows squeezed together. "A skirt?"

"I could use it as a cloak."

"You'd walk through the middle of town wearing a flowery skirt?"

"It's dark." He shrugged. "Maybe a tablecloth."

"You're being silly." She stood up and

brushed herself off. "I could clean up this mess while you walk back to your place and get yourself dressed."

"The robber might see your lights on, realize you're alone, and try again."

She stared at the dish-littered floor as if leaving a mess for a few hours might kill her. She glanced at him, but he gave her a slight shake of his head. He wouldn't back down, not this time. She was more important than tidiness.

"All right, I'll go to your store and wait while you get what you need. Let me grab the cash I hid."

He stood to test his foot. He'd have to struggle not to wince on the way back to the Men's Emporium.

She returned and passed him. "I'm ready to go."

He leaned over to pick up the rifle and hobbled after her. "Don't walk so quickly."

"You need help?"

An excuse to have her arm wrapped around his? Even though he was still not sure how he should feel about her after her keeping the store a secret from him? "Yes."

She walked back reluctantly, then threaded her arm beneath his shoulder. He squeezed his eyes shut and forced out air. Breathing was simple — an involuntary process — the lungs inflated and deflated. Proximity to a woman shouldn't be capable of derailing his respiratory system.

Then again, maybe medical texts couldn't explain everything about the human body.

Though he did need to get control of his breathing before she thought him unmanly for having such trouble inhaling and exhaling because of a minor laceration in his heel.

When they exited the store, Eliza looked back over her shoulder. "What if the robber returns while I'm gone? A busted door won't keep him out."

"Nothing costs much more than a handful of dimes, right?"

"Correct." She groaned. "I wish I hadn't destroyed so much of my inventory. What if I can't pay back Mr. Raymond because —" She pressed against him when something darted out of the alley.

He tucked her closer, watching a black four-legged animal streak across the road.

She pulled away from him a bit. "I wasn't scared of that cat."

"Of course not." He smiled and limped a little more than necessary, if nothing more than to keep her close. "I never cease to be amazed at what you're not scared of."

"Oh, I'm scared of plenty of things."

"Like?"

Her shoulders tensed. "Not being able to run this store as well as I want to. Repeating others' mistakes —"

"Telling me about your store."

She stiffened but kept moving forward. "Yes. Sorry about that, but I didn't want to hurt you more than I already was going to, and . . . well, I was trying not to let emotions override common sense. Seems I did the opposite."

"But without emotions, what kind of life would we have?"

"One without pain or sorrow or embarrassment." She shrugged. "A good-enough life."

"Ah, but only heaven promises a world devoid of the negative. If we tossed away emotions here on earth, we'd also lose out on excitement, joy, and love. To experience the good times, we often have to endure the bad."

For better or worse, for richer or poorer. He swallowed hard to contain thoughts of Eliza walking toward him in that ivory gown of hers — why get his hopes back up again if she planned to stay in Salt Flatts with her store when he'd likely never return?

But would he wish away all his past troubles? If he'd known Nancy would jilt him, would he have avoided courting her?

Some of his best memories revolved around Nancy. His first dance, the fishing hole they often took his brothers to, the times he'd pulled her pigtails in school to dip them in ink.

What happy memories might he create with Eliza?

He already had plenty of good memories of her: the feel of her hands against his chest as she batted away feathers, the smile she gave him when he complimented her on some masculine characteristic most women would pout over, their time in the alley when she'd promised not to marry the butcher's sons, the moments when he could've sworn she'd glanced at his lips . . .

"And what are you scared of?" Eliza let go of his arm and stepped under the Men's Emporium eaves.

How'd they get here already? He hadn't noticed a step of the last block.

"I'm afraid that with all my worrying, I'll miss a chance at happiness." He climbed the single stair, swung open the door, and set the firearm on the counter.

She didn't come inside, just stood at the threshold. Did she think standing outside alone in the dark was safe? He swung the door open wider.

"What would make you happy, Will?" Her

breathless voice drew his gaze to the place one momentary pleasure lay.

He pulled her through the doorway, her jacket rough against his chest. "This."

He slid his thumb along the scar across her cheek. She blinked up at him as he touched the puckered flesh he'd thought of kissing that first day — and so many days since.

She leaned into his hand a second before he pressed his mouth gently against hers.

The softness of her lips, the warmth of her in the crook of his arm, the way every worry and fear retreated with her so near — a kiss far sweeter than any of the schoolboy pecks he'd plied on Nancy. He slipped his other arm around her, and she pressed closer.

An instant later, she broke away, pupils wider in the moonlight than he'd ever seen them. "I can't be caught kissing a man with no shirt on. Everyone will think . . . Well, this is exactly why they'd gossip if they saw me with you at this time of night. Things like this could happen."

Yet she didn't leave the circle of his arms.

He couldn't help but smile at her objection. "Well, I realize this isn't the best place or time —"

She stepped away from him and grabbed

the doorknob behind her. "I can't stay in here with you."

He grabbed her free hand. "Wait." He edged closer but stopped when she put her palm out.

"No farther."

"All right." He wouldn't, though the desire to steal another kiss tempted him to hang the consequences. "But don't go outside, where I'll worry about you."

"No need to worry."

"Oh, but I am worried." He pulled her away from the door until she let go of the knob so he could take her other hand. "I'm worried that you and I'll miss out on happiness — long-lasting happiness."

"I've got my store." She glanced over her shoulder, as if she planned to return to the Five and Dime the moment he headed upstairs for his shirt.

"Will your store make you truly happy?"

She glowered. "I've worked too hard —"

He pressed a finger to her lips to cut her off.

She stood, blinking against the darkness.

"I'm not saying you shouldn't want a store and I shouldn't want to doctor, but maybe we're going about this all wrong."

"How's that?"

"In my Bible reading this evening, First

John said something about the things of this world and our desires will pass away, but he who does the will of God lives forever. I want to do what God wants, sure, but at the same time, all my focus is on obtaining finances for school. Yet look at the mess I'm in."

"You're always trying to help others. Surely God will bless that."

"But I've been acting as if I don't believe God knows what I need — as if I'm the only one who can get it."

"I didn't pay a dime for my store, as Mr. Raymond likes to point out. Some unknown person is letting me use it. If that's not God giving me a store to take care of, I don't know what is."

Will rubbed the back of his neck. She was right — her store was clearly a gift from God.

What had he expected her to do after his little Bible lesson — declare her property worthless, jump into his arms, and beg him to marry her?

Clearly, God had been speaking only to him. Maybe He was asking him to reconsider his goals, but what did that mean exactly? Give up school, the store, Eliza . . . everything?

CHAPTER 20

The glowing edge of the eastern horizon grew as Eliza rushed along an empty Main Street toward her store. She needed to clean last night's mess before opening and perhaps fix her broken door.

A face-stretching yawn scrunched her eyes so much she stopped walking. Not only had the sheriff's questions kept her from crawling into bed until a few hours ago, but ruminating over Will's kiss had stolen the rest of her night.

She ran a finger along her scar. He'd caressed her puffy skin as if such an ugly thing were endearing. She wrapped her arms tightly about herself and hurried down the road. What a ridiculous thought. Of course a scar wouldn't endear — more like engender pity. But his touch had been nothing short of tender, and his eyes had held no revulsion.

Walking faster, she forced herself not to

imagine being kissed a second time. A kiss was pleasurable, fleeting — not a promise, like an engagement or courtship. And promises were often broken . . . like her mother's vow to commit to her husband and be there for her children.

Promises were nothing. Kisses were meaningless.

She'd no longer pretend that Will refrained from asking to court her because he didn't want to, but something held him back. Her store and his schooling most likely; they couldn't be together and maintain both dreams. Last night, he'd made that clear by insinuating she'd find real happiness if she gave up her store, that she couldn't have both him and the Five and Dime.

She stopped in front of the Five and Dime. The front door was ajar. Hadn't she locked it? Ignoring the shortness of her breath and her prickling skin, she tiptoed up the steps. Heart in her throat, she put a hand against the glass to peer inside.

Seeing no movement, she looked down the street. Should she get Will or bother the baker? Surely a robber wouldn't sneak around this close to daylight. Pushing the door open enough to step through, she let her eyes adjust to the dim interior, her ears ready for any sound encouraging her to run.

Near the front counter, Will sat slumped in a wooden chair — a rather uncomfortable chair she'd found hidden upstairs. His head lolled to the side, and a soft snore escaped.

She let out a shaky breath and closed the door quietly behind her.

Spying the rifle across his lap, she stopped midstep. Could she wake him without getting shot?

"Will?" she whispered.

He hummed, a little smile curving his lips, yet his hand gripped the gun tighter.

She gritted her teeth and took a step back. She'd never awoken anyone but family, let alone a man with a gun.

No broken dishes littered the floor in the middle of the store, and a few plates and one lone teacup sat in the middle of the table she'd knocked over.

He'd cleaned? She swallowed against the lump in her throat. Just a few days ago, she'd accused him of trying to sabotage her business — more likely a reflection of what she might have done rather than Will. And yet here he slept after straightening everything.

Easing herself against the table holding children's playthings, she half leaned, half sat. These items sold so quickly, she had plenty of space to sit. She should put two, maybe three, more tables of these popular items up front.

Another of Will's snores ended with a slight whistle.

Was watching a sleeping man wrong? But trying to sneak out or wake him didn't seem wise either. Might he startle awake, ready to fight an imaginary foe, like her father used to? Or would he try his hardest to keep his eyes closed as long as possible, like her brother often had? Or maybe he awakened with a cheery attitude as soon as the clock chimed six, like her mother once did?

The morning sunlight penetrating the front windows slowly crept up to Will's knees. He couldn't be comfortable draped over that tiny chair. Why hadn't he gone home? He'd known she'd taken her cash with her and planned to return early to clean.

And why guard her store? A robber wouldn't return for towers of five-cent teacups and fistfuls of penny candy, but the guns under his counter would certainly entice a thief, along with his cashbox and more valuable merchandise.

Not so long ago, she'd doubted Will's integrity, along with the rest of the towns-folk. She hadn't trusted this man who slept in a wobbly chair, guarding the very trinkets undermining his sales, the doctor who bothered to save a stray dog's life, the brother who made his little sisters' eyes glow at the mere sight of him.

She should find something else to look at, but as the sunlight crept up his chest, causing the sheen of his navy tie to cast a blue shadow on his stubbly chin, she couldn't take her eyes off him. Playing with a loose strand of hair, she let herself look.

Nothing about him stood out if she forced herself to be objective. Sure he was handsome compared to her, but was he more striking than average?

She rolled her eyes at herself. Yes, he certainly was. Even if God hadn't blessed him with an attractive face, the caring in his hands as he'd stitched her up that first day, the kindness in his eyes when he talked to a patient, the mess of hair on his head, as soft as it was thick . . .

But the look in his eye the day of the pillow's demise had not been kindness — it had been something she shouldn't have seen from a man about to stand beside her groom.

And she'd run straight to him last night. Not home, not to the sheriff. To him. Knowing he'd help, but who wouldn't he help?

How often had she witnessed Will give advice, medicine, and necessities away without a glimmer of indecision in his blue-green eyes?

Had she ever helped anyone if she'd lose something to do so? She regularly gave a portion of her income to the church, but often with a smidgen of misgiving, especially when she was under financial stress. And once or twice she'd allowed customers to buy from her despite being a penny short — but not without irritation.

The sun hit Will's eyes, and his eyelids scrunched against the brightness. He rubbed a hand down his face and stretched in his chair.

His eyes opened for a second, drifted closed, then popped back open. "Eliza?"

She stiffened, but thankfully, his grip didn't tighten around his rifle. "Yes."

He made a charmingly silly noise as he yawned and shook his head to chase away sleep. "How long have you been here?"

"Not too long." At least he hadn't asked how long she'd been staring at him, memorizing his every feature, contemplating his compassionate heart.

He rubbed the heels of his hands against his eyes. "Well, I certainly failed at guarding anything if you walked in unnoticed."

She shook her head. Only he would apologize for not helping enough when he had gone beyond anyone's expectations. "I still appreciate it. Nothing else has been stolen and you cleaned. That's something." More than something.

"And I fixed the back door."

Of course he did. "Thank you, Will."

He pushed himself out of the chair and took a lopsided step forward. He rotated his ankle and rubbed a lazy hand over his stomach, wrinkling his shirt more.

She should do something to let him know she was grateful for his guarding her store, cleaning up, coming to her aid at midnight — all of it. "You hungry?"

He shrugged.

Right. When wasn't he? "Since you saved me from cleaning this morning, why don't we have coffee and pastries next door before you head to work?"

One would think he'd been offered a thousand dollars by the smile filling his face. "You're eating with me?"

"I normally don't breakfast this early, but we can take our time." Or maybe he couldn't? "That is, if you don't need to return to your store any time soon."

"Oh no." His smile made strange things flutter inside her. "I'll sprint down at the last second if need be." He slapped his pockets. "Oh wait, I don't have any money."

"I'll pay."

He frowned.

"Consider it reimbursement for guard duty."

His frown deepened.

She stuck her hands on her hips and mirrored his features. "You'd take a pie from an old woman for inspecting her bunions."

"But that's an old woman." He let his gaze travel over her, and strangely she didn't shrink away or cross her arms to guard against his perusal. Did he find her attractive despite her unembellished dress? And why did she wish all of a sudden she owned a nicer wardrobe?

"All right. But I'm not letting you pay because I watched your store." He held out his arm. "I just don't want to waste five minutes away from you."

She took his arm, her own shaking a bit. He wanted to be with her that much?

Her pulse pumped hard as they walked next door. If she were to commit to Will, when he went west, she'd have to relinquish her store when her contract obligations with Mr. Raymond expired. If she couldn't do that, there was no reason to entangle their emotions any further. She let her arm slip out of his. She'd not damage his heart like her mother had devastated her father's.

They stepped inside the bakery, but no one stood behind the high counter topped with two muffin platters. Her stomach grumbled.

Will stopped in front of the fresh baked pastries. "Mr. Allison?"

A boy not much thicker than a French bread roll popped his flour-powdered face around the back doorjamb. "Father's not here. What can I get you?" He looked at her, then back at Will, and his grin widened. "Both of you?"

"Coffee, and we'll just eat from the muffins you've got out." Will looked to her and winced. "Unless, of course, you wanted something else?"

Knowing Will hadn't meant to choose for her but rather make the baker's life easier, she picked up a muffin. She hoped the dark spots weren't raisins. "These will do, I'm sure."

"Great." The boy disappeared for a second, then returned with two mugs and a coffeepot. "Rice muffins are on the left. The others are vanilla egg muffins with dried berries. Hot rolls are coming out next." He set the coffee on a table near the counter. "Unfortunately, you'll have to pour for yourselves. I have to get something out of the oven." He nodded at Will, then disappeared.

Will pulled out her seat. "What kind would you like?"

Surely the baker's son would have mentioned raisins if they indeed contained raisins. "I'll try one with the berries."

"Those do sound good." He snatched five, set them on the table, then folded himself into his chair, this one as dainty as her store's chair was uncomfortable. He bowed his head.

"Lord, thanks for the protection you offered Eliza last night and that she didn't suffer much loss. I pray the sheriff catches the thief. Please help the thief learn that he should rely on you for provision rather than wrangle it for himself — like I need to learn myself. Thank you for the baker who provides for our stomachs and for the woman across from me who's admirable in so many ways. Amen."

Admirable? What on earth was admirable about her compared to him?

Will snatched up one of his muffins and took a huge bite, then closed his eyes and hummed.

Having stared at Will minutes ago made it difficult to keep her eyes off the man who far surpassed her in things that mattered more than an impressive business record. She pinched off of a piece of her muffin's crumbly top and stared at the steaming mugs on the table.

"What's wrong? Upset about last night?"

"No. Er . . . depends on what part." Before he brought up the kissing — something she would not discuss in public — she leaned forward. "Do you really think it's Axel?"

He shrugged and grabbed a second muffin. "If he needed to finance himself by stealing, he'd know this town. Some of the things I'm missing point to him."

"But he has money from the robbery and who knows what else."

"The money wasn't all his."

But he had other money. "Did you know he was running liquor?"

Will stopped chewing. "How would you know that?"

She bit her lip and rolled a crumb between her fingers. "He told me."

"I should've guessed." He frowned, but then raised an eyebrow. "And you were still going to marry him?"

She nodded reluctantly, knowing her willingness to marry a lawbreaker couldn't improve her character in Will's eyes. "He

393

said he'd quit but couldn't right away. Said you can't just stop working for those kinds of people."

"All the more reason to think he's still around then." Will's munching slowed, contemplating his muffin as if the pastry might reveal the whereabouts of his friend. "I can't believe I was so blind." Will set down his breakfast and rubbed the back of his neck. "Or so . . . gullible."

"I'm not sure if you're gullible or just kinder than most."

"Well, kindness can keep you from pursuing what you want." He glanced at her mouth, and she bit her lip. How long had he wanted to kiss her before last night?

"I don't think I've ever been kind, not truly. Not like you anyway." She fidgeted in her seat. "I've basically been given a store, and yet I worry kids will pocket penny candy, never thinking they might be stealing because they have nothing to eat."

"If they need food, they shouldn't steal taffy and lemon drops." He threw a heaping spoonful of sugar in his coffee. "I'm certain if the opportunity to help someone presented itself, you would help them gladly."

Would she truly? How often had she missed helping someone in need because she was focused on herself? "I can't think of anyone I could help."

"What about Axel's mother? Mrs. Langston said she needed somewhere to sell her clothing." Will swirled his coffee before taking a sip.

Mrs. Langston had embraced her like a long-lost daughter, offered hospitality, gushed over the wonderful things Axel had said about her, begged her to visit often.

And not once after Axel left town had she dropped by or offered help, though only she, Will, and Axel knew her desperate need. Eliza shoved her muffin away.

Will eyed her discarded pastry. "Not that you have to. Nobody would blame you for avoiding Axel's mother."

"That's not it." How could she have overlooked Mrs. Langston's need when she could help her better than anyone else?

"Is there a problem with the muffin?"

"It's not sitting well in my stomach." By no fault of the baker. She pressed her hand against her churning belly. The more she probed her character, the worse her insides agitated. She stood, bumping the table. Her untouched coffee sloshed over its rim. "I'm sorry to leave you since I invited you to eat with me, but I need to do something before I open."

Will stood, taking the napkin from his lap

to wipe up her spill. "That's all right. Thanks for breakfast." And though he agreed, the light in his eyes dulled. Once again, he deferred to someone else's wants above his own.

She couldn't leave him thinking she didn't want to spend time with him. She wanted to — now more than ever. "Perhaps you could come to the boardinghouse tonight to check on Irena? She took to bed again this morning."

Will wiped his hands on his now-damp napkin. "Sure."

"Then maybe you could stay for dinner?"

Had she just asked a man to dine with her alone?

"All right. Anything special for dessert?" He winked, a mischievous look glinting in his eyes.

She glanced toward the kitchen to see if anyone had witnessed Will's roguish expression. She suddenly felt as if the baker's son had thrust her head into an oven rather than loaves of yeasty dough. "I guess a rhubarb pie isn't what you're hoping for?"

He shook his head slowly, his eyes on her mouth.

She backed up and hit another chair. "Depends." She needed to leave before she made a fool of herself in front of the baker's son. Before Will kissed her in the middle of the bakery. Before she decided that would be all right. "I'll see you tonight."

The second she opened the door, she breathed deeply, hoping the morning air would cool her face enough that passersby wouldn't notice her flushed countenance. She marched to her store and straight to the back to find paper. After scribbling out a makeshift sign telling customers she'd be late, she hung the notice in the window. She needed to scurry across town and talk to Axel's mother quickly if she was to have any chance of returning anywhere near her normal opening hour.

Of course, she could visit Mrs. Langston another day, but would tomorrow be any less inconvenient? And with each passing hour, the conviction prodding her forward would be easier to ignore.

Though clothing was more expensive than what one ought to carry in a five-and-dime, she'd offer to sell Axel's mother's wares in the upstairs balcony. And she'd refuse any of the profit. She didn't need money as badly as Mrs. Langston.

William felt Irena's pulse. "I'm not detecting anything more worrisome than what we've dealt with before. Perhaps it's a bout of melancholia." He fingered the tincture of opium in his medical chest but couldn't make himself pull it out. Dr. Forsythe had given Jonesey opium years ago, after he'd purged his friend — neither procedure had helped in the long run. "Maybe we need to look past medicine to whatever lifts your spirits. What might entice you to go downstairs despite the pain? Music or painting or prayers . . ."

Irena shrugged. "The birds outside are plenty cheery. I like watching them."

Yet bird-watching wasn't getting her out of bed. "There's no one to talk to in here."

She laughed a little and turned sad eyes toward him. "How many visitors do you think I entertain? I can't even get someone to lodge here unless they're desperate."

"Eliza's worried about you."

Irena grabbed an extra pillow and picked at the pilling. "I'm worried about me too. I just can't shake how I feel. But it comes and goes. And the fact that my joints won't let me walk much . . ." She stared out the window again. "It's a shame I've only just met Eliza. I've lived my whole life pretending my condition hasn't changed me, but it has." She kept her focus outside the window, her voice low and rough with unshed tears. "Being shunned from the elite social circle I grew up in was difficult. I'm fifty-five now, but I've been gray since shortly after my pregnancy. No one wanted a gray-haired twenty-one-year-old lady with a beard and midget baby over for tea."

She swiped at the wetness cresting in the corner of her eye. "Then when my husband gambled everything away, I did the best I could by joining the circus, but it hurt to be seen only for the beard on my face and the boy I'd brought into the world — another sideshow attraction like me. I thought retiring here would change things. For a while I forced people to do business with me as a bearded woman until they could look past the disfigurement, but then someone new came to town and I had to do it all over again." She sighed. "So I gave in and hid my face. I told myself it was for their sakes, not mine, but . . ."

Will pulled at the hair at the nape of his neck. "I hope my little sister didn't offend you when —"

"She's just young." She patted his hand. "I've never been uncomfortable with you, but I figured that's because you have such a great medical mind, maladies and deformities are your business. But Eliza? She's the first person who valued me despite the one thing about me I can't change. And now look at me." She ran a hand through her bed-mussed hair. "I can't find the strength to eat dinner with her."

"Then that's what you need to do." He waited until she looked at him. How many times before Eliza came had Irena taken to her bed with no one the wiser? "Do whatever it takes to get down to that table every day. Eliza's what you need."

She's what he needed too.

Irena shook her head against the pillow, mussing her hair even more. "You got a pill that'll convince my mind to force these fat achy legs down the stairs?"

"No. But perhaps we could move you downstairs so you can't use them as an excuse anymore." He smiled, wishing she'd smile back. "I'll pray for you too."

"I guess that's the best I can get. I only wish your powders worked better for the pain."

"I do too." He frowned. "You want me to call Dr. Forsythe or the new doctor?"

"No, I trust you. You care about me, whereas those men don't." She indicated the door with her head. "Now, go have supper. Something tells me my presence tonight would complicate things for you anyway." She looked pointedly at his tie and slicked-back hair.

Should he expect difficulty? He'd been hoping for an evening of not second-guessing himself.

Irena winked. "Get on with you. I'm tired."

He shouldn't let her remain in bed, but he would quit badgering for now and check on her next week. Maybe Eliza could improve things in the meantime.

He squeezed Irena's hand and stood. "I'll have Eliza bring you something. She says you're not eating well, and that needs to stop."

"Just because I'm letting you doctor me doesn't mean I'm obedient." She rolled her eyes, a hint of orneriness gleaming in them.

He wagged his finger and gave her the look his mother used to whenever he sassed, but Irena only closed her eyes and turned her head away.

Collecting his medical supplies, he tried not to look as defeated as Irena. Were there any alternative treatments for melancholia in his books?

On the way down the stairs, the scent of roasted garlic enticed him toward the dining room. But the second his foot crossed the threshold, he stopped.

Eliza stood beside the table decked in a dark red print dress, complete with ruffles and lace and a cinched waist. She'd piled curls upon her head, one strand entangled in her pearl necklace. She cocked her head to the side. "Is everything all right?"

His lips attempted to say yes but failed.

"I suppose I'm too dressed up?" The color in her cheeks seemed high, whether from his staring or perhaps the reflected shade of the dress, he couldn't tell.

"No, you look nice." More than nice. Should he compliment her after she'd once said she didn't want men to notice her? But then she'd let him kiss her last night, invited him to dinner . . . "You look beautiful, actually."

She ducked her head a little.

He walked over and took the vegetable platter she held in her hands. He waited for her to look up, but his stomach rumbled before she did.

"Let me get the biscuits." In a wink, she disappeared into the kitchen.

He slid the food onto the center of the table beside a vase of irises. The flowers' sweet fragrance overpowered the smell of the roast, but he wouldn't complain. He probably wasn't going to taste much with her sitting across from him in her new getup anyway.

Eliza returned carrying a plate piled high

with biscuits. Without waiting for him to pull out her chair, she sat.

He huffed at being thwarted from performing that courtesy. All dressed up like that and she wasn't going to let him be a gentleman?

She raised her eyebrows, glanced at his seat, then pulled at her collar. He'd not increase her discomfort by pointing out how he ought to have seated her.

He snatched a biscuit and sat. "I'm glad I'm here."

"Me too." She didn't quite look him in the eyes. "Would you pray?"

Will dropped his biscuit as if it were brimstone, and Eliza bowed her head.

Quiet settled around her, then lingered. Had he fallen asleep?

She peeked up, but his lips wriggled as if he couldn't decide what to pray. She smiled a little before bowing her head again.

"Lord, help Mrs. Lightfoot find hope in you. Let her not give up on life — but find joy in being loved by you just the way she is, despite her failures and deficiencies. Let me, Jonesey, and Eliza realize that too. Let us not judge ourselves by our successes or failures but according to how you judge us — redeemed and set apart for good works.

Let not our weakness of mind and unbelief keep us from following your plan. Help us look to you for guidance, that we may bless others and be blessed ourselves. Amen."

Eliza stared at her empty plate. He hadn't thanked God for the food, but what did that matter? She should take prayer as seriously as he — even dinnertime prayers — in which she rarely voiced more than a routine blessing.

Just weeks ago, she'd started praying again and had prided herself for that, but her prayers were nothing more than asking God for what she wanted. And Will's prayers were so . . . knowledgeable. He probably read his Bible every day too. She'd felt as if she hadn't the time now that God had given her what she wanted . . . not that she'd read daily before she'd had the store.

Will dragged the green beans closer, and his tongue poked out to lick his lips. He stopped, the spoon hovering in midair. "I'm sorry. Did you intend to pray as well?"

She shook her head before he could set down the serving spoon. What could she add right now that wasn't blabbering about how she wasn't good enough for what she had . . . or what she wanted. "I was just thinking about you."

"Good things, I hope." His smile grew as

soft as the whipped butter.

"Does anyone think poorly of you?" Unlike with Axel, she'd never seen anything but smiles or high regard when others talked about Will.

His face fell. "Plenty, I think."

"In what way?" Would he honestly lay out his faults before her? Both of her former fiancés had done nothing but build themselves up — and neither turned out as grand as their boasts.

"Well, my inability to get to medical school has caused some to question my intelligence. I've also made plenty of mistakes people believe I could've avoided." He glanced up at her for a second. "No one thinks highly of a failure."

"I thought you just prayed we shouldn't care about our failures."

He stopped chewing. "Yes, but —"

"Maybe people are pushing you toward school not because they can't stand to see a failure, but because they know what a success you'll be if you do go." Eliza grabbed the potatoes and dished herself a small mound. "Irena didn't want to see anyone except you, though two qualified doctors reside in town."

"Right, two," he mumbled through his mouthful.

"Yes, two. Yet she chose you. She wanted your talent, your kindness — you."

For years, she'd fought for men to acknowledge her talent, but what about her kindness? This morning, Mrs. Langston had been excited over Eliza's proposal to sell her clothing at the Five and Dime, but if she hadn't been shamed by Will's perpetual generosity, she'd never have offered. "You're so good-natured, everyone likes you."

"They take advantage of me as well." He cut a piece of meat on his plate. "At some point I need to stop worrying about others or I'll get nowhere . . . or at least that's what some say."

Yesterday she would have enthusiastically agreed, hoping he'd start insisting on payment for his doctoring, but now . . . "We need more people like you, not one less. I like that you think about others ahead of yourself."

And that was just one thing she liked about him. She let her chin drop onto her palm, not heeding the fact that her elbow rudely perched on the table.

His perfect, slanted smile was another thing, and —

"So, with Mrs. Lightfoot . . ." He grabbed the salt.

Had he missed the warmth in her voice,

the look in her eye she couldn't help?

"I need you to try to raise her spirits." He kept eating.

She blinked. Maybe it was best he hadn't noticed her infatuation.

You're not good enough for him.

And you can't have both him and the store.

She picked up her fork and pushed her potatoes around. "I've tried countless times to get her out of bed."

"Good, but she needs to *want* to get out of bed."

"What better way to encourage her to do so than to get her outside to feel the sun and smell the flowers?"

"How long do you sit with her at night and talk?"

Eliza took her time cutting a potato. He'd probably not like her answer. "I figured forcing her to eat and coaxing her out of bed was intruding enough. I am, after all, only a guest."

"You're not a guest."

She raised a brow at him.

"You're the brightest spot in her life right now. She'd love to dine with you — in her room if she can't find the strength to come down."

Eliza stopped chewing. Of course. After all the nice things Irena had done for her,

407

she should have thought to eat with her upstairs without Will's suggestion. She forced herself to finish chewing so she could swallow the shame lodged in her throat.

"At least *I'm* finding dinner with you quite pleasant." His plate was already clean.

She sighed. Even though she'd neglected to do what any decent person would have done, he still considered her a worthy dinner companion. "Well, hopefully my apple pie will be even better." She got up to take his empty dish. "Unless you want a second helping first?"

"No need." He grabbed his plate before she could. "I can clean up after myself and bring out dessert while you finish."

She couldn't sit back down. "Do you always think about others more than yourself?"

"Well, I'm always thinking about you." He stepped closer. "Since the day you arrived actually." He straightened, smiling mischievously. "And I thought you told me you were making rhubarb."

She swallowed hard. "I thought you might want something sweeter."

He leaned down and gave her a small peck on the crown of her head. "I've already tasted the sweetest thing here. Anything else would be sour in comparison."

"Especially since I used tart apples to make the pie."

His laughter made her want to bake him bitter desserts for the rest of his life.

He set his dirty plate back on the table and grabbed both of her hands. "You know, I really don't need pie." His gaze dropped from her eyes to her mouth. He lowered his so slowly she couldn't help but press forward to meet his lips.

He merely brushed his mouth across hers and then drew back. She forced herself not to frown at such a short kiss.

He cupped her cheek, letting his thumb run along her scar. "But I'll get us some pie anyway." He winked, picked up his dirty dish, and then disappeared into the kitchen.

Will was very wrong about one thing.

The privilege to have savored the sweetest thing in Kansas belonged to her.

But if they couldn't figure out a way for him to doctor in Salt Flatts, had she the right to kiss him at all?

CHAPTER 21

Will's damp lower eyelids made it difficult to decipher Dr. Forsythe's penmanship scribbled across Mrs. Lightfoot's death certificate.

Head affection?

Will swiped away a tear and faced the doctor. "What's head affection?"

He shrugged. "She had enough exterior maladies — she likely had plenty on the inside as well." He glanced toward the door Eliza had exited in search of dry handkerchiefs. "Sometimes you don't know what went wrong, boy, and it doesn't help to draw things out. Besides, she's got no family around here. It makes little difference."

Little difference? How could he think Mrs. Lightfoot's death made no difference?

"I've got other patients." Dr. Forsythe scratched at his neck. "I suppose you could arrange for the undertaker and the like?"

Although Dr. Forsythe's indifference annoyed him, Mrs. Lightfoot would be treated with more dignity if he and Eliza saw things through. "Yes."

"Good." Dr. Forsythe awkwardly patted Will's shoulder and left him with the old woman's body, eerily still under a faded blue sheet.

If he hadn't been so distracted by Eliza last night, would he have examined Mrs. Lightfoot more thoroughly and discovered what had taken her life?

Awaiting Eliza's return, he reviewed every disease he knew of, but nothing fit the symptoms he'd observed better than melancholia, yet that couldn't have been her only problem — that wouldn't have stolen her breath nor stopped her heart.

Mrs. Lightfoot had trusted his doctoring and he'd failed.

Since he wasn't a doctor, he couldn't call Dr. Forsythe's prognosis into question. And who besides Eliza would encourage him to dig for the real cause? He'd heard enough whispers about Mrs. Lightfoot's beard being the mark of the devil that her death might actually relieve many townsfolk.

He rubbed his face. He needed schooling or at least more time to read his medical texts, no matter how long and arduous the process.

Eliza's feet dragging sounded behind him. She shuffled over to the stool where she'd silently cried as Dr. Forsythe examined Mrs. Lightfoot.

More soundless tears cascaded down her face, but she didn't look in his direction.

Will reached over and took her hand. She clamped on, crushing his fingers.

He'd have to inform the undertaker sooner rather than later, but for now, he held on tight. Nothing he could say or do would make today better, so he would let Eliza mangle his hand as long as she wanted.

Stifling her tears, Eliza reluctantly accepted the shovel the pastor handed her. She held her shawl tight with one hand, but the wind still seeped in. Had a day in May ever been so cold? She stepped forward and got a shovelful of dirt to overturn atop Mrs. Lightfoot's casket sunk deep in the earth.

Her throat constricted seeing the small pile of soil atop the pine box. The only people who'd bothered to come say good-bye stood beside her: the preacher, her lawyer, Mr. Raymond, and Will.

Just five.

How could the townspeople shun such a delightful woman? Will's parents would have attended the ceremony and perhaps some other country folk had they been in town, but only five from Salt Flatts? Even Dr. Forsythe hadn't stayed to pay his respects. All because of a disfigurement.

Mr. Raymond gently pried the shovel from her hand and propped it against a gravestone.

Will stood behind a nearby marker, looking into Irena's grave as if he believed he deserved to be buried himself.

If she hadn't enticed him down for dinner last night, would he have spent more time with Irena and possibly prevented today's mourning?

Mr. Scottsmore approached her, and Mr. Raymond sidled closer. He'd hovered near her throughout the ceremony, darting quick glances between her and her lawyer for some reason. Feeling like a defenseless rabbit watching a buzzard's claws circle closer and closer every time Mr. Raymond glanced her way, she turned her attention to Mr. Scottsmore — a pleasant chap who'd assured her the paperwork she signed with Mr. Raymond gave her a fair deal.

"Miss Cantrell, if you don't mind, I'd like you to stop by my office before you return home." Her lawyer looked over his shoulder toward his buggy. "I need to pick up Mrs. Langston to attend as well but could meet you there soon."

Eliza wiped the corner of her eye with a rough handkerchief. "Can't we talk another day?" Not that she wanted to return to the empty boardinghouse, but discussing business wasn't on her agenda. She didn't even plan to open her store.

Mr. Scottsmore sucked air through his teeth. "I know this sounds insensitive, but I'm afraid my schedule demands we discuss the will today."

The will? She turned toward the gravedigger rushing to fill the hole before it rained. Had Mrs. Lightfoot left something for her? She didn't deserve anything. She'd only known the woman for a few months and hadn't done enough for her during her last days.

"It'll be all right, Eliza." Mr. Raymond laced his arm through hers and squeezed. "I'll escort you over." He turned to the lawyer. "Anyone else needed?"

"No." Mr. Scottsmore sized up Mr. Raymond with a glance, then shrugged and shifted his gaze to her. "I know this isn't the best of times, but if anything is going to cheer you, this meeting might. If we can't visit now, we'll have to reschedule two weeks out, because I —"

Eliza held up a weary hand. "If it's better

for you, then I'll be there." Just yesterday she'd decided to consider others' needs above her own. Apparently God was testing her resolve already.

She shuffled along with Mr. Raymond toward his buggy, then took his hand as she climbed the wheel while wrestling with her stiff mourning dress.

The second the buggy started rolling, she turned to look for Will. She should have said good-bye.

He was walking behind them, hands in his pockets, staring at his feet. He'd said nothing much since Dr. Forsythe had left the boardinghouse.

She slumped against the seat and held a hand to her head. She hadn't spoken much either, shocked that her friend was gone with so little warning. She prayed Will believed her when she'd said Mrs. Lightfoot's passing wasn't his fault, but since he felt responsible for his little sister's death and the other's awkward gait, he probably blamed himself for Irena's demise too.

God determined a man's days — not Will, not her. Even if she'd checked on Irena before turning in last night, that didn't mean this morning would have been different.

Though she might have been able to ease

her friend's passing.

Eliza swallowed hard against the lump in her throat and looked at her lap, trying to thwart the threatening tears with copious amounts of blinking. The happy faces and gleeful conversations of those traversing the streets beside them only seemed to darken the day.

Too soon, the team halted in front of Mr. Scottsmore's small brick house, his parlor serving as his law office. A few weeks ago she'd excitedly climbed his steps for advice on her business deal with Mr. Raymond. Now she'd rather be anywhere else.

Mr. Raymond helped her down and almost didn't let go of her hand when she tugged.

"I'll stay outside and wait. I can take you home afterward."

She shook her head without meeting his gaze. "No need. I've walked to the boarding-house in worse weather than this."

"This is no day to let a woman trudge the streets alone."

She attempted a smile but failed. The man wanted something from her, or Mr. Scottsmore, or both, but she hadn't the faintest notion what. "As you wish."

As the dark clouds on the horizon crept closer, they stood together in silence waiting for Mr. Scottsmore to arrive with Axel's mother. Irena had never talked about Mrs. Langston. Had they once been friends?

Mr. Raymond paced, allowing her to breathe easier.

She knew of no connection between the banker and Mrs. Lightfoot, excepting probably a bank account. Did he hope to inherit her reserves on the basis that Irena had no friends and his bank was in possession?

Mr. Scottsmore's buggy turned onto Apple Street, and he guided his team to a stop.

"My dear." Mrs. Langston stepped onto the ground, then extended her hands to Eliza. "I'm so sorry for your loss."

Was she the only person people would give their condolences to? Would Irena's son and husband return and mourn or simply drag themselves back to divvy up her property? To have lived life unloved . . . No wonder today had turned unseasonably cold. It was as if God were chastising them all.

"Come, ladies." Mr. Scottsmore unlocked his door, and they followed him inside.

Mr. Raymond looked as if he would tag along, but after he hit the top stair and the women passed in front of him, he clomped back down to the sidewalk.

The door slammed shut.

Mr. Scottsmore turned to face them, rubbing his hands together briskly. "That north wind is a mite chilly. Bet we'll have a good storm, and tomorrow it'll likely be hotter than the Fourth of July." He gestured for them to enter the parlor and take the chairs in front of his desk.

Eliza sat and turned to Mrs. Langston, but the woman looked as bewildered as she.

Mr. Scottsmore picked a file off his desk and slid out a crisp paper. "Mrs. Lightfoot was a wealthy woman, as you might have figured since she could remain in a practically empty boardinghouse for eight years. She did invest a good deal and such, but that doesn't involve you two. However, she left you ladies something —"

"Us?" Mrs. Langston looked to Eliza and shook her head. "I understand her leaving something to Eliza, but I've only had one or two conversations with the woman. Perhaps she meant someone else?"

He shrugged. "I can't interpret intention. Your name, however, is clearly written in the will she signed. You are Fannie Langston, are you not?"

"Of course I am."

"Then you are the beneficiary." He smiled a little. "She's left you the boardinghouse. When I return from my business trip to

Atchison, I'll have you sign everything. I wanted you to know before I left, so you can decide what to do with the property. That way, whether you choose to sell or not, I can help you with any additional paperwork based on the decisions you make."

"She gave me the boardinghouse?" Mrs. Langston squirmed on the edge of her seat, wringing her gloves. "Why?"

He glanced at Eliza. "I think she heard you needed some income."

Eliza bit her lip and didn't look at Mrs. Langston.

"I'm sorry I didn't talk to her more." Mrs. Langston settled against the back of her seat. "I don't deserve this."

Did Irena change her will to accommodate different people's needs whenever she heard of them? Had she realized this sickness would be her end? Something tightened in Eliza's throat. Why hadn't she done more for Irena? She'd been so busy with her store, and then just when she realized she should be caring more for Irena instead of focusing on herself . . .

"Miss Cantrell." Mr. Scottsmore turned to her. "You've been given the properties on the three hundred block on Main Street."

"My store?" She put a hand against the hollow of her neck. "She was the owner?"

419

"Yes, your store and the two shops abutting."

"The bakery and confectioner?"

"Those shops are yours as well. When I return, I'll need to know whether you want to continue renting those buildings or sell. I'll come back before their next payment is due, so it shouldn't be difficult to change things over, but I've already been paid for legal counsel to —"

Eliza waved her hand. "Mr. Scottsmore, don't bother yourself any longer." Right now was hardly the time to make decisions anyway. "I have no doubt you'll help things transition fairly and smoothly once you return."

"Thank you." He rose and glanced at the clock on his mantel. "Now if you don't mind, I must be at the depot within the hour. I'm packed, but with taking Mrs. Langston home, I've only just enough time."

"Let us not keep you any longer." Mrs. Langston stood. "If we have questions, they'll keep."

He tucked away his file and hastened to hold open the front door for them to exit.

Eliza stepped out of the office and blinked against the sun now peeking out from behind the clouds. Maybe rain wouldn't fall after all.

Mr. Raymond shot off the bottom stair where he and Will sat.

She glanced at Will, his smile the only thing remotely cheerful about him. Had he stopped by for her? Surely he had no idea what Irena had willed. She cut her eyes toward Mr. Raymond. But he would. He'd known Irena was her mysterious benefactor all along.

Why hadn't she figured out her backer was Irena?

She'd wanted everyone to see her as a capable businessperson despite her gender, and in all her pondering on who had let her the Five and Dime building for free, she'd never considered Mrs. Lightfoot . . . because she was a woman. Eliza grabbed the railing to keep from plopping in a miserable heap on the stair. How could she be so prejudiced?

"I'm assuming you've got good news?" Mr. Raymond wrung his hands furiously.

Did he think they'd lost the store?

Mrs. Langston stepped around her, a hand against her heart. "To think I didn't even know her."

Mr. Scottsmore lugged a trunk out his front door while Mrs. Langston clasped her hands together, smiling more than anyone should on a day like today. "She gave me the boardinghouse. *Me.*" She bit her lip. "That might not make Jedidiah happy, since our separation will become apparent, but maybe, just maybe, he might move with me."

Eliza grabbed Mrs. Langston's hand and looked her in the eye. "Don't let your husband walk all over you if he does. You don't deserve the way he's treating you."

"I haven't treated him well either." With a quick glance at Mr. Raymond, Mrs. Langston shook her head. "I'll take what the good Lord gives me, though I'd rather not have gotten it this way. The income couldn't have come at a better time." She lightly squeezed Eliza's hand. "I hope you'll still let me sell my clothing at your store, though."

Mr. Raymond's eyebrows hit his receding hairline.

"Of course. I have no need of that space for now. But if we ever do," she said, glancing at Mr. Raymond, "we can renegotiate then."

Mr. Scottsmore dashed into his home, came back out with a satchel, then locked the door. "Mrs. Langston, are you ready?"

"Yes." She turned to Eliza and gave her a hug. "Don't worry about a place to stay. I'll have to decide how to run the place before

I take on boarders. Feel free to stay until then. Though I'd be honored if you became my first tenant. I'm sure I'll enjoy your company as much as Mrs. Lightfoot did." After a final hug, she walked toward Mr. Scottsmore's buggy.

"Now, wait a minute." Mr. Raymond dashed over to the lawyer. "There was nothing in that will for me?"

Mr. Scottsmore's face turned blank. "No, sir. If so, I would've had you attend. These two ladies and Mrs. Lightfoot's family are the only ones privy to the will's contents. I'd suggest you not bully either woman into giving you information —"

"I don't bully." He turned to Eliza and stepped so close she had to tilt her chin to meet his gaze.

She squared her shoulders. "I'll tell you what you want to know, Mr. Raymond." He'd wanted her building so badly — what would he do when she told him? "The store is mine."

Mr. Raymond had started shaking his head before she'd finished speaking. "How can that be legal?" He turned to Mr. Scottsmore. "You know of the agreement between me and Mrs. Lightfoot. You witnessed it."

Mr. Scottsmore frowned. "I figured I'd

tell you when I got back. The contract simply states if Miss Cantrell managed to maintain a profitable business for five years with you as her supporter, then you'd have the opportunity to purchase Mrs. Light-foot's property. However that opportunity no longer exists."

Mr. Raymond's eyebrows furrowed, and he huffed. "Because she's dead."

"Unfortunately."

"Truly, unfortunate." Mr. Raymond seemed near tears. Though clearly mourning the brick edifice upon which he'd pinned his hopes — not Irena.

Eliza wanted to kick him in the shins as badly as she'd wanted to kick Axel on the train after he'd split her cheek. Couldn't Mr. Raymond think of anyone besides himself? She glanced at Will, whose face registered concern as he glanced between the two of them, but he'd yet to utter a word.

But how could she be angry with Mr. Raymond's distress? She would've felt the same a few days ago.

Mr. Scottsmore rubbed the bridge of his nose, his jerky movements indicating how much he desired to leave. "The building now belongs to Miss Cantrell, who may allow you to purchase the store, if that's her decision."

Mr. Raymond pierced her with his eyes.

She looked to Will. Her choice affected their future together — what little chance they had of one. A future she'd not considered until a few days ago. A future she might wreck with her next words.

Should she sell such a valuable income source to chase an attraction? Her mother had given up her aspirations for a man she'd loved, but in the end, she couldn't resist the theater's pull. Even two children hadn't kept her from running after an irresistible dream.

Since Eliza had turned nine, she'd wanted to own a store and had done everything in her power to acquire one — despite the terrible consequences of some not-very-well-thought-out plans. How could she relinquish her dream the moment God plopped it in her lap?

What if she couldn't focus on the family she and Will might one day have, but rather pined for her lost dreams? Would she be just as selfish as her own mother?

She couldn't do that to her children.

"No, Mr. Raymond, I don't intend to sell."

Mr. Raymond's chest filled with air, and his shoulders turned rigid.

Will stepped between them. "This isn't bad, Mr. Raymond. You still have a wonderful business partner. Eliza will make you both lots of money."

She swallowed against the lump in her throat. She didn't deserve Will's defense — didn't deserve him at all.

Turning his palms up in defeat, Mr. Raymond released a short puff of air. "She has as good a chance at succeeding as the shoemaker I financed last week. I wouldn't have helped her had I not believed she could pay off her loan, but I wanted the building." He looked toward Main Street as if he could see the coveted store.

Though Eliza kept her back stiff, her shoulders drooped a little. "Let's not become combatants over something we can't control. I'll still work hard, and you still own fifty percent of the company."

"But none of the building." Mr. Raymond turned a suddenly sparkling eye toward Mr. Scottsmore. "Wait, what about the shops on either side she owned?"

"He can't tell you, but I can." Eliza crossed her arms. "All three are mine."

His head bobbed in defeat, his shoulders slouched, and his chest seemed to cave in on itself. If a man could crumple while remaining standing, Mr. Raymond held the honor. "Then I have no worries about you defaulting. We'll be in business together for a good long time."

"Yes, we will, Mr. Raymond." She stuck out her hand, and thankfully, her partner shook it before excusing himself. She couldn't look at Will, though. She'd never leave Salt Flatts now, but he would. . . . The tears she'd pushed away on the ride over fought to return.

Mr. Scottsmore gave them both a small bow. "If you'll excuse me, I really need to leave. You can stop by to discuss everything with me once I return." With that, he hopped in beside Mrs. Langston and drove away.

Will's face sported neither a smile nor a frown, but a deep sadness permeated his eyes as he watched both buggies speed down the street. "I'm sorry you had a tiff with Mr. Raymond today of all days, but he'll get over it." He held out his arm, and she laced hers with his, relishing the feel of his sturdy dependableness.

They shuffled together toward the boardinghouse. Will believed in and cared for her. Possibly the only person that did, now that Mrs. Lightfoot had passed. "And here I'd thought Mr. Raymond believed in me."

"Of course he believes in you. The hope of obtaining a building wouldn't have lured him into a bad business deal. He ensured that by reserving a full half of your business."

The corner of her mouth twitched. Mr. Raymond was justified in having half since his money was at stake, but how like Will to twist that into meaning Mr. Raymond thought well of her.

At the boardinghouse porch, they stopped and stared at the windows. They seemed darker, despite the sunshine breaking through the clouds.

"I should have checked her more thoroughly earlier this week, exerted more effort to read through my books, at least gone to Dr. Forsythe to ask —"

"No, Will. Stop. I don't blame you for —" The sudden hot pain behind her eyes abraded her words. Tears spilled out despite blinking repeatedly. "I need to lie down."

Will released her arm reluctantly. "If you need me for anything, you'll let me know?"

She nodded halfheartedly, so he'd leave without asking more questions. No matter how badly she wanted to invite him inside to hold her while she cried, she'd never have the right to be curled up in his arms — not now that she'd made her choice. "Goodbye, Will."

Will leaned against the front counter. The

flurry of business created by his coupons had dissipated, leaving him time to think between customers again. Though thinking wasn't exactly welcome at the moment. He'd stayed up late last night reading, trying to figure out what he'd missed with Mrs. Lightfoot. When the words had clustered and mixed together so much he couldn't continue, his mind strayed to Eliza.

This week he'd walked her home from work each night. And each time she'd been unusually quiet and standoffish. He tried to convince himself she was simply grieving, but she likely realized as well as he that their chosen vocations made them incompatible.

What a generous gift Mrs. Lightfoot had given her, definitely something Eliza shouldn't surrender to slog after him while he cared for sick miners or bedded down in cattle towns farther west. Because that's what he'd most likely have to do to make a living doctoring, degree or not.

The door opened and Mrs. Graves bustled in. "Good afternoon, Will."

He hadn't the heart to talk about how not good the day was, and Nancy's mother had never been adept at making his day brighter. "Mrs. Graves."

"I've come to pay down on my account as you asked." She pulled out her purse. "And let you know how wonderful I'm feeling."

He did try to give her a smile. "I'm glad the powders are working."

"Oh, they did some, but Dr. Benning has assumed my care, and what he gave me yesterday has lifted my spirits overnight." She leaned closer to whisper. "And took care of that troublesome rash thing." She leaned back and studied him. "But I do still have your medical coupon, so could you come by to fix Mr. Graves' ingrown toenail? You could do that easy enough."

Right. Relegated to insignificant, not-so-pleasant medical drudgery . . . though that's all he should be doing without a medical degree.

"I hope you don't mind my going to Dr. Benning now." She shoved $3.50 toward him. "He's got your bedside manner and Dr. Forsythe's knowledge — the best of both in one."

And there went Will's hope of returning to Salt Flatts to doctor someday. "You need to do what's best for you, Mrs. Graves. But maybe you'd want to save the coupon for a future visit for your granddaughter?"

"Oh no, Dr. Benning will visit Millicent if necessary. Unless you want more involvement in that little girl's life, that is." Mrs. Graves' eyes twinkled. "Nancy wouldn't mind seeing more of you. What better way to get over past misunderstandings than to spend time together talking?"

Just what he needed. So now instead of listening to Mrs. Graves drone on about every imaginary symptom she'd acquired, he'd become her matchmaking project. Even after he'd told Nancy he wasn't looking to court anyone at the moment.

However, he'd honor his coupon. "How about I see Mr. Graves tomorrow night?"

"All right." She waved out the window at a lady passing by. "Are you going to the dance next week? It's for a good cause. Nancy hopes to see you there."

Or rather her mother did. He scratched at his arm. "I can't go."

She gave him that disappointed-parent look. "You should reconsider. Available young ladies aren't often available for long."

Thankfully, Mrs. Graves exited without waiting for him to reply.

Maybe he should get to know Dr. Benning. He wasn't opposed to working under a doctor who was qualified. Being an apprentice in Salt Flatts would be easier than going to medical school, but then he'd just be here longer, watching Eliza from afar.

If he couldn't stay and doctor here in Salt Flatts, where Eliza would now permanently reside, why stay, why toy with courting her? A single woman in this town would draw interest from many men if she wasn't claimed. What if she started sparking with someone he knew before he left?

Lynville Tate and Micah Otting walked through the door with big smiles on their faces.

Lynville. Will scowled. What if she took up with him?

"Why do you look so down in the mouth, William?" Lynville leaned against the counter. "I bet a twirl around the dance floor would cheer you right up. Don't you think so, Micah?"

Had Mrs. Graves prodded them inside to convince him to attend the dance with Nancy?

The butcher's eldest son smiled. "We're helping raise money for the Millers, so —"

"I'm afraid I don't have much to donate." He'd only managed to tuck a few bills back into his new leather pouch yesterday. He pulled a silver dollar from his pocket and handed it to the men. He couldn't afford to part with the coin, but the Millers certainly hadn't chosen to have lightning burn down their barn either.

"That's enough for one ticket." Lynville pulled a paper stub from his pocket. "But not for a first dance. Those go for five. As do the last dances."

"A ticket for a dance?" Since when had they gone back to dance cards and such?

"Well yes, I figured you'd heard. Sarah, Nancy, and Eliza volunteered to dance all night to raise money — that's what we're in charge of coordinating. So which girl you want to take a turn with?"

"Now hold on. Do you have these girls' permission to sell them for tickets?"

Lynville huffed like an affronted bull. "Of course we do. They were happy to oblige. Besides, we can't have you hogging Nancy. There's only so many single ladies in Salt Flatts."

Eliza had agreed to dance with other men all night long — after their two kisses last week? Will swallowed against his dry throat. "I don't like this."

Micah shrugged. "Of course you don't, but us other fellas don't exactly like how Nancy will probably turn us down at every dance, waiting for you to fall back in love with her, so now we get a shot to win her — and for a good cause too. What's a more fun way to donate than taking a girl for a spin?"

"Besides, Eliza's been walking around in a gloomy cloud lately." Lynville lifted his hat

433

a bit to scratch at his hairline. "She needs a man to cheer her up. If we hadn't concocted this paid dance thing, she'd have likely sat out or not come at all. And that's no way to get over Axel."

Right, because an ostracized bearded lady's death had nothing to do with Eliza's mood. He glared at Lynville. Not that he wanted the man to be sensitive enough to win Eliza's heart, but he ought to be a little more understanding. "How many dances are you selling?"

"Now, that's the spirit," Micah said, thumping the counter. "As many as we can. How many you in for?"

"Surely you mean to let them rest." He couldn't afford to keep Eliza dancing all night, and judging by Lynville's wide grin, he and Micah had reserved some tickets for themselves as compensation for setting things up.

"Of course we do." Micah winked. "We want them in a good mood for all their dances — otherwise it'd be no fun."

A night of watching every man in town dance with Eliza was not his idea of fun.

Micah flipped Will's silver dollar in the air. "So who do you want to dance with?"

"None of them." He rubbed at the ache emerging between his brows. "Just give the coin to the Millers."

"Well, aren't you a stick-in-the-mud." Micah pocketed the dollar. "You can't butt in on their dances though, since everyone else is paying."

"I don't plan on going." He couldn't imagine holding Eliza in his arms for a few agonizing minutes, then handing her over to someone else, knowing he couldn't take her back into his arms after the dance and keep her there forever.

"Suit yourself." Lynville tucked the ticket stubs back into his pocket. "See you around."

As soon as the men left, Will busied himself with straightening the shelves to avoid thinking about some stupid dance. However, the longer he fiddled with the merchandise, the harder it was to keep from running after Lynville and Micah and handing over every last coin in his purse.

Could he work for Eliza as her husband, knowing she couldn't quit to focus on mothering because he'd ruin the store while she was otherwise occupied?

Could he give up doctoring — what he'd believed all his life God wanted him to do?

And if Eliza traipsed west with him, she'd face hardships she'd never have to endure as a shop owner.

Were his feelings for Eliza enough to commit one of them to a life they didn't want?

Maybe his feelings, but not hers.

Years apart if he attended school would help them figure out whether being together was more important than their vocational dreams, but he wouldn't ask her to wait, preventing her from finding someone here. He sagged against the shelving. Lynville and Micah wouldn't have a hard time selling dance tickets for any of the ladies. Plenty of successful Salt Flatts men whose feet were firmly planted in Kansas soil wanted a wife.

The tinkle of the bell forced him up front.

Dr. Forsythe stood by the counter, wiping his forehead.

He ought to scan his medical volumes for a condition that caused exorbitant sweating. Perspiring that much couldn't be normal.

"Good, you're here."

Will scratched his temple. Dr. Forsythe rarely dropped in. "Can I help you find something?"

"Did you hear Kathleen Hampden had her baby late yesterday?"

"No." He smiled. "Did you catch the babe or did someone off the street get dragged in for that privilege?"

"Carl alone attended."

Will huffed with appreciation. Carl could

evidently come through when necessary.

Dr. Forsythe dragged himself to the chair by the checkers table and groaned as he lowered himself into the seat. "However, the baby won't survive."

Will blinked. "Did Carl do something wrong?" If he felt guilty over losing his baby sister, how terrible would Carl's pain be if he'd caused his son's or daughter's death?

"No, nothing Carl did. I've actually never seen anything like it before." Did a tear glisten in the doctor's eye or just sweat? Dr. Forsythe pulled out his rag again. "Benning has, but not quite like this . . ." Dr. Forsythe cleared his throat and looked far off. "You should attend Mrs. Hampden now."

Will lowered himself in the chair beside him. "If you and Dr. Benning don't know what to do, why do you think I would?"

"Of course you can't do anything, boy. It's the woman who thinks someone can. And for some reason you calm patients enough to listen to reason." He stuffed his handkerchief back into his pocket. "Though there's no need to reason with her. She'll find out soon enough."

Will moved his tongue around his suddenly dry mouth. "What's wrong with the baby?"

"I don't know." The man stood abruptly,

knocking a few checker pieces onto the floor. "I need to get to Fossil Creek." The man barreled through the other chairs and out the door.

If Dr. Forsythe wasn't lording his medical knowledge over Will by expounding on a patient's affliction in unsympathetic detail . . . something was terribly wrong.

Hurrying to the back for his medical box, Will tried to push away the dread of having to hold another dead baby in his arms.

Lord, let Forsythe and Benning be wrong. Because if they aren't, how can I help?

But he would help any way he could — his heart wouldn't allow him to do otherwise. He stopped at the front counter to get his keys.

The longer he stayed in Salt Flatts near Eliza, the more miserable he'd be later. No use asking Dr. Benning to take him on. He couldn't continue pursuing Eliza knowing they'd never be together, and the more attached he became, the more tempted he'd be to give up on his vocation.

Could he really go? Give up on Eliza and move away from his family forever? Eliza had only recently stolen his heart, so that ache would likely dull in time, but his parents and siblings? Nettie?

He'd be happy staying in Salt Flatts

forever . . . if it didn't require ignoring what God had for him to do — and that would be doctoring somehow.

He flipped the Closed sign. If only Axel would return so the store could be sold. Regardless of Axel's conviction, he'd probably come out with something — and then he could leave.

Maybe he should just leave the sign flipped over permanently and let Pa deal with things for him if Axel was captured, leave immediately for wherever people needed medical help desperately enough to retain an unlicensed doctor.

No. He couldn't do that to Pa.

Will rubbed his temples. He didn't want to live in Salt Flatts with Eliza any longer knowing he could never live with her there forever.

CHAPTER 22

The Hampdens' store was dark, but the doorknob turned without difficulty. Will expected the sounds of mourning or chaos, but a stillness blanketed the air.

A child talking in hushed tones grew louder as he threaded his way to the back room.

Amongst crates, merchandise, and other inventory clutter, Gretchen stacked blocks and Junior played with a carved horse. Eliza sat beside them on the floor, her arms wrapped around her knees, her face tense, eyes red and glistening.

She looked up. "Will?"

"Yes . . ." How it would hurt to converse with the woman he loved but now knew he'd never marry. To see her hurting but not hold her in his arms.

He cut his eyes toward the back stairwell but could hear nothing from the apartment above. "I assume their parents are upstairs?"

She nodded, her throat muscles struggling to swallow.

Squatting beside her, he ruffled Junior's hair, then smiled at Gretchen until they resumed playing. "It's that bad?" he whispered, taking in the lines surrounding the eyes she wouldn't turn toward him.

She nodded again. "They want me to take the children to the boardinghouse, but Junior doesn't want to go until they can kiss the baby . . . good-night." Her voice trailed off, her lip quivered. "We'll go eat soon and come back to say good-bye." A solitary tear escaped and ran down Eliza's face.

His heart ached to pull her against him, but he had to go upstairs. "Will you be all right?"

"Don't worry about me." She tucked a stray hair behind her ear, attempting a surreptitious wipe at the tear struggling down her cheek. "You need to help Kathleen."

"I don't know how much help I'll be, considering how I failed Mrs. Lightfoot."

"Don't." She shook her head fiercely. "It's not your medical knowledge or lack thereof they need." She hastily swiped at her eyelids, then ran her tongue across her lips as if to unseal them. "It's the peace that comes with you, Will. The other doctors leave when their weaknesses are exposed, but you know you're weak and seek God's help. And He's the only one able to do anything good right now."

"Then Kathleen doesn't need me, but rather God —"

"You won't abandon her like Dr. Forsythe or Dr. Benning did when they realized their inability." Eliza's intense whisper made Junior stop playing with his toy horse, but she overlooked the boy's troubled expression. "That's why she needs you."

"But Carl —"

"He needs you too." She rubbed at her nose and sniffed.

"Are you hurt, Liza?" Junior frowned as he pushed up off his stomach.

"No, child. My nose is just running." She turned wounded eyes toward Will. "I can't talk anymore, but I'll be praying. When we return, I'll see if it's all right to bring the children up." She gripped his arm. Was she trying to find strength or encourage him with a squeeze? Maybe both?

He reached over and smoothed the hair near her temple, refraining from placing a kiss against her hairline lest the gesture loose the tears rising in her eyes.

She turned away and scooped up a fallen block. "Let me help you, Gretchen." She cleared her throat — probably to rid her voice of its warble — and handed the baby the red rectangle. "We should go eat now." She hoisted Gretchen and held out her hand for Junior.

Will pulled in a steadying breath. He waved to the children as they left the storage room with Eliza, then forced himself toward the stairs.

He knocked on the three-room apartment at the top of the landing and announced himself. Nobody responded, so he opened the door a crack.

Carl sat in a chair, staring out a window that faced the brick wall across the alley. The waning afternoon light slanted into the room but didn't chase away the deep shadows or the heavy weight of sorrow infusing the apartment.

"Carl?" Will stepped inside.

The man limply turned his head, his eyes empty. He shrugged and returned his vacant gaze to the window.

"I'm here to see your wife and baby." He closed the door gently behind himself.

Carl nodded once but said nothing.

"Can I do anything for you?"

The man blinked, completely dry-eyed.

Without knowing what was wrong, how could he talk Carl through whatever grief had struck him dumb?

Will padded across wooden planks to the inner room where he'd delivered Gretchen, leaving his friend wrapped in the silence he seemed to want. The door stood slightly ajar, the low hum of a woman's voice filtering through. He gripped the doorknob, widening the crack a little. "May I come in?"

No answer but the low notes of "Brahms' Lullaby," though the tune was stilted and slightly off-key.

Propped against an iron headboard and pillows, Kathleen tore her eyes off the overly large bundle she clutched to her chest. Her face mirrored Eliza's. Eyes red and wet, lips pursed and trembling — yet she didn't stop humming the wooden notes except for a sharp intake of breath to start the refrain again.

Will slid inside, gripping the handle of his medical box tighter. "Is the baby already . . . gone?"

She shook her head. Her humming cut off abruptly. She laid the thick wad of bunting on her knees. Surely all those layers were overheating the babe. The room was positively stifling.

He cautiously sat on the edge of the bed. "Would you like to talk, have me examine the child, or . . . ?" He took a quick glance at the babe's face. Angel-like in sleep, deep red lips pressed firmly shut, a fall of dark lashes across healthy, fat cheeks. Beautiful for a newborn.

With shaky hands, she untangled the mess of blankets wrapped about the infant. "I suppose you should see him." She unlayered her son as if jostling him would disturb his slumber.

When the last swaddling sheet still lay tucked loosely about him, she stopped and sucked in a breath. "The doctors said they don't know what's wrong." Her hopeless gaze held more sadness than he'd ever seen. "Is there any way you might?"

"Probably not." He laid a hand atop hers.

She snatched her hand away. The baby whimpered at the sudden movement, but quickly quieted. "He hasn't nursed since last night, and he hasn't cried since Dr. Forsythe forced a syringe of something into him about two hours ago, but he must be hungry." Her crimson-rimmed eyes welled with unshed tears. She picked up the baby and held him out in front of her. "Be careful with him. I'm the reason he has a big sore on his back. I tried rubbing him to wake him enough to eat, but I didn't know." A sob escaped, which she quickly stifled. "I didn't know."

Will wrapped his large hands lightly around the baby and set the boy on his lap though the flannel swaddling was wet through. A perfect face belied everything they were telling him. He peeled away the light blue blanket, the child resting between his legs.

Beginning at the boy's upper thighs, massive red sores ran down to his ankles. His lower legs hardly had enough skin to cover the bone. Several blisters bubbled on top of large areas of his skin. The baby's little hands were balled up and shiny red. Will turned the baby gently over to assess the damage Kathleen assumed she'd caused. A small section of his skin had sheared off below his ribcage.

However, the worst thing seemed to be the fever and other signs of infection. How could he possibly keep a child with so many wounds free from contagion?

"Dr. Benning said he'd once seen a girl who had sores and blisters on her hands and face and other places — but not quite like this. Said she died when she was three." Kathleen's voice sounded hollow.

Rolling the infant over carefully, Will examined the boy's cherry red mouth. He coaxed the baby's lips apart with the soft pad of his finger. The interior of his lips was redder than the outside and quite puffy. Will tickled the corner of the babe's mouth for a few seconds, but the boy wasn't tempted to root.

"He's tried to eat, but the last time he cried I could see —" Kathleen pressed her lips together hard, which pushed up more tears — "that his mouth was . . . full of sores." She wadded a discarded blanket against her eyes and wiped harshly. A heartrending sob wrestled its way out of her chest, making it impossible for Will to keep his own eyes dry.

With such a fragile bundle in his lap he couldn't gather Kathleen to him. Why wasn't Carl in here? Will laid a hand on her shoulder until her tears subsided enough that he could shift his attention back to the baby.

He gently removed the soiled blanket from under the boy's chapped body and exchanged it for the one his mother had christened with tears. Though certain the child breathed, Will brought the boy's chest to his ear, the sluggish heartbeat and shallow breaths barely discernible over his mother's repressed weeping.

Dr. Forsythe must have administered some pain medication with the syringe Kathleen mentioned. Whatever he'd given the boy must account for his slumbering so peacefully.

With outstretched arms, Kathleen took her son back.

"Don't wrap him so warmly. I'll get something for his fever and open the windows and get some cool water on him. Wash his wounds." He roamed about the room getting things ready, but infection, wounds both internal and external, and a baby refusing to eat . . . no wonder Dr. Forsythe had given up.

The baby roused enough to cry nonstop while he rinsed his delicate body. Then Will ladled enough willow-bark tincture down the baby's sore throat to hopefully ease the boy's pain. He returned the baby to Kathleen, who held a cool cloth to his head and shushed him.

Once the baby fell back asleep — after only nursing for a few short minutes as Will cleaned up — Kathleen stared at his little face, caressing his eyebrow with her fingertip, tears silently rolling off her cheeks in quick succession.

Will sat down to take in the baby's face, so precious, so fragile, nothing more than a vapor that would linger for a little while and then vanish before they even knew him.

Kathleen let out a heavy sigh, harsh with

the sound of tears clogging her throat. "What did I do wrong?"

How could he let the same question that haunted him for years trouble her any longer? "If he'd had brown eyes instead of blue, you'd not blame yourself for producing the wrong colors. And if he were blind or lame, you'd not be at fault. Jesus once told the disciples a blind man was not born blind because of his parents' sin or his own."

"But why my baby?" Her voice was barely intelligible.

Will stared at the sleeping bundle, the face almost pristine enough to pretend nothing was wrong, then he turned to look out the small alley-side window.

Do you have any answer for me to give her?

A flicker of golden light raced across the windowsill before another cloud covered the sun. Nothing but the moan of relentless wind and Kathleen's shudders filled his ears.

"I don't know, Kathleen."

She stared at the boy in her arms. "How long does he have?"

"I don't know that either." No wonder Dr. Forsythe and Dr. Benning had left. How hard to have no answers. Absolutely none whatsoever. "But you should mother him every day he has left."

Though tears still coursed down her

cheeks, she restarted her strangled lullaby.

His presence unneeded for a while, Will rose and placed his medical box on the dresser. "I'm going to see Carl." The man ought to be in here sitting beside his wife, spending time with his short-lived son.

The suffocating dread that had shrouded him upon entering the apartment weighed heavier with each step he took toward his friend.

Will sat in the rocker beside him and fiddled with his hands between his knees. Surely Dr. Forsythe had briefed him about the baby's prognosis — and none too gently.

Carl sighed. "You don't have to say anything."

"I think I do. You ought to be in there with them."

"Just to watch my son die?"

"No, to love him every second he has left. To support your wife." Will stared out the window like Carl, afraid to look at his friend in case either of them turned teary-eyed. "You'll regret not staring into his perfect face for however long you have him. He's a fine-looking boy."

Carl only licked his lips and sniffed.

"I'm not going anywhere, Carl. I'll stay and pray and work to rid him of infection. If I can manage that, then maybe . . ."

Maybe what? Will pressed his lips together before promising anything. He'd never seen a baby missing skin; surely that wasn't curable. "When he gets fussy, I'll give him something to help him endure."

Carl ran his thumb along the lower lid of his suddenly wet eye. After a minute of sniffing and swiping at a few traitorous tears, he stood and marched to the bedroom door.

Once he disappeared, Will leaned back in his chair and blinked his hot eyelids, readying himself for a long night, and hours — or maybe days — of prayer ahead of him.

First Mrs. Lightfoot, now this baby. As soon as his time with Carl and Kathleen ended, he'd start devouring every medical text he could get his hands on. No matter how long it took him to read each page. No matter how much the words and letters refused to cooperate. Perhaps one day he'd have enough information crammed in his head to diagnose and treat people before they died — to give hope to a family instead of affirming their despair.

For a long time, I've known you wanted me to focus on caring for the sick, but I just couldn't trust you'd help me with everything else. I've been focusing on providing for myself instead of relying on you to get me the education I need, and look what distrust has gotten me.

In love with a woman he couldn't have, drowning in a business he couldn't manage, taken advantage of by a crook, and failing at medicine.

He let out a sad half laugh. He'd done well looking out for himself, all right.

But had he enough faith to put his insecurities aside and trust God to help him learn medicine? He ought to get over his pride and learn from whatever doctor was willing or just plain study more and trust God to give him enough to live on.

He glanced at the room where Kathleen's strangled lullaby continued, now accompanied by a grown man's sobs, which escalated with gut-wrenching intensity.

Deep down, was he simply afraid God would require more from him than he was willing to surrender?

Could he deal with sorrow this deep his entire life? Choose a profession that would bar the woman he loved from his future? Move to a town where he'd have no family to comfort him after shouldering someone else's unbearable suffering?

A crowd ten times larger than the five who'd come to Irena's funeral gathered in front of the newest little grave in the corner of Salt

Flatts' cemetery. Eliza held a handful of wild flowers and joined the men lining up to ceremoniously cover the child.

Kathleen, unable to staunch her crying, had left with Gretchen and Junior the minute her husband shoveled the first pile of dirt upon the small coffin. Carl stood stoically by the tiny hole as men took turns quietly laying more dirt upon the simple casket, then the shopkeeper shuffled away without saying a word.

After tossing her small handful of flowers upon the unnamed baby, she stepped back. The world swam as she attempted to maneuver over the uneven ground. Someone grabbed her upper arm; his smell and reassuring squeeze told her instantly who kept her from stumbling.

If only she could turn and bury herself in Will's arms. But she hadn't that right, and now that she owned Irena's stores, the only way they could be together was if Will worked for her — something she wouldn't ask him to do, not after watching him with the Hampdens this last week. She wouldn't hinder him from going to school whenever that opportunity arose so he could become the doctor he needed to be.

Will's hands disappeared from her arm, the hot summer breeze frigid against the skin he'd left bereft. She rubbed her arms and turned to see him fidgeting beside her.

What could he say? What could she say? Their sorrow was nothing like the Hampdens', and yet it was so deep she couldn't voice anything worthwhile.

Will touched her lightly on the shoulder, and his hand ran down her arm for an instant before he turned to head back toward the row of chairs where his entire family sat. Even little Nettie. Though death happened so often, should his little sisters be in attendance? Did they need to know God had chosen not to save a baby despite many, many prayers? That He allowed such misery?

Rachel beckoned to her, and her feet shuffled forward.

The moment she sat, the older woman's arm curled around her shoulders. Rachel's squeeze conveyed the same message as her son's solid grip — genuine concern *for her.* Not for themselves, but her.

After her mother left and her father died — what she wanted, where she'd go, what she'd do had been all she thought about. Had she ever truly focused on someone else until this terrible past week?

Reverend Finch scanned the crowd that remained, all silent except for the random bouts of sniffling. What on earth could he say that would do any good?

He cleared his throat, but said nothing.

The sniffling around Eliza turned into grim silence despite a pair of birds twittering happily in the branches of a nearby catalpa tree. Its sun-warmed white blooms covered the mourners with a thick floral perfume. Oh, why did the sky have to be terribly cheery blue? Eliza pulled another dry handkerchief from her pocket and wrung it in her hands.

Reverend Finch opened his Bible and stared at a page. His mouth opened silently a time or two before he cleared his throat again. "Today, let us not focus on this child's suffering, but rejoice that it has ended. Our lives cannot compare to what the child is now enjoying in the presence of God. So if you aren't longing for the time you too may leave this world and join him, let the words of Matthew stir you to have more sorrow at your own plight than this babe's.

" 'Fear not them which kill the body, but are not able to kill the soul: but rather fear him which is able to destroy both soul and body in hell.'

"As I stare at this tiny grave, the word *unfair* echoes through my mind. Unfair. Utterly unfair. I want to cry out for justice for this innocent. But then I think of myself and I *crave* injustice because I don't want God to punish me for what I know I've done wrong. I want to be with this innocent child in heaven though I am far from blameless."

The pastor picked up a handful of dirt. "Jesus said, 'I am the resurrection, and the life: he that believeth in me, though he were dead, yet shall he live.' God loved us enough to let Jesus pay for our sins so He can remain just and fair in allowing us to follow this innocent babe into heaven if we trust in Him." He let the dirt crumble between his fingers and drop into the tiny hole. "Each of you still have today to decide whether or not you'll meet this babe in glory — Christ is your only hope."

Without a closing prayer or another word, the pastor walked through the crowd touching shoulders, then departed with his wife on his arm. One by one, people stood to leave in silence.

The Stantons each gave Eliza a reassuring touch as they passed by, but she couldn't leave without praying her heart out. It didn't matter that she'd prayed all night — all week, really. Her tears flowed as she beseeched God. To aid Kathleen in finding the strength to mother two children while grieving her newborn's death. To help Carl continue running his business and caring for his wife while in mourning. To keep the town from turning their backs on God because He hadn't saved a defenseless child. And to bolster her fledgling selflessness as she attempted to perceive people's needs and fulfill them like Will did.

With no more words left in her heart, she looked up to find every makeshift bench empty.

Will took a seat beside her. "Can we see you home?"

"I thought everyone had gone." She looked over her shoulder. Will's family stood quietly around their wagon. "I didn't mean to keep you. Surely the children are antsy to leave."

"They're all right, and Nettie didn't want to leave you alone."

"You've got very special sisters."

He nodded, but his eyes didn't hold the same gleam they usually did when he talked about his siblings.

Nettie wriggled out of her ma's hold and toddled toward them, her peculiar walk pronounced in her rush to get to them. She climbed into Will's lap. "Why you and her so sad? The baby wif God."

Will slowly exhaled. "I *am* happy about that, but I'm still very, very sad."

"Watch me." She slipped out of his arms and with her hands extended, Nettie took one firm step devoid of her usual stagger, then another. She turned, and with heels firmly planted on the ground, took several more steps, her awkward gait hardly noticeable. "Did my walking good make you happy?"

His Adam's apple bobbed, and the second Nettie came within arm's reach, he smashed his sister against himself in a fierce hug. "It sure does, sugar." His low, hoarse voice made Eliza feel like an intruder, so she rose silently and headed to the others.

At the wagon, she hugged Rachel and the other two girls. "Thanks for waiting, but there's no need to inconvenience yourselves for me."

"At least let Will walk you home." Rachel's commanding voice indicated she wasn't asking.

She'd not even attempt to disobey. "Of course." Though her tears weren't yet dry, she managed a smile.

Walking away from the wagon to allow Will to say good-bye to his family, she leaned against the cemetery's stone wall and stared at Irena's grave shadowed by a solitary cedar.

The tears she'd thought she'd spent rose up again.

"I'm sorry I couldn't have done better by her." Will hitched a leg on the wall, his gaze lost somewhere on the horizon. "By either one, actually."

"Nonsense." Eliza fished out her last handkerchief and dabbed at her wet cheeks.

"So you don't blame me for thinking Irena was simply melancholic rather than about to die?"

"Don't make me say *nonsense* again." She pulled herself to sit atop the wall and waved at his little sisters as they went by. "Do you blame me? I could've attended her better, been there when she passed away, possibly gotten help in time to keep her alive."

He slouched against the wall, his hands in his pockets, staring at the grass at his feet.

"But it seems *you* blame you."

He remained silent.

"You're not God, you know."

"Obviously not. I can't foresee death or diagnose what's wrong with a baby, let alone save anybody."

"Didn't Dr. Forsythe say training your sister to walk on her heels was a waste of time?"

The happy look he'd given his little sister

after she showed off her walking didn't re-appear. "Nettie wouldn't need help if I hadn't been the one to deliver her."

"Or she might be dead if you hadn't delivered her. I'm sure every doctor has to deal with death and sorrow regularly like you've done the past two weeks. And what doctor would've bothered with your little sister's walk? But you helped her without having one of those fancy degrees." She nodded emphatically, as if the harder she moved her head the more he'd believe her — and the less painful it would be to tell him what they both already knew. "You should be a doctor, a practicing doctor."

"I can't compete with Forsythe and Benning."

No, he couldn't. But the alternative meant Will would leave and she'd stay behind. Sooner rather than later. She licked her lips, her throat suddenly tight. She knew what she had to say. Knew what lay between them. Asking a man to stick around for her when he was meant for greater things would be the ultimate selfish request, and she wasn't going to be selfish anymore.

So why were the words so hard to form? She'd never before had trouble blurting obvious truths. But then, she'd never dreamed of a future with a man the way she dreamed of one with Will. Had never received attention from a suitor of his caliber. Never been kissed by a man as if she were the loveliest thing he'd ever seen.

Were romantic notions and the pitter-patter of her heart worth dragging them both down? Her heart might say one thing one day and something different the next. Especially since the organ was torn in two different directions. She sucked in a deep breath. Yes, she'd force herself to utter the words, because they were best for Will, and for her.

"If you can't compete with Salt Flatts' doctors, then you should sell the store to get money for school. Let Axel pay his own debts and use the talent God's given you to glorify Him."

"Even if I could sell the store, it wouldn't do much good right now. But I've already decided to go." He rubbed at something imaginary on his hands. "Soon."

The pinprick of hope that he wouldn't leave faded into black. She pressed her eyes shut against a stubborn bout of moisture. She'd not be ridiculously emotional over some foolish dream that never had a chance. She had plenty to cry over as it was.

"I'll travel west — either find a doctor I respect who needs my help or a town so desperate they'll be thankful for any aid."

No school? Would people not view Will without a degree as one of the many quacks and snake-oil peddlers doctoring the desperate and gullible? He was so much better than that. Though of course he'd do a world of good as he was, and if God called him to doctor that way . . . but why wouldn't God equip him to do his best?

"Let me talk to Mr. Raymond." She should be able to get the banker to work something out. Though that would hurt because Will would leave that much faster . . . But he needed her help. What better way to prove her heart had changed than by being selfless when it truly cost her? "He'll help."

Will chucked a piece of the rock wall into the street. "I've tried him already. The man doesn't believe in me enough to bother."

If her heart had its say, she'd pretend she couldn't get him to school immediately and choose to believe the effort was indeed futile. But Will's heart was more worthy of getting what it wanted than hers.

She'd talk to Mr. Raymond tomorrow.

CHAPTER 23

The bank was locked up for the day, but Eliza knocked again. Harder.

Mr. Raymond appeared behind the window and turned the bolt. "We need to find another way for you to contact me after hours. Your pounding is unsettling after everyone's gone."

"A key, maybe?"

He laughed and waved her through the lobby. "How about inviting yourself over for supper? A woman without anyone to cook for ought to enjoy a free dinner."

A woman without anyone — she'd definitely remain that way if he agreed to her plan. "Maybe I'll do that."

He waited until she sat in his uncomfortable office chair before he perched on his desk. "So what urgent matter requires my attention this time?"

Should she butter him up first or ask right out? She cleared her throat. "We need more merchandise, and I know of an entire store's worth we could buy for cheap."

He scratched his chin, his gaze making her squirm. "You're talking about Mr. Stanton, aren't you?"

"Yes. He only needs enough to attend medical school. We'd be eliminating competition, building our inventory, and gaining his customers, along with —"

"Your sales model is a five-and-dime, Miss Cantrell. The majority of his stock costs well above that."

She refused to fidget under his intense glare. "So our store will be more of a discount shop for a while — bargains of any kind will draw customers. We can buy him out for way under value and put most everything upstairs with Mrs. Langston's ready-made clothing."

"An addition to the business I was neither asked about nor approved."

She held her chin up. No need to defend herself against a charitable decision. "Mrs. Langston's clothing will build our customer base, and we have plenty of floor space."

"*You* have floor space." His upper lip flinched.

How could losing a building he'd never possessed bother him so much? The store still served his purposes. "*We* still have floor space. I just happen to be the landlord."

"But now your business profit is my only gain, so I want the business run efficiently. Buying merchandise not suited to our store and taking up space is not smart."

She gripped the armrests to keep herself seated. This wasn't going as she'd envisioned. Why was he so stubborn? "But we'd be rid of competition."

He crossed his arms and cocked an eyebrow. "The Men's Emporium is not competition."

Not much, no. "We can't always be money hungry. This is a decent deal — everything for less than cost."

"Since you have no money, you're asking *me* to cough up the capital to buy him out . . . unless you're here to sell me your buildings so you can have your own capital?" The fake innocence in his eyes tempted her to roll her own.

She'd not even take out a loan against them. "No."

"Then he'll have to wait until you're able to purchase everything yourself." He crossed his ankles and gripped the desk's edge, leaning slightly forward. "Have you considered why you're asking me to put out money for little return?"

She refused to break eye contact despite

his close proximity. "Because it's the right thing to do."

"Is it? I'm not even sure I could buy the emporium until Axel returns. What about his portion? If the sheriff ever captures him, buying Will out for cheap would keep Axel's victims from recovering much."

Surely most of them no longer expected to get back anything. She didn't. "Axel might have the stolen money on him. The store might not even be affected."

"A thief hoarding his loot instead of spending it on booze and —" He cleared his throat and didn't quite look at her. "And um . . . other entertainments is highly unlikely. No, the real reason you're asking me to make a bad investment is because you've let your emotions undermine your reason. That's why most men feel partnering with a girl —"

"You mean woman." Narrowing her eyes seemed to have no effect on him.

He shrugged. "Emotions make for bad decisions. That's why Mr. Stanton makes them all the time. He can't keep his emotions at bay. Women are even more susceptible to following their feelings instead of their minds. Though even I'm not immune to foolish choices, since I fell victim when Mr. Stanton begged me to give you a chance." He crossed his arms and exhaled loudly. "Because I thought I'd get a building out of the deal."

Something heavy filled her gut. "Will asked you to give me the loan?"

She'd not impressed Mr. Raymond herself? He'd not been interested in her five-and-dime idea because he'd heard a smart, capable woman talking good business?

But of course Will had pled to Mr. Raymond on her behalf. That's what made him Will. And why she loved him — and couldn't have him. The man needed to spend the rest of his life helping others, not running a dead-end store.

"You have a good business plan, Miss Cantrell. I'll give you that. But you have to stick with it, and therefore . . ." He leaned closer still. "I'll not fork over capital to purchase the Men's Emporium."

He settled back against his desk and tugged at his necktie. "Could you make a profit? Yes. Is it worth tying up my assets? No. Next time you approach me with a business proposition, throw away your heart. I want to hear only well-reasoned plans from now on."

She turned away to look out the front window. If she looked at his hardened jaw any longer, she might shed an errant tear.

He was right, of course. She could easily list more reasons it wouldn't make good sense to buy Will out. But if she saw why a bad deal was worth the sacrifice, surely Mr. Raymond could. "If you recognized my ability to run a store, surely you can see Will needs to be a doctor."

"Of course he does." He sighed. "But I don't buy things out of pity. I don't fund charity cases."

She blinked. "I thought you were a church-going man."

He crossed his arms. "I don't see what that has to do with anything."

"Your tithes fund charity. Why not fund something that will benefit others just as much?"

"You didn't come here asking for a hand-out on behalf of Mr. Stanton."

"Would you consider my proposal if I did?"

The clock on the shelf announced the quarter hour. *Lord, let him agree.*

When the chimes fell silent, Mr. Raymond closed his eyes. "I'll decide where my money goes, Miss Cantrell. You worry about handling your own."

More badgering would only reduce her footing with him, if it hadn't already. "Then I'll not bother you further."

468

She stood, determined to escape the bank before the warmth behind her eyes exposed her as a sensitive female to her hardhearted partner.

Will flipped over in the bed upstairs and crumpled the pillow under his head, awaiting another roll of the thunder he thought had awoken him. The air hung thick. How would he get back to sleep? He couldn't shut out the wind blowing across his perspiring brow if he wanted to doze off again, and he was too tired to get up and close the windows, maybe if he could just count —

Thump. Thump. Thump.

Not thunder.

He rose and slipped on his trousers and shirt. He'd been awoken in the middle of the night a few times to tend a patient, but ever since Eliza had been robbed, he worried she'd get caught up in paperwork and forget her promise to go home at a decent hour. But surely she hadn't worked this late. It had to be near three. "Coming!" he yelled, shaking away the weariness. He buttoned his shirt, lit a lantern, and headed downstairs.

Through the front-door glass, a silhouette definitely too large to be Eliza was highlighted by the moonlight. Should he grab a firearm? But what thief boldly knocked on a door?

Still . . .

Swiping a hammer off a shelf, he approached slowly, hoping his eyes would adjust before he reached the door. "Who is it?"

"Jedidiah. Open up!"

Frowning, Will laid the hammer on the counter and unlocked the door. "What's wrong, Mr. Langston?"

"I shot my son." The man stumbled in, a limp body draped across his arms.

A lanky man with sunny-blond hair. "Axel." The tension in Will's muscles leaked into his stomach. Of all the ways he'd envisioned meeting Axel again, he'd not thought up this.

"I didn't recognize him in the dark. I told him to identify himself, but he grabbed my money box and hopped the counter. He should've told me who he was." Grief and tears choked the older man's voice as he stumbled forward. "I wouldn't have shot him."

Will guided the Langstons forward, steadying Jedidiah. The man needed to snap out of his shock to be of any assistance — if Axel even needed help . . . The way he hung flaccid in his father's arms didn't indicate a living man.

"Of course you wouldn't have, Mr. Langston. But what's done is done, and Axel should've answered you." He'd need Axel on the counter if he had to extract a bullet. After swiping off the papers and other items from the countertop, Will helped lay his former business partner down.

A groan emitted from Axel. Alive.

His heartbeat turned up a notch. He had work to do. "Light every lantern. I need to get some supplies." He raced upstairs and grabbed his box and a blanket.

When he returned, he cringed at Jedidiah's trembling hands attempting to seat a glass globe on a lantern. The man might set the place ablaze if he wasn't careful. Despite the wavering flames and a close call, Jedidiah soon surrounded the counter with light.

Will felt Axel's forehead. Clammy. "Where'd you shoot him?" He scanned his body — no blood.

"I don't know." Instead of coming over to help, Jedidiah lowered himself into a corner chair and buried his face in his hands.

If Axel had been running away from his father . . . Will rolled Axel onto his side. Blood stained his friend's lower back, so

471

Will gently turned him over onto his stomach.

Axel didn't moan, so he checked his pulse. Still there.

"When I went to him, he called me Pa —" Jedidiah let out a long shivering breath — "and said your name. But then nothing. I thought he was dead. Until he mumbled your name again."

Will pulled Axel's shirt from his waistband and found the bullet's entry hole right below his ribs.

Not much he could do for such a wound. Will closed his eyes tight and took a steadying breath. He'd hoped the bullet had grazed his side or maybe lodged in his hip, but in the gut? Will pressed the blanket against the seeping blood. He'd never extracted a bullet before. And what could he possibly do about the likely irreparable damage?

Will ran a hand through his hair. Maybe the bullet missed every organ. Could he hope for such a miracle?

"I know I've not been good to him. I know it. Because he's not mine." Jedidiah clamped his hands on the seat of his chair. "She spouted off our wedding vows knowing I'd be stuck with someone's by-blow."

Will's hands stilled. No wonder the Langstons had been at odds for so long. Mrs. Langston's illegitimate pregnancy would definitely explain why she'd been so desperate to marry Will's pa when he'd only written her one letter through a mail-order bride service so long ago. Had his ma and pa figured out Axel's illegitimacy and kept it from him?

He looked at Axel. Could he hear? Had he known?

"Maybe we should leave the confessions until after he pulls through." Not that Axel had much of a chance, but should his father's accusations be the last thing he heard before dying?

"Axel already done knows. I wanted to hurt her, and he was my weapon." Jedidiah folded his hands between his knees and groaned. "I'm the reason he's the criminal he is."

"We make our own choices, Mr. Langston." He moved a lamp closer. "You'll answer for yours. He'll answer for his." Axel's more likely sooner than later. Will laid out his instruments while keeping pressure on the wound.

"Uhhhh." Axel's face scrunched in agony against the hard wood. "Will?"

"Mr. Langston, come hold him down." Will poured a cup of whiskey and turned

Axel's head enough to drink. Thankfully, he swallowed whatever didn't spill out the side of his mouth.

Easing him down, Will beckoned for Jedidiah to stand near his son's head. "Talk to him." Whether Axel heard or not, if Jedidiah needed to tell him anything, the time was now.

"I got nothing to say. No excusing what I've done." He stood at his son's shoulders but didn't touch him. Didn't reach out to soothe him.

Axel's face was paler and sweatier than when he'd first arrived. He was fading.

Will clenched his teeth. What could he do to save him? "Maybe you should get Dr. Forsythe."

"Axel asked for you." Jedidiah looked at his son's back. "What could Forsythe do that you can't?"

Actually, Dr. Forsythe would declare him a fool for trying anything. Would summoning Dr. Benning be worth the hassle? Should he even attempt to help? He might put his friend through unnecessary pain, making his death even more excruciating.

He rubbed the bead on his ring, still facing inward. Most likely he'd not be turning it face out tonight.

Why was he up against death again so

soon? Why must he fight another battle he was certain to lose? How much longer should he tend the sick and dying without a degree behind his name? Someone more knowledgeable, more experienced, should be standing over Axel's body right now.

Why had Eliza thought him better than the other doctors?

Because he knew he was weak.

God, I know I don't have enough medical knowledge to help Axel. This has to be you.

Axel's hand slithered against the counter. "Don't." His eyes focused on someplace far away, his face tense with pain. "Don't want to live."

Will immobilized Axel's arm by wrapping the edge of the blanket around him. "It's not in my hands whether you live or die, but God's."

"You're not God, you know." Eliza's words had rankled the other day. Of course he didn't think he was God — he was far from that arrogant. He'd never take credit for his patients' recovery.

So why do you shoulder the blame for their deaths?

Will blinked. He rubbed his thumb against the little clay bead.

Axel would certainly be dead within a few hours if he did nothing.

But if he botched a procedure he'd never done, Axel could be dead in a few short minutes.

His friend's glassy eyes opened and locked onto him. "Don't bother." He coughed, a heavy hack, which spread the blood farther across the blanket. "Not worth it."

"Stop talking, son. You're making things worse." Jedidiah's face blanched as pale as his boy's.

Was Axel worth the effort? The Hampden baby did nothing but come into the world, afflicted with excruciating pain, and died for no explicable reason. Mrs. Lightfoot had been shunned for something she couldn't help, yet even in her death, she provided for Axel's mother.

Axel had stolen, lied, maimed, and possibly worse.

However, a man like that needed a chance to repent. Will picked up his bullet forceps. "Hold him down, Jedidiah."

CHAPTER 24

A gunshot startled Eliza awake. Where was she? Blinking against the darkness, she made out the ledger under her elbow. Her office. In town. A gunshot.

She held her breath, letting the seconds tick by as she stared at her office door. Nothing except darkness showed under the crack at the bottom. No night sounds. Nobody's breathing.

She rubbed at her tingling cheek, where the heel of her hand had left an indentation. Slowly, she rose from her chair and tiptoed to the door to listen. The clock read 2:45 in the dim lantern light. She couldn't walk home this late — especially if she'd indeed heard a gunshot.

Last she remembered, the time was nine o'clock. Her records hadn't cooperated as she'd searched for every possible way to scrimp enough to buy Will's property.

Opening the door a crack, she scanned

the store for intruders. All seemed quiet.

What should she do? She couldn't hide in her office knowing someone could be in trouble. Especially if that someone was Will.

But the irons she'd armed herself with last time would be worthless against a rifle.

Finding nothing else in the store worthy of throwing, she grabbed an iron anyway, stuffed a jackknife into her hidden pocket, and quietly pushed the front door open. Seeing no one on the street, she stepped outside.

What direction had the gunshot come from? Down the street, a pool of light spilled out onto the sidewalk from Will's store. Her heart crammed itself into her throat. Had Will heard the gunshot and turned on his lights? Surely no robber would use that many lamps to ransack a store . . . unless he'd killed the owner and was brash enough to think no one would notice.

The image of Will face-down in a pool of blood flickered in her imagination. She swallowed against the lump in her throat.

No. More likely he'd heard the gunshot too.

Please, God, let that be why his lights are on.

Watching for any movement or disturbances in the shadows, she scurried across the street, then crept along the sidewalk, iron clutched tight in her right fist. Once she reached Will's store, she flattened herself against the exterior wall until she came to the window's edge. Slowly, she leaned her head over to peep inside.

Will and Mr. Langston were standing beside a body on the counter.

She closed her eyes and let her head fall back against the wall. At least Will wasn't the one lying on the counter.

But a shooter — possibly a murderer — lurked somewhere outside Will's store. She clutched the iron tighter in her hand.

Return to the Five and Dime or go inside the Men's Emporium? Maybe she could assist Will, and with Mr. Langston there, who'd question her reputation?

Taking a quick breath of night air, she reached for the door handle and plunged inside, setting the door's bell to ringing.

Will turned. His gaze latched onto hers, his eyes wide as if panicked.

Should she not have come inside? "I heard a gunshot."

He glanced at the iron in her hand.

She tucked the makeshift weapon behind her. "I was worried."

"What's a woman doing wandering

around town at three in the morning?" Mr. Langston narrowed his eyes at her.

She tried not to grimace at his blood-covered shirtfront or sneer at him for his absurd suspicion. Surely he didn't think she was the shooter.

"I fell asleep doing paperwork. I probably shouldn't have left my store to investigate a gunshot, in case a killer was on the loose, but I didn't want to leave someone alone and hurt either."

Jedidiah let go of the man on the table and rubbed his forehead.

Will wiped his perspiring brow with his sleeve. "No killer. An accident."

"So it wasn't a robber?" She loosened her grip on the iron.

"Oh, it was definitely a robber." Will looked down at the body stretched out in front of him.

The man on the counter groaned, his face smashed against an impromptu pillow of a rolled-up bloody shirt. Blond hair . . . Mr. Langston . . .

Axel.

Her whole body trembled at the sight of the blood-soaked blankets and Will's crimson-stained hands. Jedidiah's face looked as lifeless as his son's. Would his son die tonight? Would Will lose another patient?

"So you were right — he came back." Oh, why had he returned? Axel was nothing but bad news for Will. And lying on a table dying? Even worse. How would Will get over a third death if he couldn't save Axel either? Especially since they'd been friends since childhood. "Who shot him?"

"I did." Jedidiah's groan held more agony than his son's. "I told him I'd shoot, but in the dark, I saw nothing but shadows. I didn't know it was him."

Will stared off into space, a long scissor-like thing seemingly forgotten in his hand.

She crossed over to him and laid her iron down. "What's wrong?"

"I just put him through a lot of pain, yet failed to find the bullet. I don't know if I should try again."

What might help him? "Do you want me to get one of the doctors?"

His shoulders slumped. "That'd probably be for the best. I shouldn't be attempting this. . . . I can't do anything worth —"

"Stop it." She pressed his face between her hands. "If anyone can, it's you. You're plenty capable on your own. You hear me?"

Will's jaw moved under her hands as he swallowed, but he nodded ever so slightly.

All her life, she'd searched for someone to believe in her. And though her father, brother, two fiancés, and her own business partner questioned her, Will believed in her without a doubt. He'd proved his faith by implementing her business suggestions to the letter, and he'd somehow convinced Mr. Raymond to partner with and loan her money — the exact thing she'd failed to do on Will's behalf only yesterday, despite all her business know-how.

He needed someone who believed in him the way he believed in her. "You're thoughtful, careful, smart, and resourceful. There's no better doctor in this county, no matter how many fancy papers hang on Forsythe's or Benning's walls." She rubbed the stubble on his jaw with her thumbs. "I've seen your mistakes, as you call them, and I still believe in you."

Axel groaned. "Ma?"

Jedidiah cleared his throat.

Eliza dropped her hands and felt her face flush. She'd forgotten anyone else was present. Dropping her chin, she took a step back.

"Ma?" Axel called again.

"I think Fannie should be here, in case . . ." Jedidiah's voice clogged.

Swallowing against the heartbeat in her throat, she took in Axel's ashen, sweaty face.

He might not live much longer. "I'll get her."

"Thank you." Will glanced between her and Axel. "Mrs. Langston's presence will help if he pulls through."

She shook her head. "No need to thank me."

Will selected a different instrument from his box. "You'd best hurry."

God, no matter the outcome, let him feel he did his best. "I'll pray for you."

"I'll need it." He licked his lips and swallowed, no longer looking at her, but at his patient — at least he was going to try.

She squeezed his arm and left lest she distract him from what he was meant to do.

Will finished scrubbing his hands the moment the downstairs doorbell jangled. He still needed to change his gory shirt before going down to talk to Mrs. Langston. He'd found the bullet on his second try, but whether he'd done anything useful remained unclear. Yet Axel was still breathing. Perhaps he had a chance.

Throwing on a clean shirt, Will buttoned up as he walked downstairs.

Fannie sat on a stool beside her son, running a fluttery hand across his forehead and down his cheek. "Is he sleeping?"

"He's passed out, Fannie." Jedidiah cowered in a shadowy corner.

Will raked a hand through his still bed-mussed hair. Should he tell Axel's mother that he might never wake again?

Fannie glared at her husband. "You never did give the boy a chance."

Eliza stood near the doorway, her arms crossed about her middle. He sighed, thankful she'd returned. Her nearness was the only thing that would make this morning bearable. Especially if he had to endure a marital spat over the unconscious body of his friend.

When he reached the end of the aisle, Fannie pulled her attention off her son and pierced him with teary eyes. "Will he live?"

The very question he'd asked himself every second he'd moved his bullet probe around Axel's gut. "I don't know. Depends on the internal damage." Which he'd likely exacerbated by removing the bullet. But the fact that Axel hadn't died during surgery was somewhat promising. If he woke up, he had a chance.

Will took a sidelong glance at Eliza, who gave him a reassuring smile. Extracting the bullet was all he could do. Would God let him save anybody this month? Eliza said she believed in him, but what if he never succeeded with anything but intermittent fevers and stomach upset?

What if he had no talent, but only a personality that made people believe in him? Guess that'd keep him dependent upon God — as he should be.

Fannie leaned closer to her son's ear. "Honey, can you hear me?"

Axel made no move or sound.

She looked around the store. "Can we put him somewhere more comfortable?"

"I'd like him to wake first." He rubbed his brow. Moving him would be the worst possible thing right now, and comfort wouldn't change the outcome. "I ought to inform the sheriff he's here."

"No!" Fannie stood but then plopped back into her chair. "I mean, of course he should be told, but what if something bad happens? Axel needs you."

Axel moaned.

"See?"

A moan? Would Axel actually make it? Will walked over and felt his friend's head. Warm. Could he give him something for a fever, or was he overmedicated already? Maybe he should open the front door to let the night air revive him.

Had he done something medically right?

"I'll get the sheriff." Jedidiah rose from

485

his chair. "I'll have to explain how things happened anyhow. And, well, he's a wanted man. . . ." He approached his wife, reaching out a hand to touch her shoulder, but stopped shy of doing so. "I'm sorry, Fannie."

She kept her back to him, staring vacantly at her son. "He was a good boy no matter how he was born. He didn't have to turn out like this."

Eliza took a step toward Jedidiah. "Since you're going past my store, I probably should return with you."

"Stay," Will blurted, then clamped his teeth onto his tongue and stopped himself from walking over and grabbing her. Maybe she needed sleep. He sure did. "If you can, that is."

"Please." Fannie motioned her over with her handkerchief.

Eliza dragged Jedidiah's seat next to Fannie as Axel's father left the store. "Why don't you nap, Will?" Her eyes blinked wearily, but the proud light shining in them made him hope Axel would pull through so he deserved her admiration. "We could wake you if something happens."

Exhaustion marred Eliza's brows, and shadows haunted her eyes. How could he sleep while she kept vigil next to the man who'd hurt her? "I'll be fine."

"He shouldn't leave. Axel's stirring." Fannie smoothed her son's hair away from his face and his eyelids twitched. "Darling, wake up. We know you've done wrong, but no one wants you to die. Not even your father."

Axel's lips curled into a faint sneer. "Pa." Even in unconsciousness, the animosity between father and son dripped from the single word. How might Axel have turned out if Jedidiah had loved and disciplined him and Fannie hadn't spoiled him?

But wait, he'd said something! Will opened his medical kit. Was there anything else he could give Axel to help him recover?

"Your pa's not here right now." His mother squeezed his hand between hers. "But I am. Why don't you wake up so I can see those pretty blues?"

Axel's eyelids fluttered, and Will held his breath. Had he saved someone after all?

His friend blinked several times and smacked his mouth, so Will carefully raised his head, placing a cup of water to his lips.

He swallowed and groaned. "I hurt."

"Of course you do." Will shook his head, but the smile on his lips grew. Some in town might wish he'd let Axel bleed to death, but perhaps with correction and prayer Axel might live long enough to turn his life around. "I'll give you more laudanum."

"No." He turned pain-filled eyes toward his mother. "I should've helped more." His voice was feathery soft, making the three of them lean closer to hear. "I tried to get enough."

She patted his cheek. "You helped me plenty, and Miss Cantrell here is letting me sell my clothing at her store. I've already earned more for my clothes there than at the seamstress's."

Will shot a curious glance at Eliza, who dropped her gaze to her lap.

If Fannie was making more than she had with the seamstress, Eliza couldn't be making much.

Business-wise that didn't make sense.

He smiled.

"More importantly, I own the boarding-house now, so don't you worry. Fess up to your sins and take your punishment. No need to gallivant around doing whatever you've been doing anymore. You and I'll make it together."

Will stepped closer. "Where's the money you've stolen? If you turn that over to the sheriff, the judge might be lenient and you can see your mother again sooner than you think." Not that Axel could live in this town

488

again, but he'd not bother mentioning that detail.

Axel tried to shake his head. "Lousy gamblers . . . cornered me . . . took everything."

So the thief got robbed? "Then what about the rest? If you told the judge where —"

"Don't know. Not mine." He reached for his mother's hand. "Behind . . . post office . . . wagon. Supplies." His head lolled. "Take them."

He had a wagon parked out back? He'd been leaving? How would that have helped his mother? "What about Nan—" Will glanced at Eliza. "What about my grandmother's ring?"

"Wagon. Just trying to get enough . . . to leave." He coughed, then groaned with pain. "Sorry."

"For the ring?" Will measured a strong dose of medicine. Axel might not want any, but the less pain he felt, the less wriggling he'd do. And right now, he needed him as still as possible — he didn't look right.

"For being no good. You always believed me better."

"But you can be good, Axel." Fannie held out her hand for the laudanum and helped him drink. "You can start over."

Axel worked hard to swallow. After his mother laid him back down, he peered over at Will with murky eyes. "Not your fault."

"What's not my fault?"

"Death." Axel's rattling voice set Will's teeth on edge. Axel closed his eyes and lay quiet.

He jostled him.

Axel's eyes struggled to lift, slammed shut, then widened again like a drunk's trying to stay awake.

"You're not going to die." Will took in the man's suddenly stricken face, then noted the blood seeping out on the counter below his torso. "Stop moving around so much." He grabbed a handful of rags and butted them against the blood-soaked bandaging.

"I'm sorry, Ma." The words slurred through his fast-graying lips.

"You're forgiven. You'll be all right." She smiled at him and caressed his cheek, but the tears streaming down her cheeks belied her words.

Axel's eyes stopped blinking. No. He couldn't just wake up and then die!

Will searched for his pulse and exhaled. "His heartbeat's weak, but it's because of the bleeding. I need to stop the bleeding." He scrambled to the back room and grabbed a jar of ground yarrow. Why hadn't he packed the wound before wrapping him? He'd used carbolic acid, sure, but he should've used everything at his disposal. Prevented this from happening.

Returning to the counter, he pulled out a pair of scissors to cut through the strips tied tight around Axel's torso.

Eliza's hand gripped his. "Will?"

He tried to extract his hand, but she held on tight. The sad droop of her lips and languid, glistening eyes wouldn't discourage him. "He'll be fine."

"Will."

He looked at Axel. His eyes vacant. His labored breathing halted.

Fannie had placed her head on Axel's chest. A wet spot grew across her son's heart as she whimpered.

He slammed his fist on the counter. "No." But the loud noise failed to rouse Axel.

And neither did the door bell. Jedidiah rushed in with Dr. Forsythe behind him. "I couldn't find the sheriff, but I figured the doctor should come."

Too late. Will sank against the counter. He should have never listened to Axel and Jedidiah — he should have carried him straight to Forsythe or Benning.

The doctor cleared his throat. "There's nothing for me to do."

"You could make sure that whatever Will did was —" Jedidiah halted, his eyes glued to his son's face. A face unmistakably without pain.

"What did you do, son?" Dr. Forsythe's voice sounded far away.

What had he done? "I killed him."

"You did not," Eliza spat. She turned to the doctor. "What would you have done on a bullet wound that —" She turned to Will. "What all did it hit?"

"I don't know. The bullet lodged somewhere in his intestines I think, but I got —"

"A gutshot with intestinal damage?" Dr. Forsythe shook his head. "Jedidiah, the boy was lost. The fact that Will tried anything is because he's a saint. You didn't need me."

Mrs. Langston's whimpering grew louder.

How many saints never performed a miracle? "I'm not a saint."

"That you bothered with him tells me you really ought to be a doctor. But one day you'll tire of it." Dr. Forsythe yawned. "If you ever decide to get off your duff and go to school, I'll write you a recommendation. Maybe get you a good doctor to work under after lectures."

School? He didn't dare dream of that any longer. "I'll never get to school, sir."

"Humpf. Well, I know you don't want to

work with me again, and Benning doesn't want to take on anyone for a while — I've asked — so . . ." He rubbed one of his eyes with a fist. "I know a few army surgeons from the war. If you want to sign on at a fort, I'll write to a few post surgeons and see if one could take you on as an assistant contract surgeon."

"Really?" Could he make that happen?

He shrugged. "Why not? Now, if you'll excuse me, I'm going back to bed. I got in late. Some woman's birthing just went on and on for hours." He rolled his eyes and yawned again. "Will can take care of his own dead patients."

Dr. Forsythe trudged out the door without a word to the grieving parents. Fannie's crying turned into unabashed wailing. Jedidiah sat down beside her and wrapped his arm around her shoulders.

Leaving them to grieve without an audience would probably be best. He beckoned for Eliza to follow him outside.

At the store's porch railing, he slumped against a post. The orange hues of a new day imbued the horizon, erasing the evidence of Axel's last night.

"Are you all right?" Eliza moved closer and placed a heavy hand on his arm.

He swallowed but could only shake his

head. Another loss, but a compliment from Forsythe, regardless.

"Are you going to go?"

"Go?"

"Since Axel's gone, you could sell the store and probably pocket a profit after giving the Langstons their share."

"You think so?" She wanted him to go? But he'd thought . . . He rubbed at the ache in his temples.

She stared at the darker horizon. "An apprenticeship at a fort would allow you to keep the profit from the sale for the thin times."

Back to business. How he wished he didn't have to think about the store anymore — how he wished she didn't care. "Someone still has to buy it." But why stay any longer? Did he trust God to provide or not?

"I don't have enough."

"I didn't mean to ask you to buy it." He'd rather ask her to join him, wherever he went, but a woman thinking of buying him out was not a woman in love. And only a woman desperately in love would follow him west with no guarantee he could provide for her adequately.

She hugged a porch column, still staring off into the distance. "That's what I was doing when I fell asleep — calculating my ability to buy you out. But I couldn't figure a way to do it anytime soon without huge risk."

He rubbed a hand across his brows. What was sadder? Another death on his hands or the woman he loved trying to find a way to help him leave faster? She didn't need to know he probably couldn't have sold it to her before today anyway. "Thanks, but I could just give you the store."

She gave him that look — the scrunched eyes and the twisted lip — that indicated he'd said something she couldn't fathom. "Giving me your store doesn't help you buy supplies."

"I can take stuff from the store."

"You need money too. You'll find a buyer, I'm sure." Eliza stepped off the sidewalk and into the street, her arms tight around her middle. "Walk me back?"

Before he made it off the porch, she'd walked away. Striding to catch up, he ignored the pull to touch her. He might beg her to ask him to stay if he did.

She glanced toward him. The tears in her eyes caught him up short.

"Are you all right?"

"No." She wiped at her eyes furiously. "I just realized someone's son and friend died, and all I'm thinking about is how that affects *me.*" Her voice broke on the last word. "When did I become so selfish?"

But she wasn't selfish. "You left the safety of your store armed with only an iron to help an unknown victim."

She glanced at her empty hand. He'd return the implement to her tomorrow.

"You gave Mrs. Langston a deal selling clothing. You helped me with the Men's Emporium the day you arrived without complaining and without any pay."

"No, Will. I did none of those things out of goodness." She walked up the exterior glass hallway of her store and opened her door. "I've done fairly well for myself, haven't I?"

Why had she changed topics? "Who wouldn't have expected you to do well? You're good at business."

She huffed a laugh. "I certainly got what I wanted." She swiped at a tear wandering down her cheek and swung the door wide open. "Alone with everything I ever wanted."

"You don't want to be alone?" Was the store not enough for her anymore?

She swallowed hard. "I deserve to be." Leaving him without a good-bye, she marched inside.

He laid a hand on the knob for a second

but let it slide off.

She didn't have to be alone, but she couldn't have both him and the Five and Dime. And if he asked her to give it up . . . No. He couldn't do that. She'd worked too hard for it, had wanted it for too long. Maybe she would say yes if he proposed. Maybe, just maybe, she'd pick him over her beloved store, but for how long could he make her happy? How many days and weeks and months would it take of her living in an army fort before she grew tired of . . .

He couldn't ask her to marry him. He didn't need to add the memory of her turning him down to take with him out west.

In time, some other man would win her heart without requiring her to give up the Five and Dime.

As Will strode toward the Hampdens' store, Jonesey waved at him from across the street. His jolly, clear face was at least something sunshiny this week. Storm clouds had rolled in within hours of Axel's death and lingered for days. No rain had fallen since he'd awoken, but the sky appeared grayer than normal for five in the afternoon.

"Think the rain will stay away for the Millers' charity dance?" Jonesey bounded up onto the sidewalk.

"Clouds seem to be breaking up out east." He didn't care if the rain stayed away or not. Watching Eliza glide in and out of the arms of eligible men would be nothing short of torture. He wasn't going to the dance.

"I'm sorry about Axel." Jonesey looked to the Hampdens' second-story windows. "And the baby."

What could he say? Sympathy for him wasn't necessary.

"I hear you're leaving soon?"

Will nodded.

"Then I'm glad I caught you before you left." Jonesey shoved his hands into his back pockets. "I wanted to tell you that you were right."

He snorted. "Now, that would make my mother's day, but I have no idea what you're talking about."

"The medicine and God stuff. I'll be going to church on Sunday."

"Good." He slapped Jonesey on the back. "Hope you keep going."

"I'll find someone to drag me in if I don't." He scuffed his boot on the wooden planks. "I didn't want to admit my failures to you, let alone God. I blamed Lucinda for everything without repenting of my own sins. Stupid, eh?"

Will only smiled. Jonesey didn't need to

hear his answer.

"Just wish I hadn't taken so long to admit medicine wouldn't fix my soul."

"Don't be so hard on yourself." Will jiggled his shoulder. "You figured things out."

"Everyone else in my life has turned their back on me, except you." Jonesey's shoulders slacked. "You worked a miracle, so I thought I'd ask you to pray for another."

"I'm obviously not responsible for miracles, but I can pray."

Jonesey swallowed but looked away. "I want my wife back."

"That would be a miracle." Hadn't Jonesey said he didn't know where Lucinda was? She'd been gone for six years. She could be dead and he'd never know.

"At least I want her to write me, so I can ask her forgiveness, but if she refuses to forgive me, can you pray I don't retreat from life again?" Jonesey scratched at the hair behind his ear. "If you hadn't checked on me every now and then over these past six years . . . I might've ended everything."

He'd been suicidal? How had he missed that? He should have paid more attention. "I'm relieved you didn't."

"I didn't because I knew you'd care." Jonesey cleared his throat. "The other doctors abandoned me once they realized the problems were all in my head." He glanced at the store's upstairs apartment again. "I bet you're the only one checking on Mrs. Hampden."

Will shrugged. A doctor ought to follow up on his patients.

"God knows the Hampdens need you, as much as I needed you." He smiled. "Just wanted to tell you thanks."

"You're welcome, and I'll certainly pray for you."

"Good luck out west." Jonesey shook his hand, then whistled as he walked away.

Will stared at his retreating back. Something he'd done had saved a life? Maybe not in the normal doctor way, but saving someone from suicide had to count for something. He looked at the windows above the Hampdens' store. Was that why he felt compelled to come here daily despite having nothing medically worth checking on — was Kathleen feeling that low?

Did God care less about his caring for the body and more about his ministering to the soul? He'd thought caring for souls belonged to preachers, but maybe God could use a lay doctor like He used a lay minister.

Will forged into the busy mercantile and waved at Carl, who was counting spools of thread. The man nodded, but his face was so downcast he'd probably not crack a smile again for a long time.

Without bothering to ask for permission, Will went into the back room, climbed the stairs, and knocked.

"Come in." Kathleen's monotone voice made him frown.

Only the joy of the Lord would improve Kathleen's disposition . . . in time. Since he was leaving Kansas this week after he got everything settled, he ought to ask Eliza to continue the visits until Kathleen regained her smile. Could he drag himself into the Five and Dime before he left? Could his heart take seeing her one last time?

"Hello, Mrs. Hampden." He didn't bother asking how she felt. The grim lines around her mouth and eyes as she watched her children playing on the floor told him the whole story.

"Have a seat." She pointed to the chair across from her in the little front room. "I was hoping not to see you today."

"Why not?" Was dropping by so often making things worse?

"A young man like you should be preparing for the dance instead of sitting with me. Tell me you've bought a ticket to dance with Eliza."

"I'm not going." He gritted his teeth and crossed his arms. He wasn't there to talk about the dance. "I'm here to see how you're doing, not talk about me."

"Well, I'm talking about you. That girl likes you, and you ought to take a turn with her on the dance floor."

He rolled his eyes. She was as meddlesome as his mother. "I'm leaving Kansas, Mrs. Hampden." Why prolong the agony?

"I know. Eliza told me. Are you sure now's the best time to go?"

He rubbed at his eyes. Questions like these had stolen enough of his sleep. Did he have to debate this aloud all over again? "God's pushing me to be a doctor on His terms, not mine. I can't ignore His direction, especially if Eliza . . . doesn't love me enough to go with." If she loved him at all.

"It's one dance, Will, and it's not like you to ignore someone's feelings." A slight smile deepened the wrinkles about her mouth. "Don't you want a good memory to part on? Give her a dance to remember?"

If he held Eliza in his arms for one second, he might not go where God wanted him to. "I don't want a turn with her."

He wanted every turn.

"I heard Dr. Benning bought two tickets. Lynville Tate three."

"How do you know this?"

"Eliza told me." Kathleen leaned forward, eyebrows cocked in question. "And when I asked her how many you bought, she couldn't look me in the eyes. She couldn't understand why you didn't buy at least one."

He groaned and shoved his hands through his hair. Didn't she understand? He couldn't dance with Eliza just once.

But how could he leave her thinking he didn't want to dance with her at all?

Chapter 25

Eliza sat under the church eaves picking at her smoked pork as the crowd laughed and mingled around her. Silly to hide, but the prospect of having to dance with anyone but Will made her slink into the shadows farther. If she hadn't obligated herself, she'd have stayed home.

With Irena gone, Kathleen refusing to leave her room, and Will avoiding her, how could she get through the evening?

She pressed her eyelids together to keep from crying. Why hadn't he come by to see her this past week? She'd overheard the livery owner discussing his imminent departure, so why not say good-bye here? Dance with her once?

No. She should be thankful he wouldn't put her through such torture.

She straightened and set her lips in a firm line. Salt Flatts was where she must find contentment, where she wanted to be, where she'd done quite well for herself.

Except for being utterly alone.

Men and women congregated around the dance floor, and the band busily tuned their instruments. She couldn't pick at her meal much longer before having to step out there, plaster a smile on her face, and pretend everything was grand.

Could she hand the Millers twice the amount men had paid for her tickets and leave?

But that wouldn't help her make friends. She pulled the lengthy dance list out from under her plate and stared at the long column of names. How would she last all night? Though with this many men taking a turn with her, she should be able to find one who'd befriend her . . . believe in her as Will did.

Who could doubt her business acumen now that she had property and her profits were growing?

The names ran together because none were William Stanton, the man who'd believed in her before she had anything.

She crumpled the list and dipped her head. Did her mother stand in front of an audience with a false smile pinned on her lips? Did she recite her lines with the loss of loved ones lodged so tight in her chest it hurt to breathe?

Did the Five and Dime matter with Will no longer a block away?

"Miss Cantrell?"

She opened her eyes. The unfamiliar young man looking down on her smiled as if he'd struck gold. Blond, muscular, and better looking than either of her fiancés had been.

But he wasn't Will.

"The music's started, and I do believe I have the first dance." He stood waiting, his smile more charming than most.

And she accepted his hand. Because that's what she had to do.

Lynville Tate swung Eliza around in a fast gallop, preventing Will from cutting in. The music soon died, and Micah moved forward to capture her hand.

Will tugged on his vest and waited for them to waltz past.

Her printed calico skirt twirled round and round, closer and closer. She offered her partner a halfhearted smile despite the overly handsome grin Micah sported.

Will stepped forward, bumping them to a halt. "Mind if I cut?"

Eliza's head snapped in his direction, her

cheeks beautifully pink, her full lips slightly parted.

"Yes, I do." Micah tried to waltz past him, but Will stepped right into the middle of his path.

Micah looked him up and down as if he stank. "You need to talk to Lynville if you want to buy in. Otherwise there're other girls who aren't dancing to raise money."

Will sidestepped a dancing couple about to push him off the floor. "How about I don't require payment for helping you get rid of that terrible case of —"

"All right already." Micah scrunched his nose as if he'd caught a whiff of something infinitely worse.

Will wouldn't have gone into too much detail — a doctor kept confidences — but it was rather difficult not to smirk at the young man's panicked expression.

Micah dragged Eliza out of the swirling crowd that had bunched up behind them. "But I only bought one dance with her, and I thought you didn't charge for visits."

"I think Dr. Forsythe normally charges five dollars for a case like yours, but I'll take a dollar."

"Then, sure." He pushed Eliza forward.

Will took her against him and pulled her back into formation. Her hands warmed his, her perfumed hair tempting him to pull her in closer. But she didn't belong tucked into his arms, no matter how perfectly she'd fit.

"You promised not to marry one of the butcher's sons." Scraping out the words left his throat raw.

"I hardly call a paid dance a step toward engagement." Eliza tripped, so he gripped her tighter, her skirts wrapping around his legs. Too close for dancing properly, but he couldn't loosen his hold.

She nearly stumbled again, her feet tripping over his. "I thought you weren't coming."

"I wasn't."

He fought against releasing her when they had to exchange partners for a turn about the floor, but they were soon separated.

Oh, why had he come? Seeing her in the arms of a stranger was worse than he'd imagined. He didn't know who he held in his arms at the moment, but thankfully, the seconds until he reclaimed Eliza weren't interminable. When she came back around, his hands latched onto her waist and pulled her too close.

They bumped into the couple in front of them, so he forced himself to slow down. *Get ahold of yourself, Stanton. Don't drag her away. . . .*

As soon as they reached the stage, he'd have to release her again. He'd done so once, had done so before coming to the dance. He could do it again.

But the feel of her in his arms, under his palms, beneath his skin. He shook his head.

He couldn't do it again.

Eliza tried to pull away to exchange partners, but his hand — and his heart — wouldn't comply. The couple behind them faltered.

"You're supposed to let me go." She looked over her shoulder at the elderly man waiting with an open hand in ·the middle of the pattern.

"It's harder than I thought."

She swallowed and tugged on her hand.

He released her but simply stood amidst the sea of dancers waiting for Eliza to return.

"What's wrong with you? You're messing us all up!" A pretty little brunette not much older than Ambrose glared at him, her brown eyes flashing indignation.

"Everything." He turned to look at her. "Everything's wrong." His not going to school, the death of so many friends, moving away from family, the woman who made him lovesick dancing in the arms of another man.

The brunette huffed and tapped her foot impatiently as they waited for what must have been her grandfather to return with Eliza. Several couples staggered around them as they remained unmoving in the middle of the floor.

Eliza gave the young girl an apologetic shrug after leaving the older man's arms. She hooked her arm into Will's. "You're not making this easy."

"Neither are you."

After being bumped from behind, she pulled him hard to the left. "Dance, Will."

He waltzed her around the dance floor, his gaze roaming every inch of her face to the detriment of a random dancer's feet and Eliza's as well.

But she didn't complain.

Then the music stopped, and blessedly, so did they.

She cocked her head at him, her chest heaving, likely more with bewilderment than exertion.

"Howdy, Miss Cantrell." A squat little farmer who lived near his parents sidled up beside them and pulled off his hat. "My name's Larry Putnam. I believe I'm next."

"Mr. Putnam." Will pulled Eliza behind him and faced the other man. "You have forty dollars of store credit you owe me."

Larry blinked at him, his face tightening. "You know last year's crops did poorly, and you weren't none too worried about it afore." He scanned the dance floor. "And this ain't the time to talk business."

Will held up his index finger. "For every ticket you get a man to surrender for taking his turn with Eliza, I'll take two dollars off your account."

The caller announced a quadrille, and the other dancers moved to pair up, but he didn't move or let go of Eliza's hand.

Her breath near the back of his neck tickled his skin. "What does it matter since —"

He squeezed her hand, and she quieted.

Larry smoothed his beard with a thoughtful hand. "But how do I do that? I haven't got the money."

Will narrowed his eyes. He'd certainly found a dollar to dance with Eliza. "Barter."

"I'll see what I can do." Larry glanced at Eliza before marching away.

Will hastily pulled her into a square with an unpaired couple.

"I thought you planned to sell the store and go west?" Eliza frowned.

Would she beg him not to? "Doesn't hurt to get the books into better shape beforehand."

She kept silent as they made a few passes between partners, but neither of them danced well at all. Eliza completely flubbed her steps with another partner and blew out a breath when that man shoved her back into Will's arms. After another awkward turn on the floor, she sagged. "I don't want to dance anymore."

Spinning her out of formation, Will threaded their way off the dance floor. "I don't want to dance at all."

"Then why are you here?" Her eyelashes blinked overly quick. She looked about as if afraid everyone was staring at them — which many were.

"I don't know." He swallowed.

No, he did know.

Dragging her farther out of earshot and away from prying eyes, he faced her beneath the shade of a tree on the other side of the church. "I can't offer you anything, Eliza. Nothing you want, anyway. My store's in shambles, I'm a terrible business partner, and I'm about to wander off to I don't even know where, with no guarantee I can keep myself fed or clothed or even healthy."

Her fingers slipped from his. "Why would you offer me anything?"

Why indeed? He pulled a strip of bark off the trunk. "I've got nothing you need —

you're worth more than I have."

She wrapped her arms about herself. "I'm not worth that much, Will. I'm selfish, and . . . and I'm not good."

"You're braver than anyone I've ever known. You're smart, determined, resilient." He took one of her hands, staring at the leafy shadows playing across her knuckles as he rubbed his thumb over her soft skin. "You'll do better with your Five and Dime than Mr. Raymond expects, and within the year, I doubt any man in Salt Flatts will ever again believe a woman can't best him in business." His guts were twisted up as tight as his lips were pressed together . . . but the words refused to stay bottled inside. "And I love you."

She staggered back a step, but he grabbed her other arm to keep her upright, to keep her close — for at least another second. "I just wanted you to know before I left. . . ."

He'd never have another chance to show her how hard it was to leave her.

"Will, I —"

He pulled her against him, dug his hands into her hair, and silenced her lips.

She melted against him like spent wax, and he sank deeper into the glue that held him to her. No other woman could replace her — not Nancy, not anyone he'd yet to meet.

She was the first woman he'd really loved, whose mere presence captivated his every thought, whose skin beneath his fingertips made him fight against the flames that wanted to consume her.

Kathleen had insisted he give Eliza a final good memory. Well, he'd certainly remember the time he'd kissed a woman like she ought to be kissed.

When he shouldn't have.

When he couldn't do anything but.

His hands slid down to wrap her against him, though he struggled not to squeeze her so tight she'd break. His restraint caused his arms to ache almost as much as his heart.

He couldn't break away from her lips — not after a second, a minute, two. This moment had to last him a lifetime.

A man cleared his throat. "Um . . ."

Eliza broke away, staring back at him like a frightened kitten. Will's hands lingered at her waist despite the unwelcome company breathing down his neck.

"I believe this next dance is mine?" A portly gentleman Will didn't know scratched at his prematurely balding head.

He'd followed them all the way out here

and still wanted to dance with Eliza after witnessing her kiss another man?

"But I guess if that's not —"

"No." Will's throat clogged and his fingers slipped from the soft fabric of her shirtwaist until he no longer possessed her. "I can't keep her . . . any longer." If this man was still interested in Eliza after he'd kissed her in public, he hadn't hurt her chance to marry — and she'd likely do so within the year.

Will shook his head, trying to find the air to speak his last words to her. "Good-bye, Eliza."

Without waiting for her to repeat his farewell, he stormed off into the crowd.

Coming to the dance had been a mistake.

One far, far worse than he'd imagined.

Some man — whose name Eliza hadn't caught — tried to twirl her under his arm, but all she ended up doing was jabbing him in the side with her elbow. He smashed her toe, trying to readjust.

"Are you all right, Miss Cantrell?"

She shook her head. Answering him would release the tears she'd barely stifled through the last two dances.

She tried to follow his lead, having no idea where they were in the reel, yet bobbled an entire set of steps.

The man pulled her out of formation. "Did you drink some of the punch at the far table? They weren't supposed to be giving it to the ladies."

She raised an eyebrow. Someone put moonshine in the punch for a charity dance? "I haven't had anything to drink."

"Well, maybe that's your problem. It's too muggy to dance all night with nothing to drink." He tucked her arm around his and led her off the dance floor. "If you're parched, I'm not going to force you to dance just because I bought a ticket."

"That's kind of you." She ducked her head to hide her flushed face. Why were men still lining up to dance with her? At least one had seen Will kiss her like . . . like a man starving. And surely others had heard about the kiss or seen them on the dance floor. She'd never before danced so terribly, but the second Will had taken her in his arms, she couldn't get the steps right for anything.

A hot tear escaped, so she yanked a handkerchief from her pocket to keep her escort from asking if she was all right again.

A matronly woman behind the table smiled at the two of them, but cocked her head after perusing Eliza for a second.

She must have looked a fright.

Her dancing partner gestured to the punch bowl. "The lady needs a drink."

A lanky man, thumbs around his belt and hat jauntily cocked to one side, moseyed up next to Eliza as she awaited her lemonade. "Howdy, Miss Cantrell." He glanced over her head at the man whose arm tightened about hers. "I was wondering if I'm up next. I've lost count of the rounds. I'm George Mason."

The man on the other side, growled over her head. "The music isn't quite over, George."

"Just checking, Marvin."

She pulled her crumpled list from her pocket and blinked at the names. The long, long list of names. Her hands shook as she tried to find either of them on her paper.

The cowboy poked his arm over her shoulder and pointed. "There I am. Got two more to go."

The short farmer who'd interrupted one of her dances with Will came huffing up beside them. "I got some men to give up their tickets, Miss Cantrell. Thought I'd tell you who, seeing as you're taking a break. Where's William?"

"Gone," she whispered.

"What?"

She closed her eyes and handed over her list. She couldn't have said it louder if she tried — her throat had closed up.

Mr. Putnam took a stubby pencil from his pocket and started scratching off names. "George, don't suppose you'd trade a dozen eggs or maybe a rabbit for your dance ticket with Miss Cantrell here?"

Mr. Mason leaned over the paper. "No. Especially now that I'm up next." He took her free arm.

Marvin clasped her other arm. "She needs to rest."

Mr. Putnam held out the list. "That's seven men times two dollars. I'll be needing fourteen dollars off my account. Where'd you say William was again?"

"He's gone elsewhere, Mr. Putnam." A female voice chimed behind them.

Nancy pried Eliza's arm from Mr. Mason's. "And I agree with Mr. Jamison here. Miss Cantrell needs a breather. She and I intended to sit one out together, so we'll do so now." Nancy put a hand against Eliza's back and smiled cheerily at the three men surrounding them. "But I'm sure she'll take her turn with you, Mr. Mason, when the time comes. . . ." She took the list from Mr. Putnam. "Two dances from now, as previously determined."

Pulling Eliza away, Nancy bustled across the lawn toward the solitary bench where Eliza had eaten alone earlier.

"Thank you." She took back the list and crammed it into her pocket.

"I figured you needed rescuing from all those knights in shining armor."

Nancy probably expected her to laugh, or at least crack a smile. Probably didn't expect a frown accompanied by a sniffle.

"How did you get out of dancing this round?"

"I'm not nearly as popular as you are." She let go of Eliza's arm and sat.

Eliza lowered herself onto the bench beside her, fighting the urge to roll up in an unladylike ball on the stiff wooden planks. "You're far more attractive. Your list should be longer than mine."

"I'm also a well-known jilter, and I have a sickly stepdaughter to care for." She patted Eliza's knee. "Though I've got male interest enough to be nursing plenty of calluses on my feet tomorrow."

Eliza took a sip of her lemonade, then ran the sweaty glass around in her hand.

"Want to talk about it?"

She shrugged. "You probably wouldn't want to talk to me about Will."

"It's all right. I've had my suspicions." She

gave Eliza a sad smile. "And so has my mother. And, well . . ." She played with the ruffle on her skirt. "I saw him kiss you earlier."

Eliza's cheeks warmed. Her reputation was likely shot. How many people had seen her melt into him like an ice block trying to hold back a wildfire? Yet she wasn't at all angry at Will for kissing her like that.

Why hadn't she realized how deeply he felt before now? Every action since the day they'd met had shown he cared. His other two kisses had been sweet, but that one . . .

Instead of allowing herself to love him back, she'd followed her mother's example. She'd put her dream above all else — family, friends, love — and let him walk away.

She'd never wanted to become her mother, and yet she'd managed to turn out worse.

At least her father had ten years to love his wife, ten years of memories. Will would go out alone, with only a handful of stolen kisses from the woman he loved.

"I've made a mistake, haven't I."

"How's that?"

"I let him go."

"After he kissed you like that?"

Eliza put her hands to her cheeks hoping to cool them down. She took a glance at

Nancy. "Do you regret leaving him?"

"Yes." She swallowed. "And Will *never* kissed me like that." She looked at the clouds above, growing orange in the dusky light. "No man has ever kissed me like that."

Eliza closed her eyes. How had he kissed her exactly? Like a man saying good-bye to his most treasured possession, placing it on the altar and stepping away. "But we can't be together. We can't both have what we want if we were."

"Then you should be happy."

He sure didn't seem to be, and this was the least happy she'd ever felt.

"Did you get what you wanted most?"

"I don't know," she breathed.

"Did he offer to marry you?"

She shook her head. "If I'd given him any indication I wanted him to, he probably would've."

"My husband died within a month, leaving me widowed with children, each one following him into heaven except Millie." She rubbed at her finger where a ring ought to be. "There's no assurance you'll be blissful for long. God doesn't promise us a life void of hardship."

Eliza rubbed her temples. She knew that full well after losing her parents, her store, her brother, her money. If she chased after

Will, she could end up like Nancy, a widow with nothing to fall back on.

Me. Me. Me.

What about him?

Did he not need her? Did he not love her? Even if they were together for only a month, she could care for him as he deserved.

And she did want what was best for him.

Because she loved him. More than anything.

CHAPTER 26

Mr. Raymond ushered Eliza inside his office. "What brings you here this morning?"

She wrung her hands and plopped down in his uncomfortable, pretentious chair. "I need to sell the business."

He shut his door, dampening the noise of the customers out front. "Pardon me?"

"I need you to buy me out," she said with more conviction this time.

"I don't want to buy you out." He perched on the front of his desk. "I'm a silent partner. I've no interest in finding someone to do your job, and I'd rather have you pay off your loan than own a business I don't want."

"Even if I include all three buildings?"

He rubbed the creases in his forehead. "Why?"

"No one's helping Will get to school, but I can."

Mr. Raymond's eyebrows squeezed together. "I thought I'd asked you not to come in again if you're going to let emotions overrule your brain. Within a year, your tenants' rent alone would likely cover his expenses — no need for you to sell at all."

She rubbed the chair's arms. She couldn't be persuaded to change her mind. The temptation to look out for just herself was still enormous. "No, I'm selling."

Mr. Raymond's sniff jolted her gaze back onto him. "If you're stupid enough to give up everything — which you've yet to spend a dime of your own on — I won't partner with you again. I won't take you back."

Was greedy Mr. Raymond trying to talk her out of selling him the buildings? "You don't want the property?"

"Of course I do, but what good is an empty store? You're making me guaranteed money right now."

He wouldn't resist if she offered him a really good deal. "I talked to Dr. Benning this morning. He said some medical universities like the one he attended in Michigan don't charge tuition. However, out-of-state fees are higher. He thought three thousand dollars for three years of education would be sufficient. Of course, Will would need money to travel —"

"Miss Cantrell —"

"And that's only room and board for a single person." She closed her eyes. Would he have her after she'd rejected every subtle offer of his heart time and again? She'd need something to do while she waited . . . if he'd accept her.

Her every scheme had turned awry, yet God kept blessing her. What would He want her to do with the businesses He'd freely given her?

"Pay me bottom dollar for the buildings and inventory minus my loan." She stood. "Or I'll find someone else to buy them."

The clock ticked a few seconds before Mr. Raymond let out a quizzical exhale. "All this for Mr. Stanton?"

"Yes." She sat back down and clasped her hands in her lap. The fluttering in her chest grew exponentially, but the sudden panic over selling everything wouldn't deter her. "All I ever wanted was for someone to believe in me. My family, Axel, you. But no one did. Not like Will. He'll give up what he wants most to make sure I have a chance to succeed." Her lips quivered and her eyes grew hot. "Though everyone takes advantage of him, no one helps him. Not even you."

Mr. Raymond let his crossed leg thunk to the floor. "Now, wait a minute."

"Don't tell me you've not paid far less for his medical services than they're worth."

One of his eyes drooped warily. "He doesn't ask for much, and it's common practice to trade for medical services."

"But you wouldn't dare come into my store and tell me you had a desperate need for a teacup and try to pay me with a handful of beans two years later."

"That'd be ridiculous —"

"So is having Will nurse your wife for several days and think his medical coupon sufficiently covered his labor."

"Now, hold on. I didn't get a coupon. He offered to visit if I helped you. He made the bad business decision, not me."

"And that's why he needs me." She thumped her chest, the tears coming to her eyes unbidden. "I can keep him from being taken."

Mr. Raymond sighed. "I've told the boy countless times he needs to give up business and work in medicine."

"You could've helped him get to school years ago."

He flung out his hands. "But I'd get nothing in return. I'm not a charity."

She pulled in a slow, steady breath. Hadn't she thought similarly not that long ago — everything always centered on what she would gain? Not until Will's generosity shamed her had she looked for ways to help others, and she still fought against her nature to open her hand and freely give. "Well, I'm not asking for charity now, only a cheap price on real estate. You're out nothing but future profit sharing, but I'm positive you can capitalize on my buildings without my help."

A knock sounded at the door, which slowly swung inward with the pounding. "I'm sorry to interrupt." Sheriff Quade poked his dusty cowboy hat inside. "The teller mentioned Miss Cantrell just came in." He tipped his hat at her. "Wanted to tell you to come by the jail sometime while I'm there and collect your money."

"My money? From the robbery?" She blinked. "But Axel said it was gone."

"I suppose the loot was, but he still had the store."

"The store." She jolted out of her seat. "Will sold the store already?" To whom?

The sheriff scratched under his hat band. "I'm assuming so. Mr. Stanton came in to cover the claims made for the train robbery, the only theft we know for certain Mr. Langston was involved in. Well, besides the ones from around town, but almost all of that was recovered at his death."

"See there." Mr. Raymond crossed his arms and shrugged. "He likely has plenty of money to get to school all on his own now."

"Well, I'm not too sure about that, being he was short three hundred dollars of making full restitution. Said something about being thankful he had a shirt and Mrs. Langston had the boardinghouse. And not much later he came back in with the rest." Sheriff Quade gave her a great big smile as if that information should make her extremely happy. "So everyone gets their money back."

She folded her hands in front of her face. Will had surely sacrificed that three hundred from his own pocket. "Where did he go next? The train depot? Is there a train leaving soon?"

"Well, that was yesterday. I went with him to my brother's afterward. Charlie's been trying to sell his bay for a while. Gave Will a deal on her and the old farm wagon. Can't say I know Will's plans though."

He'd already been set to leave before he came to the dance? And surely he didn't plan to take a wagon to school.

"Good day, Miss Cantrell, Mr. Raymond." The sheriff pushed his hat back down and slipped out into the foyer.

"See there, he figured out something for

himself."

"He didn't get enough." She pulled out the deeds to her store. "Now, should I seek another buyer or can I strike a deal with you?" If Mr. Raymond wouldn't budge, was there anyone in town who'd have the cash to buy her out before Will traveled too far? Would she even be able to find him?

Eliza loosened her grip on the reins when a familiar-looking cabin and a scattering of outbuildings appeared on the other side of a stand of trees.

Anchoring the hair that had blown free behind her ear, she slowed the horse and let out a breath. Thankfully, she'd chosen the right turn at the fork, since she'd not paid attention to how they got there weeks ago.

Will wouldn't have left town last night after the dance; he'd have had to set up camp before getting a mile out of town. But he could've reached his parents' before nightfall, and he'd not leave his family without saying good-bye. He had to be there. Unless he'd said good-bye to them earlier in the week . . .

No. God wouldn't have let her give up everything and miss Will. Would He?

And here she was, still thinking about what she deserved to get. Will would've given up everything for her had she asked him. Even if he got nothing in return.

Could she ever get past her selfishness? She swallowed hard and smeared away tears. Did she deserve to find him? It would serve her right if she couldn't.

The closer she got to the farmstead, the more her stomach jittered and the harder it was to keep from pushing the horse into a full gallop.

She clenched a fist to her roiling stomach. As much as she wanted to present herself to him as an integral part of a deal, she would offer him the money with no stipulations. Show him she believed in him . . . without her. Loved him . . . enough to give him up so he could pursue his dream — just as he'd given her up so she could live hers.

When she pulled into the Stantons' yard, Will's mother came out onto the porch and shaded her eyes with her arm, a batter-covered spoon in her hand and a mixing bowl tucked against her side. "Eliza?"

She stopped the horse and tried to gracefully descend from the buggy. Where was his wagon? It must be there. "Please tell me Will's here." What if Rachel gave her an answer she couldn't handle?

His mother's gaze was unwavering, measuring . . . silent.

"Please." Eliza kept her clenched fists in front of her stomach, lest she do something as pitiful as folding her hands and begging. Groveling wouldn't change Will's location.

"He's having a hard enough time leaving as it is."

He is here!

Eliza raced up to grab Rachel's flour-covered arm. "No, I'll make it easier, Mrs. Stanton. I promise."

Rachel looked at her askance. "I can't fix everything for my children, but I don't want to cause them extra heartache either."

She stepped back to give the older woman space. "I hope never again to cause him heartache." She forced herself to look into Will's mother's eyes despite the fire creeping up her neck. "I love him."

Rachel's weary face relaxed, her lips twisted into a small smile. "Yet you haven't told him?"

"No." Oh, she'd known she liked him, cared for him, maybe even loved him. But until last night, she hadn't known she loved him enough — and then she'd proven it by putting pen to paper and signing everything away this morning. "But I'd like to."

"Then, he's at the pond." She pointed her spoon at a small rise to the west. "That way."

"Thank you." Eliza spotted Ambrose and

scurried over to him. "Would you look after the horse?" Without waiting for an answer, she headed toward the rise as fast as her skirts allowed.

Nearing the willows and pines reflecting peacefully in the pond's surface, she slowed. Yet nothing but waving grasses and the buzz of bees hovering around a honeysuckle vine caught her attention. Where was Will?

Circling a clump of juvenile cedars, she frightened away a handful of robins. A lengthy dark figure lying in the grass grabbed her attention.

Will lay by the bank, his thick head of hair cradled in his arms bent beneath his head. His chest rose and fell evenly, eyes closed. A fishing pole lay at his side.

Not wanting to startle him, she padded slowly around thick grass clumps until her shadow fell across his face. He didn't stir.

As silently as possible, she settled herself beside him, smiling at a second chance to watch him sleep. So peaceful and handsome and spellbinding. No wonder princes in fairy tales couldn't keep from kissing their sleeping lady loves.

And why not?

Just because he might not take her to school, or wherever he chose to go, didn't mean she couldn't show him she loved him as he'd done for her last night.

With shaky fingers, she unpinned her hat, then propped herself beside him on her elbow. The scent of mud and grass and man enveloped her as she placed her free hand on his heart, the smooth linen of his shirt under her hand as distracting as his heartbeat. She waited for a second, but his eyelids remained placid, his mouth soft and relaxed. Taking in every inch of his face, she leaned over to brush her lips against his.

He hummed lightly and smiled against her mouth. His head lifted, his responsive lips moving against hers.

Then his eyes flew open. "Eliza?" His head fell back with a thump. "Uff."

"Yes?" She smiled at him, her lungs completely out of breath.

He scooted back, propping himself up with his elbows, his brows furrowed. "What are you doing here?"

"Kissing you." Could someone's whole body flush? Her skin felt hotter than if she'd sat outside in the sun all day. "And telling you I'm not my mother."

He blinked, his brow still stiff.

"And that you're worth more than I have — could ever have." She snapped off a plantain leaf and rolled it between her fingers, finding it easier to look at the crushed plant than his frown.

"No I'm not." He pushed himself up the rest of the way.

She pulled out a four thousand dollar bank draft made over to him. "I made a sale this morning." She smoothed the paper against her leg, then placed the draft in his lap, glancing into his eyes for only a second. "I talked to Dr. Benning. He spent about two thousand to graduate from the University of Michigan, but now they're making it a three-year degree, and I figured you'd need at least four thousand to pay for your school and travel, and anything else unexpected."

He picked up the draft between two fingers, as if the paper was a delicate wisp of ash. "You sold your store to Mr. Raymond?"

She nodded, trying not to think too hard about it. "All of them."

"That's not enough money." He crammed the paper back into her hand. "Go buy them back. I'm a bad investment. I've told you about my reading. I might not even be able to graduate."

"You're not a bad investment." She pressed the draft against his palm.

He stared blankly at their clasped hands.

She could tell he wanted to go, that the

bank draft was tempting. "If you're worried about the risk I'm taking, I have another proposition for you to consider." She swallowed hard, not able to look at him. She wasn't worthy of his saying yes. "I sold all of them because . . . if . . . if you would consider taking me along as your wife, I wouldn't be tied to Salt Flatts anymore, and I could go along to make certain my investment panned out."

His fingers relaxed, but he didn't pull his hand away from hers. "That's riskier. A lifelong commitment with no guarantee of return. I might not turn out much different than I am now, even after thirty or fifty years."

"Then you'd still be the most loving, thoughtful, self-sacrificing man I know?" She was the one getting the better deal. "A man who paid off a criminal's debt with money from his own pocket just to make sure I got back all that I lost, though God had given me plenty?"

His eyes met hers, cautious yet beseeching at the same time.

She moved closer, cupping one hand against his jaw. "That wouldn't be so bad."

He shook his head, his stubble scratching against her fingers. "Carl bought the store from me, and I've given the Langstons' their due . . . and taken care of Axel's robbery, though the lawyer told me it wasn't necessary." He shrugged, eyes downcast. "I couldn't leave without doing so."

She couldn't help the smile on her face, as if he needed to be contrite about doing such a thing.

"So if I can find somewhere without competition and plenty of need, I have enough if I'm careful." He pressed the bank draft harder against her hand. "You don't need to do this for me."

She pushed back. "Would you rather go west than to school? Are you against me going with you, no matter where you go?"

His jaw tensed and he closed his eyes. "Even with an education, I still might have to go to some poor western town to find work. I might never be able to bring home enough to buy you a new hat, let alone afford what's necessary. I might have to leave you alone for days or weeks to attend the sick and might very well die from one of the illnesses I've committed to expose myself to for the rest of my life."

"I think that's covered in the 'good times and bad' part of the vows." She let her fingers travel back to the unruly lock always begging to be tucked behind his ear. "If you're worried about me, I have a second bank draft to cover the cost of starting another business, so I can occupy myself while you're gone. So I can afford my own hat, if I wish." She gave him a sad smile. As if not getting to buy some future hat was a concern.

Should she say more? A tingle at the audacity made her feel hot and cold at the same time. "And I hear children are awfully time-consuming."

He opened his eyes to search hers but said nothing more.

She smiled tentatively. "Have I told you I love you yet?"

His eyes turned dark and warm, and the corner of his mouth rose. "You showed me when you gave me this draft, but it's still nice to hear the words."

She curled his fingers around the draft. "There's this story about a man who found a priceless pearl and sold everything to obtain it." She closed her eyes and exhaled. "I wish I'd realized sooner you were that one precious something on earth that could make me happy."

"If you believe I am" — his voice rumbled rougher than she'd ever heard — "then I'll do everything possible to prove you right."

"Partners?"

He grabbed her hand and pulled her

forward until their foreheads touched, his mouth but a whisper away from hers. "Lovers."

His breath teased her lips, creating a heat that rambled all the way down to each finger and toe. She forced her lungs to work. "Care to seal our agreement with a kiss, then?"

Cupping her jaw with his gentle hands, he pulled her closer, as if to breathe her in. His lips met hers, gentle and soft at first, but quickly escalating into the intense passion he'd shown her last night. His lips and arms claiming her as his own.

Perhaps every business owner in the world might think her a fool for cashing in her assets for love, but owning a store had never done this to her heart.

She closed her eyes tight, banishing every thought of money or stores or contracts, and concentrated on Will, losing herself in the feel of being cherished and desired by a man. Burying her hands into his thick hair, she pressed closer. She never could've loved him as much as he deserved if she hadn't surrendered her dream for something better — him.

Putting a hand against his pounding chest, she broke away and cleared her throat. "I believe that's enough to seal the deal . . .

uh, engagement."

He pressed a kiss to each of her eyelids before resting his forehead against hers. "I'll never tire of making certain this deal stays sealed. For richer or poorer, in sickness or in health . . ."

She grabbed both of his hands and squeezed. "No matter the sacrifice."

EPILOGUE

Michigan, 1884

Will hurried to catch the front door as two women struggled to back out of the corner shop with bustles and bags and children. He pulled the door wide with one hand while pressing the box he'd picked up from the post office against his side with the other.

From behind her mother's full skirts, a curly-headed girl with her thumb in her mouth peeked up at him as she toddled out of the store and then waved good-bye with pudgy little fingers.

His heart twisted and his smile drooped a little. Nettie's sixth birthday had been yesterday. Ma'd written that she was proving to be quick . . . and that she worked hard to walk properly so her big brother William would want to come back and see her.

Rubbing his suddenly itchy eyelids, he

forced himself to smile at the next lady, who thanked him for holding the door. He batted at a horsefly, but the pest made it past, likely attracted to the floral scents wafting out of the store.

He stepped inside and let the door shut behind him, setting the chimes to tinkling again.

His wife stepped out from behind the shelving at the end of the aisle, dressed in a dark red floral dress, cut attractively. The ruffles of the underskirt peeped out from under fancy gathers, falling straight down to her black pointed-toe boots. Her hair was an extravagant pile of curls. The diamonds surrounding the opal on his grandmother's dainty ring glinted on her ring finger.

All dressed up to mirror the upper-crust clientele she chose to target for her home-and-hearth shop.

He glanced around the store full of flowers and kitchen gadgets and anything else a fine lady might want, and seeing no one, he held out his empty arm. Eliza smiled and glided down the aisle straight into his one-armed embrace. She plied a peck on his lips before looking at the package tucked under his other arm.

Yes, yes. Business hours were for business. "Thanks for the kiss. And yes, the package is for you."

She kissed him again before taking the box and flipping it over to read the address. "Wonderful."

"I'm jealous. Shouldn't I be the one receiving a package from home? It's been months since Ma sent me anything."

"This isn't from your parents; it's from Julia. What would you want from her?"

He shrugged and followed Eliza back to the counter where he mixed herbal tonics and tinctures and added scents to lotions for his wife's customers. He frowned at an empty space on the shelf behind the counter. "Did you move the blue bottles I prepared this morning? Mr. Isenhard was supposed to come by this afternoon and —"

"Yes, he's picked those up already."

He frowned. "How much did you charge him? I hadn't thought to tell you the price before I left for the hospital clinic."

"Oh well, that." She used a dainty letter opener to slice through the rough twine securing her package. "He told me about how his wife had to find a job even though their girl's sick and she can't care for the apartment like normal. And, well, he seemed so careworn . . . and then I caught a glimpse inside his purse and figured you wouldn't mind if I didn't exactly charge him. I mean,

I might have made him pay more than you needed to cover the cost of —"

He cut off her excuses with a sound kiss.

When he pulled away, she didn't remove her hands from where she'd grabbed onto his shirt to steady herself. "What was that for?"

"I love it when you don't make a profit."

She rolled her eyes and playfully pushed him away. "Well, I won't be giving *these* away for free." She pulled out the quilted, lace-edged mittens Julia Cline often sold at the Hampdens' store.

"You bought some of Julia's silly oven mittens?"

"They'll sell." She walked them over to the kitchen section.

"Enough to cover eight dollars' worth of medicine?"

She slowed, a nervous tic batting at the corner of her mouth.

He licked his lips. "Not that Mr. Isenhard's tincture cost that much. I was just wondering."

Her lips pressed tightly together, but he caught the slight shake of her head and the mirth in her eyes. She'd not admit to the hours she would've tossed and turned tonight if she'd actually given away medicine that expensive.

She came sashaying back toward him, her narrowed eyes unable to shield the mischievous glint dancing in her pupils. "Well, I'm certainly glad I didn't give that much medicine away for nothing. We'll need every cent we make with me adding to the family."

He blinked. "Adding to the family?" But she hadn't asked him about . . . hadn't mentioned any symptoms indicating . . . His mouth grew dry, and his heart pounded.

She walked right past him and through the curtain into the back room.

"Now, wait a minute, Eliza!" He swatted at the curtain and scrambled after her. "Don't you leave me without explaining —" A crate hit him square in the gut. "Oof."

"I figure since you doctored up those other two strays, you wouldn't mind helping with this one too."

In the corner of the box, a fluffy marmalade fuzz ball wriggled on a scrap of wool.

He shook his head and exhaled slowly to decrease his heart rate.

She poked the kitten, which mewed pitifully. "Miss Johnson brought him in. Evidently the others didn't make it, and the mother abandoned this one."

He picked up the delicate thing. "Oh,

honey. It doesn't even have its eyes open yet."

"Well, if anybody can save him, you can." Her eyes peered up into his. He could almost reach out and touch the pride shining between her lashes.

Did he even deserve this woman? "I'm not a doctor —"

"You've only got two more months before you can't use that excuse anymore. You may not have your degree yet, but you're almost there." She poked him in the chest, then set down the box and took the kitten away from him. "Do you want me to do anything besides try to get milk in his belly? I hope you don't mind that I swiped one of your glass droppers to feed him."

"I can do it. You have a store to run."

"You've got studying to do." She rubbed the bawling kitten against her cheek and shushed it. Obviously this cat would not be going to back to Miss Johnson. "We won't keep you."

He sighed. He did need to reread *Burnett's Treatise on the Ear* for tomorrow. "Have I told you how thankful I am for your hard work? I couldn't have gotten through school without you."

"Yes, I'm quite indispensable — remember that."

"Oh, there's no forgetting. I need you more every day." He pulled her close and bumped up her chin. "Not to mention, you're rather irresistible as well." Lightly caressing the very faint pink line across her cheek, he placed a kiss against the corner of her mouth. "And very desirable." He followed the scar line with more kisses, one hand pressing her closer, the other about to get into trouble for messing up her fancy hairdo. "And extremely —"

The front door bell chimed, and she pulled away.

"Later, sweetheart." She pressed the kitten against his chest and gave him a wink before bustling out into the store.

"Good afternoon, ladies!"

Will rubbed the top of the kitten's head to hush his pitiful mewling. "It's all right, buddy. When she flips over that Closed sign in an hour, she's all mine."

And then he could keep her breathless for as long as he wanted.

AUTHOR'S NOTE

The Internet not only makes researching a book easier, but it brings the real world to me as I sit in a corner of my house creating a fake one. Because of a friend's Facebook like, I learned about Easton Friedel. He was my introduction to the rare disease of epidermolysis bullosa (EB) and Butterfly Children. I knew I needed a medical disaster in my story that my hero couldn't fix, and after a few months of crying over the trials of these children's families while I was hugely pregnant (therefore I was plenty emotional already!), I realized they were my answer. Writing the nameless baby Hampden would be my small way of increasing awareness of "the worst disease you've never heard of."

Imagine yourself in their bandages; imagine having a newborn afflicted with EB you couldn't cuddle in your arms. Would you take a few minutes to learn about EB from

http://irefuseeb.org/ or http://www.debra
.org/; pray God gives these families grace,
endurance, and a cure; and donate your
time or money to help these families?

ACKNOWLEDGMENTS

I am deeply grateful for the people God has put into my life who love me and are proud of what I do.

I'm thankful for:

My husband and children — who put up with me, especially since writing takes time away from them and often makes me tired when I stay up way too late writing.

Naomi Rawlings — whom I rely on so much for strengthening my stories. She suffers through my long emails because I abhor the phone and my ugly first drafts. She's invaluable.

Glenn Haggerty — who is one of the nicest guys on the planet. He helps me tighten my stories in more ways than one.

549

The people in publishing who work hard to make my story become even better — Natasha Kern, Raela Schoenherr, Karen Schurrer, Dan Pitts, and others at Bethany House who work with my books behind the scenes.

My readers — who actually like what I write and ask for more. What fun that is! You spur me on.

DISCUSSION QUESTIONS

1. In Chapter 4, as co-workers, Eliza and Will clash over job methodology. Consider Colossians 3:23 and Romans 12:18. If you have co-workers whose personalities and/or work approach differ from yours, what can you do to make your work environment a peaceful, positive place? What works and what doesn't? Is it more important to get along or be productive?

2. In Chapters 5 and 6, Eliza tries to discern Axel's character through others' opinions. Boaz got a full report about Ruth before allowing himself to become romantically attached (Ruth 2:11), and reputation is sometimes an important consideration (Acts 6:3, 1 Timothy 3:7, 5:10). In light of Eliza's discoveries, should she have called things off?

As a woman of the 1880s, do you think her decision was sound? What are the dangers of trying to discover a person's reputation?

3. In Chapter 8, I'd originally written Everett's speech on capturing thoughts as though Christians can defeat their sin nature with will-power and the clever use of tactics — but Paul failed to completely conquer his own sins (see Romans 7:15–20). Do you approach life more by trying to earn God's acceptance, or by asking for and receiving His forgiveness and depending upon His enabling (Philippians 2:13, Luke 10:39–42)?

4. For most of history, a woman's quality of life depended upon the quality of her marriage. In Chapter 10, Eliza is struggling between two men who have caught her interest — one who'd proposed and possessed the store she wanted along with some nice-sized flaws; and another she'd only just met, felt attracted to, but who'd not offered her any promises. Consider Genesis 2:18, 1 Corinthians 7:8–9, and 2 Corinthians 6:14. What are the

most important considerations for marriage: a man's character, his spiritual condition, security, or mutual attraction? If you were Eliza's friend, how would you advise her? Would you advise a modern woman differently? Why?

5. Have you ever been uncomfortable with someone your loved one got engaged to? What did you do? What were the repercussions of your choice? What would you advise others to do in a similar situation? Should you tell someone you think they've made a mistake?

6. In Chapter 13, because of circumstances, Eliza and Will are both tempted to give up their dreams. Have you ever given up on a dream? How do you know when to bail on a dream and when to keep striving for one despite setbacks and disappointments?

7. When I heard of the condition epidermolysis bullosa, which the baby in Chapter 22 has, I struggled with its unfairness, and I'm still not sure why God would allow such a disease to exist. After 9/11, Billy Graham was asked why God allowed such a

terrible thing to happen. He quoted 2 Thessalonians 2:7 and essentially said evil was a mystery and that he didn't know. What is your answer for the reason terrible things happen to good people? How do you keep your faith when terribly unfair things occur? (Other verses to consider: Genesis 1:26–27, 31, 2:16–17, 3:4–6, 17–19, Matthew 23:37, John 3:16, Romans 5:12, Romans 8:18–23, 2 Samuel 12:22–23, Revelation 21:4.)

8. At the end of Chapter 23, Will helped the undeserving Axel. How involved are you in helping people who need Christ's love the most? What holds you back from helping the "unlovely" or the "unworthy"?

9. In Chapter 25, Nancy reminds Eliza that God warns, even promises, that Christians will face hardship in this life. How do you endure hardship? What have you learned or attained during hardship that you wouldn't have gotten any other way? Is fear of hardship driving your choices today? What might staying comfortable rob you of (James 1:2-4)?

10. Have you ever done something foolish in the eyes of the world for love
of another, as Eliza did by selling
her store for Will's medical tuition?
How do you know when someone's
situation is worth the sacrifice?
Consider what God gave up to save
sinners (Philippians 2:3–8, Romans
5:8, 1 Corinthians 1:18). In light of
His "foolish" sacrifice, how should
we live?

For additional discussion questions, search
for *A Bride in Store* on the Bethany House
website (bakerpublishinggroup.com/
bethanyhouse) and select the resource
Readers' Discussion Questions.

ABOUT THE AUTHOR

Melissa Jagears is a stay-at-home mother on a tiny Kansas farm with a fixer-upper house. Her passion is to help Christian believers mature in their faith and judge rightly. Find her online at www.melissa jagears.com, Facebook, Pinterest, and Good-reads, or write to her at PO Box 191, Dearing, KS 67340.